I0636178

A Soldier in the Borderlands

Dry Uramésha, Volume 1

Arwen Spicer

Published by Arwen Spicer, 2025.

A SOLDIER IN THE BORDERLANDS

First edition. November 15, 2025.

Copyright © 2025 Arwen Spicer.

ISBN: 979-8991207621

Written by Arwen Spicer.

To my mother, Patricia Spicer, for fifty years (and counting) of love and support.

Chapter One

The sun balanced red on the horizon. In the wide field of solar panels, the scraping persisted, like a gnawing rat. It seemed louder now the chatter of the boys was receding. The panels caught the evening like a second sky, and the falling sun dusted the desert with firelight.

"Go on, Ash. I'll finish up," Tan told his brother.

"You go, I got it." Short for eleven, Ash stood on tiptoe, at war with the grime, the tilted panels peaking a little higher than his head.

"I'll finish it faster," said Tan, three years older and taller. "You head back." The quicker it got done, the quicker they got supper.

Ash gave him a rueful look. "I'm not going to run, Tan."

"I know."

But he knew nothing of the kind. The desert plain bled into the low hill country. The sun was failing, the nighttime floodlights not yet on. This time of day, a lone person might just make it to those hills and hide—or at least imagine hiding. If Tan turned his back, it was the perfect opening.

With a resigned look, Ash handed him the scraper, its handle hot from his grip.

"If you jog, you can catch the others."

"Yes, Tan." Ash trotted off toward the rest of the unit. Fragments of the other boys' talk snapped back to Tan.

"—gross fucker. Why are you cutting your finger?"

"It's my home sign."

"Like the fish."

"—some barbarian shit."

"—'s just jealous—"

"Jealous, my ass!"

Laughter peppered the desert.

Tan scraped the rest of the dirt off the panel and gave himself a moment to breathe.

He watched his boys, spots in a cloud of dust. A quarter mile beyond them rose the quiet monster of the Citadel. The sun's last rays edged its southern face in gold. Two massive orbs, one on top of the other, gazed blindly at Tan. From this angle, the tower looked like a gargantuan bull's head slammed sideways in the earth, one horn sunk out of sight completely, the other rising skyward above the ashen eyes. He found its spirit bleak and beautiful.

A hundred yards north of the silent tower, the train began its nightly music. A horn moaned. Two cars cracked into motion, and wheels squealed. He closed his eyes for a moment and leaned into their song, the breeze fanning his face. Then he set off after his cadets.

The two nearest columns of the shield generator stuck up like white chopsticks near the Citadel's base. Just inside their perimeter, the sculptures of the He and She were gray swoops of metal.

He'd almost caught up when something hit the ground with a smash behind him. He spun to face the panels. Shadows moved in falling light.

Drawing the handgun at his hip, he yelled, "C-16, fall in! Panels under attack."

He glanced back to see if they'd heard and saw them pounding toward him.

Ash reached him first.

"Stay behind me," said Tan. "I'll take point, you cover." As the boys neared, he called out, "Water formation. Sho, give the alarm." At least, he could pull the ten year old out of the fighting.

"Yes, captain." The blond boy peeled off and ran for the Citadel, shouting, "Barbarian attack!" at the top of his lungs.

Tan dashed back toward the panels, his boys spreading out per the flanking formation, thirteen and fourteen year olds in front, eleven and twelve year olds behind them. He counted seven men, though it was hard to be sure, ducking and smashing among wide rows of canted panels. Not bad odds against the thirteen in his unit.

An arrow thwacked near him. Another swooshed by his ear. The barbarians adhered to tech limitation, but an arrow could still kill you.

"Use the panels as cover!" Low down, his boys would have the advantage, easier to aim a gun than draw a bow.

As Tan ran for the panels, a guy blocked his way, masked face a slate with eyes. Tan skidded to a stop and shot.

He missed, he dodged.

Another arrow thunked close by. He zagged, glancing behind him for his brother.

"Stick close, Ash!"

Shots rang. One of the boys to the east of him squawked.

He and Ash reached the solar array and ducked down. He felt more in his terrain now, sheltered by the panels, able to pick out his targets and aim. Someone's leg moved, barbarian by the tunic's swish. Tan sighted him, pulled the trigger. The man fell, trying to scramble away. Tan shot him again, in the side, then the back.

His brother's gun went off behind him.

Tan half turned. "Get him?"

He couldn't hear the reply, but he could see the consternation on Ash's face, his eyes locked on a dark lump, crawling. Tan shot it, and it went still.

"Keep to the periphery!" Keskan's voice, Tan's second-in-command. "You get in there in these shadows, and we can't tell you from the Kiri people."

Damn it, he'd called them Kiris on purpose, to remind the cadets that half of them were shooting their own kin. He wouldn't have said it if any officers had been there. He was right to hold the periphery though. Hide among the panels but not too deep in.

Tan could see the legs of his boys fanning out around the struts. Good. Well trained.

One of the Kiris moved. Tan shot and missed.

Time elongated, as always.

Watch, target, shoot, move. Listen.

The arrows swooped between the gunshots. His boys yelled to each other, the Kiris didn't, silent, sharing nothing. After all, some in the Citadel knew Kiri speech.

There was a gap in their perimeter, Tan's ear caught it: a quiet to the north where the guns should have talked. He could see the lanky frame of Ordan, all outsized hands and feet. Of course it was Ordan—conscious, crouched, but not firing. Damn Keskan, he'd put it in Ordan's head that he was fighting his own people.

He signaled Ash to follow him and moved to close the distance. When the barbarian rose up and aimed at Ordan, Tan fired fast, clipping his shoulder. The man reeled, just as the arrow flew.

The floodlights came on.

The world leapt into white light. In that instant, Tan lost track of the barbarian, then spotted him a second later between two panels, scrabbling for his bow. Tan got on one knee and aimed. The lights crackled and went off again. He squeezed the trigger, and the report rang loud. But he couldn't tell if he'd hit him.

He scampered to Ordan, groping for him in the dark. The boy was hit, clutching his right arm as the blood streamed, a deep slice from the arrow. He started as the floodlights flashed on again.

"Stay still." Tan yanked a bandage from the pouch on his belt.

Ordan gave him a blank look.

"Ash, wrap his arm. I'll cover." But when he turned to toss the bandage to his brother, Ash was missing. "Ash?"

He looked around wildly. The panels spread out like a deadly game board, shadows weaving above and below. He saw the stocky form of Muned near him, barbarians weaving among the panels, Keskan further off—and beyond him, his brother, running for the hills.

ꙮ

For a moment, Tan was back there, in that hell a year ago, that evening roll call and the instant he had realized Ash had vanished.

That night, he'd just bleated to his boys, "Stay there!" and shot out of the barracks, abandoning them—no protocol, no guidance. He'd pounded off across the gravel to the hole under the fence. Sheer luck he'd tackled Ash to the ground before he could wriggle through it.

This time, he clamped down the panic.

"Muned!" he called. "Look after Ordan." He dropped the bandages on the ground and sprang like a hare after his brother.

Ash's form disappeared behind a panel, then flashed out again, past Keskan, who was yelling orders to his flank. Tan careened toward Ash, making an arc to skirt Keskan.

But suddenly Keskan was right on top of him—

Tan sprawled flat, legs tangled up with his lieutenant's.

"Damn it, Tánashen! Watch your fucking position."

"Ash!" Tan kicked Keskan off and scrambled up, his brother's figure dwindling.

Tan raced after him, but he'd lost ground. Amid the crack of bullets, the Citadel's siren began to bellow, the blind bull summoned from its sleep. Tan sprinted on, gaining—but too slowly.

Then, Ash crashed to the ground.

By instinct, Tan hit the dirt, scanning the chaos for the barbarian who'd shot him. But it was all shadows and shouting—unless...

Yes, there was a man half obscured behind a panel. Tan aimed and squeezed the trigger twice. The man doubled over, clutching his gut.

"Ash!" Tan was up and sprinting to his brother's side.

Blood flowed freely from Ash's neck. Bandages—he'd left them with Ordan. He groped at Ash's belt and pulled a bandage from his kit, shaking as he pressed the cloth to the wound and watched it redden.

"Damn it, Ash. Why'd you have to run?"

Chapter Two

The lights were on the fritz, due to panel damage presumably. The ceiling lamps had the murk of twilight, and their dimness made the mess hall bigger, its curved wall receding to a fuzzy horizon.

Tan trembled as he stood in the food line; he couldn't make himself stop trembling.

He'll be all right, he told himself. *The bullet missed the artery, so get yourself together.*

He brought up the rear of the line, goddamn Keskan directly ahead of him.

Tan put the youngest of their unit first, and some days the other units snickered about it: *Check out C-16, ass backwards again.* In the Citadel highest ranks went first. But when Júzian was captain, he'd put himself last, and when Tan succeeded him, he preserved the tradition: How can the captain eat till knows everyone else has eaten? The protector keeps watch on his chicks.

Cadets were asking, "Where's Fendo, where's Ordan, where's Ash?"

"Alive," said Tan and left the details to others.

Tarnto stood up on his stubby legs to make sure the other tables saw him and gave a grizzly description of Ash's wound, as only an eleven year old could tell it.

Gomu, a year older and formidably scarred around the face, threw an arm around him and pulled him down. "Nah, it was a flesh wound. Fendo got it worse. Got it right in the gut, the scrawny fucker."

The server handed Tan his tray: half an okra, an embarrassed carrot the size of his little toe, a bowl of potato-turnip mash from dried flakes, the usual cup of water—

Something thundered deep beneath them. A second later, the room shivered. Tan grabbed his cup by instinct before it could slosh.

"What the hell was that?" said someone.

On all sides, the boys started jabbering.

"Wait. Quiet," said someone else; no one paid attention.

"Shut up!" cried the captain of C-10. "Listen."

For a moment, the room sank into stillness. No further booms. From way down deep came the faint whine of strained metal. They waited. Nothing.

One boy started whispering, then another. Soon their voices were back to the usual roar.

Tan joined his unit at their table. He ate the okra first, guessing correctly it would go down like slime.

"Think a bomb went off?" asked Codo. By age, he was third in command, but that bucktooth grin did nothing for his authority.

"What, like an attack from inside?" said Keskan. "The Kiri rescues revolting or something?" Though his tone was casual, his thumb tapped his spoon in excitement. Tan sized him up, as he did several times daily: a month younger than Tan but half a head taller and already broadening into a man at fourteen.

He tackled me to keep me from reaching Ash, and he damn well knows I know it.

Tan kept his voice even. "If they'd revolted, alarms would be going off."

"Maybe that's the plan, to take out the alarms."

"If they took out the alarms, we'd get the loudspeaker."

"Maybe the loud—"

"Then they'd have people shouting in the halls. Come on. It's an equipment break or something."

"Think someone set off a bomb by mistake?" said Muned.

Keskan laughed. "Wouldn't want to be that guy. 'What'd you do on munitions today?' 'Nothing much, blew up the place.'"

That got him a few laughs. Tan forced a smile and plowed into his mash, tasteless but it eased his stomach.

"Hey, C-16, how big was the shootout?" called someone from another table.

"There was at least twenty!" said Tarnto.

"Not a chance. Twelve tops," said Tan.

"You mean you nailed twelve, huh? Let the rest get away?" The captain of C-8.

"Meaning?"

The captain threw up his hands. "Hey, no offense. If I was a barbarian unit, I'd probably do the same thing."

"Watcha mean a barbarian unit?" said Tarnto. "I'm not no barbar." He was Citadel born, seven of the thirteen were.

Keskan stood. "You want to meet this Kiri head to head?"

"Sit down," said Tan on cue. "Try again, C-8, when *your* boys beat 'em back."

The captain laughed. "I'm just saying—"

"And while you're at it, learn the difference between a Kiri and fucking barbarian." Tan was done. He'd let his boys handle it from there. The challenge wasn't serious anyway. The captain of C-8 was a tester, not a thug.

Bickering followed and grumbles and jostling. Tan watched, ready to step in if things looked headed for a fight.

Tarnto would tackle anyone, but Gomu usually held him back. If Gomu got into it, Keskan would yank him out. Keskan picked his fights strategically. Like waiting for his captain's flight-risk brother to run...

A voice crackled out of the loudspeaker. "Cadet Captain Tánashen, report to Commander Shonco."

Tan downed the carrot and chased it with his cup of water.

With a secret little sense of vindication, he stood up. Keskan had gone too far this time. He'd assaulted his captain, now he'd answer to Shonco.

"Keskan," he said, "you have the unit. Finish supper, then get 'em back to the barracks."

Keskan smirked from across the table. "How would I figure these things out without you?"

Tan shot him an unamused glance and went out.

☙

But his resolve flagged on the clanging stairs. If Tan said Keskan tackled him, Commander Shonco would ask why. And the answer could not be *to help my brother desert*.

The darkened stairs lay like an ambush. Usually, the Citadel's interior beamed. Even after lights out, the main stairwell was fully illuminated, showing a broad space of circular floor that split off into hallways radiating out from the center like the sun. Now the stairs, floors, walls fell into shadow, punctuated by the floodlights from outside. At the far end of each hall, narrow windows looked onto the desert. Tan could hear a few voices from down that way, but all he saw were puddles of yellow where the floodlights trapped the floor paint.

The bell tolled third night hour, an hour until lights out. It reverberated down from the Citadel's pinnacle, humming through the stairwell's railing underneath Tan's palm. The voices paused for the tolling, then took up again.

Shonco didn't have to know about Ash, Tan reflected. Tan could say he lit out after a barbarian and that's when Keskan tackled him. And Keskan couldn't say Ash deserted because that would mean confessing he'd helped Ash desert; it would escalate him from insubordinate to traitor.

Tan clapped down the hallway and buzzed at the door.

"Yes?"

"Cadet Captain Tánashen reporting, sir."

The lock clicked and Tan went in, clapping his right fist to his heart in salute.

Shonco presided at his metal desk like a pine that had been potted there. He was a man fashioned of in-between spaces. When Tan had met him four years ago, he'd considered him old, but he was not. Though his hair was thinning, he kept a young man's trimness. Though he was of the Citadel, his slight frame and tapered chin betrayed his Kiri blood. A seasoned officer, his eyes were as big as a woman's. Tan suspected his smallness had made him a target as a boy. He had the poise of someone sharpened on ridicule. He could be a strong ally if appealed to the right way.

"Sit," he said, shuffling papers. "That was good work this evening. Out of the thirteen barbarians we took down, it looks like your unit got seven. Three casualties on your side, Fendo, Ordan, Ashtyn—Fendo's pretty bad, I hear."

He flipped a page and poised his pen to write.

"He was in surgery for an arrow in the intestines," said Tan. "But the medic thinks that he'll recover. He was very brave, sir."

Fendo was Shonco's nephew, so Tan figured he'd be worried, even though he'd never show it. He was too good at his job to show it.

Shonco's pen scratched away. "Have you talked to Ashtyn and Ordan?"

"Not since they got taken into medical, sir. I had a few words, you know: 'You'll be all right,' that sort of thing. Then, I went to make sure that supper got sent to them. I'll go see them. I was planning to."

"I'm sure you will. It's not a criticism. But it's unfortunate they both got shot—a new rescue and a known flight risk."

"Yes, sir."

"But since their wounds are superficial, you can take them back to the barracks tonight. It's best not to leave them alone in medical to talk."

"Yes, sir."

He went on to other questions, typical questions. What had Tan seen and heard? How had his unit performed?

Tan omitted Ordan's freezing up. Of course, he omitted that Ash had run. But as for that smug fucker, Tan wanted him gone, demoted to border patrol or some miners' unit, or anywhere but C-16.

"Keskan—" He began but then had second thoughts.

True, if he turned Keskan in, Keskan couldn't pin the blame on Ash. But not every one of the boys was that tactical. Gomu, Tarnto, they'd leap to Keskan's defense. What if Tarnto said, *Ash was running away again, and the captain tried to catch him and bumped into Keskan.*

"Something bothering you, Cadet Captain?"

Shonco's words from a year ago were burned into his brain: *If you ever let him run again, there will be no more mercy.*

"Keskan asked a good question, sir. About the solar panels—is the damage related to that boom we heard?"

Shonco hesitated. "A small problem with the water pump. Repair teams are on it. It won't interfere with North-Going Celebration."

Tan nodded.

"Keep up the good work and sooner-than-later it'll be your unit we're celebrating."

"Thank you, sir."

He couldn't turn to Shonco. He had to handle Keskan himself.

He started downstairs toward Medical. First, he'd check in on Ash, Fendo, and Ordan. That poor sucker, Ordan, wide-eyed as a fish, no clue how to be a soldier and pining for home.

Tan stopped and considered.

Did he dare...?

Yes, he did. It would be a risk but not an uncalculated one. In taking care of his boys, the small things mattered, and there was a small thing he could do. He turned around and started back up the stairs, past the commanders' level to the women's quarters.

Chapter Three

He'd lived in W-16 for three years before graduating to C-16. Even so, the way up the stairs felt alien, shadows thick in the low lamplight. Since leaving those doors four years ago, he'd only been sent back a handful of times. Boys weren't supposed to mix with women, not till they were old enough to be assigned someone to mate with.

At level 7, a footman stopped him. "Just where do you think you're going, wet pants?" He was muscular but a low-level grunt, only one red sun ray to mark his rank.

"C-16, Cadet Captain Tánashen, sir. Commander Shonco sent me to W-16 to let the aunts know their sons survived the barbarian attack."

It was a plausible lie the guard had no reason to question. With a warning to mind himself, the man waved him through.

He could recognize the pattern on the door that meant "W-16." It looked like "C-16" but with a different letter on the left. He pressed the buzzer and waited.

After a few moments, the slot in the door clacked open and a pair of eyes looked out.

"Oh, so finally you bother to... Tánashen? Is that you?"

The door swung wide, and Aunt Tson swept him into her embrace. She had the same fancy blond hair piled in curls, the same ample figure in a sleeveless dress but, gods, when had she gotten so short?

"Look at him. Look how he's grown." She held him out at arm's length.

A flock of women and kids descended on him. Faces out of memory in the honeyed light, aunts who'd raised him, girls who'd become women in his absence. One girl, just a few years older than him, was pregnant. That surprised him somehow, though realistically it shouldn't. New kids had been born, kids he'd never met. In the background stood the stony-faced Grand Aunt.

But he couldn't see the one he'd come for, the Kiri aunt. Where was Ferthi? Stupidly, he'd imagined he'd just ask for her and they'd get her. He hadn't expected to be mobbed like this.

"What the hell's going on out there, Tánashen?" said Aunt Tson. "Why are the lights down? Why was the siren on? Nobody tells us anything." She paused. "Why are *you* here? Are my boys all right? And little Ashie?"

"Is Fendo, is Muned...?" Their names flooded out of a half dozen mouths.

A kid cried out, "Who's he taking? Who's he taking?" thinking Tan had come to escort one of the women to a footman.

"There was an attack," Tan said. "Some of the solar is down; I guess they're sparing the batteries. But everyone's alive. Sho and Codo are fine, Aunt Tson. Ashtyn's—fine." He would be. He scanned for Fendo's mother and spotted her near the back, her thin, inverted triangle face a female version of Shonco's. "Aunt Togi, Fendo got hit, but he's going to be okay. He had surgery, and he's going to be fine."

From the look on her face, he might as well have said *he's dead.*

"Come in. Tell us everything," said Aunt Tson, leading him into the wide, familiar common with its work tables and play mats.

"Don't be ridiculous, Tson." The Grand Aunt stepped up and barred the way. "He came to deliver a message, not crawl back in the nest." She was Gomu's grandmother, an imposing block, like him. "Thank you, Tánashen. You can go."

"Uh, actually, there's one more thing."

She fixed him with her baleful eye.

"Commander Shonco said—he thought it would be a good idea... Is Aunt Ferthi here?"

"Ferthi? Somebody wants *her*?"

The cluster of women and kids drew back, and then he spotted her, a stick figure seated stiffly on the couch. She stood up, a full-blood Kiri, her braided hair as black as his, her eyes as piercing black as Ash's.

"Commander Shonco wants *me*?" she asked with that Kiri accent. She arrived at the Citadel almost grown up and had never shaken it off.

"Uh, no," said Tan. "No, it's one of the wounded, a Kiri rescue. His name's Ordan." Ordan was never in the women's quarters; he arrived at the Citadel at twelve, two years too old to be with the women.

She looked at him intently.

"But he's from Silver, same as you, Aunt Ferthi, and Commander Shonco thought it would help him recover faster if he had a little food from Silver, the way you know how to make it."

"Did he indeed," said the Grand Aunt coolly.

"What kind does he want?" asked Ferthi.

It was a long shot in the desert but... "Fish?"

"Fish," scoffed the Grand Aunt.

"Oh come on now, Grand Aunt. We do have *some*," said Aunt Tson.

"The tanks are a shambles."

"But they're spitting out a few fry. We can spare one." When she grinned at Tan, her face looked very much like her son, Codo's. Then, with a very un-Codo-like grace, she swept away into the kitchen, three little children tumbling after her.

The Grand Aunt crossed her arms. "Togi, is this the sort of thing your brother would order? Priest's food for an Oak-slave rescue?"

Fendo's mother looked up out of her thoughts. "What?"

The Grand Aunt repeated the question.

"Yes, why not?" She turned to Tan. "If he's worried about this other boy, then Fendo must not be so bad, yes?"

"They say he'll be fine," repeated Tan.

"I snagged one," called Aunt Tson from the kitchen.

"I'll fry it up," said Ferthi.

❧

Medical was a big bay on the ground floor, just inside the main doors. If the Citadel were ever invaded, it would be the first place hit. But no one invaded the Citadel. The barbarians had nothing but hammers and bows. And as for Oak, if they ever bombed the Citadel, the shield would deflect the blast.

The bay opened out into a giant bowl-shaped window, one of the Citadel's blind bull eyes. In the day, it let in a translucent daylight. Now, the floodlights spattered it, so it glowed like a portal to the Gods' Realm in scripture. The room was blue but looked steel gray. The rows of beds, with a scattering of wounded, cast shadows like a checkerboard, eerie as a crossing at the edge of life.

He could hear voices behind one of the curtains, one of them Keskan's. Of course.

The blue-belted duty medic sat at the corner desk where Tan was supposed to check in. Having been waved in by the guard, he stood just inside the doorway, listening instead.

Keskan's voice was hushed, but Tan caught a "can't blame 'em," and Ordan's reedy accent, "—get home?" It was a question. He couldn't catch the response, but there might have been a "plan" or "damn" and then "Batty Hyrax." Batty Hyrax was the village Keskan came from. Another voice answered—Ash's, but he couldn't make out the words.

More talk of deserting: Keskan, Ordan, Ash, all three.

When he'd heard enough, Tan checked in with the medic and made his way through the rows of cots.

In the corner, Fendo was out cold, a drip going into his arm, his open mouth and shadowed eyelids making an inky triangle.

Keskan sat on Ash's bed, facing Ordan. All three got quiet as Tan came up.

"I told you to mind the unit," he said to Keskan.

"Don't worry. I made sure they all know how to piss and sanitize."

"Go back to the barracks."

Keskan leaned back, casual. "Or what, your world's going to explode?"

"Follow your orders, lieutenant."

Keskan sized him up with that smug little smile. For a horrible moment, Tan thought he'd refuse. But then he shrugged, and tipped Ash and Ordan a wink.

"You guys take care," he said. "If you get yourselves killed, I'll kill ya."

He got up, a little stiffly, Tan thought, favoring the side where Tan had kicked him during their tussle.

As he sauntered off, Tan forced a smile at Ash and sat on his bedside. Time to drain the poison that flowed out of Keskan's mouth. Ordan had his arm wrapped, and Ash looked like a toddler with a winter scarf around his neck. But their color was good; they'd be up tomorrow.

Ash returned his smile weakly, no doubt waiting for the tirade. But Tan wouldn't win Ash back by yelling.

"I brought you guys food." He took the small food box from his jacket pocket.

It held two dried figs, bummed off Aunt Tson, and a fried fish the length of Tan's pinky finger. He handed Ash one of the figs and gave the greasy fish to Ordan. Then, quickly, he got up and gave the other fig to the medic "with Commander Shonco's compliments." The man nodded, his watchful face softening a little.

Ordan stared at the fish in his hand. "How do I pay it?"

That was not a question Tan expected. "Pay? You don't have to pay for it. It's just to help you get stronger."

Ordan studied the fish and then slowly crunched it, bones and all. There were tears in his eyes. "How—where do you get it?"

"There's an aunt in W-16 from Silver—from Blue Gums." He inserted the Kiri name to make it sound more home-like. "Her name's Aunt Ferthi."

Ordan sat forward. "Ferthi? Nutrattler Ferthi?"

"Shh," said Tan. "We don't have those names here."

The medic was listening, several beds away, poised motionless over an IV: four cadets in a corner, dusty-haired Fendo down for the count, the other three all Kiris. To a Citadel man, they probably all looked like cousins: those black haired, black eyed, little people. Those foreigners, he'd think, they were never really One with us. Who wouldn't think they were plotting something?

"She's dead," said Ordan. "She died in a raid, I had four years maybe. The traitors killed her, my mother said."

"Maybe it was a different Ferthi," said Tan. "Or maybe the Citadel rescued her, like they did you."

Ordan gave Tan a dubious look.

"Maybe she got hurt and needed treatment, like you did. You know the Kiris with their tech limitation, they don't know how to do real medical stuff."

He glanced at Ash, who was savoring the last bits of his fig, eyes on fingers, giving nothing away.

Ordan nodded. After a moment, he said, "Here smells like home, this room."

Tan didn't understand what that meant; it smelled like antiseptic.

Ordan brushed away a tear with his greasy fingers, though he was several years too old to cry.

Embarrassed for him, Tan nodded at Fendo. "He sure looks like shit, doesn't he?"

"He'll die," said Ordan.

"Nah. He's on antibiotics: that's stuff that keeps you from getting infected. The medic said he should be all right. And you," he said to Ash, "you gave me a real scare. I thought you were a goner."

Ash grinned, genuinely this time. "Me too. I thought, 'This is it,' and I thought, 'It could be worse, you know.' Just for a minute."

Something knotted in Tan. *Yes, it could be worse,* he thought. *It could be me without you.*

He smiled at Ordan. "You're a *davnor ferthe*." It was a Kiri phrase, "lucky uncle." Sitting here with two Kiris, he had to show he remembered. "I'll give you the week off heavy lifting for that arm."

Ordan eyed his bandage. "Wish it had went deeper. I want out a long time."

Tan thought about a joke and decided against it. "I know. We got a hard job. But if we serve good, like we did today, they'll send us back to the Garden. *I Kyolen*." Tan let the Kiri name escape him. "The Borderlands, Ordan. Once the Citadel drives Oak out, we can all go home again. You'll get fish all the time."

"I rather be home now and have Oak," said Ordan.

The jolt of rage hit Tan like an electric shock.

"Watch what you say," he whispered, hoping Ordan followed the way he flicked his eyes to the medic.

Hard experience had taught Tan about Oak. They were burners and butchers and rapists. If Keskan had convinced Ordan to side with Oak, his poison went deeper than Tan had imagined.

He had to fix the situation before it spun out. But how? What moves did he have to play? It was a battle for status in the end; that was all. Tan had to cut his legs out from under him, to shame him till nobody listened.

Chapter Four

Celebration days, they ate outside at the west of the Citadel, the back, they called it. To the east were the main doors, the statues, train station, solar array, on the west, nothing. The plain stretched away to the hills, but the morning sun threw a spear of shadow, and men crowded at its edges like yellow jackets drawn by a trickle of water, hundreds of them in a steady roar of conversation, broken into lines around several tables, piling their plates with the holiday feast.

The morning dehydration clamped Tan's head like a vice, but the echo of coolness that clung to the dawn helped him beat back the headache and focus. He stood in the endless food line, eyes fixed on Ash, a few cadets ahead of him. He wasn't about to let his brother out of his sight, but his eyes could watch on auto while his brain reviewed his plan.

At the border of the sun and shade, some footmen were erecting tri-color, gold-blue-red posts to mark out a staff boxing ring. It had been Tan's suggestion; it was his best sport.

Ash walked past him, tray loaded.

"Ash. You're on me like glue. You know that, right?"

Ash sighed and fell back into line beside him, chewing on a strip of jerky.

By the time Tan made it to the buffet, the food was severely picked over. But he still got some mash, a slice of bread folded around raisins and dried apple, and a soggy piece of jicama. You'd be lucky to see that kind of a haul twice a year. He managed to pocket two small squares of jerky and six additional raisins in case of need.

They poured just half a cup of water in his canteen, a fourth of the usual ration.

"The pump still down?" he asked.

The server shrugged. "How the hell do I know?"

If the pump was down, that could be a bad problem, but it was also out of his hands. Right now, he had problems of his own. He scanned the throng for Keskan, found him out on the fringes of the crowd, huddled with Ordan, his gestures emphatic.

He threaded his way toward them through the knots of men, Ash in tow.

"Not a good idea to stand out in sun," he said.

"Feel free not to," said Keskan.

Tan shrugged. "Your own lookout."

They'd all been issued sun hats. They were all standing bare-headed in the sun. Tan wasn't going to be the one to blink and put his on first.

"Is the train really going to the River?" said Ordan. He'd spoken Kiri except for "train." *Lan Savra*, the River, rang like the voice of the dead.

"You know better than to talk Kiri," Tan said.

"It is though." At least Keskan spoke Citadel. "All the way to the river. By train, it won't even take a day."

"Ordan," said Tan, "go check on Fendo. If he's awake and the medic says it's okay, go take him some mash, and then stay in medical yourself and rest up."

When Ordan had gone, Keskan folded his arms and waited, that slight smile on his face.

"Don't make him miserable," said Tan.

"*I'm* making him miserable?"

"I know he misses Blue Gums." He used the town's Kiri name. "But he can't go home until he earns his way. If you want to help him, help him earn it. Help him become one of them." He nodded vaguely at the footmen loading crates onto the train F-12 was going to take North.

"Stirring words, Tánashen. You're such a helper."

Tan gave a sigh and sidled off.

Then, though he hadn't quite planned it, it dawned on him that now was the time to make his move. As soon as he spotted a suitable mark, he called out to him.

"Hey, C-2! You and me in the posts." He nodded at the gaming ring.

C-2's captain frowned but gave a thumb's up. If you said no to a challenge, you got branded a coward and then even first years would beat your ass.

As they made for the ring, Keskan challenged C-6.

Sometimes he was very predictable.

☙

C-2's captain was taller than Tan but relied too much on his long reach.

Tan stepped into the bounds, half in sun, half in shadow. The hard shift between black and light was one of the contest's challenges. Someone handed him a cloth-wrapped staff, his favorite weapon, though he preferred it unwrapped and quick.

C-2 leered at him as they bowed in and took their stances, four simultaneous matches ranging along the length of the Citadel's shadow.

The bell rang.

He ducked and swung hard at C-2's feet. The tall boy stumbled but still caught Tan's back in a glancing blow. Tan absorbed most of it by going flat and rolling deeper into the shadow. He sprang up as C-2 turned and cracked his shoulder. As the boy's staff went askew, Tan smashed down on both his arms. His staff fell in the dust, and Tan stomped his boot on it.

"Down," called the referee.

C-2 didn't meet his eyes when they nodded to each other. It was tough to be trounced by the little guy, but Tan learned a long time ago to bite hard. He got in fast and gave no quarter because every damn one of them was bigger than him, and if it came down to stamina and muscle, he'd go down. He was already winded and headachy from thirst, sore from the blow on the back of his ribcage. But he had enough for one more bout, and that should be all he needed.

Keskan won his round, of course. And, like clockwork, the referee paired them up: two Kiris, one unit battling itself. Usually, that was a pain in the ass, but today, it was just what Tan wanted. It gave him a match-up without having to challenge, coincidence, like he had nothing to prove.

He and Keskan knew each other's styles inside out. Keskan struck pretty fast but relied on force. Tan tended to strike low because he was short; that was where his maneuverability lay, and Keskan would be expecting it. Instead, he'd stay high, go fast, go hard, like his life depended on it.

The bell sounded. He went in close, straight for Keskan's middle, relying on speed. He felt the staff catch Keskan's arm. Keskan stumbled back a step, and Tan moved like lightning. High, low, left, high...

Keskan parried each attack, but Tan kept him on defense, his mind amped up to that murderous place that accelerated reflexes faster than thought.

He caught a knee, and Keskan went down on one leg. But as he lurched forward, he got a clean swing at Tan's head.

The blow cracked hard despite the padding. Tan reeled, light flashing in front of his eyes. He was out of the shade in the bright of the sun. When he spun around, Keskan was a mass lunging out of the shadows. Tan parried twice by instinct and then he went down, his staff ripped from his hands.

He'd gambled and failed.

Keskan had won.

Chapter Five

T an got up, the back of his skull still pulsing. He hadn't heard the referee call him down, but he must have. He nodded to Keskan, ignoring his grin, and took a swig from his canteen, watching as Keskan squared up against the next contender. Ash was silent at his side. What the hell could Tan do now? What was the next move? There was always a next.

He took stock of his boys. Keskan's gang were cheering him on. Muned, who had a good heft with a staff, was in his own match against the C-12 lieutenant. Good. Sho was playing tag with some first years. Good again: neither witnessed Tan's defeat.

Ordan was in medical. What about Lavan and Dradam, C-16's other Kiris? Kiris were most at risk to run.

He spotted them playing cards with Dezdenec at the base of the Citadel. Dezdenec kept glancing at Tan. He had a chiseled face and striking, pale gray eyes. Those eyes were on him a lot these days, or was it Tan's imagination?

Tan meandered over, nodding for Ash to follow.

"Deal us in?" he asked Lavan, positioning himself so he could keep an eye on Keskan.

They were playing fake-out with the deck Dezdenec got from his father, who was a big-deal scholar. Tan assumed he'd given Dezdenec the cards so he could think about the gods on their faces.

Tan got shit cards: one weeping face of Loss and two angry faces of Loss's mate, Inner Fire in her fallen form. Luckily, he had a talent for faking. For some reason, guys thought he never smiled, even though he smiled a lot. So all he had to do was flash a subtle smirk to convince Dradam he had at least one Owner. Dradam folded, which spooked Ash out of the game.

Dezdenec folded on the next draw, but Lavan called him—turn after turn, the game tightening into a staring match. Lavan had a hell of a stare when he wanted. He was heir to the headman of Low in Mouth—no, think in Citadel—the leader of Soruc's Town, the Citadel's oldest Kiri ally. If Keskan pulled that Kiri-versus-Citadel shit, would he be smart enough to understand that his strength lay in alliance with the Citadel?

They ran through the whole deck and showed their cards, Lavan winning with two Owners.

Tan grinned. "You stand strong. You'll make a strong ally in Soruc's Town someday."

Lavan returned the grin. "Go again?"

"Sure."

"Captain," said Ash, "I don't feel too good."

Tan looked at him, really looked for the first time since breakfast. His eyes were pits; he'd lost too much blood yesterday.

"You need to go to medical?"

"Can I just rest a bit, you know, away from the crowd?"

Back in the staff boxing ring, Keskan had won his next round, but lost the third, against a footman from A-4. He was sitting with Codo now, drinking from his canteen, probably too worn out to get up to much shit.

"Sure, Ash." Tan stood and pulled out four of his raisins. Might as well play them now.

"Snagged these." He handed them out, one each.

Dradam's thin, dark face lit up. "Like home."

"Yeah. Let's go, Ash."

❧

Tan found them a spot far up in the tapering shadow—as far away from the Citadel as he ever got without orders. But halfway there, Ash teetered and put a hand to his head.

Tan steadied him. "You okay?"

"Bit dizzy."

"We're going to medical."

Ash dug a hand into Tan's sleeve. "Can I just stay out here and rest?"

"We got to get you checked out."

"I'm just hot and thirsty."

"What's the big deal? It'll be cooler in there."

Ash shook his head, not meeting Tan's eyes.

"What is it, Ash?"

"I just—I don't want to be there with Fendo. I don't want to be laying next to him if he dies."

"He's not going to die."

Ash said nothing.

"The medic said he'd be okay." Well, he'd said probably.

"I just don't want—"

"What?"

"I don't want to hear him breathing the way he was last night. Sort of gurgling—"

"Okay, I get it. Let's go sit down."

Ash leaning on Tan, they settled at the tip of the shadow.

"Eat these." Tan gave him the last two raisins. They'd been Ash's favorite since he was tiny, back home. "I'm going to check your bandage anyway."

He unfastened the folds around Ash's neck. The stitches looked clean, the bandage pretty bloody, but there was no active oozing. He fastened it back in place.

"Here." He handed Ash his canteen. "Drink the rest of my water."

"The rest?"

"I'll be fine till dinner."

Ash took it uncertainly and drank.

The buzz of the crowd was mellowing as the sun climbed.

"I like it out here," said Ash. "It's too hot, but I still like it." His color was already better.

"Put your hat on," said Tan as the sunlight crept closer.

In the conical space where the Citadel cut the light, the footmen were staff boxing to shouts and grunts. In the other direction, beyond the tip, the plain of sun-bleached rock fanned out to wavering blue hillocks. It would be peaceful if his head would just stop aching.

"I could imagine just walking out there," said Ash. "But I'm not going to run," he added hurriedly. "I know there's nowhere to run."

He had tried to run just yesterday, but it would do no good to say it. Ash would deny it, say he was chasing a barbarian or something. Then they'd argue...

"I can imagine it too," said Tan.

They gazed across the rocks for a couple of minutes.

"Tan, will you tell me a story?"

The request caught him off guard. "I guess."

Ash lay down with his head in the crook of Tan's hip. They probably looked like idiots, but they were brothers and it was a day of rest.

"Years back, when our grandparents were young, there was a big war, and the Oak men nuked the West men. I guess the West men had been protecting us Kiris because, as soon as their city was destroyed, the Oak men started raiding our villages. They were led by a fierce king they called the Burner. Everybody knew him by the scar across his face and 'cause one of his ears was missing..."

"You're telling me that story because you think I'm going to run."

Tan stopped short.

Ash wasn't wrong. The Citadel was harsh because it had to be, but Tan had hoped to remind him the real enemy was Oak. The man who'd terrorized their folk for decades, the man who'd murdered their parents—that man was the king of *Oak*. Tan had been seven and Ash only four, but old enough to remember the screams, the suffocating darkness of that cart. They would be slaves of Oak now if the Citadel hadn't rescued them. Yet Ash was so keen to desert their best hope.

"Tell me a happy story," said Ash with a yawn.

Tan was quivering with anger. He made himself stop. "'Bout what, chickadee?"

"About the Garden."

The Garden. About home.

"Okay. Okay, so one day, when Oneness spreads far enough, all the people who are hungry here will go back to the Garden. I don't know how well you remember it, Ash, but it's the most beautiful place in the world. In the spring, the green grass covers everything and it's sprinkled with little dark blue flowers and up on the meadow, where it's dry and the grass is short, it's dotted with tiny flowers that are all these shades from white to pink. And in autumn, the grape leaves turn dark red, and the hills are the color of... of celebration, like the red and gold tassels of the Way and the passing..."

A gentle snore interrupted him.

Ash slept in his lap till the sun hit noon and the commanders called them indoors for the official siesta.

❧

He started awake in his bunk to the tolling of the fifth day hour. His eyes shot to Ash, and he breathed easier to see his brother there, safe in the amber glow, his typical wheeze-snore turning to a yawn as he shuffled out of sleep.

Per the schedule of the celebration, Tan took his cadets back outside. The day, still hard and bright, splashed on the unforgiving turf, and the heat rolled up and over till it smoked you and claimed you like Oneness.

By this time of day, the Citadel's shadow bent east, and the troops stood in the shadow of the front court. Nearby stood the He and She, two mighty twists of steel, each high on its dais, He made of angles, the She of curves. They were very old, the stairs leading up to them rutted from generations of feet, the rock grouted brown from use. Tan didn't know what they represented, but he knew it was their function to hurt or reward, and today, thankfully, was a day of reward.

Footmen had hung ribbons from the lampposts that led to the train: crimson, sky blue, and saffron—death and healing and the Golden Way. Out by the panels came the clank of repairs. A motor cart trundled from the maintenance door, laden with panel components.

"Face the Way," called the high commander.

That meant east, toward the birth of the sun, a reminder of the gods' power. All the units currently stationed at the Citadel were assembled except those on essential duty. Row upon row: there must have been six hundred of them. C-16 fell in by the Citadel's steps, all but Fendo and Ordan in medical. They gazed at the flecks of solar panels in the desert, the repairmen moving like termites among them. The day smelled of sweat.

The high commander strode out before them. "Unit F-12, step forward."

The thirteen chosen men stepped up, two of them with a Kiri look, their red footmen's belts accented by a saffron sash. They saluted with fists to their chests.

"You have served well, and now you are rewarded. You are bound for the Garden, to farm the haven towns in peace." He turned toward the Citadel's great front doors. "Step forward, women and children. Today we celebrate you, messengers to the Garden."

Five women emerged, three of them with small children, all wearing red and saffron sashes over plain work clothes. Tan felt for those women in a river of men and boys. He could see the tension in their bodies as they stood beside their men, the way they clung to their children. From what he'd seen, there were at least twice as many men in the Citadel as women, and the women never walked outside, except to and from the train. But soon they'd be free. Soon they'd be in the woodlands, these Citadel women, who had probably never seen a tree outside of their greenhouses.

The wave of yearning ambushed him, the lupin and the woodpile and sawhorse by the yurt.

But then the horn of the call began to rumble, and its vibration in his chest swept him up. The loudspeaker spat static and a voice intoned:

How can it be we walk through fires yet remain?
That the sundered is restored to its primeval Oneness?

Out at the white columns, the shield crackled, a lightning of electric blue. And then a man stood by the columns who had not been there before. Tan suspected it was just an image, but who knew? Who knew what the Landowner was capable of? Maybe he really did have tech to transport his real body. Or maybe the gods transported him. He was close to their kind, so Tan could believe it.

The Landowner did not look remarkable, a man dressed in a loose, white shirt and trousers. His pale hair marked him as a priest, but that didn't seem to matter to him; it was cropped so close that this far off he almost looked bald.

When he spoke, his voice did not come from the loudspeaker—or from a hundred paces away. It resounded all around, yet it was soft, right by his ear.

"My brothers, my children, today I am well pleased. Our enemies seek to disunite us, but we overcome barbarity. They seek to cripple us, but we beat them back. Such is our Oneness. By our Oneness, we will overcome them. By our Oneness, we will win the Garden."

The ranks of men repeated, "By our Oneness, we will overcome them. By our Oneness, we will win the Garden."

"For it is written," said the Landowner:

> *Landowner's phantom entered the heart of Loss.*
> *And Loss embraced him as brother, as self.*
> *Wondering and human in his tears, unsundered.*

As the verse drew to a close, his voice became an echo. The music burst from bow and strings and the horns crested. In an instant, the Landowner was close, walking before them like an officer inspecting his troops, his face ordinary, no longer young. But his eyes shone out from the plane of the gods, their unearthly blue—the color of the evening just before it fell to black. His eyes understood, and at the touch of his eyes, their souls fell into the Ocean.

That was how Tan always thought about it afterwards. That's what the ocean must be like, a whirling, circle space like stars, a froth of dark and light. The call pounded through his jaw, lifting him not with sound but Oneness. In the Landowner's mind, they were united. He could *feel* Ash—and the space where Juz had been. But it didn't hurt; it was just a space. He felt his boys and Commander Shonco and all the men on all the levels of the Citadel behind him, the nice men and the wicked men, the low footmen and new rescues, the priests and scholars in their vaulted halls. He felt the aunts and the little children, high above in their secluded chambers. He felt Keskan. He felt Keskan feel him, and it was right and it was simple. They were blown beyond anger and fear and self, beyond plots and lies. They were One with each other, One with the gods, One in the god clamor that purged all division.

It faded quickly. As the horn grumbled its last note, they reeled and leaned against each other, back in the closed world where their minds were sundered.

When they came to themselves, the Landowner was gone, but an echo remained. They were still One. They'd keep Oneness together, somehow, Ash, Keskan, Tan—C-16 was One.

The F-12 men said goodbye to their comrades, the earnest exchange of words, embraces, old friends parting till the day Oneness unsundered them. The women bounced their whining children and looked up at the walls that hid their mothers and sisters and friends.

They stilled as one of the priests came out, in saffron robes, his blond hair glinting like tassels of maize. It was Sho's pa, round-faced like Sho.

He lifted his arms in blessing over each of F-12, murmuring words for them alone.

"Thank you, Owner," they responded, eyes down and shuffling their feet anxiously.

"Glad I'm not no priest-born," whispered Codo. "Good luck with that, Sho, being treated weird all the time."

Keskan shot him a smile.

Also the son of a priest, Codo had failed the test of telepathic strength. Every priest was blond, but not every blond man had the talent to lead Oneness. Sho hadn't taken the test yet.

When the priest had gone, an officer began to sing in a high, yearning voice:

I cried and sighed and split in two,
Till I myself was rent in two.

Shortly after sixth day bell, the train jerked to life. Trumpets peeled through the loudspeaker, and F-12 filed out to the train station, waving goodbye to sleepy cheers and incongruously energetic music. Tan hoped the trumpets would stop before the train's departure—and they did. The Citadel understood music well. They let the train make its own farewell, banging and moaning out of the station, then roaring off like a dwindling snake into the north. Tan sat with Ash in the shade and watched, calm as Oneness always calmed him.

A step clipped beside him, Commander Shonco.

"Sir." Tan started to rise, but Shonco gave a dismissive wave and crouched beside him.

"C-14 is going to pack up the dishes. You boys will have cleanup at eighth bell. After cleanup, you have the rest of the day." He stood. "Fendo looked rough this morning."

"I'll go check on him, sir," said Tan.

ॐ

Fendo was awake but loopy with drugs. Ordan, however, was not in medical. Fendo didn't even remember him visiting, and the medic who'd just come on duty knew shit. But Fendo kept mumbling "Can't have any mash yet," which told Tan that Ordan had, indeed, come with the food.

Why hadn't he stayed as ordered? And where was he now?

Tan made his way back out to the courtyard, quiet in the dregs of afternoon. C-14 was packing up food containers.

Tan scanned the thinning crowd. He scanned it again, did a circuit, poked in shadows, but nothing paid out.

Ordan was missing.

Chapter Six

In the westering sun, the Citadel's shadow lengthened while the evening glittered with dust. The boys moved with the purposeful randomness of scouter ants, sweeping and gathering debris. He counted them off again in his head: Keskan, Codo, Dradam, Lavan, Muned.

"Gomu, Tarnto, stop fucking around." They were off in the shadows doing gods knew what.

Ash, Sho, and Dezdenec were washing up in the kitchen.

"Ordan in the kitchen?" he asked Keskan.

"I don't know. Did you order him there?"

"Lavan," said Tan, "go check around for Ordan. He might be in the kitchen or supply room. Muned, check the barracks and the bathroom—"

Gomu snickered. "Think he's got a guy who's gonna roll him, captain?" The bathroom was where everyone went to fuck.

"—then report," finished Tan.

Out in the floodlights, workmen hammered at the panels. "Codo, go see if Ordan went out to the solar array."

"Solar array? Why'd he do that, captain?"

"To check on repairs? I don't know." He waved Codo on his way.

Keskan was being unobtrusive, quietly sweeping the stairs. That meant he knew something. Tan took a step toward him and then thought better. Keskan would deny and bicker and waste his time. No, he had to focus on finding Ordan.

He did a sweep of the train station. No Ordan hiding under the platform, nowhere else to hide.

Muned came back in about five minutes. "With a pappy."

"Shit," said Tan. "You mean Gomu's right?"

Muned shrugged. "Well, there's a belt on the wall." Hanging your belt on the peg in the barracks was the universal sign of being claimed for a fuck. "I don't know if it's Ordan's, but he's the only one missing, right?"

Why the hell didn't Ordan stay in medical? If he stayed like Tan told him, he'd be off-limits to pappies. But that was all moot now. Ordan would just have to deal.

❧

He didn't show for supper.

In the cadets' quarters, electricity was still on backup, the lights down at a brown smear. The boys fumbled for hand sanitizer in the bathroom and sloshed the gray water, as they washed in the gloom. The cool water was nice if you didn't smell it. Tan felt the sweat slick off his face. The tenderness of his neck said he'd picked up a sunburn despite trying to keep his hat on in the sun.

A card game in the barracks got dealt and called off. The low lamps made the suits too hard to read.

Why wasn't Ordan back? That was a long time for a Pappy to keep a cadet. Plus, who'd want a pimply job like Ordan, with that scar on his throat where they'd cut out the tumor?

Keskan sighed. "How splint-handed are the work crews not to fix the panels yet?"

Pulled from his thoughts, Tan said, "They've got to be at least part way fixed. They're probably prioritizing charging batteries."

"And fixing the water pump," added Dezdenec.

"How much water's in reserve?" asked Ash from his cot.

"They got tanks," said Tan. "You seen 'em. Up by the women's quarters. I think they're just rationing to be safe."

Keskan flopped onto his bunk. "Not too smart, huh? Having one damn water source the whole place depends on, one that needs electricity to run."

"It'll be up in a day or two." Tan sat against the wall, his favorite place for surveying the room. "It's not like this is toppling the Citadel."

"Yeah? Who's thirsty in here?"

A chorus of "Me!"

"It feel smart to be thirsty?"

"Hell no!"

"Fuck that!"

"Yeah, I'm thirsty too," said Tan. "But do you think the Kiris have some paradise? Down here, the barbarians can barely scrounge food. Up there, the villages are just squares on a Go board. The only question's who's going to win them: the raiders from Oak or the farmers from the Citadel."

Keskan chuckled. "I seen plenty of raiders, but *farmers*? You guys seen any farmers around here?"

"Seen a solar farm," said Codo. "It got busted though."

"Seen a bone farm," said Gomu. There was no such thing.

Sho raised his hand. "They're on level twenty." Gomu and Tarnto sniggered. "They are. When I was a kid, my mother took me up to a farm to pick tomatoes."

"You got me, Sho," said Keskan. "They're with the women and tomatoes on level twenty." His eyes were laughing at Tan.

"So you're saying we're not farming up north?" said Tan. "All that food we unload from the train, it just magicks into existence on the train, huh?"

"Yeah sure, all right, we're farmers, fighting the evil raiders of Oak."

"Damn, Keskan, if I didn't know you, I'd think you were being a sarcastic fuck."

Casual, Keskan pulled his pocket knife out. "Just a guy trying to figure shit out." He went back to carving that bloody ring shape around his finger. "Like if Oak's so evil, why haven't they nuked us?"

"'Cause they know we've got a shield; it's not a secret. The generator pillars are right out in the open."

"So they're not even going to try?"

"How the fuck do I know? That's why we got officers to figure it out."

Keskan eyed him coolly. "If you're going to let other people figure everything out, you could be taking orders the rest of your life."

Tan got up and started undressing for the night. "Well, when you become Landowner, let me know. You can tell me what it's like not to take orders." Weak joke, but it got a chortle from Tarnto and a grin from Muned.

Keskan didn't smile. "Not everyone follows the Landowner's orders."

"Meaning?"

"Barbarians don't. The Oak men don't—"

"And that's a *good* thing?" said Dezdenec.

Tan stopped unbuttoning his shirt. "Funny how it sounds like you're suggesting deserting. I know you would never suggest that."

Keskan gave a short laugh. "Not suggesting anything. Just thinking about the world." He put his knife away and licked the blood off his finger.

Discussion terminated, thank the gods. Tan hated teetering on that line. Too much talking bred insubordination; too much silencing did too.

He folded his shirt and stashed it under his bunk. He felt freer in his undershirt with the air on his arms. But as he stood there, his mind went back to Ordan. He couldn't go to bed till he knew Ordan was okay.

He threw his shirt back on.

"Okay, Ordan's been gone too long. I'm going to tell the commander."

"Oh, come on," said Keskan. "Don't be such a mama. Who goes telling their commander when some guy's getting fucked? When the commander bags you, we don't get in the way."

The commander didn't, but since the rumor protected him from other pappies, Tan let them think what the hell they liked.

Tan peered at Keskan, lolling there on his bunk.

He does know something.

If Ordan was out this long with a pappy, Keskan ought to be worried for him. He liked Ordan, at least well enough. He'd tackle Tan to let Ash run for the hills, but with some guy doing who-knows-what to Ordan, he was suddenly, *Let's talk philosophy about Oak...* diverting attention from the topic of Ordan... who was a fellow Kiri, a kid fresh from the North. A prime target for Keskan's treasonous shit.

And Tan had fallen for it.

But if Ordan wasn't with a pappy, where was he? Run out into the desert with no water or...

How long had it been since Tan had actually seen him? Just after the staff boxing. Hours before F-12 left.

"Keskan, I need to talk to you in the bathroom now."

"I didn't know you felt that way about me."

There were a handful of titters.

"Not a word out of you shits," said Tan. "Ordan's not with a pappy. He's missing. Stay alert."

He jerked his head for Keskan to follow and banged out the door. The seconds beat like hours as he waited to see if Keskan would obey. The door opened. Keskan sidled out.

Tan strode before him into the bathroom and rounded on him.

"We need to get him back before they find him."

"Before they find him with some guy who thinks he's a good fuck?"

"Don't prevaricate with me, Keskan." He said it in Kiri, just like his mother used to.

Keskan folded his arms. "Okay, Mummy, what do you think happened?"

"You sent him off on the train."

Keskan laughed. "*I* did?"

"He thinks he's going to escape back into the Borderlands. Maybe even you think he's going to, but he won't. They'll find him. They always find you."

Keskan wasn't laughing now. "If your brother rats you out."

Tan let that slide off him. He couldn't think about Júzian now. He'd done what he had to; he'd do it again.

"I told him to go and see Fendo. He did. Maybe he saw him all laid out and it scared him. Maybe you and him already had your shit planned. Either way, he was off position by midday. Or we could tell Shonco he snuck on the train just before it left, which means he's only been gone since half-past seventh day bell. But even then, he's already been gone six hours. At best he's got ten hours left before he's an official deserter. Ten hours *max*. If they time it from midday, only seven hours."

"Impressive math chops, Tánashen."

"So if you care about saving his life, cut the crap and tell the truth. Do you know a way to get a message to him on the train?"

Keskan scoffed. "Sure, I'll just break into the radio station and telepathically tell Ordan to break into the train's radio, so I can send him a message. Or maybe I'll just send the whole thing by telepathy. I had no idea you thought so highly of my powers."

"*Can* you access a radio? Do you have any cronies who could tell him to give himself up?"

Keskan cocked his head and said nothing.

"Because there are only two other options. We tell Shonco and they catch him before his sixteen hours is up. Or we don't tell anyone, and they catch him."

"Or they don't."

"They always do. *You* may not do telepathy, but the priests always find you."

Keskan eyed him in the dark. "I don't think he's on the train."

"We don't have time for this."

"As much as I enjoy seeing you twist up in knots, he's not on the fucking train. You really think Citadel security's that lax?"

"After he went to see Fendo—"

"I saw a footman bag him, okay? He said, what were his exact words, 'You're just the kind of skinny newt I'd like to squeeze something out of.'" He shrugged. "So there it is. He's getting squeezed, and I'm not crazy about what's probably happening to him, but it's out of our hands. Right?"

"What was his name?" said Tan. "The footman."

"I don't know."

"What did he look like?"

Keskan sighed. "Oh, you know, big guy. Bit priest looking."

"Newts come from Kiri lands." He'd even used the Kiri word. Tan didn't think they had a word for "newt" in Citadel. "How'd a priest-looking guy know that word?"

"He probably heard it when he deployed north. How do I know?"

Tan made no reply, and the silence between them had the shape of Tan's dead brother. Keskan stood still as a stalking cat. *He knows he has to take me down before I can tell Shonco.* The door was a strip of glow tape behind Keskan's left shoulder. What the hell had Tan been thinking letting Keskan own the door?

But then Keskan stirred. "So what're you going to do? Wake up Shonco, make a big fuss—"

Tan stopped listening. He'd said this before. *He can't attack me*, he realized. If Keskan assaulted his captain to keep him from reporting a desertion, that made him an accessory. It could cost him his life, and Keskan wasn't ready to give up his life. He was playing the long game; that much Tan knew. But he wasn't going to let him go either, was he?

"Go back to the barracks," he said.

"What, and leave you here alone with your crazy—?"

"That's an order."

Silence again, and the third presence between them. Keskan took a step toward him so the difference in their heights stood stark. "Between you and me, Tánashen, I don't really care about your orders."

Tan did a mental survey of the room: sink beside them, bottle of cleaner, floor dry but smooth enough to be slick.

"I cared about Júzian's orders."

Good. You go on distracting yourself with Júzian.

"But the guy who got him murdered—the guy who murdered him? That guy doesn't have any claim on my respect."

Tan would only have a few seconds, so he'd better play this right. He gave a frustrated sigh and moved to pass him. When Keskan blocked him, he twisted sharply and kicked, sweeping Keskan's feet from under him. Tan had hoped he'd hit his head on the sink, but the quarters were too close and it clipped his shoulder. For a second, he was half on the floor, gripping the sink to keep from falling. Tan reached over him and snagged the bottle of cleaner just as Keskan shoved at his feet.

He went down. His elbow smacked concrete, his grip on the bottle wavering. Keskan's elbow socked his gut, but he got both hands and sprayed, right into Keskan's face.

Keskan recoiled, shouting, "Fucking hell!"

Tan coughed and scrabbled for the door, got up and out the room, still clutching the cleaner. Bile stung in his throat.

He pelted down the hall, calling, "C-16, emergency!" so the night guard wouldn't shoot him.

Chapter Seven

"Cadet Captain Tánashen, by your own account, you knew Cadet Ordan was missing by eighth day bell. Yet you didn't report it till after fifth night. Five hours lost. It's like you wanted him to suffer." Commander Shonco stood before him, hair uncombed and shirt askew.

Despite the power rationing, the lights in the barracks glared full white as a reminder there was no hiding.

Tan said nothing. There was nothing to say.

Shonco paced on, eying each of the boys. His yellow officer's belt was standard issue, but in this moment, it seemed touched with priesthood. "And in those five hours, the train arrived at the Grid. The passengers disembarked. Cadet Ordan, if he was on that train, left it. Now, he is unaccounted for."

He paused in front of Keskan and peered at his red and squinting eyes but asked no questions. A good commander knew when to enforce and when to leave things alone.

He passed on. "They will find him. He has been claimed by Oneness. The priests know the call of his mind. The only question is whether they'll find him before his grace period is up. As we wait, as we hope, carry this on your shoulders: if you had spoken sooner, we would have found him on the train." A strain crept into his voice. "He was new. He might have been shown leniency. I expected more of all of you."

"I'm the one who failed, sir," said Tan.

Shonco faced him.

"I didn't notice he was missing. I didn't report it when I did. My boys just followed my lead."

The commander struck him, hard across the jaw. He reeled into Keskan's shoulder, which yielded slightly to absorb the blow.

"That's for your failure."

Tan righted himself. "'S sir."

His eyes stung and his body quivered with the need to react. He did not look at Ash, but he could feel him, four cadets away, eating every detail.

That was the game they played, Shonco and him. Tan stepped up, Shonco let him have it. It made Tan look brave, it cemented his leadership. He was relieved to get slugged. But it wouldn't save Ordan.

⁂

Shonco left the lights on, which meant no hope of sleep. The boys sat sullen, Keskan presiding at the card table like a king, Codo on one side, Gomu on another. But he rubbed absently at his puffy eyes and gazed inward. That was unusual for him.

Tan got up from his cot. "All right, listen up. If any of you had any hand in helping Ordan desert, in encouraging him to desert, I don't want to hear it." He kept his eyes off Keskan. "He did it on his own, got it? He was a stupid Kiri rescue, barely dry behind the ears, and he made a stupid decision. That's all." He released a calculated breath. "There's still a chance they'll find him and let him off with a quick death."

"He's a wet-ass," snapped Keskan. "You just said so. He could get off with a beating and a little prison time. Even the commander said they'd show him leniency."

Tan faced him. "We can hope."

Keskan stood, and Tan began to feel he'd made a tactical error. He'd wanted to impress on them how serious this was, but he may have overplayed his hand.

"You don't hope so," said Keskan. "You don't want him let off."

"If they let him off, I'll be the first—"

"You want him dead."

"Don't be an idiot."

"Because if they let him off, it means they might have let off Júzian."

Tan's eyes snapped to Ash—just an instant but enough to show his weakness. "Júzian was our captain," he said. "You think they'd stand by and let a captain desert? You think they'd stand by and let *me* desert?" He addressed the room, and ten pairs of eyes looked back gravely.

Keskan took a step toward him. "They *did* let you desert. They let you live because you ratted him out."

Tan locked eyes with Keskan. "He was the traitor. He ran out on all of you."

Keskan's eyes bored into Tan. "What really happened, Ashtyn? You were there."

Tan held his breath, forcing himself to keep his eyes on Keskan.

After a hideous pause, Ash said, "Júzian tried to force me to desert. Tánashen rescued me."

Tan let out a sigh of relief.

Keskan gave Ash a hard look but said nothing.

The room was about to crack. They couldn't wait hours like this.

"Lavan and Sho, go grab cleaning supplies," said Tan. "As long as the lights are on, we'll make this room shine."

As the room began to breathe again, he risked a glance at Ash. He sat on his cot, cross-legged, shaking, stuck in memories Tan wished he could wipe away.

❧

In the morning, they were ordered to work on the water pump. It was deeply fucked, its pipes corroded, brown fluff every which way.

When they'd tried to turn the power back on, the strain must have snapped the damn thing in half.

C-16 sat in the cold, filing off rust so replacement parts could be attached.

"Bet they'll have to rebuild the whole pump," said Keskan.

"Is that bad?" said Dezdenec. "Then we'll have a new one."

"Yeah, but how long, Dezdenec? Thing's huge. They don't have much steel on site, not no how. It'll take tons of mining, building up solar capacity for smelting..."

Tan stayed out of it. Today was not the day.

The day bells tolled dim in the lower reaches—third bell, fourth bell, humming through the pipes beneath their fingers. The work stretched on, no word of Ordan.

Five bells, six bells vibrated through his fingertips. One day ago, they'd been celebrating. He filed at jagged edges, even in the cool, his head tight with thirst, his gut cadaverous.

When Ash had to piss, Tan walked him to the bathroom, not trusting what he'd do.

Seventh bell.

"Shit," whispered Dradam.

"Maybe he got away," said Lavan.

"Watch your mouth," breathed Tan, his eyes on Ash. "That's treason."

Lavan gave him a dark look. "I'm not no traitor."

Before eighth bell, feet clanked above them. Every boy went still. Shonco's face was its usual mask, his slow step resounding heavy.

Tan stood and saluted, his boys following suit.

"The priests found him," said Shonco.

❧

The black slash of the Citadel's shadow had fled. Late afternoon threw the sun on their noses as they stood hatless at attention, awaiting the train. Before them, the He and She stood high, each on its dais, their shadows reaching out to the boys like arms in supplication.

"Here it comes," whispered Codo.

Tan could hear the faint chug too, far but he had no idea how far. He'd never had to simply stand and wait in the quiet, listening.

When the doors of the Citadel opened behind them, it took all his will not to spin and look. Some boys did.

"Eyes forward," he ordered them with a sick sense of déjà vu. He'd said those words before, just over a year ago. It had been his first real command as their captain. It shouldn't be happening again. He'd turned Ordan in to stop it happening, to retrieve him before it was too late. He should have reported him sooner.

Now as then, Keskan stood beside him like a mountain, Ash three cadets to his right. Ash should not be here to see this again. At least, Fendo was still in medical, drugged and sleeping.

The ground shook with the train's coming. For a couple minutes, its rhythm blotted his heartbeat and swathed him in artificial calm.

At the station, it screeched and complained to a halt. Quiet fell. His nose burned, the top of his head blazed hot.

He expected screaming. There was no screaming, just the sound of steps. Commander Shonco went to meet them.

When the figures came into Tan's range of vision, he let his eyes shift and track them. Two footmen held Ordan's arms. He stumbled between them, eyes wide and cheek bruised, Shonco walking a little before them. They brought him to stand before his comrades, front and center, face-to-face with Tan, not more than ten feet between them.

"I didn't understand," Ordan blurted in Kiri. "Tell them I didn't understand. Captain, tell them."

Of course, he didn't understand. Keskan lied to him with his fantasies of escape. But did he think misunderstanding was an excuse? Did he misunderstand that much?

"He didn't understand," said Keskan in Citadel.

"He didn't understand, Commander," Tan echoed. He said it not because it would help—it wouldn't. He said because it would undermine him to let Keskan be the only one who said it.

Shonco ignored Keskan and took a step toward Tan. "Whose fault is that, Cadet Captain?"

"Mine, sir."

A silence followed. The next move would be for Tan to offer himself in Ordan's place. His eyes were locked on Ordan's chest, heaving below his dirt-stained shirt. He could feel Ordan's eyes pleading but did not dare to meet them.

Tan was not prepared to face his death for Ordan, not willing to bequeath his unit to Keskan, who would get them all killed the same damn way. Tan would not break his vow to look after Ash.

But he and Shonco had a game they played.

"I should be punished in his place, sir."

"Maybe you should. But every deserter must pay for himself."

Tan allowed himself a little gasp of relief.

At Shonco's nod, the footmen dragged Ordan to the dais where the He rose in sharp, crisscrossed angles. Now the yelling came, the struggling, the tumble of Kiri words, among them, "Put me down, put me down!"

They chained his arms and legs to the metal. They stripped open his shirt. Then, for a moment, they stood back and waited. His sobs wracked the silence. Then, the loudspeaker boomed:

I will pay my enemies as they have paid me.
I will blast them asunder and you, my king,
Shall rivet back their pieces and chain them fast
So that She—the piece torn out of me—will come to me
again.

Tan found himself glancing at the She, still and empty on her dais, swooping curves and shadows waiting.

"He who is destroyed now," called Shonco, "will be reborn in the time of Oneness."

He drew his knife and plunged it into Ordan's gut. Ordan screamed like a deserter—nothing else screamed like that. That piercing cry haunted the Citadel's walls, the price of violating Oneness.

Tan forced himself to watch. Flesh wasn't easy to cut, harder when writhing, alive. As the blood poured over Shonco, Tan thought dimly, *He'll need a new uniform*. Blood leaked from Ordan's mouth as Shonco stepped away and left him there to scream.

Every instinct said to put him down. Tan could feel his hand twitch by the gun at his hip. He ought to. He should have for Júzian. He had to.

Then the shot rang out—right by his ear but not from his gun. From Keskan's.

Ordan coughed two or three times, then convulsed—too long, pheasant-like. Then he slumped, blood coursing down his chest.

Tan felt his body unclench.

Shonco was shouting, but his words were wrapped in felt. Hands floating red against the desert and the vein in his temple straining at Tan, Tan couldn't hear him, but he could only be saying one thing.

"I shot him, sir." Tan's own words a whisper behind the buzzing in his ears. He said it because he had to, because it should have been him, because a captain had to protect his boys.

Shonco yanked Tan forward with a gory hand, seizing his gun from its holster. The footmen were unchaining Ordan. The angles of the He loomed as Shonco led him toward it, sharp and black as bat wings. The blood rushed in Tan's ears; it was all he could hear, that pounding rush.

He thought, *I failed*.

He'd leave Ash now, leave his boys, desert all of them.

And he knew no one would put him down, not now, knowing they'd be next. Or maybe Ash would—let it not be Ash.

"Stand strong," he called out—for Ash but it went out to all of them.

He wondered how long he would scream till he died and if the screaming made it more bearable. Was that why they did it? To bear it?

The dais stank. It slicked beneath his boot. They held him up. They chained him, arms above his head. The ground around him smelled like shit.

He waited for his embodied self to be torn into pieces—he waited and waited, time suspended. It didn't come. He was alone now on the dais, uncut, shirt buttoned.

Shonco was far away, talking at the boys, pointing at Tan.

"...are all One." He caught those words. "If you fail each other, you all pay each other. No one is exempt."

Shonco turned and looked at him. They all looked. Ash looked, the bandage at his neck blazing white. A few minutes ago, when they'd stood together, he had not been able to see Ash or hear him. He had sensed Ash only as a worn-out promise. Suddenly, he was real again, a boy standing thirty feet away, with that blank look boys wore to survive.

It was a game. It had to be. If Shonco planned to kill him, he would be dying now. It was a punishment and you got through it and survived. All his boys looked at him, their faces one, Ash's blankness no different from Keskan's, no different from Tarnto's or Codo's. They were waiting it out. He could wait it out too. He gave them a little smile, a nod.

Dezdenec smiled back, only him, thirteen years old and serious as a priest, though he'd never be a priest; it seemed unfair his hair was brown.

Heat built at Tan's back, not just from the sun but the metal. If he bent his shoulders back, he could keep his flesh off the steel. If he let his hands sink on his shackles, they were hot but he could rest his arms. He took a breath and forced a kind of relaxation. If you sank into it, you could bear the heat. It could even be pleasant. Become One with the desert, with the He, the part torn out returning. Even a small sense of wonder.

Then, it got harder to ignore the dehydration, the ache where his neck met his skull and snaked around to his eye sockets. The heat began to sear his skin, even without touching the metal.

He found Dezdenec's eyes again. They were cool gray and sustained him, like a thread between them, like a water pipe irrigating Tan. Those eyes were pools but he couldn't reach them. He slipped off them and wandered over shadow and heat. His boys became patterns in beige, statues, mirrors. He stood stalwart.

He began to shake.

His arms hurt, hands tingled. A sharp pain grew where his right shoulder met his back. They were clay baked in the sun, those figures standing before him, though some of them shook too and sweat had begun to melt them.

But his move must be to stand and take it.

Thirst ate the back of his throat. It must be eating at all of them. How long would Shonco keep them there in the sun? Longer than it would have taken Ordan to die? He couldn't let the whole unit collapse. Ash, Sho, Dradam, they were physically small. They had no spare fat to protect him.

Tan began to shift in a sad, chained dance, hoping for relief in motion.

His eyes fell on Keskan, stiff and unsmiling. Probably he didn't dare, and Tan hated him with a molten fury. Inside, Keskan must be loving this—Tan's humiliation, his helpless, stupid, futile dance steps to escape the inescapable sun. The restitution.

How long had he been here? Half an hour? More? Less?

Gods, his head hurt. His shoulder hurt. He could feel the sun blister the back of his neck.

How long would Shonco leave him here? Shonco liked him. He wouldn't punish him harder than he felt he had to. He wouldn't—

Then, his head opened up and he understood. He almost puked there onto the gore. Maybe Shonco had already delivered his mercy. To die whole, not be eviscerated. Perhaps that was the only mercy he could give.

Tan found Ash's black bead eyes like a lance in his head.

Why did the right side of his head hurt so much?

Something had changed. Shonco was giving orders to Keskan. Keskan was marching the boys inside. The courtyard was clearing. The courtyard had cleared.

Only Tan remained.

☙

His trembling muscles kept bumping metal. His shirt provided a little buffer, but the bare skin of his forearms sizzled. Ordan's blood had dried in his feet. His boots were ovens. His throat stuck and he couldn't swallow.

He waited for Shonco to save him. He tried to stop waiting, to let hope escape. He might end here. The idea slid around his edges, terrifying and simple.

He gave up wondering if anyone was watching, gave up worrying about humiliation. He started whining in time with the pain. He let himself whine—or perhaps he couldn't help it. He only knew it was easier than silence.

A door clicked. He started up, thumping his back into the He. A man came out. This was it, his rescue.

The man glanced at him and made for the train, disappearing into the station.

He whined. Like a puppy. A cousin had had a puppy back at home to herd the goats. Back home in Naughty Vines. In Naughty Vines, there were trees and flowers; white came first in the winter, blue and yellow in the spring. In early summer, purple winked in the dry grass, but you napped in the cellar in the heat of the day—down in the earth on the rug with its pills of lint.

His neck was killing him.

The horrible thing about dying was the destruction of a perfectly good system. Tan worked. His brain worked, his body worked. Ordan had worked. A few hours ago, he'd been a living, breathing boy with decades of life ahead of him. Now he was meat—and crusted lacquer on the stones.

Was there a way to maximize the amount of shadow his body stood in?

He tried. He found it almost futile, a little relief from keeping the nape of his neck out of direct sun.

But you'd die fast in the desert in the sun with no water.

It could be good to surrender. Sunder. Surrender.

It could be good to let it end.

His neck and shoulders became a flayed cape. His hands were puffing. He felt them swell like a busted gut going purple. The sun had moved; it was back on his neck.

He twisted. He yelled, one low, hard bark. It felt good. It made him laugh, but the laugh got stuck to the roof of his mouth.

He gave up resisting and fought, smashing his body into He. Wrists cracked, elbows shuddered. His foot slipped and lightning shot through his arms as the chains caught his weight. He yelped and scrabbled back onto his feet.

The day darkened but heat endured, so it must be his eyes that were darkening.

The man crossed back from the train, a moving blot on the pale concrete.

Gods, the Citadel was mighty. He looked up at its towering divinity. Like a bone stuck in the Earth, like a dragonfly on its head, huge eyes tapering to a tail lost in the sky. His eyes couldn't reach its pinnacle.

He slipped and found himself again. His throat closed, as if a ball had been thrust inside it. The day became forever, the sun standing still. It seemed he started to fall asleep. Slip and tumble, jolt and fire. That rhythm became his clock.

Chapter Eight

C ool radiated into his back. In the dark, he would have been comfortable if it weren't for the dead weight of his arms. They lay, sacks of meat, islands of heat in the cool. It was the prickling of his blood that really woke him. Sand flowed in his veins, inching life back into his fingers.

He looked up and saw a ceiling. He was lying on a floor, something cushioning his head. He flexed his hands and rolled over to find himself face to face with the metal legs of a desk. He'd never thought about them before, the way the sturdy posts sprouted a decorative lattice near the join with the desktop, the side facing him dipping down jagged, the side at a slant to him smooth and round: the He and She at right angles, separated by the metal bar of the leg, close but still sundered.

The door clicked, but before Tan could turn to look, Commander Shonco stooped and pressed a damp cloth to his forehead.

"Get up," he said. "I have broth."

He took Tan under the arms and hauled him into a chair. The damp cloth lay on the desk before him, and a large cup—two times, three times the usual size. He got his tingling hand around it, wrists scraped and bloody. It surprised him that his hands looked all right, not mangled, not blackened, not falling off.

"Sip it," said Shonco, sitting behind his desk.

Tan tried to pretend his gulps were sips. His tongue leapt hungrily after the salts.

Shonco peered at him—not disapproving, Tan thought, but assessing the pieces, face, hands, and so on. He poured some cleaner on the towel and handed it to Tan.

"How do you feel?"

Tan didn't think he'd ever gotten that question from Shonco. He wasn't sure what to say. Should he be strong? Should he be honest?

"Not at peak, sir." He rubbed caked blood from his wrists.

"I need to know, Tánashen. Do you need to go to medical?"

Tan listened to his body, to the blood rushing in his ears. His head throbbed, bits of skin stung. "I'm all right, sir, just dehydrated and a little burned." It was true; he'd come through his ordeal essentially unscathed, as Shonco must have known he would.

Shonco nodded. "There's a clean uniform on the shelf there. Put it on. Then, finish the broth."

Tan hesitated. Despite what all the boys thought, he'd never changed clothes in front of Shonco. Any boy knew what it meant to strip in front of any man. Another time, Tan might have felt excitement—even relief, to be wanted, finally. Now, his head felt thick and dizzy. He just wanted to lie on the floor.

The commander sighed. "I'll step out. Let me know when you're done."

It seemed unreal, Tan alone in Shonco's office. He stood, rusty, like a clockwork boy, and slowly peeled off his clothes.

When he opened the door, Shonco was leaning on the wall, lost in thought. He came and took a bottle from his desk.

"Water," he said, topping Tan's broth. "You'll need your strength."

Tan sat and took a drink of the diluted broth.

They sat there a long time in silence, Shonco staring somewhere past his desk, his motionless frown profoundly sad. As for Tan, he didn't know how he felt. Tired. Nothing. The lamp gave off the same light as a foggy morning. Mornings Mum would say, *The air's off the River*, and it would not be a hot day.

"I admire what you did," said Shonco.

Admire him? For...? Taking the blame for Keskan's bullet? No, Shonco didn't know that. He thought Tan had shot Ordan. He admired Tan for being Keskan.

"A piece of me wishes for your courage," said Shonco, "but if you had a different commander, you'd be dead. The Citadel survives because we act as One. And because some do not understand that, we need discipline to uphold our Oneness. You need to keep a grip on your people."

"Yes, sir."

"That boy is dead because you didn't."

"Yes, sir."

"I'm glad we understand each other." He opened a drawer and handed Tan a gun. It was Tan's own, he knew it by the silver ding in the handle. "Your cadets are waiting. Help them finish their punishment."

&

When he entered the mess hall, the murmuring stopped. Eleven pairs of eyes snapped on him, even Fendo in a wheelchair. Tan's body did not feel his own. His shoulders sat like wings askew, his hands leaves of grass, his feet muffled.

I'm not going to make Fendo eat, he thought. *They can't make me, not with his intestines sliced.*

Ash came up to him. "Are you all right, Captain?"

Thank the gods. He'd said, *captain*. Yes, Tan was the captain, and he'd damn well stay that way.

"I'm fine. Let's get this done."

His boots squeaked as he walked past them, the sound amplified by the big, empty room. His key clacked in the kitchen's latch, and he swung the door open.

The smell struck everyone. He heard swearing behind him.

The smell came from everywhere. Where was Ordan? Tan glanced around and—there, behind the table, laid out on the floor.

"We'll get him stripped and washed first," Tan said.

Keskan strode past Tan, side-stepping the corpse. With a single sweep of his arm, he sent all the bowls and platters crashing off the prep table.

Tan jerked, hand straying to his gun.

The metallic clatter resounded into silence.

"All right, Captain," said Keskan quietly. "You get his feet."

Tan gave him a curt nod and got his hands around the booted ankles. As he hefted him, his arms felt about to fall out of their sockets. But it was only a few moments and they had him on the table.

He should assign a team to clean. No, there was no point in cleaning till all the blood had already fallen.

Tan started untying Ordan's boots. "Codo and Dezdenec, you sort clothes for reuse or scrapping. Dradam, turn the fan on. Tarnto, heat the oven."

"We can't do this." A soft voice, bewildered, incredulous. Sho. "We have to stop. We have to stop!" He held his hands to the sides of his head as if to keep his ears from ringing. "It's got to stop. My pa will make it stop!"

"Your pa made this happen," snarled Keskan.

"You don't fucking know that," said Codo. "What if it was my pa, my pa's a priest too."

None of them could know which priests had found Ordan. But Keskan meant all the priests, that was clear enough—dangerous enough.

Tan crossed to him in two steps. "They're listening," he said. They had to be. Keskan met his eyes coolly but shut his mouth.

Codo was holding Sho, rocking him like a baby.

Quietly, Dezdenec said, "He was a sacrifice to Loss."

"The gods want this?" said Dradam.

"You don't understand. No one *wants* a sacrifice. The gods don't want a sacrifice. It's the sundering that drives them mad, the rupturing of Oneness, Loss and Inner Fire—He and She sundered, Loss and Owner, the two faces of the one god, sundered—"

"Dezdenec." Tan cut him off. "We're not scholars."

Dezdenec fixed Tan with those clear, gray eyes. "You've met Loss too."

Met Loss? Did he mean being strung up... or Júzian?

Tan looked away.

"*Gudgánta*," muttered Keskan in Kiri. *Goatshit*. He started slicing Ordan's shirt, yanking it in strips with gory hands, like Shonco's. "Are we going to eat his face?"

"We're going to do what we have to," said Tan.

ەﻻ

They gutted him and minced the guts quickly for compost. That might raise an objection; some could have been used for sausage or condoms, but Tan would take the reprimand. He figured that even without the guts, they were paying the price for their comrade's desertion.

Keskan took the lead in carving him up, not a word of complaint, not an upward glance. Carve and pass a piece to Dezdenec to shove into the oven.

But when it came to the pieces of his face, Dezdenec gagged.

"I'll do it," said Tan and took up his position. The alcohol cooled his hands. Then the blood and muscle warmed them.

The saw cut the bone like firewood. It was that sound, not the sight, not the smell, that made Tan's throat close. A memory shot through him—Dad in his dark blue tunic at the saw jack. His stomach turned, and for several seconds he had to concentrate on his breathing.

From the counter where they were mincing him, Tarnto let loose a peel of laughter. "Fuck, his nuts were tiny."

"Shut up!" roared Keskan. In the sudden silence, he handed Tan an eyeball.

Tan took it, but Keskan's slippery hand grasped his wrist.

"Burn him," he said.

Tan looked at the eye. He thought of the sun just outside these walls, still blazoning the metal of the He. His shoulders ached and his hands still felt gloved, and every show of weakness in resolve had its cost.

"I will," he said. "Just carve enough to feed us."

"Fuck that."

"It's all the food we'll get today. Anyway, oven's not designed to burn that hot. It'll be obvious if it's his whole body."

In the corner, a whimper turned to wailing, Sho.

"Take him out," said Tan. "Codo, take him out."

"Where?"

"Mess hall." Where else? If he left the hall before the meal was over, they'd be liable to be punished again.

But Sho slumped like a sack of mash and writhed when Codo tried to lift him. He tried once, twice.

"It's okay. Let him be," said Tan.

Tan baked Ordan's tongue to the sound of Sho's wailing.

❧

At the table, Tan stood and mumbled the ritual words. "Those who deny Oneness in spirit will relearn it in the body."

He heard a scoff from Keskan and let it pass.

Then, in the silence, Dezdenec recited softly,

I saw my children captured, beaten,
Cudgeled in the desert sand. I heard my loved ones cry.

*In secret towers, they cried at night and in the day, they
toiled,
Until my heart sank beneath the sands,
And cried and sighed and split in two,
Till I myself was rent in two,
Till I myself was sundered.*

"This is the Golden Way," the boys replied.

They ate without speaking, chewing as if on rawhide. Fendo sipped at the broth Tan had given him. Broth made of Ordan. Dezdenec threw up. Muned got up to clean it.

Tan held it down somehow. Ever since he'd been taken down from the He, his body had pulsed as if his blood strained for breath. His heart throbbed in his forehead. His body felt like a pipe clogged with shit.

He started at a clang of metal: Keskan slamming his knife on his tray and getting up, half empty tray in his hands.

"Lieutenant—"

"Stay off me." Keskan's eyes bit into him, weirdly bright—with tears, Tan realized. It hit him as an alien intrusion. He'd known Keskan seven years, Keskan didn't cry. When Tan made no move, he took his tray into the kitchen.

He was still there when the rest filed in to wash up, leaning on the counter, his hand pressed to his mouth in thought.

"All right," said Tan. "All the scraps into the oven."

"Scraps?" said Keskan. "Is that what he is to you?"

"Don't do this, Keskan."

"Do what? Tell the truth?" He stood up, tall and imposing. "You gave the alarm. You led them to him."

"They would have found him. They always find you. If they'd found him before his grace period—"

"But they *didn't* find him! The priests didn't even fucking know he was gone until *you* ratted him out."

"You told him to run! That's on you, you fucker—luring him on with the *train* and the *river*." Tan nodded savagely. "But you're right, it's my own damn fault. It's my fault for not turning in your sorry ass. It should have been *you* strung up, not him."

Keskan lunged at him.

Tan made a feint by muscle memory, but he was slow and off his balance. Keskan kicked him to the ground, and his shoulder erupted in flames. He scrambled to block the next blow—

And a siren exploded.

Tan crumbled, convinced he'd been punched in some nerve, his brain breaking down into pummeling sound.

"*Attention. All units to the emergency shelter.*"

The voice snapped him back to life. He crawled to his feet, years of drills taking over.

"To the bomb shelter now. Keskan, carry Fendo. Run!"

Chapter Nine

Commander Shonco pounded toward them down the hallway. "Go, go, go!" He fell in step beside them.

"Fucking drill," panted Gomu.

"No!" shouted Shonco. "No drill! Go!" He gave Gomu a shove.

The clanging bells blotted the pelt of their feet. Shouts fell muffled across the din.

As they reached the stairway, Tan ground to a stop and counted off his boys as they ran past him.

Where was Ash?

There, half obscured behind Gomu.

Keskan came last, breathing hard, with Fendo over his back.

Shonco nodded to Tan and they raced down the stairs and through the steel door into the dim, wide bunker. Shouts rang off the walls, multiplying the cacophony. Dozens of women and children clapped through the door to join men and boys.

"Down!" yelled Shonco.

They dove for the floor.

Tan threw one arm over his head and the other over Ash. The ceiling thundered above them, and improbable shocks of pink and blue snaked down the walls. The lights went out. The floor beneath them trembled.

The alarm stopped.

Its absence made Tan weightless, like he'd fallen through the floor, but the wailing of the little children tied him to reality. Ash, solid and hot beneath him, tied him. Tan held him close and breathed along with the rise and fall of his brother's breathing.

For maybe a minute, a thunder rolled like the train, the room sporadically lit by lightning in the walls, like veins on fire. The shocks did not touch the floor, and it came to Tan that the floor was made of some padding, nonconductive. There were four bomb shelters, and this one pulsed with some five hundred people packed arm to arm.

Rarer now and sharper in the quiet, the snaps and pops continued, the sounds of breathing ringing louder in the stillness.

A handful of voices began to whisper.

"Stay down," said some officer.

"Shon," hissed a woman's voice. "Shon, where's Fendo?"

A little way from Tan, Shonco raised his head. "Keskan, is Fendo...?"

"He's alive, Commander."

"Bless the gods." Fendo's mother scrambled across the floor to her son, ignoring the curses of the people she crawled over. She sat there, cradling his head while he moaned.

"Keep down, damn it, Togi," came the voice of the Grand Aunt, but Aunt Togi gave no sign she heard.

It cracked something in Tan. He couldn't look. He pressed his head against Ash's shoulder and held him tight. Ash was safe in his arms, so there was nothing to fear.

"What's going on up there?" someone whispered.

"It's all right," said a quiet voice near the door. "It's over. Our shield has withstood the attack." His voice was not amplified or altered but Tan knew it to the root of his brain.

The lights went on, white. And when Tan dared a glance, he saw the Landowner standing there, deceptively ordinary in his loose white clothes, his hand still on the light switch. He was human now, no flickering phantom, but his eyes still blazed an inhuman blue.

"They're treacherous, these Raiders. No doubt their spies informed them of the barbarians' attack, and knowing our weakened state, they thought they could crush us. They've failed." He rubbed a hand across his mouth, the tired gesture of a man whose people thirsted and whose enemies were closing. "But their declaration is clear enough. We would not have chosen this moment for war, yet Oak will not find us unprepared for it." He paused for a moment and in a low voice sang a fragment of scripture:

> *I will pay my enemies as they have paid me.*
> *I will blast them asunder...*

Tan shuddered with a baffled mix of terror and elation. The Citadel would make Oak pay, and the *Citadel* understood punishment.

The Landowner's voice trailed off, as if he were lost in thought, and on padding feet, he went up the stairs.

❧

In the heat of the setting sun, Tan dragged a bent steel pole toward the recyke heap. Gods, it was heavy, his hands dry as sand. A wave of dizziness came over him. He stuck the pole in the dust and leaned on it, took a sip of water from his quarter-filled canteen.

As he caught his breath, his eye strayed up to the towering horn of the half-buried bull's head. It had stood in the desert a thousand years, proof against the weapons of Oak, like the ancient skull of a spirit passed indelibly into the land.

Bathed in sweat, men and boys plodded the courtyard, gathering up hunks of twisted metal; hammers clanked and short-range trucks trundled across the wreckage. The train station was shattered, half the solar panels too. But inside the shelter of the shield's pillars, the Citadel stood unblemished.

He remembered the aunts teaching that the Citadel was once a space ship. They taught how it had fled the infidels and sailed on the waves of space till it reached its haven here, on the planet Uramésha. He did not remember learning the word "citadel," but the aunts must have taught him that, too, because he knew it meant an impenetrable building. He'd known it a long time, but only now did he think about what it meant: how long the Citadel had stood, how it would always stand...

This is what it means to be a citadel.

Tan threw a scrap of rail tie into the junk cart. As he turned, his eyes fell on the He and She, untouched within the circle of the shield's protection. He could see a trace of brown on the dais, the blood of Ordan.

Had that been only yesterday? First night bell had recently sounded—about seventeen hours since Ordan had died. There was Keskan, loading detritus into a bin. For good or ill, he was part of their Oneness. At the same time, he'd helped Ordan desert.

And Tan couldn't turn him in because it would implicate... Ordan, he realized, not Ash. No one would mention Ash running after this, not even Tarnto. No one wanted another Ordan. And Ordan was dead; no more harm could come to him. The game board had suddenly opened up. Now, he could turn the fucker in without implicating his brother.

☙

"Commander Shonco." With the grudging permission of the sentry, Tan had been waiting outside the conference room in the inky battery light for an hour.

Now, as the officers filed out, Shonco started at his name. "What are you doing here, Tánashen? It's lights out. You should be in bed."

Yes, he should be. Though he'd set Dezdenec to keep an eye on Keskan, he'd left his boys alone too long.

"I have to make a report, sir."

"Now?"

Before Tan could reply, Shonco waved him into the conference room. It had a huge, round table and at least twelve chairs, receding into the low-lit gloom.

Shonco sat and ran his hands through his thinning hair; he'd aged a year since yesterday.

Tan stood and began without preamble. "Commander, I have to report that Cadet Keskan helped Ordan desert. In fact, I think he planned it."

Shonco showed no surprise. He showed nothing at all. "Evidence."

"Yesterday, I overheard them talking about going to the river—and the train, how fast the train could get there. Ordan was asking questions. Keskan... was very encouraging."

"That's all?"

"He tried to cover for Ordan by lying and saying he'd seen a pappy take him. I knew it was a lie because he described the man as Citadel but had him saying Kiri things. A bad lie."

"If you knew it was a lie, why didn't you report it then?"

"I did, sir. That's when I reported Ordan missing." He paused. "As for Keskan—I was thinking about Ordan, sir. I guess he didn't occur to me."

Shonco leaned back and crossed his arms. "Hard evidence?"

"Sir?"

"Did anyone else hear this? Do I have anything besides your word?"

Tan hesitated. Ash had heard some of it, but what if Ash sided with Keskan? "No, sir. But I think you know he's a troublemaker."

That sound might have been a laugh. "Yes, it's obvious he's making trouble for you."

"Sir, I am not making this up."

"I believe you, Tánashen, but if I act on that belief, it will pulverize your authority. You see that, don't you? You come to me, I have him killed, and you are the weakling who could not put down dissent."

Yes, Tan saw that clearly. It was the equation that had kept him mute month after month. But it shamed him to hear it from his own commander. He was keenly aware of his head pounding with thirst.

"Commander, Ordan is dead. I can't let that pass."

"And Ashtyn might be next."

That froze him proper. He stood stuck to the floor as a statue.

Shonco rose. "You did right to come to me. I'll put eyes on him. You keep eyes on him, too; use the boys you trust. If he's a canker, we'll burn him out, but the denunciation cannot come from you."

"Yes, sir." Tan turned to go.

"You'll need a cover story for seeing me."

Tan hesitated. "I hung my belt up."

Shonco barely cracked a smile. "Here's a better one. It'll be announced tomorrow anyway. I summoned you to tell you that we're being deployed North. To obliterate Oak."

Chapter Ten

As the train plodded north toward the Grid, Tan fought off ghostings of nausea. Once, he'd had a strong stomach. No matter how frightened, how disgusted, how guilty, his emotions didn't translate into that kind of sickness.

Then, a year ago, he'd eaten Júzian.

Ever since then, at odd vertiginous moments, his stomach would pitch. He felt it now, as the flat desert gave way to bigger hunks of rock. It fled through his mind with words like "Ordan" and dwarf pines behind desks—and the realization that soon Oak would be vanquished and the Garden free, or he would be dead with the rest of his boys.

Ash leaned against Tan's sprained shoulder, his breathing deep and abrupt with sleep.

Outside the window on a distant hill, a splotch of blue-green caught his eye. Up close, he knew, it would resolve into a patch of lupin, those weird, big blossoms that dominated here south of the River.

There was life here. Why couldn't they all share it, the Kiris and the Citadel. Even Oak? Was lupin edible?

"Captain."

Tan glanced up at Dezdenec, sitting by the aisle on the other side of Ash.

"It wasn't your fault," said Dezdenec.

It took a moment for his words to register. Tan managed a smile and flashed his eyes toward Keskan. Dezdenec nodded.

🙵

Still miles outside the Grid, the train ground to a halt. Ash stirred sleepily. Old metal creaked, while the boys chattered low.

Tan looked out the window to see if he'd missed something. The hills stretched to the horizon, punctuated by higher crags in the distance.

"Why do you think they stopped us, Captain?" Muned scratched absently at the dent in his nose, where the skin cancer had been cut out.

"Bomb scare?" said Lavan.

"Are they going to nuke the train?" asked Dradam.

"A nuke for a *train*?" scoffed a guy from C-15. "You barbs even know what a nuke is?"

Several boys broke out laughing, but the jerk in their movements was taut with fear.

"It's not a bomb scare," said Tan. "If we knew a bomb was coming, we'd be rolling, not a sitting target."

"If we knew," said Keskan.

"So what is it?" said Muned.

"I don't know," said Tan. "They'll tell us what we need to know." He got up on one knee and leaned over his seat. "Just stay in your seats and hang tight."

"Your bits look pretty tight, Gomu."

Gomu gave Tarnto a shove. "You want to find out personally?"

Tan could feel Keskan's glare on his back, but he also saw the keen exchange of glances among his own cadre: Dezdenec, Muned, Dradam, Lavan, watching him for signs of treachery.

After a few minutes, Shonco entered the car and stood with one hand on the guard rail.

"The priest has located a group of deserters out of Soruc's Town." Lavan's home town. Tan glanced at him; Lavan's face was grim. "They're Kiris," Shonco went on, "but they'd been brought into Oneness and chose to reject it. They're sneaking supplies west,

toward Oak. We've been tasked with intercepting them. C-15 and
16, you're with me. C-13, 14, you'll stay with the train. Clear space
for wounded. Clear space for cargo. Have first aid unpacked and
ready to go. C-15, 16, get your packs and clear them of everything
but your arms, water, one ration bar, and first aid. We'll be carrying
back what we can of their supplies."

※

The midday sun beat on their helmets, but a breeze from the
north brought some relief. Tan loosened his top button to invite it
in. C-16 marched between Shonco and C-15. No one would trust
them to bring up the rear, a deserter's unit and half-Kiri. No one
would give them a chance to slip away among the rocks. Tan came
last in his unit, Ash directly ahead. He didn't trust his unit either.

The rocks were splattered with meat. Though memory said the
orange and red were lichens, they struck him now like grease and
blood. He remembered once feeling this land was clean. He had
breathed it with a sigh of anticipation, the Citadel behind him, the
Garden ahead. The Garden was still ahead, he reminded himself.
They'd get there if they played their parts.

They began to crunch uphill. Untold years had whittled out
excrescences of rock, leaving shards of every size, from great boulders
to the gravel beneath their boots. Here and there, blankets of lupin
sprang out luminous blue. Up close, they were tall chains of purple
and white, arching up over palm-shaped leaves. They were not the
lupin of home.

Something moved to Tan's left, and he started. But they were just
little balls of fur, hyraxes sun-bathing on a far-off slope.

"If these guys want to meet up with Oak," said Muned, "why
aren't they heading north?"

"They're idiots," said Tan sourly. Júzian had fled into the south;
he'd been an idiot.

"The north between the River and the Grid is too well guarded," said Shonco. They hadn't meant him to overhear and got quiet when he answered. "They'll skirt the Bridge and cross farther on. They may even be carrying boats."

After a silence, Dradam whispered to Lavan, "They must be headed to Dip." Dip—or Naimu's Town—was Dradam's home.

Lavan nodded stiffly. "Fucking deserters."

Low in Mouth—Soruc's—was Lavan's home; those deserters were betraying not just the Citadel but the headman, Lavan's father.

"But maybe they're just traders," said Dradam. "Commander," he said a little louder. "Maybe they're traders. Naimu's and Soruc's trade all the time."

"They're not," said Shonco. "Citadel trade goes through the Grid. If they're heading cross-country with a caravan, that means they're trading off-Grid and they're agents for Oak."

⁂

They'd been walking for about an hour, when abruptly and for no clear reason, Tan's heart began to knock. It couldn't be fear of battle; marching always soothed that. It was the place, something familiar. That stone. What was it about that great upended stone? Then he recognized the rough grass, the hint of far-off trees.

It was the route they had taken on the day they had run, that day of rocks and dust. They'd found water trickling in a crack in that rock. Ash had complained of a headache. Tan had had a headache too—he remembered it but couldn't recall how it felt. He'd been hungry, but he couldn't recall how that felt either. He just remembered the water and Júzian's voice. *Be quick, we need to keep moving.*

He ordered himself back to the present, disowning the wave of nausea.

After a time, they went slower and crept low, keeping to the cover of the boulders. They could hear the wagon wheels now and the occasional voice, male, furtive.

Commander Shonco signaled for them to halt and crouched a few feet ahead, watching.

"Seven wagons, seven camels. Five men in sight, but if they're smart, they have backup off the road or riding in the wagons. Remember, arrows kill, knives kill, rocks kill. Don't get cocky just because you have a gun. They may have guns too. They may have stolen them from us. Shoot the men. I don't see any women or children, but if they're stupid enough to bring them, try to take them unhurt. The camels are meat. We'll pince three ways. Captains, you'll deploy your soldiers."

At least, Tan was still trusted with that.

Having given his orders, Shonco left them. Per the pincer maneuver, he'd backtrack till the caravan was out of sight, then dart across the canyon and hide in the hills on the far side.

C-15 moved up ahead, aiming to attack the caravan from the front.

C-16 kept pace with the caravan, skulking above them and ready to hit from behind. Tan motioned his marksmen to stay high in the rocks: Codo, Dezdenec—and Fendo, who was only an average shot but already breathing hard from the walk.

"You're strictly backup," Tan had told him. "It's fine. You're still healing. If you get a clear shot, take it. If not, don't try anything ambitious."

The littler boys—Sho, Ash, Tarnto—would support the older, ready to shoot low or dash under the wagons, those things little boys were best at.

He pulled Sho aside. "Stick to Muned and don't fire unless you have a clear shot." Sho was just shortsighted enough for his aim to be a little hazy.

They inched down. As they wove in and out of sight, they could see the row of wagons wending through the canyon. He'd worried that wagons might be covered, like nomad habitations, but they weren't. They were merely large carts, tarps thrown over goods. A man might hide in there, but no more than one per wagon if their goal was to transport supplies.

Then someone's boot slipped. A rock the size of a camel's head thudded down the hillside.

Everyone froze.

From his vantage point behind a boulder, Tan could see a Kiri man draw a gun. The only good thing was that it played partly to plan. They were supposed to give Shonco a diversion as he crept in close, but not for another few minutes and not with such a dramatic cascade.

Shonco's voice came from too low down and too far back, but it rang out self-possessed and certain. "You're carrying property to our enemies, comrades. It will go better for you if you surrender it now."

The men pulled the camels to a stop. Tan raised his head enough to make out five wagons. Two men darted back into view. Easy targets. At least two hunkered between the wagons.

Tan couldn't see the leader but heard him answer, his Citadel speech accented even more than Ordan's. "We do not take to the enemy. We take to Dip. What you say 'Naimu's Town.'"

The commander whistled as if he found their story ridiculous. But that was the signal. Tan counted down from five.

"If you were headed to Naimu's, friend," said Shonco, "you be going through—"

"Fire!" The two captains called together.

Their first volley rang out and they were on the move. Amid the shots came yells and the wailing of the camels. That camel sound stuck in his breastbone. At least four of the deserters drew guns. They had plainly given up on tech limitation. A C-15 boy fell. Three of the deserters were down. A shot cracked the rock beside his head. He ducked and tracked backward, darted behind another rock, sighted a man and took him down.

"Ash?" He glanced around, relieved to see his brother crouched close beside him.

It went fast, the initial barrage of shots already reduced to an occasional clap, echoing around the valley. When he risked a look up, he saw five Kiris dead—and Lavan in a crevice between rocks, clutching his side.

A sharp whistle came from Shonco, ordering them to secure the wagons. As they surged down the rocks, an arrow winged by and a gunshot cracked.

"Stick close, Ash," called Tan, as he dashed across the canyon and skidded down behind a wagon.

Then Keskan broke ranks.

Tan saw him sprint toward an outlying wagon, dragged off the road by its dying camel. Tan shouted to him, but his voice got lost in the camel's keening.

"Stay down, Ash."

He sprinted to the wagon where Keskan had vanished, its wheel stuck between rocks facing a steep incline, the stones and flowers weirdly still against the groans and sounds of camels thrashing. He peered around the corner.

Keskan had his gun trained on a skinny, salt-bearded man on the ground.

"—for years, right?" Keskan demanded in Kiri. "Blast it, tell me who you're arming."

The man stared at him in terror.

Just then, something under the wagon moved. Tan took aim at it. A heavy man lurched out and grabbed Keskan's ankle. Keskan went down just as Tan fired. His position wasn't great, and he winged the big man in the side, but it was enough. Keskan scuffled and got free.

Tan raced up and shot the man in the back. Keskan's eyes snapped from his attacker onto Tan.

The old bearded guy was scrabbling away.

Tan shot him point blank and wheeled on Keskan. "What the hell? Where in your orders did it say to interrogate the meat?"

Keskan sprang to his feet, glaring daggers at Tan. Then he turned away and peered around the edge of the wagon.

"Get back on target," Tan ordered him, confirming he was moving before racing back to cover his boys.

But the guns had stilled and the shouts turned to cries of pain; the camels, at least, were mostly dead. Tan put a bullet in the head of one that wasn't.

"Get the tarps off—and careful." Shonco was out from his cover now, gun at the ready.

"Sir." Dezdenec approached him, dirt-stained and breathing hard. "Cadet Keskan disobeyed orders, sir."

That brought Keskan's head up sharp.

Tan went still. He'd told Dezdenec to keep a look out for treachery, but this wasn't desertion or aiding desertion. *Dezdenec, you're overplaying your hand.*

"Explain," said Shonco.

"He went off position to interrogate one of the traitors."

Keskan strode up. "The guy was right in front of me, sir, alive, incapacitated. It was a chance to get information on their movements."

"Cadet Captain Tánashen?"

Don't overplay. A good captain doesn't rat out his boys. "He disobeyed orders, sir. I reprimanded him. It's closed."

Shonco moved like lightning. He smacked Keskan across the face, so quick and sharp Tan jumped.

"You're fortunate to have a captain so invested in protecting you. Get back to work, lieutenant."

"Yes, sir," said Keskan.

A strange little shower of relief fell on Tan. They had all played their parts, and they'd brought the move off. Dezdenec confirmed that Keskan was trouble. Shonco confirmed it, too, while Tan downplayed. Shonco put Tan in the role of Keskan's protector, so when the time came to get rid of him, no one could say Tan just did it from malice.

If only Ash wasn't frowning at Tan.

"Come on," Tan told him. "Help me with the wagons."

Chapter Eleven

The first wagon was secured, the second, the third. Fourth wagon—when Tan went to untie the tarp, a hand flashed in the shadows. He jerked as the knife sliced his arm. He grabbed the thin wrist, shook the blade from her hand. She roared like a beast as he dragged her into the daylight, a girl about eight. When she bit his wrist, he twisted her arm behind her back and got her wrists tied to a wheel.

"If you behave, you won't die," he told her.

She screamed.

"Dradam!" Tan called. "Talk to her. You come from these parts." He'd been living in Dip just four years ago.

Dradam came and tried, the girl just growling at him.

Tan left her to him, and... mad gods, he'd lost track of his brother. If Ash was dead, if Ash had run—

Then Ash was in front him, dirty, vacant, a goose egg red on his forehead.

"You okay?" Tan checked the lump, checked his eyes. His pupils looked normal. "Come with me." He wanted to say, "Go rest behind the rocks," but he didn't dare, not with the lure of escape so close.

A C-15 boy was dressing wounds. A bullet had broken Lavan's ribs but missed his lung to judge by his breathing. He lay curled in a ball, whining.

"Can't you inject him with something for the pain?" Tan asked the boy.

"Why you barbarians all so scared of pain?"

Tan crouched beside him and rifled in his own kit. He squirreled away a vial of anesthetic months ago. "Just do it." He handed him the vial and syringe. "Or do you want to hear him crying all the way to the train?"

&

One from C-15 was dead. Lavan was in rough shape, the others' wounds superficial. Tan's arm stung, but that was nothing. All the deserters were dead but the girl, who'd gone quiet. Dradam still talked to her softly.

"Will they take her back to Low in Mouth—I mean Soruc's Town?" Tan asked Shonco.

"Probably. Best thing would be to send her back to her family, if she has any."

"Why'd they take her?" snapped Ash, as if their choice was Shonco's fault.

"Ash," Tan admonished but Shonco shrugged.

"Who knows? Maybe they're tired of Citadel discipline. Maybe they've forgotten that Citadel protection is the only reason they aren't slaves of Oak."

That day, Júzian had said, *Oak's not the problem. Oak has never been the problem.* But Júzian had been wrong. There could be more than one problem.

&

They found uncooked sorghum in the wagons—and sweet potatoes, which they could eat raw on the spot. They filled their packs with sweet potatoes. The wagons carried guns, too, and ammunition, a wealth of arrows, but only a handful of bows. They left the bows and arrows, packed as much of the real arms as they could, and hid the rest so other passing enemies wouldn't find them. Two of the wagons carried nothing but small boats.

They laid out the bodies of the men in the shadows, so they'd keep a little better till the cleanup crews came.

Commander Shonco was not a priest, but as the ranking man present, he said a few words from the scripture:

For now his enemy lay in his hands, he loved him.
With all his soul, he loved him,
Saw the little child inside him.

Not bloody likely, thought Tan, who felt tired and sick. But he folded his hands with the rest and replied, "This is the Golden Way."

"They going to make the Soruc's people eat 'em, sir?" said Gomu.

"Not for me to say, Cadet," said Shonco.

"Lavan, you're a Soruc's guy—"

"Gomu, shut up," said Tan.

Curled on the ground, Lavan still trembled in pain.

"We'll break for an hour," said Shonco. "Have a good meal. We can't carry this all back. What you eat before the cleanup crews retrieve it doesn't have to be recorded."

Tan gave Lavan half his water.

"Soruc's Town'll be lucky to have you as *lintor*." He used the Kiri word for *headman* because it sounded truer. "When you take over, you'll stop all this shit."

Lavan nodded. "My *nomo* let it happen."

Tan shrugged. "Your father's a good guy." He had no idea if that was true. "But he wasn't trained in the Citadel like you are."

Lavan winced and Tan squeezed his hand.

"Sho," he called. Sho was hovering nearby with a face like a smudged doll. "Sho's going to stay with you, okay? Sho, you stay with him. Hold his hand if he wants."

Sho nodded. Tan gave him a piece of jerky in thanks and got himself free, his head aching.

He needed to circle back with Dezdenec. Where was he? Not by the wagons, not by the wounded... there, a little way uphill, gazing across the valley.

Tan hiked up and sat beside him, receiving a small smile.

"I didn't realize you considered it closed, Captain," said Dezdenec. "I wouldn't have spoken."

"No, you done good."

Dezdenec shook his head. "No, I'm a dork."

It was such a little kid word Tan laughed out loud.

"I never feel like I know what I'm doing out here."

"You're fine. You always pull your weight," said Tan. "Anyway, you're a scholar. You were born to be with books. You'll just—I think you'll understand the cycles of destruction in scripture better because you've been out here in the field."

"You could be a scholar too."

Tan laughed again. "Me?"

"You could. I could teach you to read the scripture."

"I'm a Kiri. Ashtyn and me, we're going to go home to the Garden and be farmers and traders." He thought a moment. "But when Oak's defeated, maybe you can visit us. The flowers in late spring are blue. They're—they're..." He couldn't find the words for indigo lupin blanketing the miller's hill. "We could sit in the fields and talk scripture—or just talk."

Dezdenec returned the smile and shifted his position so that his knee brushed Tan's and, accidental though it seemed, it was not an accident. Tan's whole body jumped. Yet he didn't dare respond; he was their captain.

He had one piece of jerky left. He handed it to Dezdenec. "What you did out there, it was perfect. You took him down a notch, just what he needs."

Dezdenec's face fell. "I don't need a reward, sir. I didn't do it for that."

Tan felt chastened, like he'd made a wrong move. "It's not a reward, it's a thanks." He set the jerky on a rock. "If you don't want it, pass it on."

He got up and got out of there quickly.

*

His blood still pulsing, he climbed to a spot lightly shaded by dwarf pines and sat on a rock with his helmet beside him. He sipped his water and gnawed a sweet potato, gazing out across the canyon at nothing, dead camels, dead men. Absently, he rubbed his sore shoulder. Was it late spring yet? Back home, was the lupin in bloom?

The cleanup crews would bring wagons or maybe electric carts and get the meat. Maybe they'd make it look like those squares of jerky. Or maybe they'd use it to punish the sympathizers in Low in—Soruc's Town. Tan didn't know, and he tried not to think about it.

His job was to protect C-16, that was all. And he was doing it, right? The way Júzian hadn't. A captain didn't run out on his boys. *The boys will be okay*, Júzian said. *My first duty's to look after you two.*

The fuck with that. Fuck every syllable. Tan sat still till the hot coal of his rage sputtered out and left his brain empty. Forests of moss clung to the rocks, interspersed with lichens and a froth of white flowers. Sprigs of grass fought out between the stones. The land lived here, not like at the Citadel, even the little trees...

Those trees. He looked again. They'd shrunk. Now they only came up to his chest, and it was obvious they'd never offer cover. You couldn't run all the way to Blue Gums on all fours—

He started to his feet.

That was the place, right over there. The rocks looked like they provided shelter, but the trees opened out into a clearing, and that was where it happened, just outside his present line of view. It was vital not to go there, not to see it. Júzian had led them up the very path Tan stood on. Tan's feet had found it like a memory, and Shonco—

He spun, expecting footsteps right behind him. He was alone, his pack and helmet back where he'd left them, the voices of the boys a murmur below. Just him and—

He started. Shonco was there, sitting thirty feet away, half obscured by a rock, pretending not to be watching him. Tan glanced back toward the trees that framed the path like a gate. In his memory, he could hear Júzian's silence. And Ash—

Where the hell had Ash gotten to?

He spun again, searching. He could see the corpses by the hulks of wagons. He could see some C-15 boys, and on the rocks some way below him Gomu and Tarnto, Dezdenec, the C-15 lieutenant standing sentry. But where was Ash?

Where was Keskan? How had he dared let them out of his sight?

He started down the hillside. Stopped. Retrieved his pack and helmet. Then, he went quickly back the way he'd come, down where most of the boys sat eating; he counted them off: Sho and Codo with Lavan and Fendo, Gomu with Tarnto, Dradam and the little girl. Dezdenec sitting by himself. Where the hell was Muned? There, talking with a C-15 boy.

Tan crossed to Gomu and Tarnto. "You guys seen Keskan?" He didn't ask about Ash, his brother, the flight risk. He didn't dare show him too much attention or ever suggest he was not in control.

They said they hadn't seen him. They might be lying. How did a guy who hated the Citadel pick up so much loyalty from Citadel boys, even after Ordan?

He walked down to the canyon floor and looked back up at the scatter of C-16. Had he run? Had he burst at the reprimand and cut out? With Ash?

Then, he caught some little movement—and there they were, right in front of his eyes, by the path he'd just come down, halfway up the Júzian slope, their heads together, their eyes on him.

He strode up to them, glaring at Ash and said, "I told you to stay with me."

Ash merely looked at him. The absurdity came through so clearly. Tan hadn't been watching, hadn't spared him a thought.

"Never mind," he said. "Long day. Come on."

Keskan looked at him too, out of black Kiri eyes. He said nothing, gave up nothing.

Then, slowly he cracked into a smile, like plaster fracturing. And in that jovial voice, he said, "Brings back memories, doesn't it? Captain."

&

The priests hadn't noticed that Ordan was gone, and when Tan gave the word, they hadn't known where to find him, just as Keskan had said. How far was their telepathic range? How far away did you have to get before they couldn't sense you?

As the train rocked beneath him, Tan's thoughts spilled over.

A year ago, if they'd just gone faster, if Tan hadn't stopped to argue...

But, Juz, we still have time to go back.

That night came back in pieces, the starlight of the Ribbon sharpening the rocks; the empty sense of wandering, the half-faith that Júzian knew where he was going, the gnawing fear that he did not.

Juz, we'll only be running to Oak.

That day, the dawn had burst like a beautiful, free precipice. Ash slept on Júzian's back. Terns circled on dagger wings, like spies. Tan remembered their *bratch* and *twee*, blessedly unbroken by human voices. *Maybe he's right. Maybe we got away.* His mind had been sticky with fatigue, but the new day's clarity pricked his eyes. He had been intensely, completely alive.

"We can't be far from the River," Júzian said, "not with all these terns nearby."

Each time Tan relived those words, they filled him with more fury.

We can't be far meant he didn't know.

Not far from the River meant circling back toward the Grid.

Yes, Blue Gums was on the River too, but according to Shonco's maps, it was far out west past Dip, and there was no way they'd covered more than six miles that night. Júzian had given the last of his water to Ash. Tan had a fourth left in his canteen. They'd had no option but the River, but that meant straight into the soldiers.

Juz, didn't you see that deserter strung up in the courtyard?

Júzian had been fifteen, older than Tan was even now. He should have planned for this shit, even Ash knew it, even Ash had doubted.

He should have had some plan besides running, careless at the end, seeking nothing but speed. They'd been due back yesterday at sundown. Now, the sun hovered over the hilltops again. Now, their grace period spent, the voices of their pursuers rang startlingly close.

Júzian pounded through the pines.

But as for Ash, he *must* have doubted. At least, he must have hung back because he was right there when Tan grabbed him and started dragging him back the way they came, back to the hope of mercy.

He flailed, he yelled.

Tan thought perversely, *Shut up. You'll give us away.*

Then, Júzian yanked Ash from his grasp and ran, shouting. The impression of his words fell like blows in Tan's memory, but he couldn't recall what the words had been, the last thing his brother said to him lost in the dust.

He didn't remember tackling him either, but he must have because then they were grappling for Ash.

Then others were pulling them apart, Shonco, a footman, the priest a yellow blur. And Keskan. What Keskan might have said or done had fallen outside of Tan's memory too. There was only his face, red like death in the sunset.

Júzian's face he could no longer see.

What if he hadn't turned on Júzian? What if that was the only reason the three of them hadn't escaped?

Chapter Twelve

T he sun had fallen by the time the train pulled into the Grid. There was more barbed wire than before: four layers of fencing instead of two. As the train passed the checkpoint, Tan took in the twisted mass.

They wanted to make damn sure no one tunnels out again.

He could feel himself now, grabbing Ash's ankles, dragging him back through the hole underneath the fence—

It took a couple of minutes before it occurred to him that the reinforcement was designed not to stop deserters but to repel attacks. Priests could stop deserters... at least at close range.

As the train rolled toward the station, it hit him how much the Grid had changed, the rocky terrain he had known bulldozed to make way for steel domes, cylinders chopped in half. *Quonsets*: that's what they were called. The train rumbled past a set of geodesic green houses, the only green in sight.

Red-belted footmen teemed like termites, a scattering of brown-belted cadets among them.

"There must be a thousand of them," said Dradam.

"They're gathering for the big assault," said Tan.

The Grid was nothing like the Citadel. Where the Citadel rose as one indomitable spire, the Grid sprawled, a city over a mile wide. Up on the hillsides in the flat evening light, he could see the Old Town, a jigsaw of wooden houses with peaked roofs, so many places to run, to hide, for a while.

Above the roofs, the watchtower rose like a chimney. To the west, the geothermal plant belched plumes of steam, but not enough to obscure a runner.

"What the hell is that?"

He followed Gomu's gaze but couldn't see anything except for his spiky head blocking the window. He got up and picked his way over. Leaning over Gomu and Tarnto's seat, he saw a giant metal ribcage bent into an oval. Men were at work, drilling steel plates across it. It seemed somehow akin to the blind bull eye of the Citadel. A powerful ghost.

"Whatever it is, they're going to move it," said Keskan, also up out of his seat.

"Move that?" said Tan.

"Yeah. They're building it right by the tracks so they can load it up and haul it out to the Bridge." The train tracks ended at the Bridge.

"That behemoth?" said Gomu. "Like fuck. It'd smash the tracks."

Keskan shrugged. "Maybe not if they balance it right."

"But what the fuck is it?" said Tarnto.

"A nuke maybe?" said Muned.

"I think it's a tank," said Dezdenec.

Gomu snarled, "No one asked what you think, rat-out!" The price of informing on Keskan.

"I said it's closed," said Tan. "What do you mean, Dezdenec?"

"They're not going to haul that thing to the Bridge, they're going to haul it to the river. Look how it's curved. It's meant to hold water."

"And then they'll haul it down to the Citadel," said Tan. "It's got to be three times bigger than our biggest water tanks."

Keskan laughed. "That's some advance planning," as if Gomu's outburst had no bearing on him.

"What you mean?" said Muned.

"Well, look at that thing. The well's been down for eleven days. Building that thing took more than that."

"It is advance planning," said Dezdenec. "It's not news that we're short of water."

"Yeah, not like it's news, right, super geniusy genius," said Gomu.

"Priest-esy genius," said Tarnto.

"Penis-y genius."

Dezdenec shot a weary look at Tan.

It looked like a giant fish, that thing, a big, dead spirit from a nether time.

A few minutes later, the train clunked into stillness.

"All right," said Tan. "Get your kit and be orderly."

As he stepped off the train, the smell from the natural sulfur pools struck him like a blow, a smell from the past, an echo of Júzian. He glanced at Ash, but his brother wore a studied blankness, which Tan emulated as he marched his boys to their quonset.

❧

Oneness came the next morning on sulfurous plumes. The slanted sun threw shards at the gravel. As Tan stared at the steam from the geothermal pipes, it seemed the mournful horn was billowing it to life.

As the horn faded, the priest's voice crackled through the loudspeaker:

How can it be we walk through fires yet remain?
That the sundered is restored to its primeval Oneness?

Tan could feel his boys inside him, and they comforted him suddenly, even Keskan. They were here, they were family, C-15, C-14, C-13 and other receding rounds of people he knew and did not know but knew.

They fell into the sea together: flowers and air, stone and sulfur and people. No Ordan, no Júzian—they were spaces in between a state of being and not being, spots of light blazing out and dissipating into soft, persistent radiance.

The echo of Oneness was still soothing him when he came back from breakfast and saw Shonco on a bench.

On impulse, Tan said, "Keskan, I'll be along in a minute. Make sure the boys actually scrub themselves." They had real, clean water at the Grid.

"Should I scrub 'em personally?"

Tan ignored him and climbed the low rise to Shonco. There, he stood at attention, waiting.

"Yes?" said Shonco after a moment, his eyes on the distant houses of the Old Town.

"C-16 will be ready for orientation in fifteen minutes." That was obvious, didn't need to be said.

"Good. How's your shoulder?"

"Good, sir. It didn't need stitches or anything. Sir?"

Shonco glanced at him.

Tan hesitated, but Oneness made him open and mellow. "Is it good to be home, sir?"

Shonco cracked a smile. "Sit."

It felt strange and wrong to sit by Shonco like equals, but since there was nowhere else but the bench, Tan sat there.

"Do you see that little tip of metal above that roof there?"

He saw some dark gray points. "I think so."

"That's the local He. They're different here, the He and She. They're woven into each other as if they were already unsundered. That was the point, I think, when the work was first commissioned. We built the Grid as part of an alliance with the West Men. It seemed an age of unsundering."

"You remember those days, sir?"

Shonco chuckled. "Gods forbid, Tánashen. That was seventy years ago." He paused. "I remember when Oak bombed the West

Men though. I was four, and it was night. We had fire pits then for roasting peccary—right over there, where Quonset D is. We didn't know what it was. It came through on the security TV, like a comet climbing up the sky. I thought it was a ship, like the Citadel. Maybe I thought it was the Citadel; the idea of the Citadel was dim to me then. My sister understood it better, I think. I remember she put her arms around me. I remember the fear in the grownups' voices—my father afraid. I had never seen my father afraid."

When he glanced at Tan, his eyes gleamed like earth-dusted water.

"Then, we lost the West Men on the radio, and finally word came they'd been obliterated, their whole great city blasted to ash. With the West Men gone, it was easy for Oak to conquer the Garden, what with the Kiris refusing to use guns. We ourselves—the Grid, I mean—we had guns, but we were a weak outpost then. Now, we're strong. We've already won back half the Garden. Soon we'll win the rest."

A wind gusting off the River softened the sulfur to a rocky sweetness. Its first button undone, Shonco's collar blew in the breeze like an invitation. It made Tan uncomfortably aware of his own lips and how Shonco's skin might taste on them. Directing his eyes anywhere else, he caught a bit of white to the side of Shonco's boot, the same he'd seen up on the hillside yesterday.

"Sir, do you know what those flowers are?"

Shonco peered where Tan pointed. "Saxifrage. My mother used to mix it up as a cure for kidney stones."

"We have that in Naughty—in Reason's Town too. Not the flowers, I mean. I'm pretty sure we don't. But the kidney medicine: Grandmother Linóvi, our—" He stopped. He wasn't supposed to speak Kiri unless he had to, so he couldn't say *way pointer*. "Our priest traded for it when I was young."

"From the Grid, no doubt. Reason's Town has been a good trade partner for decades."

Tan smiled but a sadness built in his chest. "I'd like to go back, sir. Do you think, if we do earn the privilege of settling the Garden, that Ash and me could be back there?"

Shonco thought a moment. "If you want your choice of where to settle, my advice is to prove you're an asset. Prove they need you. Prove that you're a leader."

The steam jets hissed around the geothermal installation, breathing like a living spirit. Inside the plant, the sound of steam rushed loud as a sandstorm. The dome arced high above the pipes, and stairs and metal casings rose over parts Tan didn't understand.

But he understood a big pipe had ripped off its moorings. Something about slugs—whatever that had to do with thermal energy. It lay on the ground disconnected and dented.

"Your job," said Shonco, "is to move the old pipe out for reclamation, move in the replacement. Then, we'll shut down the plant, you'll get it fitted up. The engineers will install it, you'll do cleanup. Just like managing the water piping at the Citadel."

Keskan surveyed the puzzle work of pipes. "Where's their regular maintenance crew, sir?"

"Keskan," said Tan, "you don't need to know—"

But Shonco held up a hand. "Marched out for Mon's Town. We're starting a geothermal project there."

Keskan's home village. Tan glanced at him but his face was blank.

In Kiri terms, they were breaking tech limitation. Kiris believed you couldn't use big machines or electricity. But the Citadel didn't follow tech limitation, so once the Garden villages joined the Citadel, they could throw away tech lim too. It was hard for him to imagine that, and that bothered him. It should be easy.

"If you have questions," said Shonco, "the engineering team is through that door."

After he'd left, Gomu grumbled, "Through that door on their asses while we do the hard shit."

"Okay," said Tan. "Let's get his pipe on the trolley and into the hangar for reprocessing."

It was heavy work. They were soon sweating, sleeves rolled. Tan used Fendo as a foreman to guide their movements, worried lifting might make his stitches tear.

After disposing of the old pipe, they had to go down to the sub-level to pick up the new one. The elevator was a creaky metal box that fit five or six people.

"How we going to get the pipe in there?" asked Codo. The pipe must be at least four times too long.

"Shrinking machine, Codo," said Dezdenec deadpan.

"Shut up, fucker," muttered Gomu.

Tan sighed. "We'll just have to ask for instructions when we get there."

The installation ran deep into the ground, connecting with the Grid's industrial production center. The design made sense, Tan reflected. They needed a big drill to get down to the volcanic heat—might as well use the facilities that built the drill to build the other big industrial stuff. Like piping and the plates for that water tank.

The elevator descended at turtle speed, six of them standing in bored silence in the watery brown light.

Keskan had been glaring at him but looked away at Tan's glance.

"If Oak bombs the Grid," said Muned, "I guess this would be the bunker, huh?"

"Why hasn't Oak bombed the Grid?" said Keskan, casual, leaning against the metal wall. "Why bomb the Citadel, but not the staging ground on their doorstep?"

"Because it *is* on their doorstep." Tan had thought about this a lot. "If they nuked the Grid, it would contaminate the river."

"Okay. Why wait so long to bomb us at all?"

"Because we've been careful," said Dezdenec. "Because we're planners. We've been winning over the Garden towns little by little so Oak didn't see what a threat we were becoming."

Keskan smiled. "If they didn't see we were a threat, why have they been fighting us for all these years?"

Gomu chuckled like he understood, but he didn't. Keskan was saying there was no Oak. It was a hoax, a fiction. Just like Júzian had said. Like the Citadel had bombed itself, like his parents' murder had just been, what, bad luck? Wouldn't that be convenient, if there was no Oak and no war and they could all just go home?

"Look, nuking someone's a big deal," said Tan. "Not no way would they pull that trigger if they thought they could win just by fighting. That means they're getting desperate now. It means we've almost beat 'em."

"Which means they might bomb the Grid, right?" said Muned, "If they're desperate. So this would be the bunker, like I said."

No one answered.

Out of the quiet whir of the elevator, Keskan said, "Everyone's dead in Batty Hyrax."

"What?" said Tan.

"If they're putting in geothermal there, Mon's Town? All the Kiris must be dead because, the people from my town, they'd die before they'd let that happen."

"Then they'd be idiots," said Tan as the elevator thunked to a standstill.

"Or they'd be brave." Keskan pushed out past him. "I understand you don't get the difference."

❧

The technicians told them to take the pipe up an alternate exit, a claustrophobic passage ascending gradually to the surface. After more sweat and bruising, they got the new pipe on the trolley and pushed and pulled it up the dim-lit shaft, out into the steamy heat of the day, a hundred feet from the entrance to the plant.

They hauled it back to the plant and into position, heaved it up onto its struts, grappled to connect the right joints, got berated and shoved by the engineers for not lining up this thing or clamping down that.

When the pipe was finally in place, the engineers took over and the boys got time off in the breakroom, a little dugout on the first underground floor, bright lights, two aluminum tables and eight chairs.

Tan stood. If he took a chair, he ran the risk of the boys without chairs resenting him. If he sat on the floor, he looked like a lackey to the boys sitting higher. His body was tired, but standing was best. He drank from his canteen and leaned his back against the wall.

Keskan took a chair, exuding the right.

"Wonder what's in here?" Tarnto swung open a side door and clicked on the light. Tan caught a glimpse of some big pipes running down from the room with the machinery above.

"Stop messing around," he said. "You're not authorized to be in there."

Tarnto sighed and sprawled on the floor beside Keskan. "Goddamn fuckers. If those guys are so good at pipe stuff, why do they make us do all the work?"

"'Cause they can," said Gomu.

"'Cause we're kids," said Muned. "Grow up and pay your dues."

"My dues, asshole?" said Gomu. "What the hell do you think this is?" He pointed at the scar across his face.

"Oh, we're paying," said Keskan blithely. "You know all about paying, right, Fendo?"

Fendo, resting his chin in his hand, gave Keskan a tired look. He always looked hammered since the barbarians shot him.

"Lavan knows about paying." Keskan's eyes were on Tan. Lavan was in the Grid's med bay with his injuries.

"I just meant it's dumb to complain," said Muned.

Keskan ignored him. "Sho knows, right, Sho? You clocked a lot of time with Lavan after he got skewered."

"I don't mind—"

"I know you don't mind. You're good kid." His eyes bored into Tan. "You were right there by his side, while our captain was just sitting around in the hills, relaxing, you know, while one of his boys screams."

"Actually, I gave him drugs for the pain," said Tan. "But I know some things go past you."

Keskan smiled. "It really surprised me how our captain just unplugged, right up there by the corpses, like he was on holiday. Funny how the screams don't seem to bug you—as long as you're not the one screaming."

"You're out of line, lieutenant." Tan stepped away from the wall and crossed casually to the table.

Keskan lounged in his chair on the far side of the table, arms crossed. "That's right, kiddos. Stay in line. That's Shonco's little boy, hiding out behind the rules."

Dezdenec watched warily.

Gomu and Tarnto grinned.

"Do I need to take you down?" said Tan with a studied weariness.

"Funny, I was going to ask you the same—"

Without waiting for him to finish, Tan moved in, upended the flimsy table with a crash, and kicked out at Keskan's chest. The boys around them scattered. His plan was to smack him down fast, before he was properly out of chair, get his legs out from under him and get a knee in his back, get it over with before Keskan had a chance to swing back.

Only Keskan was already half out of his chair. He pushed Tan's foot aside. Tan stumbled, so his back was to Keskan. He crouched and kicked where instinct said Keskan was closing. He swept him, but as he made a move to pin him, Keskan rolled into Tan and toppled him in turn. Before he could right himself, Keskan was on top of him, pinning his right arm back so hard he heard a joint pop, left arm useless against Keskan's knee.

He was going to lose. He'd missed his chance and now Keskan's weight gave him the advantage. What the hell could he do now? Think.

Keskan's grip on his arm pushed his body to the left. It gave him just enough leverage to get his right knee under him. He wasn't strong enough to push Keskan off, but for just a second, he unbalanced him. Keskan rocked, Tan swiveled, freeing up his left arm, stuck a knuckle in Keskan's eye.

Keskan jerked back with a grunt, wrenching Tan's right arm, but his grip had relaxed. Tan broke free, rolled upright, and shoved his knee in Keskan's back, holding it there just a couple of seconds before standing, signaling—he hoped—that the fight was over. The truth was he wasn't confident he could keep Keskan pinned for much longer.

Keskan got up on his knees, rubbing his eye. "Little shit. That was a goddamn girl move."

Tan smiled. "Didn't know we were fighting by the rules." Turning his back, he righted a chair and sat in it, doing his best to hide how hard it was to make his right arm obey him. Laughter rippled through the boys.

With that laughter, Tan had won. They both knew it. Keskan could tackle him to the ground, but he'd just look like a sore loser.

Keskan wasn't an idiot. After a moment, he laughed with the rest, as if the whole thing had been a good-natured tussle, and started gabbing with Codo about something else.

Gomu plonked down in a chair next to Tan. With an admiring leer, he said, "You're a raw son of a bitch, captain. But you do what you gotta, sure as shit."

Tan glanced at him in surprise. Was that what he was?

Chapter Thirteen

They rode the train to the end of the track, a wooden station with an array of solar panels. When they got out, the wind rushed them—but there was no wind, just the sound of it, heavy and hollow beneath Tan's helmet. As Shonco marched his units toward the Bridge, Tan realized he was hearing the roar of *Lan Savra*, the River.

He'd crossed the River before, seven years ago in a cart. He remembered bodies crammed so tightly he couldn't make a move without flesh sliding on flesh. He remembered the stink of unwashed kids and the way their wailing lanced his head. He didn't remember the River's voice.

The sentries waved them past, and when they marched across the Bridge, the River's cool breath engulfed them. The Bridge was wide enough for fifteen to walk abreast, old enough that the wood had grayed and creaked beneath their feet. No wonder the train line ended at the River. The Bridge would buckle beneath a train.

They stepped straight from the Bridge onto a plaza of concrete, punctuated by a watchtower. It reminded Tan of the flat campus surrounding the Citadel. The sight surprised him—shocked him. This was the Borderlands; it didn't deal in concrete.

No, he reminded himself, it was the Garden. This was Free of Ford, it had to be. No, call it Ark's Town. Even if it didn't look garden-like, this place's power came from alliance with the Citadel. The flat expanse protected the Bridge from assault by stripping away any hiding places.

Footmen marched to and fro—and beyond them were Kiris, more than Tan had seen in years, dark people dressed like his parents used to, in light-colored, loose shirts and shorts, chatting in Kiri. Fishers boated out on the water. The Kiris scarcely looked up as the unit went by.

They walked through a large, low city of stone, its streets broad to minimize surprise attacks. The smell of fried fish from the food carts made Tan's hunger leap. Maize popped over fires. Someday, when the war was over, maybe he and Ash would stop over here and eat.

Then something remarkable happened. They did stop, right there amid the carts, and Shonco pulled out money, big old coins minted of Citadel steel. He bought them half cobs of maize dripping with butter and dried River weed made into crackers—and fish, big fish, the size of Tan's hand, like Ordan must have had in Blue Gums and never would again.

Shonco took them out to tables overlooking a pier where the River rushed, south of them now. The sun baked their helmets, but the breeze caressed their hands.

Codo got butter smeared down his chin, and everyone rushed to wipe it and get an extra lick, and they laughed, really laughed, and had whole cups of River water, and—

"Helmet, Muned," Tan called, and Muned plonked it back on. He'd taken off it to mop his brow, but his pale olive skin couldn't take the sun.

Down the street, someone strummed a dancing tune.

This was the Garden, Tan thought, everybody just living their lives, protected by the Citadel.

Shonco put a bit of fish at the end of the table for the yellow jacket people, just like Tan's parents used to. Then, he bit into his ear of maize. "Just like I remember," he said with satisfaction.

Fendo had been poking listlessly at his food. But now his expression perked up, "You used to come here with Mother as kids, sir, right?"

"Oh, many times. Our mother-side's family lived here, until the *Evagéta*." The Kiri word startled Tan, but then again, maybe there was no Citadel name for the Massacre. It was a horror the Kiris bore.

"Did any survive?" asked Fendo.

"Not here as far as I know. Your grandma, ma, and I all fled with your grandpa to the Citadel."

In the silence that followed, Tan said, "Oak killed my grandfather in the *Evagéta*." He glanced at Ash, who was silent, watchful.

Keskan sighed but held his tongue.

"Only Soruc's Town escaped," said Shonco, "thanks to its long friendship with the Citadel. Oak didn't dare try to reach that far east. When Lavan is leader there, he'll carry on that alliance."

Lavan was still recovering at the Grid.

"And you, Dradam," said Shonco. "You hope to be a trader between Naimu's Town and Soruc's, I think?"

Dradam froze like a pika in the shadow of a hawk. It was just a few days since they'd killed those traitors, right on the trade route from Low in Mouth to Dip. "Yes, sir. We'll make sure there's good trade—lawful."

Shonco smiled. "I'm sure you will. Your towns were meant for friendship. After all, the brothers hold them, Soruc Evernew, Naimu Unchanging, the two as one, unsundered."

"You mean as a symbol?" said Dezdenec. "My father says the brothers are apocryphal gods."

Tan had no idea what that meant and he suspected Shonco didn't either. The commander hesitated just a moment too long before saying with a smile, "All the gods are gods."

At the next table, Tarnto flailed as Gomu licked River weed crumbs off his fingers; Muned wisely scooted out of the way. Codo held Sho on his shoulders, gazing out over the boats on the River.

﮳

Fed and full of energy, they marched out of Ark's Town, down the boot-beaten road, through a land that looked almost like the Grid, rocky and decked with scrubby flowers. It was hard to believe this was the Borderlands. Tan remembered oaks, vineyards, and green grass. He'd expected to cross into a different world. Instead, it was like he hadn't moved—except for one small shift. The tall clumps of shimmering lupin had vanished, replaced by scatters of shorter, purple lupin, still different from home, but not as different.

They marched into the heat of midday. The River left them and the thirst came back like a bothersome old friend. Gradually, the bushes grew taller. Then they rounded a hill, and the landscape was wiped blank.

Down in the valley lay a floor of green, intense and improbable. Featureless. They were practically walking through it before Tan recognized it as maize: acres and acres of nothing but maize, fringed by rectangular buildings. It was a hole. It stirred no memory. He had never passed this way before—or rather, he probably had, but he and his brothers had been tied up in the cart. They hadn't been able to see anything except vague slits of color through the struts.

He fell back beside Dradam. "Do you know where we are?"

Dradam shook his head.

This didn't look like a village at all. It didn't look like anything. It looked like a maize factory.

A cart trundled toward them.

"Stand ready," barked Commander Shonco.

They fell into formation by the side of the road, half obscured in the maize. Two donkeys came into view.

"We are One," called Shonco.

The cart slowed. "We are One," said the driver in native Citadel speech, a brown-haired man.

Shonco came alongside, his hand on his gun. "Bound for the Grid?"

"A lot of bodies to feed."

"Thus, we reunify the pieces." Shonco waved him on.

The driver saluted as he passed, and the boys peered eagerly through the slats, about half a load of unshucked corn.

"All that food," whispered Dradam.

"That's why the Citadel needs the Garden," said Keskan.

That was true; it wasn't any secret. The Citadel needed Garden crops; it had traded for them for years. Yet Keskan's words rang like a condemnation, as if needing food made the Citadel the enemy.

"It's why the Garden needs the Citadel," murmured Tan, "so Oak doesn't come and take it all."

They plodded on, past the fields and houses and the troops fanning out among them. They passed two people hanging from gibbets, a man and woman. Tan didn't want to look close enough to discern if they were Kiri or Citadel. He thought the man might be in uniform, but it was best not to dwell.

They walked out into more rock and brambles and finally to occasional spindly trees: laurel and oaks. In time, the trees got bigger, beginning to resemble home, which meant they were not far from Oak's traditional marauding range. The sun dipped low until it blasted their left cheeks, but the afternoon brought the River wind to soothe their necks.

The plan, according to his briefing, was to make for Energia's Town. Shonco said it was in a canyon with a swift stream good for hydroelectric, so they'd focus on claiming it to set up some infrastructure. Tan guessed they'd sidestep Naughty Vines.

Right now, he couldn't imagine fighting. His shoulders sagged beneath his pack, feet sore. His head streamed under his helmet. His thoughts clapped out, he marched in a stupor, some poem Júzian used to have them chant wheeling brokenly in his mind:

On and on and ever on,
Everything but feet are gone,
But feet march ever more.

He couldn't remember the rest of it. The trees began to cluster, and rock gave way to more stretches of grass. Late-spring, he thought dimly, the grass seeds high and yellowing. When he looked back, he saw Fendo swaying with exhaustion. He scanned for a branch that could serve as a crutch. Too short, too spindly. But there—that was thick enough. He dove out the line and grabbed it. Commander Shonco glanced at him but said nothing as Tan handed it to Fendo. They walked on, the trees granting respites of shade.

❧

His brain dull with fatigue, Tan scarcely noticed when the trees gave way to more tilled fields, orderly green and brown, like chains.

And then, through his stupor, he saw the flowers, just like in his dreams: pink and white, little daubs of color on stalks so razor thin that the yellow earth showed behind them. He thought, it's Yellow Tips, the half-season after High Green. He had assumed it was High Green, though that name had not come to him. The lupin sprouted in High Green, but those little pinks only bloomed for a few days in Yellow Tips.

His heart fell into his gut.

A memory stirred, of running in a field of those flowers with Júzian, those flowers like the Ribbon of stars. Scissors, he recalled. The plants were called scissors. They'd grown in profusion on Runoff Meadow where the old man had let them ride his hill-jack. The memory pulled a sense of joy from his depths, a joy that froze when it touched this reality. He shouldn't see those flowers ever again. If he saw them, he would break.

Suddenly, he knew this flat dirt road, knew it despite the furrows of green and brown that ought to have been woodland. It wasn't the Ancestor's Meadow; that was off to the north and uphill a little. In a minute or so, he would see it through the trees—if there were still trees—a bright grassy patch on the opposite slope, uphill from the creek. This was the road to his mother's yurt, the road home.

What about Ash? Did Ash recognize it? He glanced behind him quickly, but Ash's helmet hid his face.

Tan's eyes snapped onto the slope to the north, straining after something he didn't want to see. Where was Runoff Meadow? Was it that spot through the trees? With all but a few of the trees cut down, he didn't know how to gauge it. The hills were his but he no longer knew them. There? They kept marching. He kept staring. There?

Up and up the hill they went till the road leveled off and he knew they'd passed the spot. The meadow wasn't there anymore. When the war was over, would he farm this land, these forlorn rows of green and brown chains?

Was this the price of keeping Oak out?

When the road leveled off, Tan knew they were only five minutes from the yurt. He remembered the bend where the yurt came into view. When he was three or four, it had seemed far from home out on the road where he watched the lines of ants carry seeds in summer. Around the bend they went, and his heart gave a jerk of relief: the big woodpecker oak was still standing.

Maybe Mum and Dad are waiting.

Why had he thought that? He had seen their bodies, right there, right there, where the path to the yurt had been.

That day, there had been drums and yelling. Dad had come running and told the boys to hide. Then Tan knew Oak had finally come. He and Júzian dashed out back and crouched by the side of the yurt.

Júzian put an arm around him. "It's all right. I told Dad I'd watch over you, and I'm going to, Tan. You stay here. I'm going to get Ash, and both of us will watch over Ash, whatever happens. Got it?"

Tan had said yes. He didn't remember if he said the word, or nodded, or merely stared. But his heart said yes, and he never forgot it. He would watch over Ash till the day he died.

He remembered Dad's voice close by, calling garbled words. In the midst of the screams and drums, he'd bolted around the side of the yurt toward Dad. He'd seen Dad in his deep blue shirt fall down by the woodpecker tree, blood on his head, and the Oak man in the long, beige tunic leering out his scarred face. The Burner.

Mum had run toward Dad, but another Oak man grabbed her. She kicked and fought as he'd never dreamed Mum could fight, till the Burner slashed her with his sword and she fell near Dad's feet, her face filled with blood.

Tan didn't remember what happened next, just Júzian tackling him to the ground, holding him and Ash down with all his weight, Ash wailing, and Tan thinking, *They'll find us.*

A man strode toward them. He could see his boots, nearer every step.

Júzian pulled them up on their knees.

"Run," he said. "Hold my hand and run, straight down the hill to the town square. They'll protect us." His hand was a vice around Tan's wrist.

They found their feet and ran for the footpath down the steep slope to the town. They only got a few steps before something hit Tan between the shoulder blades. He fell dazed, and Júzian toppled beside him, still clenching his wrist and Ash's. They were bound and thrown in a cart with several others. The others died or went to different units, but Júzian never let them go.

That had been seven years ago. Now, as C-16 crunched over the spot where his parents had been struck down, Tan's vision blurred, not with tears but something more fundamental: an inability to experience what he was experiencing. He wanted to throw up but couldn't. He was in formation.

He looked around, making his eyes be present in the real moment.

The Citadel had rescued them from Oak. It had won back Naughty Vines and protected it. It had trained Tan to come back and protect it.

To protect *this*...?

Mum's yurt was gone. Where she'd sat and had tea with Grandmother Linóvi there stood a large, rectangular house, and something—a grain silo?—rose behind it like an obscene gray hat. He was pretty sure it was a violation of tech limitation. He couldn't say why exactly, but in his memory the Teacher sat the children down and told them big metal things were too high tech. She had a gray Teacher's robe and long brown hair, and said, "Keep it small, like grinding this glass for my spectacles."

But Tan was being ridiculous. Naughty Vines didn't need to follow tech limitation; it was a Citadel town. Bullets won wars, not arrows, and grain silos fed hungry people.

He didn't like the way they had painted that house though. Wood was brown, but they'd painted yellow. Why? What was the purpose of that?

They passed the house and marched on down the road to Dad's grapes. At least the fields were still there. Except they weren't. The field nearest the house had been the vineyard Mum had inherited from Grandmum, though it was Dad's work to tend it. The grape vines, planted in irregular intervals, had been over a hundred years old. They squatted on massive, gnarled trunks sprouting little, pruned branches that burst into red in the autumn. They'd been torn out, replaced with even furrows of leafy something.

Off to the west, where he and Júzian used to play in the tree house Grandmum built, people worked in the fields. He couldn't tell what they were doing. His eyes couldn't fix on it. As the road ascended Mill's Hill, another gray obscenity drew his eye. A second silo? Water tower? He couldn't tell. He only knew it was standing where the old fallen tree had lain, the one they'd take Ash to on picnics so he could play peek-a-boo by that rotten trunk.

He glanced at Ash again. His little brother showed no awareness of anything but weary marching.

"Ash? Is this the Garden like you remember?" He tried to sound conversational, but he couldn't stop his voice from shaking.

Ash looked at the land as if for the first time. He shrugged. "I don't really remember."

That made Tan angry and relieved together.

Up they trudged, step by step, then pulled east. *Wrong way*, thought Tan. The old path had forged straight up the steep hill. It had been abandoned, he realized, in favor of the broader road gouged out of the hill at a gentle slope: east, then a sharp turn, then west and up. They passed—still standing—the Wood Spirits' tree, where the big metal bell had called the people to remembrance. The bell was gone, and the cairn. He couldn't even see a scattered remnant.

At the crest of the hill, they crossed onto the miller's land. Tan couldn't remember her name, only that she was the miller. The miller's woods had been cut down too, an orchard of thin young fruit trees in their place.

The gristmill was gone, the old runner stone the miller's husband had harnessed his hill-jack to had vanished. The bedstone lay disused on the ground. At the sight, indignation flared in Tan. Didn't the Citadel need to grind grain? Cutting the trees, distorting the houses, even killing the people, that might all make sense in a farming sort of way, but tearing apart a functioning mill to leave nothing but a useless hunk of rock smacked of viciousness.

They passed the spot where the miller's yurt had been—a blank of grass now. Or Tan thought it was the spot. The miller had been an old woman with small use for wild children, so Tan and his brothers had avoided getting close.

They marched down Mill's Road, which curved downhill to the high road. Tan had rarely walked it. His family, on the other end of the hill, had taken the Thistle Path by the creek. But he remembered the road shaded by madrone trees, their crisp yellow leaves crunching underfoot. They were gone. Down the road in the glare of the lowering sun, they passed some men and women with baskets and wheelbarrows, who stopped and saluted them—so many damn people.

Then they were out on the high road, just in earshot of Crow Daughter's Stream. The farmhouses were behind them. The soil—if Tan remembered right—was rockier out here and not fit for farming. And though they were marching away from his home, oddly, for a little while, the rockiness made the place more homelike. The trees still stood here, scraggly as ever, twisting branches and tough leaves on narrow trunks. He knew their smell. He knew the feel of their bark on his hands. But with every step now, he was farther away from the clarity of old memory. He vaguely recognized a sharp bend in the road, a field he'd once visited with some friends where some radish still flowered white and purple in a ditch.

Then, he didn't know the land anymore. In his mind, a piece of him screamed, *Take me back!* And a piece of him gasped in relief, as if at the sound of gunfire receding.

Chapter Fourteen

Tan woke before dawn and slipped out of his tent, feeling sick. He'd slept by the flap, in case Keskan tried to get out, but maybe Tan was the one who needed to get—

No, that wasn't a good thought.

He breathed the dewy air among the gray impressions of trees. They'd camped on the ridge of a hill with a clear sight of the road. On the far side, the stream—still Crow Daughter's, Tan supposed—was just out of earshot, leaving the dregs of night to the birds and crickets. Gradually, his breathing slowed and his stomach ceased to pitch.

He was home, so close to home, he had been home, there was no home. But he had told Ash they had to be loyal soldiers so that one day they could go home. Could Ash be happy in that trampled place? If he barely remembered Naughty Vines, would it matter—?

"You're up early."

Tan drew up sharp and saluted Shonco. "Yes, Commander."

"Well, get your boys up, and let's get breakfast going."

"Yes, Commander."

A dream was departing. The vines had been old spirits. Year after year, they sat on the hill, pruned to little knotty stumps. In the spring they leafed out the color of grass; in the summer they sagged with purple grapes... in the autumn they blazed. Now a fence of posts and wire blocked the hill, and brown-gouged rows of something grew on the graves of those gnarled vines.

Knotty vines, he realized.

He felt his face flush hot. All his life he'd heard those words with a child's understanding. He'd seen the whole world like a child. Júzian had understood.

What if Júzian had really understood? What if he'd known there was no home?

Tan existed like a flower in a vase, sucking up water and looking alive, but the life was an illusion. Why was he here? What was left?

He glanced at Ash laying out provisions by the camping stove. Ash was left, like a memento carved from a dead tree, the more precious because he was all that remained. But where would they go? Where could Tan take him?

He realized he'd lost track of Keskan. Out here in the woods was the prime chance for him to run. And good riddance if he did. Let him be the next Ordan.

Then he spotted him, striking the tent with brutal efficiency, encircled by careful watchers. Shonco had positioned C-16 in the center of a loose triangle of other units. Any C-16 runner would have to get past them. He'd have to get through Tan's cadre too, Tan's loyal boys, who were looking to him to lead them.

He pulled himself up and nodded to Dezdenec, who gave him a knowing nod in return.

Muned, however, was fishing a rock out of his boot.

Tan crouched beside him. "Sharp eye," he said softly. "We're all One."

Muned surprised him by quoting scripture: "*Fear me not but trust in me.*" It surprised him not because he thought Muned was unfaithful but because he'd never pictured him as word-smart.

Tan smiled and finished the quote. "*And all the stars of heaven will be ours to unify.*" Okay, the original said "yours to unify," but it seemed a good idea to drive home the Oneness of it.

Dradam sat motionless, pummeled. He understood what he'd seen yesterday.

Tan sat beside him. "Dip is fine. It's been trading with the Citadel forever, right? No need to change around anything there." Though Naughty—Knotty Vines had been a longtime trader too.

Dradam nodded, looking unconvinced.

"That's why they call it 'Naimu's,' right? Because it's unchanging?"

He nodded.

"Now is the most important time to make sure our unit stays together. We defeat Oak, then we rebuild, and if we're faithful...." We'll go to the Garden? "I'll definitely speak for having you sent home to Dip, and you'll trade with Lavan."

A nod.

Tan clapped his shoulder. "Keep your post then, yeah?"

Dradam swallowed and shifted so that Keskan was in his line of sight.

They drew plenty of water from the stream and ate mash boiled on camp stoves whose batteries had been charged up on geothermal at the Grid.

Fendo sagged over the crumbs of his breakfast, his head almost to his knees.

"Go lie down a few minutes. We march soon." Tan took his bowl.

"Can I have it, Captain?" said Sho.

Tan gave it to him to lick.

Over by the tents, a whoop came from Gomu, in a tussle with Tarnto.

You're a raw son of a bitch, but you do what you have to, he'd said.

What he had to, to see his boys safe in the Garden. All the things he'd had to do. He couldn't get the vines out of his head, their trunks ripped up and thrown away.

"Tánashen." He jumped at Shonco's voice. "Cadet Captains' briefing in two minutes."

The plan for the day was to march halfway to Energia's Town. Their units would have the usual role: backup for the adult units. Tan reviewed maneuvers with his boys and released them to finish packing.

٭

He had gone to the edge of camp to piss when he heard a step behind him. He whirled, fumbling with his britches, to see Keskan behind him, washed out in the dawn light.

Where the hell were—?

Yes, they were watching, Dezdenec, Muned, from the circle of the tents. Dradam, per Tan's order, was chatting with Ash.

Keskan folded his arms. "Do you really believe Oak is out there being evil, or are you playing some long game for power or what?"

"Oak murdered my parents."

Keskan barked a laugh. "For fuck's sake, Tánashen, the Citadel murdered your parents: yours, mine, our whole damn villages."

"You've really got a suicide wish."

"Then turn me in."

Tan hesitated. "I'm not out to get you."

Keskan scoffed. "Can't get me without a witness, can you? Otherwise, it's just you whining to Pappy 'cause you're not strong enough to take me."

"Took you down at the Grid."

"Anyone can cheat—but not forever."

"I know who the hell raided my village," said Tan. "They wore long, beige tunics, Oak-style. I can see it as clear as your sorry ass. Yeah, I know—" Keskan was smirking again. "It was the Citadel in disguise. You think they faked the bombing of the West Men too?"

"Could have."

"They killed the West Men, then they massacred us. They killed my grandfather. They enslaved my grandmother for two years."

"Only two?"

"She escaped, you fuck. You think that was the Citadel too?"

"Could be."

"And took her to the Citadel and just told her it was Oak? Because, guess what, it had a lot of oaks."

Keskan shrugged. "Maybe they sold her off somewhere."

Tan stared at him. "Has it ever occurred to you that if you weren't terrorized by Oak, it might be because Batty Hyrax is way out east? Has it ever occurred to you your family was safe because they got to mine first?"

That stopped him for a moment. "Even if that was true, someone did terrorize my town, and Oak didn't have shit to do with it."

"Well, I hate to say it," said Tan, "but maybe your town was full of traitors."

His face grew hard. "Don't call my *sélnua* traitors."

That was a word Tan hadn't heard in a long time. It was weird to think of Keskan coming out of a *sélnua*, a kid with a homeplace and a circle of kin.

"I got nothing against your people—"

"You. *You* are calling my people traitors?" Keskan took a step toward him. "I remember that day, Tánashen. We planned it—me and Júzian—that I'd be part of the search party, that I'd lead them away from you. I tried. Should have done better. I own that. But *you...*"

Tan met his eyes. It was all he could do.

"The way you squealed like a little pig, 'It was *him*. It was *him*. He took Ashtyn and ran! I was just trying to get Ashtyn back.' Made me want to throw up."

Tan stood and took it.

"It made Ashtyn want to throw up. I don't know how you held on to him. I thought he was going to scratch your eyes out."

"I had to keep Ashtyn safe," said Tan.

"That's a load of shit."

"You don't—"

"Yes. It is. You could have said, 'Me and Júzian made him go.' He'd be safe. Come on, Tánashen. You owe me a better lie than that."

"So I go down with Júzian, and then who's in charge of C-16? You? And the whole unit ends up like Ordan."

Keskan reached out and held Tan's chin tight. "If I beat you to a pulp right now, I figured they'd either charge me with insubordination or demote you for incompetence. Want to gamble?"

They'd charge him, Tan thought, and steeled himself. Dezdenec and Muned exchanged a glance, and then Muned was striding toward them. With a flick of his hand, Tan motioned him back.

"Sure," he said. "Let's roll the dice."

Keskan went still, eyes blazing, fingers gouging the soft skin at Tan's neck.

Then he let him go. "I don't roll dice. I play to win."

He stocked off, ignoring Muned.

Tan waved Muned away, needing a moment to himself. He had to get Keskan sent back to the Grid. Would it be enough, what Dezdenec and Muned had seen? Anyway, he'd have them report it to Shonco.

He started trudging back to camp.

Then off to the west, a boy yelled, "Dej, look out!"

C-13 exploded, boys bursting out like an ants nest.

"Ambush!" yelled Shonco. The alarm bell blared.

Tan's boys dove for their arms, Tan racing to join them.

A gunshot went off.

"Keep low." Tan slammed his helmet down over his head. "Find tree cover, fan out. Shoot when you got a clear shot. Ash, with me."

As the boys scuttled off, Tan made for the woods, keeping Ash close beside him. Keskan had dashed off according to Tan's orders, but damn it, Tan ought to have kept him in sight.

A shot rang out nearby, another farther off. Someone ran by behind him, friend or foe, he didn't know. He plunged under the bush, and Ash crawled in after him. A bowshot twanged.

Tan froze. Bows meant Kiri traitors, not Oak. Oak would certainly stick with guns.

Another arrow zinged past them. Feet crunched in the brush, but when Tan turned his head, he couldn't see anyone. A third bowshot thunked from farther away.

They waited. It was a good manzanita bush with just enough space for the two of them to crouch, thick branches curving down over them. The branches wouldn't hide them if anyone was looking, but to people rushing past, they would just be a swath of green.

With every minute the sunrise crept closer, everyone outside cover more exposed. He held his gun ready and measured his breaths.

"Don't shoot unless you have a clear shot," he whispered to Ash. "The more shots they hear, the more chance they'll spot us."

Ash raised his gun dutifully.

Tan focused on the campsite. The soldiers and the enemy had scattered and, except for a handful of fallen bodies, the campsite was eerily empty. Around the periphery, shadows moved ever more distinctly in the dawn. Guns fired at rough intervals. Arrows thunked. Now and then, a cry punctuated the gloom.

A figure moved near him, dressed in a long, flowing tunic, not a Citadel uniform, not the short tunic favored in the Borderlands.

Gods, it was Oak after all.

Tan fired. The man fell with a yelp. He continued to gasp and crawl, and basic decency told Tan to put him down, but he didn't. He wouldn't risk an unnecessary shot to alert the enemy to his position.

"Red Banner!" cried Shonco's voice far to his left. The retreat order. It meant regroup at the hill a kilometer east.

A movement to the southwest caught the corner of Tan's eye. Someone had tracked where his shot had come from.

"Move back, Ash," he whispered and raised his gun.

"No, Tan!" cried Ash for some reason.

"Shut up," hissed Tan. Now, anyone in earshot would know where they were.

But Ash wasn't listening. He grabbed the barrel of Tan's gun. "Don't shoot. It's an old woman."

Tan yanked his gun out of Ash's grip. It couldn't be an old woman, not in a middle-of-nowhere ambush. He tried to sight the figure again, but it had melted into the underbrush.

"Shit. Back behind me." The best fallback position he could spot was a depression shaded by a patch of brambles. Poor enough cover. He shoved up against Ash, pushing him back, scanning the terrain through the branches of their bush.

The branches clutched their sides, their heads. A moment later, they were out of the bush. A gunshot cracked, right on top of him. Tan hit the turf by instinct, an arm over Ash. He scanned the brush. Nothing.

Then a rustle of leaves and Keskan's face.

He's going to kill me.

"Ash, make for that stand of brush. I'll cover."

"But—"

"Run!" His first priority was to keep Ash out of the line of Keskan's fire. If his target was Tan, let it only be Tan.

Ash made a dash for it, twenty paces of open grass. The way looked clear, peaceful even but—

Something smacked into his head.

Chapter Fifteen

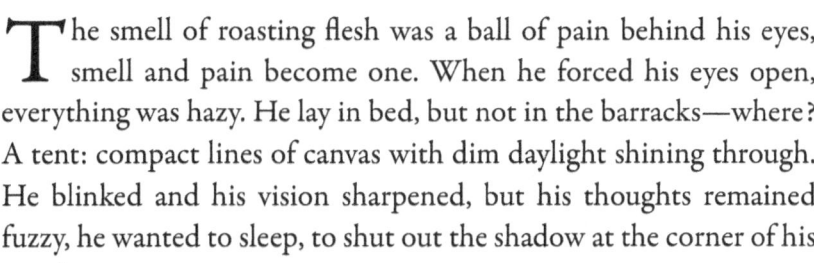

The smell of roasting flesh was a ball of pain behind his eyes, smell and pain become one. When he forced his eyes open, everything was hazy. He lay in bed, but not in the barracks—where? A tent: compact lines of canvas with dim daylight shining through. He blinked and his vision sharpened, but his thoughts remained fuzzy, he wanted to sleep, to shut out the shadow at the corner of his mind.

Outside, men were talking. Their workaday voices comforting, like Dad and Uncle conferring about pruning the vines. Was the battle over? It seemed he had already fought. Had he fought and been injured? The smell of the meat—he had to stop before the body was burned black.

He jerked, then froze, stark awake. It all snapped back to him: the ambush, hiding. Keskan.

Oak. He'd seen their tunics.

A hill-jack snorted. Then, he heard a scrape of cloth beyond his feet, right there in the tent. It was not the sound of a Citadel soldier. After years with the daily rasp of Citadel uniforms, he knew.

He kept still, only his eyes darting to take in every detail in his range of vision. He was on a blue bed roll that lay on a canvas mat. He could make out tufts of grass between the mat and the edge of the tent. The tent walls were almost perpendicular to the ground, which meant a separate scaffolding for a roof, which meant too much time and effort for a field tent, which meant slave labor. Which meant this was, indeed, Oak. No Kiri would have a tent like that, not even the Citadel would bother.

The person just out of sight stirred again, and a scratching sound started. A rodent? No. Tan knew that sound. He'd heard it a hundred times from Shonco. A pen, someone writing. It only went on a few seconds. Then the person got up.

Tan held his breath, poised to spring. Why wasn't he tied up? No matter. Good luck that he wasn't.

The man sat down on the ground beside him, knees in leggings that disappeared behind the long tunic of gray splashed with brown, slit up the sides, an Oak tunic. His hands were folded, big hands. He appeared unarmed but must have something hidden.

He'd plainly heard Tan move, no more point pretending to sleep.

Tan looked up at a square face, framed by wavy brown hair, a Citadel man. No. Oak. It was strange they looked so much like Citadel men. He was not scarred, not the Burner.

The man studied him. "How are you?" He spoke Citadel words, heavily accented.

The question stumped Tan. What was he supposed to say? I have a headache? He said nothing.

"Do you understand me?"

"I'm okay," said Tan.

The man smiled. As if they were friends. Had the Oak men smiled at Grandmother like that?

"You were hit on the head. Can I see your eyes? If they are all right?"

Why was he asking him? Tan was his prisoner. He could not say no, so he gave a little nod; it made pain shoot through his neck.

When the Oak man bent over him, Tan went stiff, scarcely breathing as the stranger's thumb gently lifted an eyelid. What if this was just a ploy? What if he was going to gouge out his eyes? Or was this some weird prelude to fucking him?

If Tan was going to make a break for it, he should break now while the man's exposed stomach was right over him. But where would he go? There were Oak voices all around, just outside the tent, at least a dozen. Was the Burner with them? Was this fancy tent his tent?

The man sat back. "It is okay. The... black is the same size. My name is Sajem, son of the *Dashor* Nermártan. What is your name, can I ask?"

Should he lie? He couldn't think of a lie. Why would it matter? He was no one. "Tánashen."

"Tánashen, I must tell our forces defeated your troops. Some ran, but some died. You are the only alive person who we found." He stopped as if expecting Tan to say something. When he didn't, the man went on, "We will not hurt you. You are a child. A child is not our enemy."

Not hurt a child? Every person in the encampment except Shonco had been a child.

The man Sajen—Sajem seemed to read his mind. "It was sad to us that your troops are so young. We did not think this camp was... so young."

Mad gods, they'd killed Ash.

For a moment, "so young" could not mean anything else. But no, he had no reason to assume Ash was dead. He'd been running for cover, good chance he'd made it. But made it to where? Naughty Vines? Most logical place to fall back.

"There is food." Sajem gestured over Tan's shoulder, but Tan did not look; he was not about to take his eyes off the man. "Please eat if hungry."

This man was going to fuck him. It was the only explanation. If he was just an enemy combatant, they'd have killed him. If they wanted him for slave labor, he'd be chained up laboring. They might be planning to extract information, but what did they expect a kid to know? No, it was like Grandmother said: they fed you and kept you in their rooms for their whims. He tried to keep his breathing even and told himself what he'd always told Ash: don't cry and don't do anything to get yourself hit.

"We cannot leave you alone," said Sajem, "because we do not know you. If you are alone, we must, what's the word, tie you. But please, rest."

Why was he explaining this?

The man got up and went back to his former position, guarding the tent flap, Tan now saw. He picked up a block of wood with paper on it and started writing again. Was that a trick? If he was a guard, he didn't seem to be guarding. Maybe he was just a guard though. Didn't *dashor*, a warden, mean a guard? If this man was just a guard's son, maybe Tan had been earmarked for someone else.

After watching Sajem a few moments, Tan took stock of the room. There was a second bed roll—of course there was—and beside his own bed, a pitcher and three slices of thin bread sat on a dish.

He needed it. Tan reached for the water, ignoring the pain in his neck, the vertigo as he got up on his elbow. He gulped some of the water and tore into the bread. It was divine, tasting of some salty oil. He'd eaten two of the pieces before it occurred to him to stash the third. Glancing at the man, who was watching him now, he took the third slice and stuck it in his pocket. So what if the man knew where he hid it? Better than eating it all now or just letting it lie. He lay down again. He needed to piss but it could wait.

The man Sajem resumed his writing.

Tan watched him and—

It hit him with a jolt. What time was it? How long had he been unconscious? He could see the blush of daylight on the tent canvas; it lit all the walls fairly evenly; that meant the sun wasn't low. Same day, anywhere between mid-morning and late afternoon, and he'd been separated from his unit. He hadn't deserted, but Keskan would claim he had. Shonco might not believe him, but he might have to capitulate, especially if they fell back to Naughty Vines and other officers were around, poised to pounce if the half-Kiri officer let his Kiri captain off again. Which meant Tan had maybe ten hours to get back before getting fucked was the least of his problems.

How long to Naughty Vines? Depended on where he was now, but it was the same day, still daylight. If he could make out the main landmarks, if he went fast with no kit to carry, at a guess five or six hours. If so, that left four hours to escape from this camp. But if he was out farther, if they'd ridden hill-jacks…?

No, he couldn't get stuck on doubts.

There were at least half a dozen men outside and one man guarding him inside. Guard him or tie him—that's what Sajem had said. Assuming he was telling the truth, tying him might be better. Left alone, he might untie himself. Depended on how well they tied him though.

No, his better bet was to take Sajem out. If the man was a guard, he was either a bad one or a genius, sitting there looking down at his paper—or pretending. The pitcher was fairly lightweight, but it might be heavy enough—

The tent flap moved. Tan shot upright, grabbed for his gun. His gun was not there.

Into the tent came an old woman, armed with a metal baton in her belt. No, not a woman—an *evan*, his body female but his clothes and his bearing a man's. And he wasn't actually old. The gray braid beneath the twist of his scarf made him look old, but he stooped into the tent with the ease of youth and sat cross-legged on the floor next to Tan, barely glancing at Sajem. He wore an Oak uniform and had an old scar on his right temple.

"This is Tánashen," said Sajem in Citadel words.

"Do you speak Keshnul?" the *evan* asked Tan.

Tan didn't know the word *Keshnul*, but the other words were Kiri. "Yes."

He went on in Kiri words, "Tánashen, my name is Jeyza. I hit you over the head. It was the quickest way to disarm you without killing you." There was an old woman, Ash had said. "You have the look of the villagers hereabouts. Do you come from this part of the country?"

After a moment, he nodded.

"What part?"

"Back there." He gestured in the direction he thought they came from if he was right about the orientation of this tent.

"What's the name of your village?"

The question made him cringe. His village was massacred, by the Citadel *and* Oak. He'd better lie. It felt dangerous to confess he came from that place.

"I—I come from Batty Hyrax."

After a moment, Jeyza said, "How long have you been with Fenorn?"

Tan frowned, he didn't know the word.

"The Citadel."

"Since I was seven."

Jeyza glanced at Sajem. In a softer voice he said, "Do you have—do you think you have family in the villages near here?"

"No," he said, chiding himself for the roughness in his voice.

Jeyza looked at him a long time, weirdly long, as if trying to solve a puzzle written on his face. Finally, he said, "You sound very certain."

"Yes."

"You'll stay with us for now as a prisoner of war."

"Jeyza!" exclaimed Sajem, as if that statement were surprising.

Jeyza gave him a cool look.

Tan couldn't figure out their ranking. Jeyza talked like a commander, but Sajem openly rebuked him. What kind of standing did *eváni* have in Oak? Tan had only ever heard of Oak men and women slaves.

"This is my tent," said Jeyza. Then, he glanced sharply to Sajem, as if he'd interrupted. Turning back to Tan, he said, "You will stay here until I come for you." He got to his feet and swept out.

Sajem glared after him, his breath quick with anger. Were they rivals, like Keskan and Tan?

"We're not your enemies," said Sajem in Kiri. If the stakes weren't so serious, Tan would have laughed. "Fenorn abducted you from the Borderlands. We have—I have no intention of doing the same. If I have my way, we'll see you sent home to Batty Hyrax."

He blathered on like that a while.

As he did so, Tan surveyed the room. Light shone at the gap between the walls and floor canvas. They were not connected, and it should be possible to wriggle out underneath the tent, at least in the middle of a wall between the posts. Most of the outside noise seemed to come from behind Sajem, behind the tent flap. That made sense—the tent would face inward toward their camp. That meant Tan should aim to escape under the opposite wall.

Were there trees? Was there cover? It was hard to tell. But once Sajem stopped talking, Tan thought he could make out a faint sound of wind in leaves and the shade that wavered over one wall had the impression of swaying branches. But he needed to know more.

"Sir," he said, "where do I go to piss?" He spoke Kiri now except for "sir"; he didn't know how to address the man.

"I'll take you out," said Sajem, "but I'll have to tie your hands."

Tan should have been tied already. That he wasn't spoke to ineptitude or some sort of trick. He nodded and held his hands out for the length of rope. The man did know how to tie a knot, snugging his hands together tightly.

I could still run though, Tan thought, and if he had the chance he would. But he suspected the camp would be crawling with Oak men.

If he ran, there would instantly be five long-legged raiders to tackle him to the ground.

He stepped out blinking onto a sparsely wooded ridge. He only spotted one other tent, half in, half out the shade of scrawny oaks, but bed rolls lay everywhere, along with packs and pots and tethered hill-jacks, taller and sleeker than donkeys. The smell of burning meat mixed with hill-jack dung assaulted his nose. A warm wind caressed his hair. It was mid-afternoon, getting toward peak heat, and most of the men rested in the shade. Some had even taken their headscarves off to let the air in. Back behind him, on the far side of a stand of trees, he could see the great fire pit crackle, its smoke wafting black into the sky.

They didn't care about being found out. Were they so confident that the Citadel couldn't assail them?

They stared at Tan but, at a small wave from Sajem, went back to their business. So he did have some rank. They were all speaking Kiri, and like natives as far as he could tell, their accents just a little different from his. Didn't Oak have a different language?

Sajem took him to the edge of the ridge line to piss, awkward with his hands tied but doable. At first glance the way looked clear to run, but no, there was a footman watching off to his left, hand on his bow. Why not a gun? They'd attacked with both guns and bows. What for? Guns were better.

He didn't recognize the terrain, rolling hills of yellowing grass patched with oak groves, little scrub. He had never been this far west: it had to be west, toward Oak, away from Citadel power. But if he headed east, skirting the fire pit, and kept the watershed to his right, he would hopefully come back to familiar landmarks. And maybe... maybe that squarish peak blue in the east was one he had seen in the west at his unit's encampment.

"All right, back to the tent," said Sajem.

But Tan had seen enough.

❦

He would use twilight to cover his escape.

Sajem was trying to engage him in conversation. "How old were you when you left Batty Hyrax?"

"Young."

"What is your life like with the Citadel?"

Shrug.

And so on.

Tan's answers were insubordinate, and at first he gave them to test the bounds. There appeared, however, to be no bounds. Sajem accepted all he said, or didn't say, nodded, waited, asked a different question. Who was this man? He seemed to carry some rank but have no idea how to wield it. In a way, he reminded Tan of Ash: careful, unobtrusive—subservient. But even Ash could snap, and this man, too, must have his trigger.

Jeyza was different. After maybe half an hour, he returned and sat. "I have some questions. First, where were you headed?" Insubordination would not pass with him.

"I don't know. I just marched where my commander said."

Jeyza scrutinized him. "Why only children? Why no adult warriors?"

Now here was a chance to sound cooperative and possibly wheedle some information of his own. "There was one adult, sir, our commander." Did he already know that? Had he seen a body?

"But the ones under his command were all children, yes?"

"Yes."

"Why?"

"I don't know." That was true enough. "We're cadet units." He used the Citadel words, as they were all he had.

"Where did you march from?"

"The Grid."

He raised a warning finger. "Don't be clever. Which village did you march from most recently?"

It was probably obvious on a map. It was a piece Tan might as well give up. "Knotty Vines, sir."

"Drop the, 'sir,' boy. Can't you recognize a woman?"

Tan had no idea how to respond. If he—if she—wasn't an *evan*, what was he—she? Women didn't dress or talk like that. She clearly had authority, but he didn't know what to call a woman in authority. In the Citadel, he'd have called her "aunt." In Knotty Vines, he might have called her "grandmother," but he had a feeling that would be very wrong.

"Why now?" He—she was saying. "Why this big incursion? Fenorn has been settling the Borderlands for years, trading here, farming there, skirmishing, yes. But why all-out war now?"

Tan frowned. *Because you nuked us.* Wasn't it obvious?

"They must have told you something," she prompted.

"I don't know," he said carefully. "I just got my orders." Then he added, "I was stationed at the Grid." If they were pretending the bombing hadn't happened, he might as well pretend he hadn't been there when it did.

"What does that have to do with anything?" she said, "being at the Grid?"

"Jeyza," said Sajem, "don't interrogate him like a criminal."

"I never said he was. That's not the point."

Tan shook his head. "They just don't tell us much."

"Well, what do they tell you?" she said irritably.

"What you said: there was going to be a big attack and they needed us to march."

She weighed him up. "How many were you?"

That was a test. The question was basic. She had a fair idea of the answer, or she would have asked sooner. The exact answer was fifty-one. He tried a low ball. "Forty."

She narrowed her eyes and nodded.

Tentatively he asked her, "How many died?"

"Of yours? Nine." That might have been a lie too.

"Little children?"

She hesitated. "Two."

Two. Ash, Sho. But the other units had first years too, and Ash had been running for cover.

He glanced at Sajem, looking for a sign. He got nothing but a look that was possibly pity. How far could he play him? How soft was he really?

"Sir," he addressed Sajem. "I'm sorry but my head still aches. I think I would answer better after I rest a bit, if that's possible."

"Yes, of course, you can—"

"Sajem," warned Jeyza.

"You can," he repeated and scowled at her. "He's a child, Jeyza."

She gave Tan a look as if to say she knew better. To Sajem she said, "Séduan wants to talk to you."

"In a while."

She sighed and went out.

Tan took a long drink of water from the pitcher. He had no means of carrying water and no idea where the nearest running creek might be. Then he lay down, making some show of massaging his temples.

"I don't wonder you have a headache," said Sajem, "both with the way she hit you and the way she kept hammering on your mind."

His mind? Tan glanced at him, frowning.

"You don't read minds, do you?" said Sajem. "It's not surprising if you were taken by Fenorn as a child. If they raised you in their religion, you'd be conditioned to read minds only in their ceremonies."

Oneness. That's what he meant. And he was right: that was the only time Tan mind shared. But the Kiris were different, and Oak, too, it seemed. Tan remembered it vaguely, Mum and Dad speaking silently if they didn't want the boys to hear, smirking over their heads. Ordan had claimed he could do it, but no one else could do it with him. Well, it was a good thing if they couldn't reach Tan's mind. They couldn't track him and catch him like a priest.

He settled on his bedroll and pretended to sleep, half expecting Sajem to attempt more conversation. He didn't. He sat and watched. He was an important man; at least, he talked back to a woman who plainly had authority. Why was he spending this day playing guard over a prisoner—a prisoner he refused to leave tied up? It would make sense if they'd given him Tan to fuck, but that didn't seem to be the answer. Jeyza plainly saw him as a source of information, but Sajem blocked the interrogation. It didn't make sense.

But it didn't matter.

What mattered was the hours peeling away Tan's chance to get back to his brother, his unit, his life before his grace was up and he was branded a deserter.

He memorized the room: the pitcher, the food plate, the distance to the back of the tent. They'd been stupid not to take his boots away.

Sajem would be going to see that man "in a while." The odds of getting another guard as malleable were zero. In Tan's head, the afternoon bells were passing; at the same time, the darker it got, the better for his escape. Time slipped by. The sun was sinking, throwing an orange glow against the western side of the tent that cast Sajem into a brown silhouette.

"Tánashen," said Sajem finally, "are you awake?"

Tan made a bleary, noncommittal noise.

"I have to go. There's a guard outside who'll come take my place. His name is Kor; he won't hurt you."

Couldn't let him go, not yet. "Sir, what do they want with me?" Tan tried to make his voice plaintive.

Sajem came to sit closer to him. "What we want is to free your people. We want to stop the Citadel's attacks on the Borderlands. Jeyza has a rough demeanor, but she's asking you those questions so that we can help the villages fight. We want to free you too; that's the goal in the end, to let you go home, or where you want to."

That was so obviously goatshit Tan barely bothered to listen. He could almost believe Sajem believed it, but it was goatshit all the same. Nonetheless, it got him what he needed. It got Sajem up close. Now if he could pull off a few seconds of a tired, old trick...

He grasped his forehead and curled into a ball. "Gods, my head."

"Is it much worse?" Sajem leaned in over him.

Tan snatched the pitcher and smashed it into his face.

Chapter Sixteen

He smacked Sajem hard three times, then scrambled back, just as the man's grunts brought concerned calls of "My lord?"

He yanked up the tent and slithered out quick. A couple of men shouted. He sprang up. It was still too light, but the day was fading, the sun soaking the grass to rust. Someone grabbed for him. He leapt free like a pika dashing rock to rock.

A smoldering bonfire rose before him, filling his nostrils with Ordan. Silver-charred branches. Charred corpses, chopped limbs. Ash—?

His boots crushed charcoal, then he was past it, his mind reeling with glimpses of carnage, shriveled fingers; black, leathered skin stretched over ribs.

He sped downhill, goat footed, scanning for cover. They had hill-jacks, so they could catch him, except brush crowded the ravine. He plowed into it, branches slicing his face. Roots caught his ankles, he stumbled. But he was deep in the brush, down in the damp bed of a narrow, seasonal creek, barely room for his own feet. At least a hill-jack couldn't easily reach him, and his smallness might help him, but the voices were so many.

Angry shouts from above, one a woman's voice, Jeyza's.

If he crashed along the creek, they'd hear him. If he went to ground, they'd find him. He was still at the doorstep of their camp, yet hiding was his only hope.

But there was nowhere to hide, just branches, leaves, rock—and voices closing. He stumbled along the creek bed, one ankle twisted just enough to twinge.

There. An overhang, two feet of turf half worn away above the mud. He slammed himself under it and pulled up rocks around him. He had no gun but if someone came close, he could kick out, trip them maybe or stun them with a rock. He found a sharp one and gripped it.

Feet crunched up above. They passed to the other side of the creek bed.

"We know you're there," called a man's voice. "Come out now and you're not dead."

Tan scarcely breathed. The feet crunched some more.

"Come on now. You can't hide forever."

"Perhaps he doesn't understand you," said another man.

"Oh, yes, he does, the little bastard. Lady Jeyza said so."

"Bloody Fenorn mute. If he had a normal mind, I wager I could sense him even if he blocked his thoughts."

The feet moved farther away, then back closer, stopped, moved again. The light in the gulley was failing fast. At least, that was to Tan's advantage. But back in the Citadel, evening bells were tolling, and he had to find his unit before dawn.

More crunching. "Blast it!" A branch cracked in the dark.

After a time, the feet receded and fell silent. *They're still there,* thought Tan. *They haven't gone. They're lurking, probably talking with their mind speech.*

As if in answer to his thought, something stirred in the brush. He went stiff but after a few moments determined it was just a mouse or something nibbling.

Night fell. In the blackness, the whine of mosquitos was sharp. He had to get moving before Ribbon rise, while he had the full cover of darkness. Gently, he pushed the rocks back from his shelter. They thunked and scraped, but maybe not much more than the mouse. He rolled himself out. The Far Stars cast only the faintest glimmer. He couldn't see the branches, couldn't see the creek bed. His only hope to minimize his noise was to make every move tentative and slow, though slowness was his enemy.

He managed a few steps with only faint knocks and whispers. On the slope above him, something crunched. He waited, went forward again. Nothing. He went on, a little bolder, or more desperate—and crashed into a bush with a great rattle of leaves.

Some way behind him now, footfalls answered.

The dark lay thick, it was sound that betrayed him. He had to get out of the creek bed onto the hillside in the open grass; it would still make noise but less.

But first he had to go slow. He crept south, one step up from the rocky bed, two steps up, backtrack to avoid a gnarled bush. The crunching still came faint behind him. Up he went, deer-like, slipping through gaps in the brush as he found them.

Then, all at once, he was out in the clear—or so it seemed. The light was so dim he could barely tell where hilltops merged into sky. But this was it, his chance. He ran.

æ

He put his trust in the earth beneath him and pelted by feel alone through the grass. The rough ground jerked his knees and ankles. He fell and ran again. A slope dropped abruptly, and he tumbled and rolled, bruised hip, grass seeds up his nose. He got up and plunged on, only marginally slower, down, down, into a rut, then up, his legs finding the upslope easily. His pursuers must be hot behind him, but he could not hear their steps over the rasp of his own.

Ribbon rise loomed in the east, framing the hilltop with indigo. He found a deer trail, more or less flat, looping in the hill and swept along it as the skyline silvered. A few steps around a bend and the Ribbon appeared, a milky swath of stars, the hilltop a black void in its midst.

That flat edge near the summit had the look of landslide; Tan thought he remembered it, though from a different angle. They had camped in sight of a tall hill like that, capped with a landslide scar. He recalled hoping their path didn't lie up its slopes. But if he got to the far side now, he could backtrack to Knotty Vines.

His breath hissed and a stitch in his side was worsening. His legs seemed to have slowed to a crawl, like a dream, but he couldn't stop. He was too close to the Oak camp.

As he came to the far side of the hill, he left the trail and plunged downhill in the direction he hoped was toward last night's camp. Oak knew where the camp was and might head him off there. Nonetheless, he needed to get his bearings. As he stumbled through the grass and into patches of brush, he tried to assess how to make for Knotty Vines without retracing the exact path Oak knew.

But he couldn't think. The damn brush snagged him on all sides, silver tipped in the Ribbon light. At some point, without conscious volition, he sank down beneath a bush and listened for pursuit.

There was none at his heels, no crashing, no voices. His breath rushed in his ears. As it stilled, he could hear nightly noises, distant crickets, some creature nibbling.

Something rustled in the grass.

Tan's whole body listened. It came again, a step. Pause. A step, somewhere upslope from him. He listened a long time, praying his pursuers would give up and look elsewhere. After a time, he began to wonder if the step was a human at all. It didn't have the cadence of someone stalking. It neither moved steadily, nor started and stopped with a measured care. It felt careless: step, step-step, stop. Step, stop, wandering along the hill. A deer. He hadn't been around deer since he'd been rescued from Knotty Vines, but his child mind recalled their nightly tramp outside the yurt.

He began to consider next steps. The night was still young, but night travel would spend it quickly. He wasn't past his unit's campsite yet. Maybe his pursuers were waiting to pounce, maybe not, but he needed to risk it and move on.

He was thirsty. He should have sifted the mud in the gulley to get some water. But at least he could eat. He pulled the bread from his pocket and ate half of it. It cleared his head and made his legs a little stronger. Bending low, he started picking his way through the brush.

❧

He probably doubled back too much; even so, by the time the Ribbon shone high above him, he had skirted the campsite and made it to the road. That, too, might be a bad idea. Oak could well have been tracking them there. Still, he had to pick his battles. He needed speed and clarity about his route, and he hadn't heard any sign of pursuit since the gulley.

That fact kept coming back to him, as a relief and a worry, by turns. It didn't seem possible he'd outrun those men: older, longer-legged men who probably knew the terrain better. That meant they'd let him go. That meant they were waiting to spring—but why? If they just wanted their prisoner back, why wait? If they were hoping he'd lead them somewhere, where? He'd already said he marched from Knotty Vines. Dammit, he'd given it away.

But they couldn't just trot into Knotty Vines; it had been held by the Citadel for years. It housed dozens of Citadel men, and from the look of it, garrisoned troops from the Grid.

Perhaps he had outrun them. Could even stealthy trackers follow him as silently as this?

After a time, exhaustion slowed him to walk. The Ribbon arced directly over his head. He could almost feel it scatter stars in his hair. Then his perception shifted, and it came to him that the Ribbon was not rising up but rather the planet spinning past it. The aunts in the Citadel had taught him that, using a lamp and ball to show it. The idea made him dizzy, like he was slipping off the skin of

Uramésha. He rarely thought of his world's name. Thinking of it now, one terraformed world among so many, he felt very small and, for a moment, almost weightless. He looked ahead into the silvery night and resumed his jog.

He went on that way for hours, jogging, stopping, listening, walking, marking the progress of the Ribbon. Behind him now, it made his shadow jump before him, long and sharp, like an imitation of the Citadel's great shadow. The sun would rise before Ribbon-down. He had maybe two hours.

A faint rattling ahead became a clear drip of water. He followed it down an embankment, his face and hands scraped by twigs. Something wet hit his foot and he tracked it back to a trickle, a seasonal waterfall well on its way to dryness. He filled his hands and drank over and over, the dirt taste awakening childhood memories of splashing with his brothers in the creek.

He stepped back. A finch twittered in the dregs of the night.

When he shot a glance at the sky, the black had thinned to a charcoal gray.

By the time he'd bolted back to the road, birds sang all around, as if they'd all woken at the same twitch of dawn. He pounded down the road as the horizon grayed, then warmed to yellow.

The sun burst into his eyes like condemnation just as he came to the bridge over the Crow's Daughter. He jogged across the creek and stopped; it came to him his feet had been headed for home. Yet home was not home.

His time was up. He was a deserter.

But he wasn't; he'd been captured in battle. Commander Shonco knew him; he'd believe it.

But did that matter? He was a deserter. Oneness couldn't bend the rules. It was a whole, unassailable. If it started picking and playing favorites, it would cease to be One.

He stood underneath the sharp-tipped laurel leaves, the creek burbling uselessly behind him. He could not go forward. He could not go back.

He took a tentative step backwards toward the bridge. Maybe he could hide and think...

"Halt. Stay where you are." A sentry stepped out from the brush.

Tan obeyed him. "We are One," he said, feeling a breath of relief that luck had made his decision for him.

"What's your ID?"

"Cadet Captain Tánashen, C-16. I got captured but escaped, sir. Did my unit fall back here, sir?"

"Escaped?" said the footman as if the idea were absurd.

"Sir, if Commander Shonco is here, I need to report to him."

The footman eyed him, then gave a curt nod. "Move on." He gestured with his gun. Two other footmen crunched out of the brush. "Got him," said the first man. "You two cover here. We've been tracking you for a mile, boy. You're piss poor at sneaking."

They climbed backward up the weird dream that had been the Miller's road, across the bones of the hills he knew, down through furrows of what must have been the Ancestor's Meadow, though he could scarcely recognize it through the seedling furrows of maize. The farmers were stirring, Citadel people and Kiris too. A Kiri woman working on an irrigation line glanced at him. It was little Davi's mother; he'd known her all his life.

They came onto a flat-packed road that did not belong, passed some square buildings, and came to an expanse of tents among chopped tree stumps. The smell of breakfast took hold of him—bread, asparagus, and butter. His mouth watered. The soldiers bustled, carting buckets of water, shaking out blankets, or eating.

Some stared as Tan walked by; most didn't. A lone cadet with footmen was unusual but not especially odd. But when they came to the cadets' tents, people knew him, and they watched and whispered.

A C-13 boy called out, "Tánashen's back." Not Captain Tánashen.

Keskan surged out of a tent. "So you did come back. Commander, I told you: he's been scheming with *them*."

Shonco emerged from the tent behind him.

"It's obvious, isn't it?" said Keskan. "They let him go so he could come back and spy."

A footman seized his arm.

"Commander Shonco, that isn't true!" said Tan. "They took me prisoner. I got away."

"Ashtyn saw him with that Oak woman," said Keskan. "He saw them together."

Shonco stood before him now, his eyes not quite reaching Tan's face.

"Muned saw her!" Keskan strode up to Tan, his eyes molten with rage and delight. "He struck a deal, the coward, like he always does."

"Commander, you know me. I serve the Citadel."

"Commander Shonco knows exactly what you are," said Keskan. "You deserted before. You deserted with Júzian. And when the game was up, you ratted him out to save your skin."

Tan could see Muned's stocky shape now. Where was Ash? Was he dead? Was Sho? He could see Gomu and Tarnto, still and blank.

Dezdenec came to stand by Shonco, his pale eyes ablaze. "You liar. You said Keskan was the traitor. You made me believe it. And all the while it was you. Just like with Captain Júzian."

"Mad gods, Dezdenec, I didn't betray you. I was captured. Commander!"

Shonco met his eyes a moment, then nodded to the footman. "Bind him."

"I'm not a deserter. I'm not a spy. You know me." He felt a length of rope go around his wrists. The corner of his eye caught a familiar face, Ash by a tent flap—unhurt, bless the gods—watching in silence as they dragged Tan away.

Chapter Seventeen

"Commander, just let me explain!" cried Tan.

Then something orange struck the ground, five feet from where he stood, an arrow smoldering.

"Take cover," called Shonco and everyone dove.

The footman holding him yanked him to the ground and started dragging him, crawling for the shelter of some crates while bullets clapped around them. Tan twisted and kicked. The footman's hold on his wrists went slack. He rolled to knees and was up and running, hands still bound, zagging wildly with no thought but to run and not get shot.

"The tent's on fire!" shouted someone. "Get buckets! Get the hose on the pump."

The camp smelled sharp with smoke, flames licking in the corner of his eye.

The face of the land had been recarved, but childhood knowledge told him where the deer trail down to the gulley lay, down the hill too steep for crops and houses. Without his hands for balance, though, he tripped and rolled, coming up hard against the trunk of a chestnut. He scrambled around it and down into the gulley, where laurel and chestnut grappled for water. He fell into the creek, two feet deeper than it should be, and splashed, groping for the opposite bank.

Then with a crash, a sheet of water drenched him. Hands grabbed him and hauled him up onto a hill-jack. He teetered like a sack against the animal's shoulder hump, hands helpless, as she snorted up the hill, dodging roots of trees. He lost his bearings almost at once.

Somewhere behind him a woman, Jeyza, shouted, "Split and go!"

She was answered by the crash of hill-jacks.

Grass and trunks, sun and shadow, his stomach crushed by hill-jack's gallop, the smell of man and jack—it knocked him into delirium.

At some point, they rolled to a stop and muscular arms dropped him, like a dead load, on the ground. The man yanked off Tan's boots and tied his ankles. Deftly, he untied his wrists and tied them again, this time in front. Then, he dragged him to a tree and snugged him to it with a rope wrapped three times around his arms and chest.

Tan stared at him dully. An Oak man, middle years, heavyset. Not Sajem. Somehow he had expected Sajem, unlikely as that was after the beating Tan had given him.

He couldn't see the hill-jack, but he could smell her. Her hooves crunched in the grass.

"Is he all right?" Jeyza's voice.

The man stepped out of his sight. "What the blast do I care?"

"Our comrades will tend the wounded."

"Luck keep them, my lady, or this boy will pay."

"Go rest, Kor."

She came into Tan's line of sight, dirt-smeared and cheek upbraided. Uncorking a waterskin, she gave him three swallows before drinking herself.

"I trust you're not going to yell for help." She sat in front of him. "You have an idea what response you'd get."

She was right, he was an outcast from the Citadel now. What the hell could he do? The next move was... what? What could a deserter do to get back to his boys and his brother?

"Are you hurt enough to need help?" she asked.

He shook his head. His body throbbed like a single bruise. His neck ached, his hands were numb, and several cuts stung, but nothing deadly wrong.

She nodded. "We'll rest here, then head back to camp."

He dozed against his tree, leaf dappled in the warm afternoon. He came back into an aching consciousness to Jeyza's voice. "All right. Let's move."

The ropes fell from his arms and he was hoisted to his feet. When he sagged at the knees, he got pulled up with a curse. The rope left just enough space between his ankles to hobble.

"I need to piss." He had forgotten how miserable it was to have imprisonment rob him of that simple freedom. He hadn't been so hamstrung since the cart, after his parents...

"Blight you," said the man.

"It's all right," said Jeyza. "Just remember, you have nowhere to run." She took the bow from her saddle and nocked an arrow, aiming at him all the while. She moved with the poise of a practiced archer.

Under the eye of Jeyza's bow, they gave him some bread and another sip of water, then tied his arms behind him again and gagged him. Finally, freeing his ankles, they shoved him up on her hill-jack, a gray, grumbling beast with twitching ears.

He was going the wrong way, every step farther from Ash. He could feel the heat of Jeyza's chest behind him and the hill-jack's hump in front. The gag was slick and hot. He hadn't ridden a hill-jack since he was seven, and without use of his hands, he kept listing, yanked upright by Jeyza.

He had to get to Ash. Ash was primed to swallow whatever Keskan told him. He'd say, *This is our chance to escape. This is our own land. We can disappear into the hills.*

But they couldn't because most of the towns had priests—

Why hadn't a priest found Tan?

Keskan told the whole division he was a goddamn deserter. So the priest must have been looking for him? Why did they only spot him a mile from Knotty Vines? He must have been out of range. They'd taken him off by hill-jack, miles and miles.

Did that mean Keskan *could* escape? Could he get far enough away to just disappear?

But disappear where? The west was held by Oak and the east by the Citadel. And say they stole some supplies, how long would that last? What could they eat this time of year? Wild onions, caterpillars, pine nuts, maybe plums if they got lucky. Not enough. If they shot an animal, the gunfire would give them away. No, Ash was dead with Keskan.

But what could Tan do? Even if he escaped and rescued Ash, they'd be equally alone in a strange, warring land. Wouldn't Ash be dead with him too? And what about the other boys? He couldn't just desert them, but he couldn't help them either.

He needed allies, time to plan, a place to land.

☙

They came to the camp in the blinding sunset, so that Tan could not clearly see the charnel bed of bones, yet he thought he caught a strange flash of yellow. When he glanced back, it proved to be buttercups scattered on the charred remains of four men and a hill-jack.

Men burst into chatter as they rode up.

"Blessed luck to see you whole, lady."

"Was he worth it, lady? Kerméken and Davan are moaning like death."

"Our men's blood for that *tapánesh* worm." He didn't know what "*tapánesh*" meant.

"If I were Lord Sajem, I'd flay him raw."

Someone pulled him from the hill-jack and kneed him in the gut. He sputtered and fell, no strength left to resist them. A fist smashed his face and he tasted blood. A boot sent a shock through his left elbow. He tried to roll up in a ball, but with his arms bound useless behind him, the rain of their blows cracked into his bones.

"Enough," ordered Jeyza. "Kor, tie him up."

The big man tied him to a tree as before. It was all Tan could do to keep track of his breathing. He wanted to gasp through his mouth; with the gag, he could barely suck air through his nose. His mouth hurt, his gut hurt, his arms screamed as Kor retied them in front of him. His right cheek was a burning mass twice the size of his left.

Campfires sprang up. The smell of Ordan. Did Oak also eat the dead?

The cooking fires blurred into little suns. His tree was near the center of the camp. No way to run. That was all right; there was nowhere to run to. The mosquito bites were easier to ignore than their fucking buzzing, but that, too, he tried to put out of his mind. Men talked and ate. Occasionally, one cursed at him, but no one hit him again. Jeyza had power. She was tough but not cruel, a bit like Shonco, Shonco who had turned him away, who had sided with Keskan—

He banished the thought. Jeyza, she was the one here now. She had seized Tan twice under the Citadel's nose. If he could make her an ally, she might rescue Ash too.

(*Rescue?*)

If he craned his neck, he could just make her out at a campfire, talking to a circle of men.

She was the only woman. Why? These were Oak men; they enslaved women, at least Kiri women. But Jeyza, with her Citadel looks, was no Kiri. Maybe they didn't make slaves of their own. But it couldn't be usual for their women to fight or else there would be others. What was special about Jeyza? What was special...? What...?

His head hurt.

What...?

It hurt and he nodded.

It was like being bound to the He, he thought. Desertion demanded sacrifice. They would come in the night and set fire to the yurts. You could hide in the gullies if you were very still. A snake had laid eggs inside his stomach; he wished someone would take her out.

When something prodded him, he started awake, and as he grabbed for his gun, his body jerked against his bonds. The pain shocked him alert, and he found himself looking into Jeyza's face. The sun's milky afterglow suffused the slopes. Tan must have been asleep only minutes.

A handful of men loomed behind her. One had a battle-seasoned face, pock-marked with a lot of skin cancers dug out, a man with a salt-and-pepper beard, who stood, arms crossed, with an air of authority. Sajem was not with them.

"I've captured you for a reason," she said. "If you make yourself useful, you'll stay alive. You know Fenorn from the inside out. Your knowledge is a valuable weapon for us. Given how they welcomed you back there, you are beautifully positioned to understand your situation. You can help us free your people from Fenorn, or Fenorn can kill you. Can I take it you understand?"

Tan nodded.

"Good. Why are they massing at the Grid? You're a smart boy. Don't pretend you don't know."

But she knew the answer. Why pretend she didn't?

"You bombed us."

"Bombed you?" said the pocked man. "King Rendyen's daughter? You make me laugh." He wasn't laughing.

The king's daughter? The king. Could he mean the Burner? Was Jeyza the Burner's daughter? He couldn't be that old—or could he? He'd led the Massacre back in the grandparents' time. Tan watched her with a new wariness.

"Who told you that?" she said calmly.

"I was there."

Jeyza raised an eyebrow. "Funny you're alive to talk about it."

"The shield held," said Tan with pride. "The Citadel is still standing."

She gave him a searching look and nodded. "Well." She half turned to her companions. "If what this boy says is true, joke's on us for depending on our bombs, eh?"

A scatter of chuckles answered. The man with the pocked face merely glowered.

"One more thing," she said, "that big metal contraption down by the River, scouts say it looks like a bullet half the size of a town, what is it?"

"I don't know," said Tan, though privately he agreed with Dezdenec that it was a water tanker. "We were wondering too. They only tell us what we need to know."

She narrowed her eyes, then rose to whisper among the men.

None of this made sense. Jeyza had seemed to know nothing about the bombing, only to turn around and affirm it. And when Tan said their assault had failed, at least three or four men laughed. Laughed at their failure to obliterate their enemy?

Twice now, she had asked why they attacked. But if you bombed your enemies and they survived, wasn't it obvious they'd retaliate?

Therefore, Oak hadn't bombed them. Her affirmation was a bluff. Keskan had always talked as if the bombing was a fake-out. Keskan, fuck him, had been right.

Chapter Eighteen

Dawn filled Tan's face like fog. All the world seemed as far as Ash, and even Ash unreal. The pain was real, though, and most of his energy directed to arranging his limbs to minimize it.

A sullen youth came up and ungagged him to give him water and bread, then untied him so he could relieve himself. His legs could scarcely support him, and when the boy retied him, his left arm cried out.

He counted about twenty men huddled over a cold breakfast. They all wore long, gray-splotched tunics—Oak's uniform—with gray or green scarves twisted up as round hats, bits of their shaggy hair showing beneath.

Like C-16, their parentage seemed both Citadel and Kiri. One man had hair as blond as a priest; another was small and black-haired, like Tan. Most looked mixed, the offspring of Oak men and their slave women, probably. There was no sign of Sajem. Surely Tan hadn't hit him hard enough to kill him?

He glanced at the extinguished funeral pyres. Above them, pika vultures circled. The characteristic gold triangles on their wings identified them. He had missed the vultures; they didn't live in the deep desert. It brought a keen relief to think the dead would pass through them; even the people Tan had killed would pass through the earth into life again.

The Garden lived. It did. If he could escape with Ash, somewhere...

Then his other boys, what became of them?

He watched the Oak men pack their gear in the bundles for the hill-jacks.

The hill-jacks were gone. The realization smacked him. The hillside was utterly bare of them. Had the balance of the men ridden off in the night—to ambush his people?

Then, he heard a bray, and man led a hill-jack up over the ridge, others following like goats. Where the hell had they been...?

He was an idiot.

They'd been down the watershed, drinking. It had been years since Tan had lived with other animals. Living things needed water, even hill-jacks with their forehumps. Any Kiri knew that. It disturbed him how he'd lost the basics precepts of... what? What was it called? There was a word, and he couldn't remember. It was like forgetting his brothers' names.

&

A quarter hour later, Kor dragged him off to Jeyza's hill-jack, and right past Sajem. The sight of him sent a jolt through Tan—relief mixed up with terror. He was alive and, bless the gods, didn't look up. He just sat on a log, massaging his head, half his face swollen purple.

"Here, boy." Jeyza boosted him onto her mount.

Sajem's nose was bashed and bloated, and Tan would pay.

The pocked man addressed the unit. "We ride down the valley. We had surprise on our side yesterday. Now the invaders know we're on them, let us ride with care."

The hill-jacks snorted and shuffled with a torpid air, but once their leaders started off, they fell in—the wrong way, away from Knotty Vines and Ash.

"Lady Jeyza," Tan blurted. "There are Kiri boys, these Kiri boys with them, an older one, one a bit younger, and a child. If you rescue them, they'll help you."

Yes, here he was helping Keskan desert, but cutting him out of C-16 would make the others safer. Obviously, Ash had to be with

Tan. He probably shouldn't have mentioned Dradam. Dradam he wasn't sure about.

"Why?" she said. "You don't want to help us."

He hesitated. "They really hate the Citadel." Well, two of them did.

"I'll take it under advisement."

"Time is important. They might already be moving—"

"Unless you want your gag back, don't tell me my work."

He shut his mouth. He should have known better. If she was the Burner's daughter, what could she feel for his folk but contempt?

"Sajem," she called.

Now it would come. He couldn't escape his punishment. He dropped his eyes as she cantered up to the man and tried to look invisible.

"I want to draft a letter to Leki," she said.

"I agree," he said around swollen lips. "We need the Convener's mandate. But if you want help from off-planet, you'll have a bloody long wait."

"We have Enátha at any rate."

"It was a stupid risk to drag her out here. I'm here, I can teach them."

Teach who? Teach what? Wounded men taught pain.

"I know you can," said Jeyza, "but we need someone with the authority to speak for the Kept Worlds." Whatever they were.

Sajem barked an angry laugh and said no more.

❧

They turned west. That would put them on the way to Energia's Town. Was C-16 under different orders now, or once they regrouped, would they be headed there too? Maybe he was going in the right direction after all.

If so, he could help them get close and grab Ash.

And what about the others? Lavan was still back at the Grid, and he'd never desert the Citadel; Low in Mouth was its loyal ally. Dradam could tip either way. He wanted out, Tan could see it in his eyes, but could he give up his dream of being Lavan's ally? Should he?

As for the Citadel boys, what could possibly stop Oak from just killing them?

Oneness could answer this if he could just find it. He realized with a deep yearning it had been days since his mind had last been called into that union. He couldn't desert C-16. He couldn't turn his back on Oneness.

But he couldn't go back to the Citadel either.

He couldn't go back to Knotty Vines, not ever.

He couldn't leave Ash with Keskan.

He couldn't side with Oak. He could use them *maybe* to get to Ash, but he couldn't side with them. The Burner had murdered his parents.

He couldn't run to the Kiris just to be crushed between Oak and the Citadel.

He couldn't help any of them kill his boys.

Each way he turned there was a wall with no gate.

He took a deep breath and made himself think. First, he had to get Ash. Then he'd worry about the rest. If he hit a wall, he'd get over it, under it, wriggling like Ash under that fence in the Grid. Like a deserter, like...

He wasn't sure what pulled him out of his thoughts, but he realized it had been some time since he'd heard the men talking. They road silently now, bows in their hands, not slung across their backs for travel. The open woods had given way to forest, a mix of spindly oaks and thicker pines, the day hushed and temperate in the dappled shade. It was a prime spot for an ambush.

As they rode on, the trees closed around them. A bird twittered and hooves clumped.

Off the trail to the east, a twig cracked.

"Archers ready!" cried the pocked man.

All the men and Jeyza drew.

"All right, all right," came a woman's voice, a Borderlands accent. "I was wondering how long it would take you to spot me."

She emerged from trees, a slim figure, dressed as a man, like Jeyza, but in a Borderlands fashion, loose goatskin trousers and short tunic, hair pulled back in a tail. She—or he?—was maybe five years older than Tan, thin in the face with large eyes that put him in mind of a moth.

"Your hill-jack take offense at your face, Oak Sajem?"

"Show some respect, girl—" began the pocked man but Sajem waved him back.

"Well met, Yowlers Fashen. What news do you bring?"

Fashen. He, then, a man's name, even if Oak said *girl*. The Kiri crossed to Sajem and handed him a paper. Sajem glanced at it and passed to the pocked man.

"We can't talk here," said Fashen. "And if you want a safe campsite, you're on the wrong road."

❧

Fashen took them to a hilltop where tall pines sprang among great slabs.

There, they tied Tan to a tree again. His left arm screamed in protest, unwilling to unbend.

"Lady Jeyza," said Tan as she snugged the rope, "the kids don't have a choice but to fight. If you could capture them—just get them out of play—it would weaken the Citadel, but they don't have to die."

It was stupid babbling, with no plan, no sense. It just came out of his mouth in desperation.

She gave him a quizzical look. "Tell me, do they still lock the women up in the tower?"

The question caught him off-guard. "Um, the women live in the Citadel—until they're sent to the Garden with their men."

"On the middle floors, yes? Around, what, floor ten?"

"Yes," he said faintly. The women's quarters were levels 6 to 10. "How do you know about the Citadel, lady?"

She sat before him, crosslegged, casual. "I've been there. My daughter was born in the Citadel." She laughed at his stare. "I don't mean I had a baby in the Citadel. I adopted her when I was there as *talanléyta*." She must have seen his confusion because she added, "The—oh, what is the word?—*stenzao*." Ambassador, like Lavan would be for Low in Mouth. "She was a problem for them, you see. Her eyesight was bad, like so many with priest blood, so they didn't want her as a breeder, and she couldn't be a scholar because women don't *do* that, do they? So to them, she was only a drain. They were happy enough to pass her off. When I say, 'they,' I mean the *Uronbezo*. Her birth mother wasn't happy—but relieved to see her live."

"You *met* the *Uronbezo*?" The Landowner?

"Of course. What do you think an ambassador does? Not talk to heads of state? I didn't meet the present one, of course. This was thirty years ago; I met with his father. The present one's a mad-bat, as far as I can tell."

Tan gaped at her, speechless.

"A strong telepath though, yes?" she said.

Strong, yes, the strongest. "His hair is almost white," said Tan proudly.

"Hair color has no bearing on telepathy, boy, though I suppose inbreeding does preserve high mind strength." She stood. "You keep quiet now. I'll get you when I need you."

"Lady Jeyza, the Citadel really welcomed an ambassador from *Oak*?" It broke his mind to think that the Citadel and Oak had ever been on speaking terms.

"Of course not. Don't be stupid. I was an ambassador for the Kept Worlds—for the Convention." More things Tan had never heard of, so many things he didn't know.

❧

Though the afternoon lengthened, they raised no tents and set no fires. Tan shivered in the cooling breeze and watched them tend the wounded, changing bandages, applying salves. Beyond the pines rose the north mountains, not the rolling hills he knew but snow-capped peaks, beyond Oak and Citadel and the Borderlands too. Beyond that, other worlds. Kept Worlds? Places Jeyza knew. She was far more powerful than he had thought, maybe even beyond her father. He, after all, was just a king of Oak.

She sat now, pensive, talking with the leaders and Fashen. Sajem was sagging, the pocked man gruff. At one point, Fashen hooked an incredulous thumb at Tan.

Eventually, at a signal from Jeyza, Kor came and untied him, pulling off the ropes so roughly it burned his wrists. With one great paw, he hauled him up and gave him a shove toward the leaders.

"Careful of him, my lady," called one man. "He's either enemy or savage."

"Even his mind is closed like a liar," said another.

"Sit," commanded Jeyza, and he sat, his left arm smarting as he lowered himself.

"Yowlers Fashen," said Sajem, "we have a spy in their ranks—if we can trust him."

Fashen raised an eyebrow at Tan.

"Not him," said Jeyza. "I met the spy the same day I rescued this one."

The same day...? And then Tan understood.

"He's like this one," she said, "one of the Borderland boys captured for a warrior."

"Keskan," said Tan.

"Very good, Tánashen. We need to know what he's like."

He was like an infection in C-16.

"He's a—" Tan stopped. As long as Keskan was their spy, he wasn't going to desert. He wasn't going to make Ash desert. They'd both stay to gather information. This could stabilize things, give him time to plan.

"He's a what?" said Jeyza.

"A Kiri, like you said."

She slapped him, not hard but hard enough to sting.

"Don't play games," she said. "He despises you. Why? Why was he so determined to portray you as a *tapáneshtor*?"

"A what?"

"Traitor." She used the Citadel word.

Tan hesitated. "I was the leader of our group of boys. Now he is."

"Will he be a good one?"

"He's a *tapáneshtor*."

Fashen chuckled. "Well, that'll either make him a good spy or a bad one."

"You grew up with him?" said Jeyza.

"Since I was eight."

"But never liked him?"

"Not really."

She gave him a small smile. "Thank you. That's all I need to know." She turned to the pocked man. "Send her to him."

"I'm sorry, do you mean me?" said Fashen. "'Send her here, and send her there'? I'm part of Dawn Rock's alliance. I don't run errands for you Oak men."

"He's right, Jeyza." Sajem turned to Fashen. "You're not under our command, but you are our ally and a tracker. This is an opportunity we can't waste."

"To head straight into an enemy encampment based on some chirping from a kid you trust so much you keep him tied up to a tree?"

"I agree with the girl," said the pocked man. "This boy's dislike is thin footing for trust, Lady Jeyza."

"This boy's dislike is the garnish, Séduan. I spoke to this Keskan, not long but long enough to peg him for a leader. I asked Tánashen if he'll be a good one. That boy's out for his blood, yet he couldn't say no. All he said was he's an enemy of Fenorn."

Sajem was studying Tan, eye squinting from the blows that Tan had given.

"So I'll go find your spy—where?" said Fashen.

"Out by Knotty Vines yesterday," said Jeyza.

He laughed. "Fantastic. I'll go meet your spy in the middle of a Fenorn stronghold, and tell him...?"

Sajem glanced at the pocked man, Séduan. The older man shook his head.

"We'll tell you later," said Sajem. "Vaníen," he called, "break out some supper."

"And I'll meet you back on the siege line at Yowlers," said Fashen.

Yowlers. Was that Energia's Town?

"You'll meet the warden at Yowlers," said the pocked man, Séduan. "Our party is headed to Blue Gums."

"What?" All trace of amusement left Fashen's face.

"When our task there is done, we'll circle back to Yowlers."

"They need you now, Marshal. The siege was holding when I left, but Fenorn men are swarming toward them." Swarming. It had to be Energia's.

"Hardly a swarm," said Jeyza and nodded at Tan. "He was one of about fifty."

"And you're twenty. Any way we cut it, we're massively outnumbered. We need every man. Look, they already hold Blue Gums. It's vital to break their hold at Yowlers."

Tan frowned. The Citadel did not hold Blue Gums. It held Low in Mouth and Dip but not so far west as Blue Gums. It just traded there and helped fight off raids. Ordan's parents got killed in a raid: Oak raids, like the one these people were planning.

"We look to you to spy, girl, not dictate strategy," said Séduan.

Fashen glared at him. "You are in *my* homeland, Marshal, and my people will dictate where your help is needed."

Kiris dictate to Oak?

The marshal sat forward. "Four of our comrades lie dead, and two wounded because we came to your aid—"

"Peace, Séduan," said Sajem.

At the word *peace*, the tracker scoffed.

"We advance on Blue Gums," Sajem went on. "Those are our orders."

"You're mad," said Fashen. "You think you can take Blue Gums with twenty men? It's south of the River. Let them keep the bloody south. If they move west, it'll be from Yowlers."

"If we're going to drive them from your land," said Jeyza, "we need to gut their access north. For that, we need Blue Gums."

"For that, we need Yowlers!"

"Afterward."

The tracker fumed and then dissolved into a long, low laugh. "Then that's when I'll go meet your bloody spy. Afterward. You free my village, and then we'll talk." He rose and stalked off, and Tan admired him for it.

But gut their access north? The Citadel's northern access route was the train line, the Grid, and the Bridge. Blue Gums was south of the River and days west of the Grid. What made it strategically important?

Jeyza led Tan back to his tree. "I'm sorry we have to bind you. But I'm sure you understand we need to measure our risks. Frankly, it's risk enough to leave you ungagged."

"If I screamed, you'd shoot me."

"That's a point."

"Lady Jeyza, why Blue Gums?"

"You worry about what *you* need to know."

❧

Night fell, and still they lit no fire. When Jeyza threw a blanket across Tan's knees, the warmth came as a sharp relief, yet he resented her for it. She had no call to be kind. She was an Oak woman, and her slap had been more honest.

But, no, she might be *from* Oak—but not *of* it. She'd scoffed at the idea of being their ambassador. She was above Oak somehow, a woman of other planets. And she knew the Citadel. She spoke its language pretty well. She'd once spoken with the Landowner's father. She'd adopted a child from the Citadel in order to save her (would the Citadel really have killed her)? If she cared that much about one Citadel kid, wasn't it possible she'd care about C-16?

She'd risked her life to rescue him. She'd picked him out for something—for information, she'd said, and maybe that was all. But it was an *in* he couldn't afford to squander. Right now, she was the ally that he needed. He just had to prove that she needed him too.

In the gray of dawn, he wolfed down a scrap of jerked fish and watched the cold camp creep to life.

The tracker hefted his pack. "You'll get skewered at Blue Gums, Warden's son."

Sajem looked up from his breakfast and rubbed at his eyes. "But now you see the sense of trying?"

The tracker sighed. "'Sense' is not the word. But I'll go talk to your spy."

A small laugh from Jeyza, petting the nose of her twitchy hill-jack.

Interesting. They'd plainly told him their plans and he approved, or didn't disapprove. What was going on with Blue Gums?

"My lady," Tan said. Better start earning his ally. "I don't know where Yowlers Fashen heard this, but the—Fenorn does not hold Blue Gums. The men are always complaining about raiders." Oak raiders, but whatever.

A chorus shouted him down.

"Don't listen, my lady."

"He's with Fenorn."

"—was born to deceit."

Fashen snorted. "It's dead quiet down there. You might say peaceful, except for the bodies."

"Bodies?" said the marshal.

"Strung up on posts like a warning. I saw five or six from my watch point in the forest. My comrades saw more."

"Perhaps there was a revolt and they subdued it," said Sajem.

The marshal, Séduan, crossed his arms. "Or perhaps this Fenorn boy's a liar."

"Or perhaps he's not," said Jeyza, "and neither is Yowlers Fashen. If the transformation is that recent, then Blue Gums is not really subdued. A veneer of silence is not the same. Broken twigs make the best kindling, they say."

But assuming Fashen was telling the truth, how could the Citadel subdue Blue Gums so fast? Lots of troops? Plausible—but if they'd just won a battle, everything would look wrecked. Fashen said it looked peaceful except for the executions. That meant traitors captured without a battle. And to track down the traitors unawares, they needed—

"My lady."

No one heard him, deep as they were in their own debate.

"My lady."

Jeyza looked up.

"I can help you, but you need to help me. Help me rescue my brother." Rescue all of them really, but it would overplay his hand to say so.

Séduan rounded on him. "What makes you think a scrounger thug is in any position to bargain, boy?"

Jeyza raised her hand. "This is the young boy who was with you when I captured you?"

"Yes. He's in trouble. Fenorn doesn't trust him because he's tried to run away. If he tries again, they'll kill him. That's why I tried to get back. That's why I hit Lord Sajem." The tracker glanced at Sajem and raised an eyebrow. "I'm sorry but I have to take care of him. If you can help me do that, I will gladly help you."

"If that's true, then show us in your mind," said Séduan. "If you're so sincere, let us see your thoughts."

Tan stared in consternation. He had no idea how to open his thoughts. His mind was only open when the priest led them to Oneness.

"He can't, Séduan," said Sajem. "His mind is trained in the *Shonac*, their Golden Way. They can only mind read together in their rituals. Once a mind is attuned in that way, it's mute to other mind reading."

"You've made my point, my lord. He's one of them."

"I saw him that day," said Jeyza. "He knew he had enemies all around him, and he covered that boy's retreat, like a brother."

"We didn't ask to be taken from—from Knotty Vines." Tan glanced at Jeyza. "I'm from Knotty Vines, not Batty Hyrax."

"His story changes with the wind," said someone.

"I'd lie too," said Jeyza, "if I came from one of the burned villages and fell into the hands of the burners."

Tan felt a surge of vindication. She knew the Burner for what he was. But she was his daughter? She was his daughter, and she knew.

"My lady," he said, "my brother's the only family I have. I need to protect him. I'm not bargaining. It's just true."

Several men retorted, but they stilled when Sajem raised his hand. "Our people's enmity was a long time ago."

Fashen huffed.

"If you can help us now," said Sajem, "we will help you rescue your brother."

Tan nodded. "They've assigned a priest to Blue Gums. If you want to win it, he's the one you need to kill."

Chapter Nineteen

In the afternoon of their second day riding, muffled gunshots rang across the woodland.

"That's Yowlers," said Jeyza. Energia's Town.

"Luck keep our kinsmen," said the marshal.

The intermittent pop of guns followed them for an hour before fading. An hour later, the River came into view, a golden road flashing through the trees, like a Golden Way, the way of Oneness, Tan thought, but the words rang flat.

They stopped by a creek. Tan slurped the cool water with his hands still tied, right hand dragging the left, though it hurt to bend his arm. Then he caught a new voice, a Kiri accent like his own. He whirled.

There were five of them, three men and two women. A stout gray-bearded man with a purple sash and deerskin hat was talking with the Oak men. From time to time, their eyes flashed to Tan.

"Tánashen." Sajem called him over. "Dawn Rock Ren, tell him what you told us."

The man in the sash gave him a measuring look. "It's like day to night, lad. Last year, when our alliance made a play for Blue Gums, true, half the Blue Gummers sided with Fenorn, greedy traders, who'd give up their homeland for Fenorn metal." He sighed. "We should have seen that coming but never mind. Half sided with us. It was chaos. Now, though, now, it's ghastly quiet."

A seed of vindication took root in Tan. That attack a year ago, it had really happened. The Kiri traitors *had* attacked, and the Citadel rescued Ordan. That, at least, was not a lie, not fully.

"This quiet, Tánashen," said Sajem, "that's because of the priest?"

Tan explained as best he could. "It's because of Oneness. Once you're part of the One, the priest can find you."

"Find you how?" asked Dawn Rock.

"Mind reading. I don't know exactly."

"What is this One-ess business?" asked a lean woman. Tan realized he'd said the word in Citadel; there was no Kiri word.

"It's... everybody being One," said Tan.

"It's a kind of experience of unity, fundamental to *Shonac* practice," said Sajem. "As far as I understand, it's a group mind-reading bonding guided by a single priest."

"So how does that take over the village?" asked Dawn Rock. "The Blue Gums folk aren't *Shonac* people."

"They can bring in you," said Tan. "I knew a boy from Blue Gums. He became part of the One."

"You mean he converted to *Shonac*?" said Sajem.

Tan didn't know what *converted* meant. "They just bring you in."

"Whether you choose it or not?"

"Oneness is. You don't choose it."

Sajem glanced at Jeyza.

"We need to scope this out," she said.

ཉ

In the dusk, Tan crept through a high bed of reeds, a rope around one wrist leashing him to Jeyza. They followed the lean woman from Dawn Rock's group, leggy and agile as a stick insect. Something Hérseji; her *sélnua* name had slipped Tan by. Sajem brought up the rear.

"We've hid boats on these shores for over seventy years," said Hérseji. "Since the West Men moved in."

They hid them from the West Men? Why? The West Men had been their allies.

"Here." Two skiffs were grounded in the reeds.

"Right," said Sajem. "Tánashen, give me your hands." Quickly, he undid the rope from Tan's wrist.

"You trust him?" said Hérseji.

"If he calls for help," said Jeyza, "he's dead before anyone can reach him. If he runs, he's dead before he gets anywhere."

"You'll need a sound plan to take the village with twenty men," said Tan. "The priest will be well protected."

They settled into the skiffs, Tan and Sajem in one, Jeyza and Hérseji the other.

"We aren't here to take the village," said Sajem.

"But I thought I—"

"Oh, we will before this war is over. But my father's orders are very clear. There's something here we need. We reconnoiter the village, retrieve it, and get out."

"Then why am I here?"

"To help us not do something stupid."

They set out in the two skiffs in the dead night before Ribbon rise. The planet Fennoc hung low in the sky, outshining any star. Still, Tan could scarcely see where boat bled into water, gray flecks of wave interrupting the black. He could hear the water kiss the boat with false promises of peace.

"What was his name, the boy from Blue Gums?" In the dark, Hérseji was a dim movement of oars. Her voice, though quiet, broke the night.

He couldn't say it. If he said it, his ramparts would fall. But that was foolish; there was no reason not to tell her.

"Ordan."

Her oars licked the night. "Far Glow Ordan? Danten's son?"

"I don't know."

She made an odd noise in her throat. "Danten was a good hunter, one of our head Blue Gums men. That ex-wife of his, though, I never thought much of, bloody medicine trader, if you ask me. She did all she could to keep that boy from his father. She coddled him, if you ask me."

"He had a tumor."

"Did he? I heard he was a sickly sort, but I figured that was just his mum's excuses."

"The Citadel cured him."

She made no reply.

"But then he died." He had to say it. It would be wrong—it would be cowardly—for him to pretend he didn't.

After a space, she said, "Some cure, eh?"

ða

On the far shore, they pulled the boats into the reeds and hid them as best they could. Then, they climbed into the woods and circled a hillside till the flicker of lamps came in view. Their feet cracked on bark and twigs, but they went slow and no one accosted them. Hérseji motioned them to a mound that afforded some cover. They crouched among dried leaves and some sort of small, hard nut.

"Can you eat these?" Tan asked.

"If you're out to poison yourself," said Hérseji. "Good for a bit of flavor though."

Sajem had given Tan back his helmet. He knew wearing it made him safer, but oddly it made him feel less safe. Perhaps it made him think of battle.

"The Blue Gummers harvest wood on this hill," said Hérseji. "But not every day, and with luck none will see us if we cover ourselves with gum bark." She was already gathering long strips in the Ribbon light.

The bark had the smell of antiseptic, just like home, Ordan had said.

"Be well," said Jeyza and moved to leave.

"Where are you going, Oak man?" said Hérseji.

"To scout out our target. I have experience in spying."

"You'll blow us wide open."

Jeyza turned to her. "No."

"We'll watch from here through tomorrow," said Sajem. "Be careful."

Hérseji watched her go and huffed. "And don't get any ideas, you," she said to Tan and Sajem. "I'm a free Borderland woman, even alone with an Oak man—and whatever you are."

"Certainly you are," said Sajem mildly.

As for Tan, he took a kind of comfort in her statement. She was worried they'd enslave her, which meant his grandmother's servitude, too, had been real. He knew the truth of his own family, whatever Keskan might say.

❧

A pang in his left arm awoke him; he'd jarred it in his sleep. Opening his eyes, he looked up at trees like nothing he had ever seen. In the daylight, they stretched to dizzying heights, moving sculptures constructed of strips: leaves like curved blue knives, narrow branches arcing skyward, and the weird ribbons of peeling bark.

Blue gums. It seemed like long ago, he'd known that gums were trees, but he'd forgotten.

The forest dipped down to the village like a road, and Tan could hear foresters some way off tramping up to the woods for their daily work. He hoped the whispering of the leaves would mask his party's own crinkling.

Sajem groaned and pressed his hands to his head. After a few moments, he sat up in his bed of leaves and got out some bread. He passed a piece to Tan, who devoured it at once.

But Sajem said softly, "The gain is ours," and held the bread up before he ate it.

Beside them, Hérseji snored softly, curled in a ball with her knife wedged in her hand.

Tan felt suddenly exposed, alone with the man he'd assaulted. "I'm sorry I hit you." Better cover his ass sooner than later.

"Are you?"

He asked it like a genuine question, like Dezdenec might have about scripture. In Tan's mouth, in anyone's mouth, those words have been sarcastic, but there was no hint of sarcasm.

"I'd say you did what you felt you had to," said Sajem, "to escape your captors, yes?"

Tan didn't know how to respond.

After a moment, Sajem said, "I was an idiot for letting my guard down. That's my shortcoming, not yours."

The words were plainly intended as comfort, but they made him feel like a thug—a thug in a world of thugs where this man was not one.

Hérseji stirred. "Oh, blast it to cinders, I feel wrapped around a corkscrew. What are you lot jabbering about?"

Sajem smiled and shook his head.

After Hérseji came back from relieving herself, Sajem took out a metal device that looked like a long cup. He pulled on it, and segments expanded till it was the length of a soldier's baton.

"Here." He handed it to Tan. "Look at the town through this spyglass and tell us what you see."

The thing was basically binoculars but for only one eye. He looked through it and fiddled with the focus until he got a decent view of the houses and the people in the streets.

"You want to know about the priest?"

"Yes, but also soldiers' movements, schedules, anything that might help us infiltrate."

"Do what?"

"Sneak in."

The village was divided into three clumps of buildings with boulders lining the streets between them. Each section looked the same. If they had separate functions, he couldn't tell. What did Oak need from this place?

"The houses look kind of like the Grid," he said. "I thought they'd be more Kiri—I mean, since the Citadel—Fenorn—hasn't been in charge long."

"How like the Grid?"

"Boxes. Peaked roofs."

"They're like that in the Oaks too."

"We've long built like that south of the River," said Hérseji.

Tan studied the foot traffic. He could see kids in the streets in cadets' uniforms. What if C-16 was there? His heart leapt, hungry for any familiar face.

But there was no one. Shonco's units had been headed for Energia's—Yowlers.

"There's a lot of Fenorn people. Maybe half. Some women. If they're moving families in, that means they don't expect much fighting."

"Because of this priest thing?" said Hérseji.

Tan had found what he was looking for and handed the spy glass to Sajem. "See?" He pointed at the village square. "I'm guessing that's for deserting."

Six makeshift He's stood at the edge of the common, crisscrosses of wood. Four were vacant, two with corpses hanging. The vacant ones were dark with blood.

"Guessing?" said Sajem.

Tan hesitated. "It's not the penalty we use in the Citadel. But it makes sense if there's a whole village of Kiris you want to make a point to."

"So they hold a whole village this way?" He stared for a moment, then passed the spyglass to Hérseji.

"If you run," said Tan, "they'll find you. If they find you... No one is lower than someone who turns her back on being One."

Hérseji handed Tan the glass. "Well, let's truly hope that what's-it—*priest*?— doesn't realize you ran away."

Tan swallowed a surge of rage. He *hadn't* run, but this wasn't the time to quibble. He went back to watching the village. The priest would probably stay in either the finest house or the most central, best protected. Nothing in Blue Gums looked especially fine, and the village had been so recently secured that the priest probably didn't feel secure. He'd keep low then, in an inconspicuous house. Tan tried to do a tactical sort of buildings.

Hérseji grunted. "Lot of Oak-looking, well, I mean Fenorn-looking folk coming up along the River."

"Near the boats?" said Sajem.

Tan lowered the spyglass and followed his gaze. He could make out a group of people with pickaxes off by the glint of the River.

"Near enough," said Hérseji. "Not right in the reeds. What are they doing?"

"Digging irrigation lines, it looks like," said Sajem. "We do a bit of that in the Oaks."

She scoffed. "Irrigation. Why, we're right by the River."

Tan went back to studying the village, but Sajem's attitude needled him. Spyglasses, irrigation lines, yet they fought with bows and arrows, like Kiris.

"Why aren't you using guns?" He forced his voice quiet.

"Tech limi—"

Tan thrust the spyglass in his face.

Sajem flinched, and it filled Tan with chagrin. It was six days since Tan had smashed his face in. And though the man's fear of him should make him proud, it didn't.

But Sajem said, "You're right. The tech required for guns and spyglasses is similar. But the Convention Treaty prohibits guns."

Tan didn't know what the Convention Treaty was. He said, "I thought only Kiris practiced tech limitation."

Sajem and Hérseji exchanged a puzzled look but made no reply.

Tan gazed through the glass again. More people were stirring among the buildings. Then came the blessed moan of the horn calling Oneness.

It sank into his chest, and he longed to fall into it, to hurtle out of hiding and prostrate himself. More than that, he felt dragged forward as if by chains. Oneness didn't force people like that; he'd never seen it work like that, yet he could feel the urge as strong as the River. He shook as if with fever and the glass slipped from his hands.

"They'll find me," he whispered. "They'll find me. Hold me back."

"He's batty," said Hérseji.

Sajem took Tan's arms and held them snugly behind him.

Without the spyglass, he could only see the little boxes and people like termites among them. He couldn't see the priest, but the voice came amplified across the distance.

> How can it be we walk through fires yet remain?
> That the sundered is restored to its primeval Oneness?

He tried not to listen but tears sprang in his eyes. He concentrated on Sajem's hands on his arms and the tree bark beneath him. But Oneness sucked him in, people he'd never spoken to—and some he knew—all souls made brother, sister, self. And there were others too, Blue Gums people, not One with them but feeling them, battered on a wave not of their making.

> Owner's phantom entered the heart of Loss.
> And Loss embraced him as brother, as self.
> Wondering and human in his tears, unsundered.

He understood those words better now. As he came to himself, he trembled with loss.

Then something changed. One face shone out before the rest, the priest, a young, blond man with eyes sharp like the Landowner, no, sharper, less grand. Tan could feel his eyes, like the sun on his naked forehead.

One has deserted us. One has betrayed.

I didn't, thought Tan. *It wasn't my choice.*

But he had, here he was, a betrayer.

A murmur rose among the people, so soft he could scarcely hear it with his living ears, but his mind knew the words, "He's deserted us."

"They're moving," whispered Hérseji, gazing through the spyglass.

Tan tried to make sense of the scene below. It might have been any day, Oneness ended, and the people going off to their appointed work, but some were leaving the village streets and heading for the trees.

"They've found me." Tan jerked but Sajem's arms held him tight. "Keep still."

"No, they're coming. They'll find us."

"They're heading this way," confirmed Hérseji.

"Blast." Sajem released him. "We have to join up with the boats." He slung his pack and bow and moved to go.

"You go," said Tan. "I'll head the opposite way. It's me they're tracking, it'll let me lead them off."

"No," said Hérseji. "Lead them to us. Ten minutes, then lead them into our jaws."

⁊

As the others retreated, Tan reached for his gun. They hadn't given it back. He grabbed a sharp stick and backtracked, looping northwest. As he crested the hill, the River fog rose up. His steps cracked in the muted white and he heard other feet crack behind him.

He hunkered down in the shelter of some saplings, igniting the lingering pain in his ribs. But hiding wouldn't help him. The priest was with them: he had to be or else they couldn't track him so precisely. The priest could see Tan like a blaze in the night. He crept fast to the east. He'd have to circle back to the riverbank to lead them into Oak's arrows.

And help Oak defeat the Citadel. Damn it. And then Oak would just go back to burning and looting. *Don't think about that.* He had to win their help to get to Ash.

He heard feet to the east. Just the way that he needed to go. He corrected, straight north for the River.

A twig snapped near him. Then a bullet broke the air.

He ran.

"Take him alive," cried a Citadel man.

He needed cover, but there was no cover. His only hope was that they wanted to torture him enough not to aim for his vitals yet, not while they thought he was alone. He zagged through the trees, trying to steer east, toward the boats.

Then something barreled into him and he was down, his left arm exploding in pain. He was grappling with a big man, big hands, relying on muscle. If only Tan could stab with his stick. But the man knocked his stick from his hand.

As he tried to twist free, a horn sounded, not the Citadel horn but high and sharp. From the River came a battle cry.

The man started.

In the moment his grip slackened, Tan broke out of his grasp, grabbed his stick and jabbed it into his ribs. As the man jerked back, Tan seized the knife from his belt and plunged it into his chest.

The man writhed and choked. But even as Tan rolled away, another soldier closed on him. Tan tried to scramble back—and then his pursuer crumpled with a bullet in his head.

"Get down." Hérseji knocked him on the leaf litter and rolled him against the roots of a tree. "Stay low." She threw some bark on top of them and they lay scarcely breathing as mayhem shook the forest. His left arm burned.

"The priest is on the hill," he hissed. "When he realizes Oak's closing, he'll retreat toward the village."

"A coward, eh?"

"Doesn't matter. He's too valuable to lose. But you'll know him by his yellow hair and yellow clothes. Even if he's dressed to blend in, he'll have a yellow something."

"Let's go." She started up.

"Wait. We have to split up. He can sense me, but he won't notice you."

"Right. You track southwest. With luck, we'll herd him toward our warriors."

Tan darted back to his attacker, who still lay shaking in the dirt. He shoved him over and grabbed his gun from its holster, then put the man down with a bullet in the head and pocketed the knife.

He sprinted through the trees in the direction of the village. The thick of the fighting had bent toward the east, and few men remained on the hill. Then, gunshots rang loud to the west. As he cleared the trees, he saw him: a young blond man with a stole of gold, flanked by two soldiers and dashing across the common.

Tan crouched and aimed. The priest was far off, but if Tan kept steady, he might get a clear shot.

He lost him behind an outbuilding. Wait for it. One second, two: he ran out of the other side. Tan took aim again. But damn it, could he really shoot a messenger of Oneness? He hesitated.

One of the soldiers beside the priest tumbled; an instant later, the priest fell too. Someone else had nailed him. Something pulled at Tan's insides, not pain or Oneness, but something residual, some thread being cut.

We are One, he thought and, for an instant, he could see the priest's life, dreamlike, a boy gazing out a high window at the desert. Then, he was Tan again in Blue Gums.

The priest was gone.

He can't find me.

For a moment, he felt blissfully invisible. Then, a bullet ricocheted near him and he realized he was exposed. He dashed back into the fringe of trees as a shout went up.

"The priest is dead!"

The cry became a chorus. "The priest is dead. Blue Gummers, come out and fight!"

The town exploded in shouts and screams and bullets.

"The priest is dead!"

"The priest is dead!" It pulsed like music beneath the noise.

Tan tried to distinguish the Citadel from their attackers. Kiris ran around on both sides with guns.

Slowly, he began to make sense of the confusion. The Citadel was trying to outflank them to the east: a snake maneuver, they called it. They'd keep low in the reeds. Tan had to warn Oak—

But what the hell were those cadets doing, scattering every which way like quail? Where was their captain? Stupid? Dead?

Tan had to go help them.

No, he had to help Oak so they'd help him get Ash. They weren't even his cadets, those kids. They were out of his division, not Shonco's boys. He knew them though. In his heart, he knew them. He'd seen them in Oneness, and they were kids like anyone.

He strained to catch orders shouted across the din, couldn't make any out. Maybe their captain was dead.

He broke from his hiding place. Hunching low, he scampered down the incline, aiming to get closer to the bulk of the cadets. He hugged the trees while he could, then darted behind a cart and peered around its edge to the outskirts of the houses. He smelled smoke. Somewhere a camel squealed.

They were vicious, these Oak men; he could see why the Borderlands summoned them. Kiris hid and took pot shots with arrows and stolen guns. Oak ran pell-mell into the fray. Off to the east, they'd set fire to the riverwood cottages. He watched the smoke curl and crackle.

Then came a blast of thunder.

A ball of fire spit chips of flaming wood. Tan clung to the ground near the wagon wheel. Fuck. They *did* have bombs, the fuckers. Fuck Sajem's tech lim, fuck Keskan. They were *Oak*, they were hypocrites and destroyers.

He could hear the boys' panicked shouts. He could see the unit in fragments, eight or nine in a disjointed dance between diving for cover and drumming up some formation. He recognized one of those faces. C-4.

A Kiri, half turned away from him, was attacking them from behind a barrel, his bowshots steady and accurate. One of the boys collapsed with a cry.

Tan inched out from behind his cart, took aim at the Borderlander and nailed him twice in the ribs. The man went down.

"C-4!" Tan called, "Fall back to Dip!" No, not Dip. Fuck. "Fall back to Naimu's Town. C-4, fall back to Naimu's!"

He broke cover and dashed to the nearest shed, closer to the cadets. "C-4, fall back to Naimu's!"

Someone else took up the chorus. "Fall back to Naimu's."

The boys ran for the east.

The Kiri archer was still convulsing. Tan put him down with a third shot, just as an arrow sailed past him. The man wore purple.

There was no more he could do, no more he wanted to do. Another bomb went off, another house in conflagration.

The gunshots came fewer now, replaced by calls of "Man the pump!"

Tan scrambled back to the trees and hugged them, edging down to the reeds. He startled two Kiri children, who ran from him screaming, and lay low while several men dashed past. When he reached the mud, he sank into its safety, watching figures fight the fire. Probably, he should be among them. But it was clear now that Oak had won, the Citadel had been routed. And he was wearing a Citadel uniform.

Chapter Twenty

From his hiding place, Tan couldn't count the corpses, but there were at least thirty and probably more. That was a heavy loss, equal to the whole force from Oak. From the clothing, about half were Citadel. Most of their force had retreated. And though the fires sickened him, he had to admit the fires were the reason Oak won. With a third of the village burned, it probably wasn't worth the effort to hold the remnants, not without a priest or a plan.

No wonder the Oak king was called the Burner.

A tang of mint clung to the smoke like disinfectant, and flecks of ash floated like insects. It surprised him that only a third of the village had burned, only one of its three sections. But perhaps that was why the village stood in three segments. It made sense to have fire breaks by a forest that rained tinder.

Getting listless from hunger, he ate a piece of jerky he had squirreled away and drank from his waterskin, not trusting the muddy water.

Then he ventured out, leaving his helmet behind, hidden. With luck, despite his Citadel uniform, the Oak men would recognize his face. He cradled his left arm with his right, finding it hurt less that way. The noon sun beat his head, as he scanned the rows of bodies for faces he knew. His thoughts flickered, like a lamp on the fritz: a man shot in the face was just an image, information; the next moment, it was the scream of an unrestful ghost.

There was one C-4 boy he knew, a friend of Dezdenec's. His father had been a scholar too, but Tan could not place his name. It was something –bo, something –lo? Soblo? Seemlo?

Further on, he caught sight of yellow cloth. The priest would no longer hold them. Oneness would no longer hold them like a mother bird beneath its wings.

I'm sorry, Owner, he thought to the priest. *I guess you never asked for Oneness to be used this way.*

He walked on. Was Sajem here among the dead? Was Jeyza?

A gray-haired Kiri was there, shot in the ribs, the man Tan had killed, the purple-sashed man. Tan stared in horror. It was Dawn Rock—Dawn Rock Someone, the leader of the scouts.

At that moment, as if sensing his guilt, a woman keening over a body looked up at him and cried, "Fenorn!"

"I'm a friend," Tan called in Kiri, holding his hands high as several bows turned toward him. "I'm from Knotty Vines." He did not want to say he had ridden with Oak, not in the ashes of a bombed-out village.

"Tánashen!" Sajem emerged from the rubble, limping and blood stained.

Tan was surprised by the surge of relief that ran through him.

"Are you all right?" said Sajem.

It took Tan a moment to understand the urgency in his voice. "Oh. It's not my blood."

"I was afraid you were dead. There are still bodies in the ruins, some are still being dredged out of the marshes. Térvelen," he called, "find him a *shulin*," whatever that was.

"I was hiding in the marsh," said Tan. It seemed Sajem didn't know he'd shot one of their allies. Good. If he was lucky, nobody had seen. He surveyed the wreckage. "You won."

Sajem's face was grim. "We drove Fenorn out, all right. For a while. Forty-one dead, as of last count, and a third of their food stores gone. They want *us* gone by tomorrow, I can't blame them."

"Then, why'd you bomb them?" Tan kept his voice calm, but Sajem jumped.

"Of course, we didn't bomb them! We used some stolen guns, that's all."

Tan's training told him don't talk back. His gut said Sajem wouldn't do a thing if he did. "They went up like bombs from where I was sitting."

Sajem's jaw twitched. "I didn't know how hot gum wood burns. And then, their gunpowder stores went up. We're lucky the whole forest didn't go up." He sat on a nearby trough, and Tan saw blood through a bandage around his thigh.

"You should lay down."

Sajem ignored him, watching people pick their way among the dead. When the man Térvelen came and placed a scarf hat in his hand, he gave a weak smile. "Thanks." He handed it to Tan.

It felt wrong on his head, wet with sweat. It was probably a dead man's, but it kept the sun off.

"Well," said Sajem at length, "fewer mouths to feed."

Tan stared at him till a shout pulled his attention.

"You come back here and pay for that!"

A woman was at the heels of two men and Jeyza. Each man carried two large sacks slung across his shoulders.

Jeyza did not even glance at the woman. "This is our payment for liberating Blue Gums, the only payment we're taking, so count yourself lucky."

More people were closing on them, crying out protests.

Sajem merely stood and watched, though Tan could see him breathing fast. Where was the marshal? Surely he'd intervene.

Then, a Blue Gums man made a grab for a sack.

"Close ranks!" Sajem shouted. "But don't fire."

At once, ten men had arrows trained on the knot of people.

"Get back, ungrateful scrounger!" cried an Oak man.

An arrow thunked, and the Blue Gums man reeled, struck in the shoulder. Jeyza already had a second arrow nocked.

"That's enough," cried Sajem, though it wasn't clear to who. Belatedly, he strode toward the knot of people. "Get out of our way, and we'll go."

A roar rose up in answer, fists shook, Blue Gummers shoved each other.

Then an older woman appeared out in front, the hat on her head decorated with rows of nuts. She said to the Blue Gummers, "Let them go. We can reckon debts later. Now, we have our dead to look to."

ॐ

As the day fell, the Oak men gathered their own dead and crossed the River. Sajem crossed last, taking Tan in the skiff with him. Tan wasn't sure why he got singled out that way. Maybe Sajem wanted to show he wasn't scared of the boy who beat him.

"Is the marshal dead, my Lord?" Tan asked.

"No, just knocked over the head," said Sajem. "But it's left me in charge, for now. Seems I'm it." He smiled limply.

"So what's the next move?"

"Rendezvous with the warden, my father."

"In Yowlers?"

A nod.

"My brother may be there."

Sajem sighed. "We'll find him, Tánashen, but not tonight."

No, not tonight, and who was in charge anyway? Who decided if a promise was kept? Was it Jeyza, the warden, the Burner—where was the Burner? Was he dead or...?

A thought struck in the pit of his stomach. What if Tan had been wrong about Jeyza. What if she wasn't from Oak at all? What if the man they called *warden* was...

Tan made himself ask, "Where's the king?"

"The king?"

Tan hesitated. "Who's the king of Oak?"

"His name's Rendyen. He was a mighty warrior once, but now he's old and has retired to the western realm across the mountains."

"It's not your father?"

Sajem gave a small laugh. "My father? No, he's a vassal, the governor of Oak, so to speak."

Tan heaved a sigh of relief. The king of Oak, the Burner, was far away. As for Jeyza, she might be his daughter, but she was cut from a different cloth, he knew it.

"So, my Lord, what's the plan? I helped you so you'd save my brother."

Sajem's bruises splotched his face like flowers. He gazed at Tan as the oars licked the water. "I don't have a plan. I have a promise. I'll convey that promise to my father, and we'll figure out next steps."

At those words, Tan's anger rose up slow and hot.

"And if he doesn't honor it?"

"He will." Sajem's eyes met him steadily. "My father is a man of his word. He is a man I trust implicitly."

Any son might say that, but something in his eyes made Tan believe him. No, it wasn't his eyes. Eyes could be liars. It was the bruises on his face, the bruises Tan had given him.

❧

They grounded their skiff in the reeds. In the waning day, Tan took off the scarf hat, the *shulin*, and stuck it in his helmet for safe-keeping.

Across the River on the south bank, Blue Gums smoldered and the distant mourners wailed. They did that in Knotty Vines too. Tan remembered back when his grandmother died and how the keening had frightened him. It had been different there though, more a dance, more musical. Here, he heard cries of "Dole!" half lost on the air. In truth, he found it soothing. It reminded him of the train wheels; he could almost feel the spirits.

"Here." Sajem took out something white. "Let me bind up that arm you're favoring."

Cautiously, Tan let him wrap it. "My brother hates Fenorn," he said. "He's always watching for ways to get at them." That last bit was more Keskan than Ash, Keskan the spy—Tan the spy. "He'd be a good ally for you."

"I'll make that point."

"He's small enough he can sneak in places."

"We'll find him, Tánashen."

"Is that something Yowler's Fashen is good at? Because it's only a guess that they're making for Yowlers."

"Yes, he's good at it. He'll find him." He broke a crust of bread and handed half to Tan.

"Thanks." Tan ate three-fourths of it and squirreled the final bite into a pocket.

Sajem folded his hands over his own bread in a ritualistic way. Then he turned it pensively in his fingers and handed it to Tan as well.

"You need to eat," said Tan.

"I've eaten."

Tan suspected that was not true. It was the sort of thing he'd lie about to his own boys. But his stomach received the gift gratefully.

"Now, try to sleep," said Sajem.

Figuring he'd better obey, Tan lay down, the reeds swaying over him against a yellow sky, the cool smell of mud alive around them. Free, and not free. So unlike the barracks.

Sajem still sat by his feet, his head in his hands. Like most things in Blue Gums, his bandaged leg smelled of mint, and the mint of fire and death.

Suddenly, the world struck Tan as sad and solitary. The reeds silhouetted in the dusk were like ghosts. This was why they called a ghost a "shade," because death distilled it down to a black outline of its self. There would be unrestful ghosts in this place, maybe Dawn Rock coming for Tan. So many ghosts. Was Júzian like that somewhere, or had he passed back into *mirya*?

Mirya. That was the word he had lost, the Kiri Way, the Way of Life, the way things became each other through death. What if Ash was dead? He pushed back the thought.

The wailing of the mourners floated up like scripture, the crisscross of the reeds a He and She. Shonco had told him that the statue at the Grid depicted He and She as One. Tan hadn't seen the statue, but he knew it wasn't true. No matter what a sculptor did, everyone was sundered. You could be One for an instant and an enemy the next. That kind of Oneness wasn't real.

"They must have been starving you for years," said Sajem.

"Yes," said Tan. "The Citadel is starving. Why the blast do you think we're farming the Borderlands?"

"But if the Citadel can't feed their own people, why are they stealing more of you?"

They rescued me from you. The words almost came out, but Tan stopped them. As long as he needed help from Oak, he didn't dare condemn them.

After a moment, Sajem said, "I didn't realize the impacts of the drought were so severe. I should have; that far south, there may be no farmland left. But I thought they were supplied by indoor farms."

"They are. It's not enough though."

"And that's why their army is surging, isn't it? Because of the drought."

If Tan had already accepted the bombing of the Citadel was a hoax, this confirmed it. The Citadel was the aggressor. The Landowner had lied. The Landowner himself had lied. What could make him lie? What weakness was he afraid to reveal? There was only one possible thing, the only condition that had changed.

"It isn't the drought," said Tan. "We always got crops from the Borderlands. This surge, it's because the well pump broke. The pump at the Citadel, I mean. And I guess—I mean, I guess they can fix it. They said they are. But I think they're having trouble, and when you don't have enough water, you don't have a lot of time."

After a moment, Sajem said, "So they had to evacuate to the Grid, and the Grid can't feed them all. So they'll take the land they need to eat."

"That's what I figure." What Keskan figured.

"That explains a great deal," said Sajem. "Thank you. Knowing what they need will help us to make peace."

Tan sat up, the skiff shifting as he moved. He peered at him in the fading light. "Are you from Oak at all?"

"I'm sorry?"

"Your people are warriors. They exist to make war. How can you be one of them and not realize that?"

Sajem didn't reply at first. Finally, he said, "I understand my people."

"I don't think you do."

A small laugh answered him.

"You talk like you're here to rescue us Kiris, but your people kill Kiris. You've been raiding us for years."

Sajem hesitated. "I'm sorry about the raids."

Tan almost laughed. "You're what?"

"I know it will take a long time for their memory to fade."

A cold anger was settling over Tan. "Yes. A long time."

The light fell, and in the pre-Ribbon dark, the planet Fennoc gleamed like a blue star in the east. Not far off in some other skiff, a man laughed, a hard Gomu laugh, the way guys did when death was near them.

Sajem said, "We're all Kiris."

Tan frowned, not understanding.

"We're all Kiris, everyone on planet Uramésha except Fenorn."

That couldn't be right. The Kiris were *Tan's* people, not their killers. Kiris followed tech limitation, but Oak bombed the West Men—unless that was a hoax too.

"You look like Fenorn," he said.

"There was a lot of intermarriage, centuries ago, before they withdrew to the Citadel. But culturally I am as Kiri as you are. Dawn Rock's hunters asked us for help because we're fellow Kiris, and we came." After a little time he said, "They told me the Citadel used child warriors, but walking into fifty children..."

He broke off and started to make a soft noise. It took Tan a moment to realize he was crying, this leader of Oak. It was an affront; he had no right to tears. Soldiers could afford no space for them.

"I'm sorry," Sajem murmured. "For all of it, I'm sorry."

The skiff shook with his sobs. Tan found it distasteful and slightly shocking.

He reached out and found Sajem's hand in the dark. "You need to pull yourself together."

The heat of their hands connected them. Then Sajem gave his hand a squeeze and pulled away.

"I'm sorry," he said again, calmer.

"It's like you've never been in a battle before."

"No, I've never been in battle." He sniffed. "I've had training, and I've fought off bandits with the border guard, but never this. They're fools to give me any sort of power here, just because I'm my father's son."

But this warden, his father, was clearly a war leader, so wouldn't his son be too?

"How old are you?" Tan asked.

"Twenty-seven."

Mad gods. "Why have you never been in battle?"

"It's been peace time."

"*Peace*?"

Sajem gave a rueful laugh. "We thought so. We were plainly fools." He took a breath. "In your opinion, what should we do?"

"Do?"

"You know Fenorn. You know the Borderlands. Jeyza saw that in you, that knowledge of both peoples. If you could fix everything, what would you do?"

What would he do? Bring everyone to the Garden, let the Citadel ruin all the villages? *No, think differently*, he told himself. *Think of your boys. One by one, think what they need.*

"I'd... let people be where they belong," he said. "Let people go home. One boy, he's the son of the headman of Low in Mouth. One boy's from Dip. One boy just wants to be a scholar in the Citadel—but he needs enough to eat to do it. Mostly, they just need to eat."

Sajem studied him. After a time, he said, "Even after their water supply's restored, Fenorn will need access to the Borderlands for food. So what are the options? They get food somewhere else?"

"I don't think there is enough food somewhere else. We raid the barbarians sometimes." In his ears, it made them sound like Oak.

"The barbarians?"

"The Kiris in the south, in the desert."

"The nomads. I see."

"But it's not enough to feed everyone." He paused. "I guess the tanker will help."

"'Tanker'? I don't know that word." Tan had said it in Citadel.

Tan waved a mosquito away. "That big metal thing on the River, it's like a barrel to take water to the Citadel, that's what we figure."

After a short silence, Sajem said, "That makes sense. Yes. Yes, that's smart. If you're going to use electric tech, you might as well use it that way. So when that—that *tanker* is ready to go, it will further alleviate the water shortage, but not enough to really give them more arable land. And so I see two possibilities: they continue to get food from the Borderlands somehow, or enough of them die that they can produce enough food on their own."

"So that's the plan?" said Tan. "Kill enough people that the food goes around? Maybe just kill half the boys from my group—"

"The plan was to come to the Borderlands' aid and help them beat back the invaders." *Was.* "But you're right. We can't beat them back and just let them starve. Leave aside the cruelty, it's a recipe for them to invade again."

"They aren't invaders," said Tan.

"Oh, aren't they?"

That hit him hard. "All right, some are. In the surge. Because they need water. But the Citadel's been in the Borderlands for years. My parents traded with them. When you people attacked—"

He stopped. It was not wise to make an enemy of his captors.

After a little while, Sajem said, "You really wanted to go back to them."

"I can't go back to them." Wrong thing to say. "And my brother, he's genuinely never liked them. That's true."

"But you," pursued Sajem. "You wanted to be there. Because of Oneness?"

Tan didn't know how to answer that. He couldn't say it was because he hated Oak. The Garden was a vanished dream. Perhaps it was Oneness.

"Doesn't matter. I can't go back. And my brother won't stay." That might be true or not. As long as Keskan was there, spying, Ash might stay—and spy and be caught and killed. "He'll either try to desert and be killed, like those Blue Gums people, or we'll rescue him... and then maybe we'll settle down if there is any place to settle."

"There will be."

"Where?"

"Many places, Tánashen. The Borderlands—or north, if you wish, in the Noryen mountains, or farther." His voice took on the lilt of story, the lilt Tan used with Ash sometimes. "My mother's family lives up in Zelár, far in the northwest of Noryen, and my grandmother's home people farther north still, in the green lands of Nivár." These names were totally foreign to Tan. They gave him a sense of the world expanding. "All these lands could be open to you and your brother. I could give you letters of passage, if you like."

Tan didn't know what that meant, but he said, "I thought your family came from Oak."

"My father's from the Oaks. My mother married him in honor of the peace between our peoples at the end of the war."

He trailed off, and by and by, he lay down. Tan thought he had fallen asleep, but then he said, "We knew that some of the Borderland villages have had good relations with Fenorn. The Grid's been there in peace for decades. That's why we didn't move sooner—but, no, I won't make excuses. In any case, the water pump notwithstanding, the drought is only going to get worse. We should have seen this coming sooner."

"How do you know it's going to get worse?"

Sajem hesitated. "They didn't teach you that?" When Tan didn't reply, he pointed up at the sky to the east. "It's getting worse because Aldu-la's releasing her grip on us."

Tan followed where he pointed. "Fennoc?"

"Is that what Fenorn calls her, after the king of the gods? Makes sense, I suppose; she's the largest planet. You know about planets...?"

"I know it's a planet," said Tan shortly. "It's a gas giant." Aunt Tson had taught them astronomy.

"She's big enough to exert a subtle pull on us when she's near us. She pulls us just a little away from the sun. But our orbits are offset so that every few hundred of our years, she falls behind us and her pull on us slackens. Then we move closer to the sun and the drought takes hold. In about another five hundred years, we'll get close again and she'll reel us back. Our descendants will enjoy a gentler world."

Tan gazed at the bright blue pinpoint, just starting to fade in the pre-glow of Ribbon rise. *Aldu-la*, Sajem had called it, the blue world. It seemed odd and unfair that something so far away could command the destiny of Uramésha.

"How bad will it get?"

"Much of life will survive it. Much of the complex terraformed life on Uramésha has already survived about six of these cycles. In the meantime... things will have to rebalance, one way or another. We might as well try to find the balance that feeds the most people with least damage. Do I know how to do it?" He gestured across the River at the wreckage and corpses. "There's your answer."

"But you're trying," said Tan.

"I'll try all my life. Uramésha is my home."

Uramésha's my home, the whole planet his home. The thought opened like a flower, and for a moment, the strife between the Citadel and Borderlands and Oak felt small.

Chapter Twenty-One

A mile from Yowlers, their party paused and listened. Gunfire popped in the distance, interspersed with the grunt of hill-jacks and a light breeze in the leaves.

"Séduan," Sajem called, "take the wounded and ride for Twelve Salamanders. The rest stand ready. They'll have need of us in Yowlers."

"My lord—"

"That's my command."

The marshal hesitated, his head absurd in its big bandage. "Yes, my lord."

"Our guns, my lord?" said one man.

Sajem sighed. "Those who have a gun may use it. At least, we didn't create them."

Tan was beginning to realize what a shifty thing tech limitation was. He counted five guns among eighteen men, not enough. In Knotty Vines, they'd had surprise on their side. But the element of surprise was gone.

Noon lay thick on the yellowing grass. The chestnuts, which lived a season ahead of all other trees, had already decided it was autumn and crinkled their leaves like baked skin. The hills looked still, but the sounds of battle echoed like the cheers of footmen at a tournament.

That's what it reminded him of: a game, not a battle. Battle was quiet and furtive till it exploded, and the explosions were quick in Tan's experience. This was different.

Jeyza told him to dismount. "Go stick with Hérseji," she ordered.

"Lady Jeyza," he said. "Spare the children."

She gazed down at him sternly from her hill-jack. "Tánashen, you know this world too well to think we won't shoot at armed warriors."

"You spared me."

"I had the chance."

"Then look for the chances, lady."

"We'll look for your brother," she said and nudged her hill-jack forward.

Tan donned his helmet and tied the *shulin* to his belt, ignoring the pain when he moved his left arm. When he came to Hérseji's side, she seemed startled, but nodded once he said Jeyza sent him.

"I want to thank you for saving my life," he told her.

"It's no more than we do." She led him off the beaten road. "We're stalkers, you and I, aren't we? Let's be ready to be useful."

Keeping low and hugging the bushes, they crept toward the fighting, a discordant, brutal loudness connected to none of the grass and leaves before them.

Then, as they crested a hill, it assaulted his eyes, a scene unlike anything his time as a cadet had prepared him for. No bands of nomads, no caravans of traitors. There must have been a hundred men, riding, running, shooting, a pandemonium that made no tactical sense.

He tried to extract maneuvers he knew, but all he could make out was that the Citadel had their backs to the canyon, precarious. Yet in that canyon was Yowlers—Energia's Town, deep by the rushing stream and perfect for hydroelectric development. That meant the Citadel held it; they'd taken Yowlers, if they could keep it.

How many Citadel troops were there? C-16 had been on its way to Yowlers, which meant Ash might be right there, if Tan could spot him. Maybe grab him in the chaos.

"I'm going to—"

But when he turned to Hérseji, she was gone. That surprised and perturbed him, but he had no time to dwell on it.

He had to get closer to identify C-16. He scuttled forward to the cover of a nearby tree and tried to sort out the units. He could differentiate two units of Oak men on hill-jacks. There were Kiris too, proper hunters under cover, breaking only when they had to.

No C-16.

Or was it...?

He could see a cadet unit, behind a footmen's. He counted one, two, three black-haired heads—a lot of Kiris for one unit. That alone meant it could only be C-16, C-3, or C-10.

Suddenly, shouts rose up. Shots flurried: a new Citadel unit, circling in from the north. All at once, the hillside that he hid on was bombarded. A hill-jack thundered past him, followed by Borderlanders on foot. He jumped and dodged to avoid being run down, lost sight of the cadets. Which way had they gone? They'd be reinforcing the footmen. He dashed forward.

There. Was that Dradam?

And Codo, and...

"Ash!" He bolted downhill as his brother's form disappeared behind a wave of footmen.

Something hit him. He was on the ground, feet running past. He curled up to avoid getting trampled. Then a big hand was yanking him up.

"Blasted fool!" It was Kor. "You think Lady Jeyza's your nurse? Come on before they skewer you."

"Let me go! My brother—!" Tan screamed and kicked out. For a moment, he broke free, but then a fist smashed his face and he was over Kor's shoulder, his struggles useless.

The evening sun broke orange through a mountain cleft when they finally let their hill-jacks rest at a clearing in the conifer wood. Up the road dogs started barking, but the Oak Men ignored them.

Hot and pummeled from the ride, Tan slumped off Jeyza's mount and stumbled like a drunkard, underfoot among twenty-five Oak men. He took a swallow from his waterskin and dodged a bridling hill-jack. His gun and his knife had been taken by Kor.

They'd lied to him and, against all he knew about Oak, he'd fallen right into their snares.

An older woman came up to them, flanked by some young people. They wore short, Kiri—or Borderland—tunics embroidered with bright thread.

"Yowlers has fallen?"

Yowlers has fallen! The echo rippled.

"They'll be on us next."

"Better make for Creeky."

"Nonsense. We're miles back behind the lines."

Leaning against the tacky bark of a pine, he took stock of his surroundings. They had stopped on a plateau in a mountain valley, near the edge of a village—Twelve Salamanders presumably. He could see yurts through dust clouds off to his left, encircling a stand of boulders, which looked too regularly spaced to be natural. The hills sloping down from the plateau were safest, bad for staging an attack, good for slipping off and hiding. He noted this in passing, his thoughts on his brother. They said they'd rescue Ash, but they had no honor. Jeyza was a liar and Sajem a weakling—

"Enátha!" Jeyza exclaimed and strode toward an oddly dressed woman with wire-framed eyeglasses, like some of the scholars in the Citadel wore.

Her big-skirted, wine-colored dress stood out against everyone's plainer clothes, and the way the Oak men bowed to her, she was obviously important. Beneath a red *shulin* flowed light brown hair;

though not priestly blond, it gave him a sensation of priest blood. Citadel-like and shortsighted, she had to be Jeyza's daughter.

Jeyza embraced her.

She cared about her daughter; she'd rescued her, raised her, a Citadel child. Well, Ash was a Citadel child too, so were all his boys. How could he rekindle that caring in her?

Sajem had followed Jeyza. Now, with an awkward start, he took the daughter's hand and kissed it. "Well met, my lady."

Who was she to the Oak men? More than just Jeyza's daughter. Sajem seemed afraid of her—in awe of her?

Enátha.

Jeyza had mentioned that name, had said she was coming. Sajem hadn't liked it. He'd called her too important to risk. Did she have the authority to make them get Ash?

"Tan?"

At the sound of his home name, he jumped out of his skin. It was Júzian calling, the voice of a ghost.

"Tan!"

He shrank inside himself. Who would be using his home name?

Then, he saw her heading toward him, a tall woman, no, *evári*, man-as-woman, dressed in white, lean and very old. It was by her wide-brimmed hat he knew her, decked with a single iridescent pheasant plume.

But she was dead, the aunts had said so. All his kin were dead, everyone but Ash.

"Tan?"

His feet stepped out from behind the tree, as if of their own will.

She held out both hands and he took them in kin greeting. "Blessed luck, it is you." Her voice creaked with age, yet there remained something in it of childhood comfort.

"Grandmother Linóvi?" The name felt wrong, as it was wrong to utter a vanished hope.

When she took him in her arms, he couldn't tell if he wanted to run or sink into them.

She drew back and sized him up. "Happy, happy luck! It *is* you, and so big. I half thought you were Juz. Is he with you? Is Ash?"

If Tan held still, he could wait out the lance in his chest. He knew that. He'd done it before.

"Juz is dead," he said shortly. "Ash is still with Fenorn—in Yowlers. He was alive when I saw him. Oak owes me for helping them at Blue Gums, and Lord Sajem promised they'd help me get him out, and Lady Jeyza said she'd look for him, but when we were there in the battle, I saw him and they wouldn't even let me get him."

She pressed his hand. "Thank luck Ash is living. That's the first thing. And Juz is out of danger, may the loss be ours."

He'd heard her say those words before, performing the rites when his aunt's-daughter died. She had blessed Ash's birth and his own and Júzian's. Here and now, voices barked and people bustled, but all that fell behind a wall while he stood with a ghost from his childhood.

"Grandmother, why aren't you dead?"

"Some friends helped me escape. I've been the way pointer here since their way pointer died. But we can talk about that later. You look like you haven't had supper in... weeks. Come on, my yurt's just over here."

"But Ash..."

She put a hand on his shoulder. "Tan, look around you. Do you think we'll get him back this instant?"

She was right. Of course, she was right.

"In this moment, Tan, *in this moment*, we are together, you and I. We're a pair of lucky uncles; let's not scorn it."

Reluctantly, he followed her, only to find Kor blocking his way. "Just where do you think you're going?"

"He's going with me," said Linóvi. "He's my cousin."

"And what gives you the right to take our prisoner, she-man?"

Instantly, several Borderlanders converged on the scene. Oak thug! How dare he speak like that to the way pointer! Couldn't he see who she was?

Tan shrank back. The last thing he wanted was to be the center of trouble.

"Kor!" Jeyza's voice cut through the crowd. "Let him go with her."

Kor gave them a glare but stepped back.

Like a shift in the wind, the Borderlanders' anger transmuted into nattering and fawning over Tan. The learned one's *sélnutor*, oh, happy luck! But dressed so oddly and so dirty and so bruised. Poor little thing. Why's he in that Oak hat? He nodded and smiled stupidly, bewildered, till Linóvi somehow made them part and led him on to the yurt.

Even without Linóvi, he'd have known it for the yurt of a way pointer, her honor stitched in rich adornment. Blue salamanders snaked around the canvas, interwoven with vines of purple grapes and autumn leaves of red.

Red Leaf. His *sélnua* name. It flashed in sweet pain across his thoughts as she opened the door to the yurt.

"Wait for me here, Tan. There's one thing I must do."

Chapter Twenty-Two

Tan watched the daylight fade from the window, the tumult outside beginning to quiet. Linóvi had said she'd be back in half an hour, and maybe that was true and he was stuck in elongated moments. Though he itched to act, he could not disobey her. She was his elder and a way pointer—and she was his *sélnuta*. He had thought Ash was the only one left.

The yurt had rafters like home, and it hurt to look at them. The warm brown of those wood spokes ignited a longing for bedtime stories with the firelight flickering among the beams. The central fire pit was surrounded by a cooking table. They'd had something like that at home, though theirs hadn't completely ringed the fire. He sat behind it, near the back wall with a full view of the door and window, the room alive now with the flicker of the single oil lamp.

He jumped when the door creaked, and rose up on his haunches, ready to spring.

It was Linóvi, as promised.

She broke into a smile. "I half thought you were a dream, and you'd be gone when I got back here."

"What's going on out there?"

She lowered her old limbs onto the cooking table, between a clay bowl and painted gourd filled with chopsticks and spoons. That felt wrong; you didn't sit on the table in Knotty Vines.

"Our hunters and warriors are regrouping from Yowlers," she said. "They expect the warden's riders any moment. Hunter Apáshan's people will be some way behind them. They're on foot. They think we're safe here from Fenorn, for the moment."

"We are," said Tan. "They've only just taken Yowlers. They'll secure it before they move further west." When had the Citadel become "they"?

She stirred the embers in the hearth. "Shall we build up a cooking fire?"

"What about Ash? Somebody needs to go back for him."

"Tan, the alliance is in retreat. Do you really think they'll send somebody back for him tonight?"

He had no reply.

"For now, you wash yourself up. There's a pitcher and bowl on that shelf there."

Tan was suddenly aware he stank. When he washed his face and hands, his cuts stung. The moist washcloth felt like the Citadel. Odd that water made him think of the bathroom there, out in the desert.

"Let's see that arm," said Linóvi once the fire was crackling.

As she shifted toward him, he stepped back. "No, I'm all right." That was mostly true; he could move it; it just hurt to. But he felt ashamed to let her see him. She'd pity him, she'd fuss over him. She didn't understand he wasn't a baby anymore.

"Well," she said. "Those clothes won't do, at any rate. They need a good scrubbing in the creek. See that basket there? There's some clean clothes there."

Linóvi was head and shoulders taller than Tan, and he had no idea how he'd manage in her clothes. But the basket had shorter shirts and pants, meaning she shared the yurt with someone. Now he looked, he could see three bedrolls rolled up against the wall.

Feeling foolish and exposed, he pried off his boots and left them off, though his stocking feet felt naked. He fumbled out of his bandage and uniform, slightly shocked to see the huge black bruise up and down his arm. As best he could, he rubbed himself down with water from the pitcher and cinched on the pale shirt and pants.

They hung loose on him, as on a little girl. But they smelled fresh and let his body breathe. A piece of him felt released.

Without a word, Linóvi took a fresh piece of cloth and deftly wrapped his arm. "Now, wash your feet and then hand me the pitcher."

She started some water in a pot on the metal cooking stand thing... what was it called? "Thank you, water, for giving us life," she said, and then to Tan, "Would you like a lie-down?"

Lying down without his boots and the Oak men still milling around outside felt deeply dangerous. "No, I'm fine."

"In that case, see that blue jar on the shelf there? Grab half a dozen onions from it and cut them up, will you? And hand me the basket beside it."

The basket contained acorn meal.

"Do you have oaks up here?" he asked. When they'd ridden up the hillside, he'd only seen scattered pines. "Oak trees, I mean, not Oak men."

"Spruce mostly. This was traded from Creeky."

The onions were sad little things, limp and no thicker than two of his fingers. They ate things like that at the Citadel, but he expected better of the Garden.

He set about slicing them in half.

The onions of his childhood had been big as his fist, and wasn't that abundance the very reason the Citadel was settling—?

"Thank them, Tan," exclaimed Linóvi.

He paused, baffled.

She put her palms together and bowed in the direction of the onions. "Thank you, onion people, for giving us your lives."

He repeated it. She gave the same thanks to the acorns and every piece of food. The memory of Mum cooking came back to him dimly.

A drumming sound interrupted his thoughts, a thunder of hoofbeats.

Why the hell were his boots off?

He dove for them. "Someone's coming. Grandmother!"

She had her whole damn head outside the window.

"They'll see you!"

"It's the warden's men," she said. "Buck my ears, there must be at least thirty of them."

An Oak men's raid. They had to run for it—but no. The Oak men were their allies.

Tan pulled his boots on and went back to the cooking table, surprised to find himself shaking. The din of the arriving men buffeted the yurt like a wind.

After a moment, Linóvi said, "My son will be so relieved to hear you're living."

"Is he fighting with the alliance?"

"Luck save him, lad, no. He's over sixty. He's in Creeky with his wife's *sélnua*."

"So these aren't his?" He indicated the clothes.

"Oh no, they're Mother Anji's. She keeps this yurt with me. But she won't mind your borrowing them. Here, add those onions to the soup, and would you hand me that jar?"

She poured half a cup of goat's milk into the pot. The soup began to rivet Tan's attention. The acorn meal mixed with milk and water formed a hearty base for the onions and some dried mushrooms—she called them chanterelles—seasoned with laurel leaves and pepper. It seemed a magic clung to it that said, *This is the Garden, the Golden Age that will come.*

But if the Citadel came here, would it wreck the place like Knotty Vines?

He pocketed the onion knife.

"Let's put it back on the shelf where it lives, lad."

Chagrined, he put the knife back. He shouldn't steal, of course, but Kor had stolen his knife, and he needed one from somewhere.

She handed him a bowl of soup.

"The gain is ours," she intoned, and he repeated the words.

It tasted like a return to life. He downed it at once, and she gave him more, and then a small square of bread to sop the rest with.

Outside feet still tramped and people jabbered, but that began to feel unimportant. It was like Tan existed in a separate plane, not the daily world, not the Gods' Realm, and not the world of ghosts, but a place enclosed in this little yurt.

Linóvi talked about safe things, the quality of the firewood and where to find the stream, the weather up here in the foothills.

Tan liked it here pretty well. And up north lay the mountains beyond the Borderlands. Noryen, Sajem had said. He said he had family up in Noryen. There was a whole world out there, peoples he had never heard of. Green places, new places for the Red Leaf *sélnua*.

He started as the door swung open.

A stout middle-aged woman bustled in with a big cloth draped over her arm. "Well, that's it. We're overrun." She stopped when she saw Tan. "And there he is, by luck, just as you told me. The gain is ours, way pointer's *sélnutor*. Red Leaf Tánashen, is it?"

"The gain is mine, Aunt," said Tan.

"'Aunt'? When did I become your aunt? I'm a Four Stones, not a Red Leaf. Four Stones Anji's my name." She put her palms together.

Tan was stuck, but Linóvi had called her... "Mother Anji," he corrected.

Anji's smile was small and knowing, like Dezdenec sometimes. She was forty or fifty and wore a coarse-spun dress slit to the thighs and loose pants, just like his mother. But her face was rounder, and he took comfort in the difference. As she studied him, she reached a hand toward his face. He suppressed the impulse to bat it away, let her fingers brush the sore spot where Kor had hit him. He wondered what he looked like.

"Poor little mite," she said. "He's a mute."

Tan glanced at Linóvi, as if she could explain Oneness, but she just said, "They all are in Fenorn, aren't they?"

Tan shrugged, surrendering under the weight of trying to explain the unexplainable.

Anji shook her head. "I don't know how we'll feed him, way pointer."

"We'll manage," said Linóvi.

"Easily said." She held up the piece of cloth, a blanket. "That Oak man, Jeyza, gave me this, said it was payment for keeping him. 'Well,' I said, 'we'll eat that then.'"

Linóvi smiled.

"Then he said, 'We'll settle up later.' That's always the way, isn't it?" She dove for the kettle, just as Linóvi reached for it. "You let me pour the tea out. Don't trouble yourself."

The tea had a tang of spruce.

"I need to go see Jeyza," said Tan.

"Tan," said Linóvi, "Oak Jeyza asks that you stay in the yurt for now."

There was no way she'd *asked* anything, yet it gave him a sense of pride to see Linóvi interpret it that way.

"Stay for how long?" he asked. "I need to talk to her about Ash."

"We will," said Linóvi. "Tomorrow. I've said so, and so it will be."

Chapter Twenty-Three

At the doorstep of Linóvi's yurt, Tan counted off his pebbles. "Roll for me. I'm mixing the rennet."

He'd waited half the morning for Jeyza's summons. Inside him, each lost hour hurt, but outside his pretense of calm was honed by his years at the Citadel.

"Here goes." The little girl, about ten, cast the stones and read their position. "Your cougar is three up. That means you can attack."

"Oh, that's lucky, isn't it, Tan?" said Linóvi, sitting beside him on the log that served as a bench.

Tan leaned over to peer at stones, still mixing as he did so. The scrape of his spoon on the cheese bowl soothed him.

"All right," he said, "I'll take on Rárian's boar." Which was dumb. Tan had never seen a boar or a cougar, but he knew they were both big and fierce. They should leave each other the hell alone. But whatever.

The girl moved Tan's stick animal up to the boy's.

"Gonna get you," said the boy, rattling his stones with gusto.

But the clatter of his stones was broken by angry shouts beyond the yurts.

"Get down." Tan grabbed the kids' hands and pulled them down behind the log.

"What's going on?" said the girl.

"I don't know. Just stay out of sight and be ready to run. Get down, Grandmother!"

But Linóvi didn't move.

A goat dog barked and goats began to bleat. Two Oak men came around a hill, one carrying a struggling he-goat around his shoulders.

A Salamander woman followed, yelling, "—and do your own hunting and your own blasted planting."

The other man chuckled and grabbed the woman around the waist. "Little girl's in quite a state. What she needs is a little pacification."

A volley of shouts erupted, Borderlanders and Oak men converging on the village circle. The woman struggled free and spit in his face. He merely laughed. And now Linóvi was heading toward them.

"No, Grandmother!" Tan leaped up and held her hard by the arm. "It's too dangerous."

"Tan!" she said sternly.

But by then, the fighting had begun, Borderlanders and Oak men yelling and shoving. He spotted Anji in the thick of it, shouting something like, "I'll show you!"

"—didn't ask *you*—"

"You can give us up a blasted goat."

"Wait—" That was Sajem, rushing into the fray. No one heeded him.

The Oak man had the goat over a slab of rock. An old memory told Tan it would be curved for catching blood. The goat bleated over and over till the man slit his throat.

Tan cringed. In the Citadel, you killed without hesitation; it was war, always, all the time. But at home, you never killed your own people without ceremony first, not goats or partridge, no one.

Behind Tan, the children were crying. Tan pulled Linóvi back, waving the kids down with his free hand. "Quiet and wait," he told them. "If Oak comes for you, run."

Then from behind, a woman barked, "That's enough." Jeyza strode past them down the mountain trail.

Some in the crowd parted for her, others kept on shouting, pushing.

She drew the metal baton from her belt and smacked it deftly into the shoulder of an Oak man grappling with a Salamander woman. He stumbled back.

"The war is over!" she cried, though the war was just beginning. "Your fathers were slavers. You are not. You are the *new* men of the Oaks."

"But Lady Jeyza," said one man, "these ungrateful scroungers—"

"Ungrateful?" said an elder woman. "We summoned you by our treaty rights."

"And we have a right to the tax you never pay," said the man who'd killed the goat.

"Show some respect, you—" started Anji.

Just then, a new voice, clear and strong, cut her off. "The Fenorn villages pay it."

Through the swirling dust, a man marched into the village circle—and froze Tan where he stood. He was bearded, his graying hair tied in a tail. Though he was not big, a furred cape gave the illusion of bulk. But the thing that tapped Tan's primal fear was the vicious scar on his right cheek, arcing up to the ear half shorn off.

That man had long lived inside him, deep down where he kept that day, the beige tunics and screams and his father falling. At the Citadel, telling tales to Ash, the man's name had slipped off his tongue easily. Now it glued his lips, as if its very shape was enough to wake the unrestful ghosts.

The man closed on the elder woman. "For years, every village occupied by Fenorn men: they've paid their taxes with no complaint."

"And in far better food than yours," said the goat killer.

Sajem said, "It's because they're breaking tech lim—"

"Sorgan, come here," said the man, the Burner.

The goat killer went to him, a large blond man, taller than the Burner.

The Burner backhanded him hard. The man stumbled, blood welling from a split lip.

The Burner marched past him to the bowl where the goat lay. "Come here," he said again.

Sorgan obeyed.

The Burner handed him a knife. "Blood for blood."

Tan's heart beat fast with the memory of Ordan. The Citadel or Oak, punishment was the same.

The man glowered but made a clean slice across the palm of his left hand. He squeezed several drops into the bowl.

"Now go to my yurt and wait for me."

Sorgan bowed and walked off. Tan felt his breath pour with relief. Was that all? It could not be all.

"Vánien."

The man who had grabbed the woman stepped up.

The Burner smacked him. "You too—to my yurt."

"Yes, Warden."

"Fenorn is coming," said the Burner. The *warden*. "Yowlers has fallen, Blue Gums is ravaged, and Salamander will be next, unless my forces stop them. This goat is dead, so cook him and make his life blood count. We have a war before us."

The Oak men moved to obey, but the Borderlanders stuck to the spot.

"I, for one, don't take orders from a thug who can't hold Yowlers," said Anji.

"Let them cook him," said the elderly woman—the headwoman, she must be. "Do it for *mirya*, and we'll honor him that way."

The warden nodded to her stiffly.

She motioned to a handful of Borderlanders, who moved to one side and formed a ring.

While the warden took the marshal aside to confer, Sajem stood on the outskirts alone, watching the Oak men bleed the goat.

"Let go of me, Tan," said Linóvi quietly.

He hadn't realized he was still holding her. He let go.

"Wait in the yurt," she said. "I have to speak the words for the goat. Children, you go home now."

"Yes, Way Pointer."

Stunned, Tan closed the yurt's door behind him, the room dark and hollow after being in the sun. Sweat streamed down his body.

The Burner wasn't Jeyza's father, some distant king. He was Sajem's father after all. The man who'd killed Tan's parents was the savior Sajem promised.

He owes you Ash, Tan told himself. *You gave him Blue Gums.*

He owed Tan everything: his father's life, his mother's, his own childhood, his brothers'. The rage boiled up, coalescing in his head like a furnace ready to blow.

But he had to be smart, or he'd lose Ash too.

He couldn't face the Burner.

He had to face him.

He owed it to Júzian to not give Ash up.

He took a kitchen knife and stepped out of the yurt. Linóvi's instructions were well meant, he knew, but she didn't understand his duty.

Mechanically, he put one foot in front of the other. The Burner drew him like a sucking void.

He needed a gun. But he couldn't use one anyway; he needed the monster's help. It seemed a wheel turned before him, and the wheel was life. The same turning that had crushed his parents would lift his brother up. Maybe he was meant to do this. Maybe he was the axis around which the wheel spun.

People were staring at him now, calling to him, parting for him like birds taking flight.

"Tánashen." Jeyza came up to him. "Didn't they tell you to stay with your kin?" Her voice rang distant, as if down a corridor.

"Warden," he said, though he did not hear his own voice.

The Burner faced him, full on, somehow simultaneously large and small, half a normal man's face and half the truth.

"Your son, Lord Sajem, made a promise to me." Were the words coming out? He could not hear them. "I helped you at Blue Gums—"

"Yes, my son has told me," said the man who'd killed his parents, his voice ordinary, matter-of-fact. "We owe you a great deal, Tánashen." He had said his name. He had no right to Tan's name. "I have to confer with my counselors a while, but I will call you to me shortly. We have much to discuss." He gave him a nod and turned away, disappearing with the marshal into a yurt.

He just turned away, like Tan was nothing.

Chapter Twenty-Four

Tan went back to Linóvi's yurt. At a loss for what to do next, he might as well bide his time by doing as they told him. After a while, Linóvi returned and said she had to go up the mountain.

"Up the mountain?" he asked.

"I have to perform the rites."

"You need to talk to Oak, to Jeyza."

"I have spoken to Oak Jeyza and to the headwoman. Now, it's the mourners and the spirits who need me. We'll talk this evening." She pressed his shoulder. "I love you, Tan, and I love Ash too. We'll work out how to save him."

The words rang hollow. Love should act. But she'd told him that he had to wait, and he knew enough to know when arguing was futile.

He watched her go out and sat, silenced.

Outside the yurt, the buzz of voices was constant—and the hammering and ax blows. When he looked out the window, he saw men carrying posts with sharpened ends—fortifications of some kind, but effective against the Citadel's guns?

Sometime before noon, Anji came in carrying a basket of beets and greens.

"Well, that's always the sort of thing, isn't it?" she grumbled. "They may say the treaty's changed things, but mark my words, when I'm a rock in an alcove, that's when I'll believe it."

Tan didn't know what that meant; it didn't matter. "Mother, did you know the Burner's with them?"

She stopped in the midst of unloading her basket. After a moment, she said, "I'm not blind as an earthworm, am I? But what's to be done? He's the warden of the Oaks, and Hunter Apáshan called on him for help, though *why* I'll never figure."

"Who is this Hunter Apáshan?"

"Who's Hunter Apáshan? Why, only the alliance leader, a fellow from Vinter's Delight. My son's with him now, heading back from Yowlers—with luck." She fell silent, pensive. "Well. Luck carry the day. Here, lad, be useful: wrap these jars in these cloths here. And careful not to spill 'em."

Tan realized she was preparing to flee. But if the Citadel came, where would they go? West? Toward the Oaks?

But this Apáshan, this hunter: if he was alive, if he was heading here, he might be the ally Tan was seeking. He came from Vinter's Delight, a wine village, like Tan's. Tan remembered Dad jeering at their bitter white wine. Maybe he'd have some fellow feeling for a couple of kids from a wine town.

🌢

Near midday, Jeyza came for him. Outside, the Oak men were skinning the goat. The sight reminded him of the kitchens and Ordan, and Júz—

The circle was set with stone tables and open kitchens, and ringed with those tall boulders carved so that giant salamanders appeared to snake around them. It looked like it should be peaceful, like the court with the He and She.

Jeyza took him to the Burner's yurt—a big one, probably made for gatherings. The animal hides that covered its walls were dyed brighter than the other yurts. This was a special place, the headwoman's yurt maybe. Taken over by *him*.

They entered it to the smell of sweat and Sajem's earnest prattling. "Yes, I know. I was ordered to get in and get out. Instead, *I* decided to scout out their priest. It was stupid and unstrategic, and I blew up half the town."

It was more like a third. And it had been Tan's idea to take out the priest.

In the circle with Sajem sat Séduan and the headwoman, and Jeyza's daughter, Enátha, too, like a crimson mushroom in her fancy dress. Tan barely glanced at them, however, for facing the door, in the position of power, was the Burner, still the overload of Oak.

"You got the oil though," commented Jeyza.

Sajem ignored her. "Father, I'm a liability. You should have me flogged and send me home. Better yet, send me back to the Teaching Keep. Make Nari or her kids your heirs and bypass me completely. Let them assign me to Noryen. Let me—" He broke off, as if he'd run out of ideas.

"Have you finished?" said the Burner.

"Yes, I think so."

The Burner fixed ice-blue eyes on Tan. "Tánashen, sit." The circle widened to admit him and Jeyza. "My son confirms you did us good service in Blue Gums. He says that in exchange for your service, he offered our help in rescuing your brother."

"Yes, my Lord."

"Then we will do so. When we can."

When we can. Which meant never. He glanced at Sajem, whose face was bleak, barely registering Tan's presence.

"And when we can depends on our ability to vanquish Fenorn," said the Burner.

Really doesn't, thought Tan. Jeyza had rescued him with a handful of Oak riders.

"He's in Yowlers, my lord," said Tan. "I saw him."

"Good," said the Burner. "Tell me, if you were sent into a Fenorn village, would the Fenorn folk recognize you, leaving aside the party you marched with?"

They wanted to use him again, deploy him as some sort of spy. In truth, he didn't know if he'd be recognized. A lot of people at the Citadel knew him; a lot didn't. Most of the grown men didn't. Yet if a priest was there, he was dead meat, at least if the priest was looking for him. Or during Oneness.

But that was beside the point. What mattered now was not the truth but the next move. If he said he was useless, he'd lose all his leverage.

"If I wore a helmet, they probably wouldn't recognize me," he said, suddenly glad they couldn't read his thoughts. "I'm just a random boy outside my group."

"Would it be the same at the Grid?"

Tan couldn't figure a way to lie about that. "The Grid's fenced." Surely they knew that? "I'd have to identify myself to get in." He paused, wheels spinning. "I might be able to fake being someone else, for a little while." Small chance, but he wanted to see what they'd say next.

"Then, we should aim for the Grid." That was Enátha.

Now Tan saw her closely, she looked familiar. Some Citadel aunt she reminded him of, a relative of hers? But he had never seen a woman in the Citadel with glasses. Yet he had seen one somewhere...

"It will be hard to break in there, my lady," said Séduan.

"But with this—" She moved as if to pull something from a pocket, but the Burner held up a hand to preempt her. She glanced at Tan and let her hand fall back. "We can defeat them in one blow, and we should do it."

"I disagree," said Sajem. "And, no, not just because of what we did to get that oil."

"I thought you were tired of burning things."

His face went still. "That's a bit nasty, Enátha."

"But isn't it true?"

"I'm tired of this whole bloody thing, but I will not abandon tech limitation."

"Sajem, this isn't—"

"Let me finish. This is the path tech limitation warns against. It's the path that brought us to the bombing of the West Men." He glanced at Jeyza. Why? "If we do this now, what about next time? And there will be a next time. The drought is getting worse. It will continue to get worse. Food will be scarce; people will fight. If we do this, we're saying tech lim doesn't matter: if one group is breaking it, another can too. What's to stop the escalation?"

"Sajem," said Enátha, "this course of action was approved under the uses of high tech in the Convention Treaty: prohibited tech may be surgically used against prohibited tech for the purposes of enforcing the treaty."

"That's still an invitation into a high-tech war."

"But if it's used surgically—"

"Its surgical use," put in Jeyza, "depends on our being able to target it surgically. From Tánashen's account, I don't believe that's viable. We'd have to infiltrate the Grid, and pulling that off is a long shot. The Bridge is more accessible—and the solution more low tech."

So *that* was it.

They planned to burn the Bridge, soak it with that explosive oil from Blue Gums and touch it off. It made perfect sense. It was the way of the burners—and it would, indeed, block off the Citadel's only roadway north.

"Headwoman?" said the Burner.

"I'm not a hunter, Warden. It's Hunter Apáshan you should be speaking to."

"And if he comes, I'll gladly seek his counsel. But he was in the thick of the fighting at Yowlers. If his hunters are dead or delayed, I don't know. I expected them this morning. But you are the one who's here."

The headwoman made a futile gesture. "Burning a bridge I understand. I'd choose it over a Teacher abandoning the teaching to violate tech limitation."

A Teacher. That's where Tan had seen Enátha, though she'd been wearing plain gray then: a thin figure in glasses who'd come through Knotty Vines years ago, teaching tech limitation.

"But it doesn't violate it," the Teacher said. "That's what I was saying—"

"Lady Enátha." The Burner stopped her. "It's settled. We'll attack the Bridge."

Her face was stony. "Lord Nermártan, you are contravening the recommendation of Convener Leki."

"I am the Warden of the Oaks," he said quietly. "It is I who command here, not my wife. Tánashen."

A jolt shot through Tan at the sound of his name.

"We will arrange for you to infiltrate Free of Ford with some portion of this oil. We will plan the attack for the cover of night. All you have to do is spill the oil on the Bridge and then jump into the River. We'll have boats waiting for you. Our men will do the rest."

Tan gaped at him. All at once, he could not tear his mother's face from his mind, his mother sliced through in the face. In the Citadel, he might be a trapped rat, a no-say cadet under orders. But even cadets got to share in Oneness. With Oak there was nothing, no union, no honor—not the slightest recognition of what this man had done.

"No, my Lord," he said.

The Burner raised an eyebrow.

"I told Lord Sajem I'd help with Blue Gums if the Oaks agreed to get my brother. I helped. Now I want my brother."

The Marshal Séduan seized him hard by the wrist. "The man invites you into the very circle of his council, and this is how you repay him? You? The whelp who bludgeoned his son?"

"Séduan!" snapped Sajem. "He's right. I made a promise to him, and I owe him."

"Enough," said the Burner. "Séduan, let him go."

With a sneer, the marshal shoved him back.

"We cannot conjure your brother out of air, boy. Compromising their power at the Bridge is the best way to defeat their surge, and we have no hope of freeing their prisoners as long as their army keeps surging."

Tan did not believe that for a moment. They'd abducted *him*—twice, right from under the Citadel's noses, with no one but Jeyza and a handful of men. He glanced at Séduan, Sajem, Jeyza, trying to size them all at once. He couldn't, not really. Linóvi should be here to speak up for Ash, but she wasn't, and he had to make a choice.

"I know what you did in Knotty Vines," he said. "I may have only been a child, but I could not forget your face—"

"Forget his face?" cried the marshal. "Lord Nermártan has not set foot in Knotty Vines these thirty-six years."

"Peace, Séduan," said the Burner, and to Tan, "Go on."

It was not the reply that he expected, but he'd say what he had to say. "You killed my parents. Never mind your son's promise. *You* owe *me* my brother."

The marshal shoved him down and put a knee in his back, sending shocks of pain down his bruised arm.

"He's a spy, my Lord, sent to sow lies and dissension."

Tan twisted to see the Burner's face and gasped out, "You will pay me back."

The killer held him with those icy eyes. In that moment, the future did not exist. They could beat him, kill him. That was out of his hands. His heart was flat, and he understood why the word for *flat* among the Kiris was the word for *peace*.

"You may go," said the Burner. "You've completed your service."

Chapter Twenty-Five

When Tan got back to yurt, Anji was bent over the fire, stirring acorn mash.

"I'm finished with them, Mother." He sat down and worried at his boot laces.

"Finished? Why? What happened in there?"

Tan shrugged. "They let me go. They won't help me get Ashtyn, so I've got to get him on my own."

"Get him on your own? How are you going to just up and do that?"

"I'm going to head back toward Yowlers."

"Now calm down, lad."

"I am calm."

"Have some soup. You can't just rush into a warzone."

He got his boots off.

"That stench! Get it away!" cried Anji, waving her hands at his feet. Did they smell that bad? Linóvi hadn't said so.

Tan went to sit on the doorstep and shook the dirt out of his boots, his feet, for the moment, deliciously cool. He would have liked to let his boots air out, but he couldn't let them stink up the yurt and didn't dare leave them outside. He put them back on.

"I'm not rushing anywhere, Mother," he told her, accepting the soup bowl she put in his lap. "I'm only doing what makes sense. If he's still alive, my brother is in Yowlers. So to rescue him, I have to go there."

"But a little mite like you!"

"I know I need help. And if Oak won't help me, that leaves me two options: Yowlers Fashen and this Hunter Apáshan. They're both Borderlanders, right? It's their work to help other Borderlanders, right? And if Fashen's done his task, he's in touch with our group's leader—our Fenorn group, I mean, who could help get my brother out."

Yes, he was talking about help from Keskan. The irony wasn't lost on him. But while Keskan hated Tan, he did not hate Ash. Keskan helped Ordan to desert after all. Why not Ash too—and anyone who would go? Wasn't that always his plan? To make everybody deserters?

Anji studied him with black, knowing eyes. "It'll kill the way pointer, lad, losing you again."

Tan looked down. "I'm going to bring her Ashtyn. You tell me Hunter Apáshan should be coming from Yowlers, so if I head back that way, I should run into his people. Yowlers Fashen was supposed to meet up with Oak. He's a tracker, so I guess he knows that Oak's in Twelve Salamanders, which means he's heading here too—probably from Yowlers. Same conclusion: that's the way I need to go if I want to meet up with him."

❧

Nobody tried to stop him leaving. No doubt Linóvi would if she saw him, but she was still *up the mountain*, which he took to mean the cliffs above the village, where the songs of mourners hovered. No, he didn't like to leave her, but he knew what he had to do.

The smell of roasting goat was like his longing for Linóvi, saying stay and go. A piece of him hoped Sajem would try to stop him. It wasn't rational; he just wanted to see him. But Sajem did not emerge, or Jeyza. The Oak men merely watched or sneered or ignored him.

Tan's service was over; the Burner had said so. He wished to hell he had a gun, but he had no immediate way to get one. At least he had the kitchen knife; maybe someday he could return it.

He cinched his left hand in his belt so that it steadied his arm and the pain departed. As he burned the afternoon in walking, the knapsack Anji gave him light on his back, his freedom caught him by surprise.

It unfolded like the purple flower of the dusk. Each sip of air, each sleepy birdcall, the thick needles on a low-hanging branch, the crunch of dirt beneath his boots, they were wholly themselves—sufficient in the moment, and so was he, there was nothing else. Alone and One became the same.

He knew it was an illusion. He had a day at most before life forced more choices. But he'd always clung to those moments of freedom. He had a sudden memory of the squeal of train wheels and the evening breeze in a high window fanning his face. It couldn't have been more than half a minute he'd stood there. Now the weightlessness stretched endless, maybe all night, maybe into the dawn.

As dark descended, he left the road and searched for a clump of bracken on the rocky earth to sleep in. He decided on a moderate drink of water. Anji had confirmed that a stream flowed down the watershed to the north, but it might be a quarter mile from here, a good way off the road, and if he left the road, he might miss Fashen or Apáshan. Nevertheless, it eased his mind to know the stream was there. Still reasonably full from Anji's table, he ate only a few slices of dried beet, rationing his food for whatever lay ahead.

The air cooling fast, he took the clean shirt and britches Anji had given him and wrapped them around his head and shoulders like a blanket. He took his helmet from the knapsack and set it beside him, then propped the knapsack beneath his head.

It was when he stilled that he heard the crunching, bracken or needles, slow and subtle, twenty or thirty feet up the road, back the way he'd come. A deer, like that night on the run for Knotty Vines? It stopped almost at once. He waited, but it did not come again.

He laid his hand on his knife, and, thus armed, settled back in the scratchy bracken, eyes wide and ears pricked.

The last gray faded. Full darkness fell. Only the blue dimness of Fennoc and a scatter of stars left gray streaks on the night. He heard a crinkling, one single step—or maybe something lying down. It didn't move like a deer on the browse, too infrequent, too careful. If it was an animal bedding down for the night, it made one hell of a coincidence, so close to him, settling at the same time he settled.

Therefore, he was being followed.

Well, that made sense. He knew too much, didn't he? He knew Oak was in Twelve Salamanders; he could describe exactly how to get there. He knew this Apáshan was on his way. They'd have to assume he might sell that knowledge in exchange for the Citadel taking him back. They didn't understand there was no return from the desertion. They didn't know how the Citadel would dispose of him if they caught him, not just a foreigner fleeing but one of their own.

But it didn't matter. He wasn't going to rat them out, so their tracker would spend a night in the woods for nothing. He'd join with Fashen or Apáshan, and there would be no betrayal.

Of course, there was an outside chance the tracker wasn't from Twelve Salamanders.

But if he came from the Citadel, if he was sent by a priest, he wouldn't be alone, and Tan would already be captured.

He tried to sink into sleep but it refused him.

A pit had reopened in his gut. Say he did find help and they rescued Ash, say they went to the mountains and began a new life, what about the rest of C-16? How many of them could Tan possibly rescue? And what about the boys for whom the Citadel was home? Sho, Muned, Codo, Gomu, Tarnto—Dezdenec, who hated him now. He pushed the thought down with a pang. How could he help them? What was his duty to them? The cold of the night had vanished, leaving his palms slick with sweat.

Maybe, somehow, Shonco had been right. He'd said the Garden needed Kiri speakers to interpret between the Kiris and the Citadel. Maybe that was Tan's role. So many things had not turned out as he'd imagined, but here he was, Kiri and Citadel both, someone, just maybe, who could help them be One. Though he had no idea how to do it, the thought gave him a kind of compass, a ghost of peace, like the train in the sunset.

❧

In the morning, he went down to the stream to refill his waterskin, and that was his miscalculation. The clatter of the water was just receding behind him when he heard the bray of a hill-jack. He stopped, listened. A few moments later, a man's voice reached him, some way off. He couldn't catch the words, but the speech was Kiri.

He pounded uphill, thrashing through the bracken with zero stealth, getting cautious only near the road, where he slowed and hugged the spruces. But the road was empty. They were already gone or—

It had been his imagination or—

They'd heard him, of course, cracking like a deer through the brush. They must be hiding just off the road. A bird warbled, hopped to a lower branch, warbled again and was answered by a distant warbler. The seconds crept.

A hill-jack snorted.

What if it was the Citadel? No, it had been Borderland voices.

He put his hand on his knife and hung back in the trees.

"I'm a friend," he called, "down from Twelve Salamanders to meet you."

No reply.

There was a right way to introduce yourself. It was...

"The gain is mine. My name is Tánashen—Knotty Vines Tánashen. I—I escaped from the Cit—Fenorn."

Almost at once came the soft crunch of a foot. "I thought it was you."

He released the breath he'd been holding. "Yowlers Fashen. I've been looking for you." He stepped out from the trees.

Fashen immediately emerged, face and clothes smeared with dirt. "Thought you were with Oak."

Tan started up the road to him. "Do you know if my brother's alive?"

"He's in Yowlers."

"Yes, I know. Alive?"

"Tune your ears, bat. Did I say he *was* in Yowlers? *Had been* in Yowlers?"

Relief flooded him, so strong it turned his bones to jelly.

"We have to go there then."

A deep laugh rolled out from the trees. "We have to go to Yowlers?" A small, black-bearded man stepped out. His bow, though not drawn, was at the ready in his hand. "Where do you think we've come from, lad? This lad wants us to go to Yowlers."

Laughter burst out like a flock of birds. Two men, then a third, came to stand just behind their leader.

"Barely got out with our lives," said one.

The leader smiled. "Keen for trouble, Knotty Vines?"

Tan walked up to Fashen's side. "Yowlers Fashen knows me."

Fashen gave a cocky smile. "I've heard some stories."

That wasn't good.

"Oak broke their word to me, Tracker Fashen," said Tan. "They said if I helped them at Blue Gums—"

"Liar!" It was a woman's voice, behind.

He whirled.

Hérseji, sharp as a crow, strode toward him from the brush. "He's a Fenorn spy. He didn't *help* at Blue Gums."

"You were there!" cried Tan. "I gave you the priest. His men almost killed me. You saved my life."

"Well, everyone makes one big mistake." She looked at the leader. "Hunter Apáshan, he's the one who shot Dawn Rock Ren. I saw it with my own eyes."

At once a dozen arrows were cocked and drawn. Somehow they'd managed to surround him. Fashen's mirth had turned to stone; he stepped back behind the shelter of the bowmen. Everything was spinning out of control. Tan could not let things slip from his grasp like this.

He held up his hands in a gesture of surrender. There was no way to lie his way out.

"I did it," he said. "I shot him. I didn't see it was him till after, but he was about to shoot a boy I knew—"

"You see, he admits it," she spat. "He's with *them*!"

The hunter, Apáshan, fixed him with stricken eyes, arrow drawn to his mouth and quivering.

"I was saving a boy's life," said Tan. "And you can kill me, but before you do, I need to save another."

Apáshan did not move, the moment a taut thread between them. He wore a purple sash, Tan saw, like Dawn Rock Ren, and in his face, Tan could see the resemblance now: the same big eyes, the same hooked nose.

"We may need him." That was Fashen, still hanging back, but he had not drawn his bow.

"For what?" said the hunter.

"Sneaking past the Fenorn guards. He's the only one we've got on the outside who can pass for them." It was exactly what Tan had told the Burner he refused to.

"That's *him*?" The hunter lowered his bow a fraction and tossed his head at Tan. "That's the one you were talking about?"

"He's poison," said Hérseji. "He'll wither more of us if we touch him."

Apáshan shook his head. "I'm sorry, Mica Melting Fashen, but Winding Root Hérseji is right. My own grief is nothing, but I can't let a trust-breaker walk among us."

"He's a trust-breaker, all right," said Fashen. "Our spy, Waxwing Keskan, says so. But his obsession with his brother's real. Our spy says that too, he has no reason to lie. If we can use that tie to bind him, we should do it. He's part of our plans. Without him, we'll have to unweave it all and start all over."

For a deadly minute, silence hovered.

Then, Apáshan lowered his bow, and at a wave of his hand, his followers did likewise.

"Hunter," Hérseji hissed.

"I know." With a savage precision, he walked up to Tan. "Dawn Rock Ren was my *sélnutor*, my mother's-sister's-son. You care for your brother? He was that to me."

Tan said nothing, showed nothing. Any reaction would drag him deeper in the pit.

"Nothing is decided," said Apáshan. "This is not done between us."

Tan gave a minute nod.

"Give me the knife."

Tan thought he had hidden it better than that. But he took it out slowly and handed it over.

Apáshan turned away and took a breath. Tan could see his shoulders heave with it.

Then he said, "Come, friends. Mad times make mad bedfellows. This boy has done us less harm than the Burner, yet I myself went to Burner's city to propose our alliance with Oak. May Ren's loss be ours, and we will mourn it when we can do. For now, our goal is Salamander before this day is over."

Chapter Twenty-Six

"Oh, thank luck, thank luck." Linóvi hurried out of her yurt to smother Tan in her embrace. "When Anji said you'd gone, I was on the verge of sending someone after you, but the headwoman said the hunter would bring you back—and look."

"He's to stay in your yurt, Way Pointer," said the man who'd escorted him. "He's to stay until Hunter Apáshan calls him. This boy owes the hunter a life."

"A life?" said Linóvi.

Tan brushed past her into the yurt, doing his best to blot out their conversation. The yurt closed like a prison, like the He at his back.

And here came Anji, bursting in with one of the hunter's men, that son of hers apparently. She clucked over the gash on the man's forehead, lathered some gel on it, smelling of Blue Gums. Everything smelled of Blue Gums. As his mother worked on him, the man glared at Tan.

"Grandmother Linóvi," Tan said. "I need to talk with Tracker Fashen. I need the details of the plan, so I can argue my use with the hunter."

"The plan to get Ash?"

"You think Dawn Rock takes counsel from Fenorn slaves?" said Anji's son. "You think he'll fashion his plans just to rescue some traitor's—?"

"Jethan. Not in this yurt," said Linóvi with uncommon force.

"Forgive me, Way Pointer, but you heard Shantan. He's killed one of ours. They tell me he's your *sélnutor*, but it isn't on you that he broke our trust."

"Now, Jeth," said Anji, "you mind where you are and who it is you're speaking to. Have some soup."

Tan addressed Linóvi. "The plan's to defeat Fenorn. But I'll free Ash too, or I'll die trying."

"He'll die trying?" Another scoff from Jeth. "In that case, I half hope the little brother stays enslaved."

Anji clapped her hand down on the bench. "Once more out of you, and you'll wish you did marry that cabbage from Vinter's, as you'll be looking for another yurt to stay in." She set a soup bowl in front of him.

"The gain is ours," he mumbled, surly.

Though Anji's words were meant for Jethan, Tan took the lesson and kept quiet. He did need to get in touch with Fashen, but he'd get nowhere till he could get away from this man.

He ate his soup; it was the same acorn mash, as if to say you've been nowhere, done nothing. You are frozen in time. All you do, all you say is a waste, a joke.

It dared to taste of the Garden, rich and buttery beside the beets and cheese, and though there was not enough to fill him, it filled him more than the Citadel. It tasted as good as the lie of the Garden, and he wondered if Ash, miles off, was getting fed now, too, really fed—now C-16 was stationed in Yowlers. Had they stolen enough of Yowler's food to feed him nuts and beets and cheese?

Anji was telling her son all the gossip since he'd been gone. Jethan was nodding, his eyes on his plate.

Linóvi's silent presence cracked open a fissure inside him. It cracked him in two—into the soldier and the child who longed to hide in her arms.

Why was Anji laughing? A moment ago she'd been grumbling about how to feed everyone. Linóvi was laughing, too, as she produced from a pocket—what was it?—a handful of wedges, potatoes or something.

She passed them out, two for each, but only one for herself, because the leader eats last.

Someone said *yam*—sweet and thick on his tongue; they were rare at the Citadel; *sweet potatoes*, they called them there. Even when speaking Kiri, they translated the Citadel, *sweet potato*, like those traitors, those Kiris, bound for Dip had carried. Tan seized his chopsticks and threw the wedges down his throat, fast as mice into their burrows, only afterwards remembering to thank the yam.

It was the laughing, though, he could not stomach. It was like sitting in the barracks with Gomu's jokes, pretending there was nothing wrong.

He had to get to Fashen. He was the only way Tan might get Apáshan's ear and circumvent the Burner. But Apáshan had asked for the Burner's help. He might be talking with him now about burning the Bridge, and Fashen saying they could use Tan, and the Burner saying *he is my sworn enemy*—and Apáshan saying *he is mine too*. Oak and the Borderlands unsundered by their mutual hatred of Tan. For a moment, he almost laughed at the perfection of the irony.

But Apáshan hadn't killed him yet because he might be useful. So he had to get around the Burner. That man pressed on Tan like a hornet on the ear. He could almost hear him buzzing now in the gathering yurt, the yurt he'd taken over, as Oak always took over, took the women, killed the goats—Anji was chuckling—demanded their taxes. Tan didn't know what taxes were, but he suspected it was a polite way of saying you asked for it: to be raided and robbed.

"—the warden's men." His ear caught on *warden*.

"Are they enough?" asked Linóvi.

Jethan, who had spoken, replied, "Well, if we can close ranks here—"

"Here?" snapped Tan. "At Salamander? What the blast are you going to do with Salamander? You can't even feed all the people here. And what if you do hold them off for a while? Either they'll keep coming or Oak wins, and you belong to Oak."

"You, boy," said Anji, "mind your manners."

"Manners, Mother, with respect, are not going to save you from Fenorn—or Oak."

"And who are *you* to lecture?" Jethan leaned toward him, his jaw twitching. "A trust-breaking, murderous little spy—"

Tan half rose, fingers clutching the table. "And who is it now in your fanciest yurt? In the place of honor, like he was the headman? I killed one man in the heat of battle, but you welcome him, the man who burned down the Borderlands?"

"The Massacre was over thirty years ago!" cried Jethan. "We've none of us forgotten, but it's *Fenorn* on us now. But, of course, Fenorn are *your* folk, aren't they—?"

"Fenorn didn't kill my folk! The Burner killed my folk! And it wasn't bloody thirty years ago—it was in front of my eyes!" He hadn't known he could shriek like that. His voice spiked back at him, throat gone raw. His body trembled as if with fever.

In the uncanny silence that followed, it was like he had just become visible to them, like an unrestful ghost rising out of a mist. Outside it was too loud for evening, too human-crowded with men's voices and ugly laughs. The whole town must have heard him, would be coming for him soon.

"Tan," said Linóvi gently. "The Burner didn't kill our folk. Fenorn did."

Chapter Twenty-Seven

He was alone in the yurt with Linóvi. He had seen Anji leave, flushing her son out in front of her, but it seemed that they had been a dream—a projection, like the Landowner in the desert, a lie of technology switched suddenly off, and it gave him the sense that all his life had been a projection, a lie, just so someone could see what he'd do. (It occurred to him that this was why they had tech limitation, just to make lying a little less easy.)

Linóvi was washing dishes. The shadows of the fire danced like ghosts across the walls, as if to say this is not the real world. Unfortunately, he suspected it was.

Calmly he said, "You're wrong, Grandmother. With respect, I saw them."

She stopped with her scrubbing. "What did you see?"

Was she going to make him say it, make these tears prick his eyes? "I saw him, the Burner, with his scarred face. I saw him kill my parents."

She dried her hands and arranged herself on the floor a little way from him. The dance of the fire distorted her face, taking pieces from it, Burner-like. Why did he feel ashamed?

"He shot them with arrows?"

A low chuckle percolated up in Tan. "Oh, I know how that goes. I say, 'No, with a gun,' and you say, 'Oak doesn't use guns because of tech limitation.' But they do use guns. Oak Sajem himself just gave an order, just a couple days ago at Blue Gums. 'Those who have guns can use them,' he said. So, *yes*, he used a gun."

She nodded in a slight and careful way, like you might nod to a raider demanding your rations at gunpoint.

"They wore Oak clothes," said Tan, "long beige tunics, same cut they wear now."

"Their tunics are gray."

"It wasn't the Citadel in disguise. The Citadel doesn't do disguise, not in all the years I've been with them, never, not once, under no circumstances. The Citadel is proud of what it is."

"They do wear beige."

Tan barked a laugh. "Maybe Oak bought some cloth from them."

The wood popped on the fire. Outside the yurt, in the embers of the afternoon, a man and woman laughed too loud. Though the ground beneath him lay flat and steady, his balance, nonetheless, was failing. It seemed to him he'd built his life like a cart with two wheels and both on the same side. He'd been working on that cart so long, in fights with Keskan, with Ash, with Júzian. He was weary of trying to make that cart stand.

"I was there during the Massacre, you know," said Linóvi.

For a moment, he thought she meant that caravan they'd attacked, the one headed for Dip, one more crime he was guilty of.

"I was already almost fifty. I lived a long time under Oak. I remember back when Rendyen ruled them."

Rendyen, Jeyza's father.

"For a while, I thought he was the Burner."

"Rendyen? He'd be old for that. The Piercer, they called him. Because he was a good archer, so I'm told. I never saw it. But I grew up under Rendyen. I must have been... ten, not more, when his people came from the west. They brought a lot of trade, that was the first thing. Oak had never traded with us before. A lot of iron from their smithies—like that." She nodded at the tripod over the cooking fire. "We used to set our pots on clay stoves before that."

"Someone said he's the king."

"Is he?" she considered. "Is he still? He must be very old. In any case, he hasn't been in these parts for years and years, since well before the Massacre. Maybe that's why he sent his daughter to Oak, as an ambassador maybe, to keep the peace, I don't know."

"But she hasn't kept the peace," said Tan. "Oak is still right here, murdering goats and grabbing women."

"You're right."

For a time, she gazed into the fire. Then, she got up and hung the kettle up to boil. She moved slowly, careful and creaking with age. It made him feel guilty for not helping, yet there he sat, not helping, as if in some silent protest.

"Would you fetch some tea down?"

Relieved by the order, he went to study the shelves. "This one?"

"Let's see it... Yes, that will do. Thank you, spring mint people, for giving your life." She pinched some leaves into a pouch for... what the hell was the word, that you did with tea?

"Rendyen was a compelling man," she said. "I saw him twice. He came through Knotty Vines twice, that I saw him. It was the sort of thing you remember."

Like the Burner killing your parents, Tan thought.

"He was—how to put it—good looking without being especially good looking. It was this presence he had that drew people to him."

"By mind reading?"

"No, no, that's not what I mean. I think Oak uses mind reading much as we do, to share with loved ones, to judge motives sometimes, but rarely with strangers, no. It was more basic than that. There were girls who were happy to go with him and his men." She paused. "There were girls who were not, but they weren't taken, usually. Not back then. They brought those fine iron arrowheads. They brought pelts from great wildcats in the west."

"Well, the Citadel—Fenorn brings iron and steel too, so..."

She nodded, and he wished she wouldn't, wished she wouldn't pretend to understand.

"Were they good to you, Tan?"

"That's a trick question."

"Is it?"

"It's an unfair question. They're in the middle of the desert, trying not to starve. They do what they have to do. They *are* good people, mostly, to people who are loyal to the One."

Shonco flashed through his head, the pools of his eyes and cool water in his office, and his knife at the He. She seemed to see through him to all of it.

"No, not everyone is kindly," he said, "not all the time. Not everyone is kind right here." He yanked off his bandage and pulled up his sleeve to show the bruising of his arm, deep purple marbling from bicep to mid-forearm. "You know who gave me this? Not the Citadel." He used their own name for themselves on purpose. He wanted to honor who they were.

She looked, though he wasn't sure she could actually see in the firelight. Far away, it seemed a train was whistling.

"There's a lot of truth in what you say." She gazed into the fire, eyes far away. "Yes, those were hard times—after Rendyen. It got worse after he took the West Men back west. The warden—the Burner's uncle, I mean—he had no respect for our folk. No respect for the West Men either, I suppose, since he ordered them bombed in the end. I always assumed Rendyen died then. How funny that he didn't and they still call him king."

Something in him jumped. So they *had* bombed the West Men. Linóvi said so. He wanted to laugh with glee. So Keskan was wrong, completely, stupidly, one-hundred-percent wrong with his it's-all-fake-the-bombing talk. The attack on the Citadel, yes, that was fake, but *this* was not; they did have nukes and damn well used them. Oak's not the problem, Júzian had said. Júzian could go fuck himself.

"They killed my mother's father," he asserted, partly to see what she would say.

And when she said, "Yes," his heart swelled with anger and something akin to joy. The kettle on the fire sang with his joy—it had been the kettle whistling that he'd heard, not the train.

"They enslaved her mother," he said.

"Yes. She told me they shot her husband dead in the very act of swinging his ax to save her. It was terrible, the people we lost that day. My sister burned in our yurt that day."

In the stillness, the kettle shrieked.

Tan took it off its hook and put the teabag into it to—what the hell was the word? The iron kettle was not from Oak. He knew the flat plates of a Citadel kettle. The Citadel did not burn people alive. Whatever else it did, it did not do that.

"Your mother grew up hating them," said Linóvi. "Of course, she did. She'd seen her father killed and her mother taken. Then, after your grandmother's escape, oh, the tales she told of the horrors of Oak."

"Like?" Somehow he needed to hear it.

"It won't help, Tan. Anyway, I think you heard them."

The scent of that herb was alive in the room, that tea herb from his childhood days. She called it *spring mint*, but he didn't recall ever hearing that name. Its smell was its name, saying *life pricks, life pricks*. He poured the tea.

"Thank you." She gripped her cup in both hands. "Your grandmother was a strong person, Tan. Like you."

"I'm not a strong person. I just have Ash to get back to."

"Well, and she had your mother." She sipped her tea.

He sipped his. The tang on his tongue was strange, not familiar like the scent, and it made him very conscious of being far from home—so far that Knotty Vines didn't exist, the vines lost in another time.

"Why are you telling me all this?" he asked. "To prove you know more about Oak than I do? I'm certain you do, Grandmother. But I know what I saw with my eyes."

"I saw him too, the Burner. In the Massacre, he was there, riding with his uncle, just as the tales say. His face was seared in all our minds. Oh, the tales retold, year after year." She let her cup close, so it steamed in her face. "But he never came back. It was a condition of the Convention Treaty, that he never come back—unless we asked Oak for protection."

"You think he cares about conditions?" Tan didn't know the word *treaty*, but he got the gist.

"I wouldn't know whether he cares, but he never came back."

"That you saw."

"That I saw. But I saw a great deal. It was Fenorn that attacked that day—Fenorn men in Fenorn uniforms, with Fenorn guns. They did ride hill-jacks, some of them, as Oak does. Perhaps you saw a scarred Fenorn man."

His mind went to Gomu. Though Gomu himself had been a child then, he was far from the only scarred soldier in Fenorn.

"I lived under Fenorn there in Knotty Vines for over a year," she said. "They have occupied our village from that day to this." She paused. "I tried, Tan. I did. I tried to speak on behalf of our folk. They beat me. I tried again. They beat me again. I didn't try after that. But I stuck to our people, trying to carry on the way of *mirya*. It worked, in its way, for a while. Then, more came from Fenorn, and they said my practices were dividing the people. They locked me up in a house and kept sending these men in to see me. Most of them didn't speak Keshnul well, and I didn't understand half of what they said. But I gathered they wanted me to pray to their spirits, to be like their way pointers. Well, I couldn't do that. Their ways are not ours. So they kept me there till my friends and my sons broke me out."

"They drove Oak out," said Tan. "They drove them out and then settled there to keep them out."

"No, Oak was not there."

Tan's head was pounding. For a moment, that pounding was all he could think about, that rusted pump behind his eyes, overextended and stupid, like a well drilled too deep. The air was thick with tea and woodsmoke; he didn't know how to breathe it. He needed to get out—outside in the night, down the road in the trees, up the mountain to the north. His stomach heaved; he needed air or he would be sick.

"Let me go," he said softly, his eyes on the floor.

"Go?"

"Outside."

"Yes," she said. "We need to go up the mountain."

Chapter Twenty-Eight

She walked with a walking stick, venerable in a long white robe. Her white hair, piled up on her head, took on a glow in waning daylight.

There were too many people, too many Oak men, stopping to stare as they passed.

"The warden should put down those scrounger clowns," said one of them loudly as they went by.

But the Borderlanders bowed to Linóvi. And when they'd passed, some hissed at Tan behind closed teeth.

Didn't matter—or it mattered only in a practical way: Tan had spent his proverbial rations on stupidity; he'd made enemies where he should have made friends. Well, at least Fashen was willing to work with him. He'd do this mountain thing and then get Linóvi to take him to Fashen.

They went up a well-worn, winding trail. The western horizon was pink, the world soaked in lavender. Thin spruce twisted up out of the rocks, curved like a She, two-dimensional as painted trees in the lowering light. They left the sounds of the town behind them, till only the loudest cries broke through—angry and sometimes sobbing. Always anger and sobbing.

As he sank into the slow rhythm of their steps, Tan's mind slipped into the past.

The day they had waited for Ordan's capture, Ash said he had to use the bathroom. Tan had walked him there, through the dim and echoing basement, that day they'd counted the hours till grace was spent.

Into the silence, Ash said, "I sure hope he escapes."

Tan found himself scanning for a supply room or maintenance hatch or anything to get out of the open hall. When he saw the mop closet, he pushed Ash inside, into an electric yellow.

"Watch your mouth. What if someone heard you?"

"No one's around."

"You don't know that. Odds are there're eyes on us like vultures."

"Sorry. It's just—it's no good here, Tan." The lamp lit up the bandage on Ash's neck like an accusation. "What if Ordan does get away?"

"Ash, no one escapes. You get killed fast or you get killed slow. We need to wait and do our duty. Then, we'll be free. Then they'll send us to the Garden."

"But is it really that impossible if we help each other?" Ash hesitated. "If you hadn't turned him in—"

Tan smacked him hard across the jaw. He didn't think; he just did it. As Ash clattered against the door, Tan hoped wildly no one heard. In the thin light, he could see Ash wipe blood from lip. Ash didn't look at him, but in the small space, Tan could hear his breath hiss.

He felt his own face red hot, but he couldn't apologize. A captain couldn't apologize to his cadets, not even if the cadet was his brother. They stood there, Ash's breathing raw, his fists clenched.

"We did what we had to," said Tan. "Do you understand me?"

"Yes, Tan." He could hear the tears in Ash's voice and felt a swell of pride that his brother had learned not to let them fall.

"It's my job to keep you alive. Don't be stupid."

He reached past Ash, who flinched, and opened the door. Without a word, he marched on, and Ash's steps had clapped behind him.

He realized now that all he'd told Ash had been based on a lie.

The Garden was a lie. Tan had known the Citadel was ugly, but it held out the beauty of the Garden as its lure, until the sight of Knotty Vines had pulverized its justifications. Tan's heart had known in that instant. His mind had just been catching up.

How odd it was that he could still see it: the tunics of Oak, the scarred face of the Burner. Even so, it hadn't happened.

Júzian had said, *Oak isn't the problem.*

Keskan had said, *Of course, the Citadel killed your parents.*

They'd been right. The Citadel killed them and tore up the vines. It had always been the simplest explanation.

As night fell, Linóvi paused to light a lamp. It threw a dancing orange on the gravel at her feet. Above them, the blue speck of Fennoc gleamed.

"Will you take this lamp, Tan? It's a bit much to handle along with this stick."

He took it, a small stone lamp with a wick dipped in oil that smelled, like everything, of Blue Gums. The flame licked in a breeze so slight Tan hadn't been aware of it till the lamp said it was there. When he sheltered the flame with his hand and it warmed him, he suddenly realized the night was cool.

They walked on through the stillness, the only sounds their crunching feet and, here and there, a cricket singing like a childhood promise.

Then, all of a sudden, there was another lamp, an amber flicker behind a boulder to the west, making half a halo of its curving bulk. When they stopped, the night filled with weeping, the choked hiccups of a child who'd been crying a long time, behind them, softer, a woman's murmur.

"Come gently," said Linóvi and led him off the main road onto a plateau, illuminated by the lamp's faint glow. It was perhaps twenty feet deep, loosely hemmed by large stones that gave an illusion of safety. The child and woman sat by their lamp, close to the sheer face of the mountain, the woman rocking the child.

When she looked up at them, Tan thought, *Please let them not be Dawn Rock's family*.

But they didn't seem to recognize him. Setting down her lamp, Linóvi pressed her hands palm to palm, and the woman did likewise. Tan belatedly followed, the gesture both familiar and foreign—like a memory that is a lie, or a truth slipped out of memory.

The woman whispered to the child, and they stood, the child, who might have been a girl or boy, wiping her eyes with pudgy hands.

"Don't let us rush you," said Linóvi.

"We were going, Way Pointer," said the woman. "And anyway, it's right to yield the night to the next mourner."

When she'd gone, Linóvi said, "Hold the lamp up to the cliff face."

Tan caught his breath. He'd stepped into a nest of unrestful ghosts. The cliff was pocked with alcoves in which stood figures chiseled of the native stone. They varied from the size of a fist to a head, most were crude but some finely sculpted. All were forms of animals. The salamanders wriggling in the lantern light stirred a very old memory: Júzian had lifted up a stone to show him the little brown salamanders... in Knotty Vines. He pushed away the thought.

The statues also depicted birds, voles, a cat, an animal with a flat nose he did not know.

Linóvi folded her hands and bowed. "The memory is ours."

Memory is a liar, thought Tan.

"The memory itself is *mirya*," she intoned. "The spirits are the memory." She bowed again. "Tan, there's a long history here, generations of Salamanders watching over their children."

"This is where they commemorate their dead?"

"We throw the bones to the pika vultures. That's a privilege of living in the mountains, so many cliffs and crevices to home the dead. But this is our commemoration, yes."

"They must run out of room."

"No, not often. The village is small, so there aren't many dead. But when we do need room, we send the weather-worn mementos down the mountain to rejoin the rocks."

Tan stared for a while at that wall. "They have their accusations," he said softly.

He wasn't sure why he said it, and Linóvi did not reply. After a moment, she walked off to the edge of the lamplight, as if looking for something.

He followed to light her way.

"Do you see the pines?" she asked him.

He jumped. How did she know about Juz in the pines? Then he looked and saw they were surrounded by them, drought-twisted dwarfs, just like those at the Grid, their needles wan as a reflection in a turbid pool, ghost reflections. It was a trap. He tried to still his breathing.

"Do you remember our ways in Knotty Vines?" she asked him.

"No."

She peered at him. "Not your grandmother's death? The wooden figures?"

"No... Yes." Yes, he remembered, the little wood carvings they hung from the trees, mementos of the dead. He remembered it perfectly now. Not animals, not in Knotty Vines: they'd been small human carvings in the likeness of the person who'd died. His grandmother's memento had her willow-shaped eyes.

Linóvi produced some string and said, "Let's tie bits of pine into figures, and we can say goodbye that way."

Following her lead with trepidation, Tan set the lamp on the ground and began to gather twigs.

"They were *sélnuti* to both of us," she said, "but they are yours first, your close kin. So you tell me whose likeness you'll form. And who should I form? Your mum, your dad, or Juz?"

"Juz," he said abruptly, caught again in the suspicion she had led him here for penance. But she couldn't have—she didn't know. Even if she guessed his guilt, she couldn't know about the Grid and the pines. "I've already said goodbye to Juz," he added by way of excuse.

He set to work on his father's figure, awkward as a child. He hadn't made stick figures since childhood.

As they worked, she hummed and her humming became singing.

> *He goes out.*
> *He goes out.*
> *May the loss be ours.*
> *No loss to him.*

He looked at the rough figure of his father in his hands, but his thoughts were on Júzian. No loss to him. That wasn't true. Tan could feel his spirit.

She sang,

> *No loss to mirya.*
> *No. No loss.*
> *No loss to mirya.*

She handed him twigs to make the form of his mother, pine needles to represent her long hair, pitch to bind them, fingers sticky. She chuckled at their sticky fingers. Tan couldn't tell if that was right. To laugh with the dead would not be right at the Citadel, but she was a way pointer.

She hung the three figures from the same branch and pressed her hands and sang their names:

Knotty Vines Red Leaf Váneki, may her loss be ours.
Knotty Vines Free of Ford Red Leaf Áfkafen, may his loss be
ours.
Knotty Vines Red Leaf Júzian, may his loss be ours.

The Ribbon silvered the eastern peaks. Tan shivered in the breeze and took up the lamp to shelter it. The world felt cool and otherly, the figures in the tree unreal and something like the dead strung up on the He.

"Sing for them, Tan," said Linóvi.

Tan did not respond at first. The words played in his head, loss be ours, loss be ours. This is our luck, our chance, to live in the time of losing, to live in *that* time...

He found himself reciting then, not Kiri but Citadel words from the scripture:

I saw my children captured, beaten,
Cudgeled in the desert sand. I heard my loved ones cry.
In secret towers, they cried at night and in the day, they
toiled,
Until my heart sank beneath the sands,
And cried and sighed and split in two,
Till I myself was rent in two,
Till I myself was sundered.

The words felt true, and they cleansed him as truth can. Calmer, he watched the figures turning softly in the breeze. They were still the spirits of the dead skewered on the He, but a trace of the wisdom of Oneness whispered that was all right. It could be what it was. He could let it be.

Could he be One without the many?

"Can you tell me what those words mean, Tan?"

What they meant? No. No other words meant what they meant, but he tried to render them in Kiri.

> *I saw my children tied and beaten,*
> *Beaten in the desert's sand. I heard my sélnua wailing.*
> *In secret... mountains, they wailed at night and worked in*
> *the day,*
> *Till my spirit sank into the sand,*
> *And they wept and sighed and broke apart,*
> *Till even I was broken apart,*
> *Till even I was divided.*

She took his hand in hers. "They are honest words."

Chapter Twenty-Nine

They were halfway down the mountain, deep in the Ribbon-silvered night, when Tan caught sight of something moving on the rocks.

He started, hand darting to a small knife he'd purloined. But it wasn't human; it was a little round mass.

"Oh," said Linóvi, following his gaze. "We don't often see the hyrax people up so high."

The blob of fur was humphing around on a slab.

"Poor mite," said Linóvi. "She's got the wildness."

Tan looked again and saw she was right. The hyrax was shuffling in a nonsensical circle, her head hanging to the side.

"Will she get better?"

"No, lad. The wildness is fatal. Don't you remember your mum saying so?"

He thought maybe he could now, but it had been so long.

"They're prone to it, you know." She sighed. "We should put her down, but it'll be a trick not to get bitten."

Tan watched the creature's sluggish movements. After a moment, he tossed a pebble her way. Her head turned a little bit toward it, still sluggish.

"No, it won't be a trick. I'll do it. Can I borrow your scarf?"

He wrapped it around his hands and advanced on the little creature. She did bite after he first stabbed her, but the cloth kept her teeth well away from his flesh. He held her down and slit her throat, and then her spirit was released.

He glanced up at Linóvi.

Her blank face reminded him of Ash, weighing, judging. Quietly, something in him broke.

He sat by the bloody corpse and laughed.

Her stance changed subtly, but it was a change he knew well, tense and watchful. She was over eighty, but if he moved on her, she was ready to bolt—or to try.

He wiped his knife on the scarf. It occurred to him he'd ruined it. If the blood was poison, they'd have to throw it away, red on white, like blood on bone.

"I didn't make this world, you know," he said. "I don't know why you're looking at me as if I'm the one who made it."

"Oh, Tan, of course, you didn't." But that was just what you said to a kid.

"I didn't ask the Citadel to pull up the vines. If I'd been there, I'd've said don't do it. But you don't understand what's like in the south. Everyone is hungry all the time. Everyone is thirsty, everyone is working sun-up to sundown to keep the solar going and the water pump and train and the cooling and the—and the—" What the hell was Kiri for *manufacturing*? "—the smithies using the machines to make the guns and pipes and glass and clothes and—and soap and water—the water cleaning and ovens—" He stopped abruptly, seeing eyeballs on plates. "When you're there, you just try to survive, to grow food and bring food and *be* food. You try to support each other. I tried to."

Linóvi sat down on a stone a little way from him. "I know you did."

"No, you don't! You don't know anything about me. You're just saying that to make me feel better, and with respect, it sounds very, very hollow. You have no idea what I've done, how many people I've killed. *I* don't have any idea."

After a moment, she said, "It's a difficult chance to be a hunter in wartime—"

"No, that's not it. *That's* the easy part. Killing strangers who'd be just as happy to kill you, that's easy. In comparison, it's easy. It's turning on your own—" He stopped.

He'd said too much. Her eyes were too keen, pits in night, full of Ash-like accusations, and it was too late to hide.

Suddenly, tears were pouring out, an ugly flood out of eyes and nose, and words poured just as ugly. "I killed him—he tried to run away and I killed him. I—I got him killed, I told them. I told them he'd run. And they strung him up, and he was—and I didn't even put him down. I just watched..., I just watched, I watched..." He couldn't stop crying. "And we cut him up... and cooked him..."

He could not force any more words out. He choked on his sobs, his shoulders heaving.

In a strange, hard voice, a man's voice, she said, "They should be torn up the roots and burned off of this planet."

Tan buried his face in his hands and sobbed harder. Because that meant Dezdenec and Sho and Muned; it meant Codo, Fendo, Gomu, Tarnto—and Shonco. It meant Aunt Tson, Sho and Codo's ma, and Aunt Togi, Fendo's ma, and maybe even the Kiris who went along, Dradam and Lavan. And Tan. Did they deserve it? Were they a plague to be rooted out?

After a very long time, his sobs receded.

He wiped at his face. "Why do I feel so bad about eating him? The rest of it, I can... I don't... But eating him—that's *mirya*, right? Starving people have to—"

"No."

"*Mirya* says eat and be eaten."

"It is a sickness in *mirya* that requires such things. It is a failure to understand *mirya* that demands it."

Tan snuffled, unable to think.

Linóvi went on. "I've heard tell that they compost their dead at the Grid. That's one thing. Some of our villages do likewise. The other thing—what you describe—is enslavement."

Enslavement? It was punishment, the price of deserting Oneness. No, the price of deserting the Citadel.

Tan's head felt heavy from weeping. He held it in his hands. "He could have gotten away. Maybe. If I hadn't stopped him, if I hadn't held him back. If I'd believed in him maybe. Maybe he could have escaped the Grid, made it down to the River, made it out to Blue Gums."

He wouldn't have, logic said. By the time Ordan got there, if he got there at all, Blue Gums would have been in the hands of the priest. They would have caught him, like they almost caught Tan. Logic said he'd been right about that—he'd been right, not Keskan, not about *that*.

But the first time, a year ago, that day up in the pines by the Grid, Blue Gums had been free back then. If Tan believed *him* when he said they could make it...

"I owed him that chance," he said. "I owed it to him—I owed it to Ash too. But I just keep—I keep being one of them. The enemy. No wonder Ash..." He looked up Linóvi, a tear-streaked silver in the Ribbon light. "What if he won't go with me? What if I find him and he won't go with me?"

She didn't answer at once. Finally, she said, "Tan, you are not the only one who wants to get Ash away from them. You are not responsible for getting Ash away from them."

"I am."

"Not alone. No, you are not. You're not the only one his homecoming rests on—or the only one responsible for repairing what's between you. As for that repair, much of that is my work." She paused. "I spent too much time on the mountain. I should have been there with you when you spoke to the Burner." She shook her head. "Never mind. As to getting Ash home, there are Dawn Rock Apáshan's hunters—"

"Dawn Rock Apáshan wants me dead."

"You need to give him time." She stood slowly and sat down beside him, the two of them gazing out over the slopes to the silver thread of stream below. "You need to give yourself time." Tan sniffed, suddenly aware of a headache dull behind his eyes.

"They don't deserve it," he said, "to be rooted out. Maybe some do, but the boys I lived with, the women, who don't even get to go outside..."

"I spoke without thinking. Tan, our choices carry weight. *Your* choices carry weight, it's true. That is their nature. But the unfairness of the burden is also real. The hunter will see that. One day, Ash will too. It may sound impossible, but someday even Juz—"

Tan jumped like a lightning rod had touched him. "Who said anything about Juz?"

She hesitated. "You said... he tried to escape..."

"Ordan. His name was Ordan. He was... he was a dumb kid." The tears slid down his cheeks again. "He didn't belong there, in Fenorn, he..." He hid his face.

"I'm sorry," she said. "I misunderstood."

He crumbled then, his shoulders shaking. He could not make them stop. He just kept on thinking, *I'm sorry, I'm sorry.*

At last, she said, "We have to speak the loss of Ordan."

"We can't," said Tan, thinking of the mementos above them. "He doesn't belong in a tree. He comes from Blue Gums, not Knotty Vines."

"In Blue Gums, they mark their dead with stones."

Tan looked up at her, bleary. "Can I send a figure down the stream, down the stream to the River? He came from a River village."

"Yes," she said. "Yes, that feels right, to send him home."

So they did, a little boy of spruce twigs, tied with grass. They went down low to the flat stones where the night was cool and silver clatter of the stream made the air soft and wet. Tan dipped his hand in sharp living current and let the figure go. It was gone in an instant.

"May the loss not be his," said Linóvi. "May the loss be ours now. Let his be over."

And for that moment, it was so.

Chapter Thirty

Tan scrubbed the washing against the rocks till his fingers wrinkled. A little way up the bank, children chased each other, using wet shirts as whips, their laughter mingling with the stream's.

He wanted to tell that little one to put her hat back on, but he wasn't supposed to speak to them.

He was no longer confined to the yurt. Linóvi said he was awaiting judgment. She didn't think it would be harsh; he was a child after all, she said. Everybody said that. But for the next few days, he simply needed to keep his distance and no one would bother him. It was a weight off to see the children unafraid to play beside him.

As the water raced across his knuckles, the dirt from his uniform pooled in his palms, then ran away toward the River. Never mind that the bloodstains would stay, the water washed it purer than the Landowner's own shirt. Maybe that's why the Citadel was dirty, because it had lost running water.

Shonco came into his head, the way his eyes were like water, the way his collarbone showed when he undid his button. He'd been raised at the Grid and they had water there. They had lupin and life, unless that was also a lie. Tan missed him without knowing if he should, his mind wrung out.

He'd heard Fashen had left. He had not spoken to him, and, curiously, now he did not feel a need to.

He laid his clothes out to dry on the rocks and bowed to the stream as Anji taught him. "Thank you, Five Sheltered Bends Stream."

❧

Heading back to the yurt with a full waterskin and the laundry basket on his back, he took the long way through the forest, because the spruce was dappled in the warm afternoon and Linóvi had said, *Don't hurry*. He heard the call of a crow and a jay—and so many others he couldn't name but ought to know. He was thinking about that when he caught voices down the hill, Oak accents, a man and woman.

He hid the basket in the brush and crept toward them, keeping to bare rocks that wouldn't crunch and the shadows of the tree trunks. They stood in the dappled light beneath an old spruce, Sajem and the Teacher, Enátha. Tan crouched behind a tree some way above and watched them.

They stood close enough to accentuate the difference in their heights. Both were tall, like many Oak people, but Sajem was one of the tallest of Oak.

He spoke in a low, strained voice. "—brought down a whole third of the village."

She squeezed his hand.

"I don't know how I can go on from that, En. I wasn't built for this. I wish I was back at the house on Green Sky."

She hugged him. They stayed there a long moment with their arms around each other. Tan found this hard to square with Sajem's hesitance to kiss her hand. Who was he to Jeyza's daughter?

When they broke apart, she said, "I know. I do, I know." She took his face in her hands and held it several seconds, and Tan had the impression they were speaking—or feeling?—with their minds. "If we used the device, it would end things quickly."

"It's a door Falling Wind's ethics always spoke against opening. She spoke against it in the Convention War."

"I don't know if you noticed, Sajem, but the Convention War was won because of a tactical missile. Yes, Falling Wind spoke against it, and if she'd had her way, we would have had a bloody war of attrition, possibly for generations."

"Instead of fifty thousand dead and a city laid waste overnight."

"We're not fighting fifty thousand now."

She was talking about using nukes, just like the bombing of the West Men.

Faint, Tan sank down in the dirt. They had been talking about burning the Bridge, but Tan had refused to help them. Had his refusal axed the plan? Were they going to bomb the Citadel because of him? Not just the soldiers and priests but the scholars, women, kids?

What about blasted tech limitation?

But it wouldn't work; the Citadel had a shield.

Except they didn't, did they? The bombing he'd experienced had been a ruse, and when he thought about it, no other machinery he had seen in the Citadel suggested technology that high, not still working anyway.

"And my mum really sanctioned it?" Sajem was saying.

"She did. She does."

He rubbed at his temple as if it hurt. "But Enátha, Dad will never condone it, not after everything he saw in the war. We have the Convention for a reason. Breaking tech lim just because it's convenient has to be the wrong choice."

"But the Convention Treaty itself has provisions—"

"I know, I know." He held up a hand. "But I can't—I really don't want to talk about this now."

He didn't want to talk about it? It was the only thing worth talking about.

But she fell silent and leaned back against the tree. After a time, she said, "Last letter from Green Sky, the troop was working up a production of time relative."

Tan tried to parse that and failed.

But Sajem laughed. "Oh, my gods, it's like another planet."

She grinned. "They wanted Nari to sing the Waker, but alas, then Uramésha went to war."

"Poor Nari."

They went on and on like that about stuff Tan couldn't follow. But one thing was clear. He had to get a hold of Sajem. However bad the Citadel was, its people did not deserve to die, and if they were talking about nuking it because Tan had refused to help them, he needed to fix that mistake right now.

❧

He returned the laundry and water to Linóvi's and went to gather firewood around the outskirts of the yurts, eyes glued to the trail the two Oak people had to take back. At the town circle, the Salamanders were cooking in the open kitchens. The smell of pheasant awoke a fierce hunger. Tan ignored it.

They arrived within about half an hour, their demeanor utterly different now. Faces calm, they walked a judicious space apart.

"Lord Sajem," Tan called. "I'm sorry, but I need to speak with you."

A piece of him expected to be told to fuck himself. The last time they'd met, he'd accused the man's father of murder. But the louder piece said that was not Sajem's way.

Sajem and the Teacher exchanged a glance.

"I'll go on ahead," she said.

Starting back the way he'd come, Sajem tossed his head for Tan to follow. After a couple minutes, he left the trail and cut uphill.

Sitting down out of sight among the spruce trees, he leaned in toward Tan earnestly. "I am glad you came to see me. I've been dying to talk to you."

Tan was taken aback. "You were?"

"I am so sorry about your brother. I made a promise to you and, so far, I've failed completely. I didn't—well, I could make excuses forever, but I want you to know that I haven't forgotten I owe you."

Tan stared.

"Everyone said give you time," said Sajem. "My father, the way pointer, even Jeyza—it makes sense, of course. And that makes it all the harder—but forget all that. Tell me what you wanted to say."

Tan started where he had to. "I was wrong about your father. I believed what I said at the time, but I know now I was mistaken."

"I'm glad you know that," said Sajem. "I wanted to tell you, but my father said you wouldn't believe it from me."

"I'm sure he wants nothing to do with me, but if he'll have me back, I'm ready to help out with the Bridge."

Sajem gave him an incredulous look, then slowly broke into a grin. "You're serious?"

"I am."

"Luck thank you, Tánashen! We need you, and I wanted to ask, but after everything that's happened, the idea of asking more of you... And yet without you as our inside man, it's cast doubt on the whole operation. And Enátha—I know she means well, but this dance around tech lim! It's a dangerous thing."

"I agree," said Tan. "Nuking the Citadel—or the Grid, if that's the plan—"

"I'm sorry, doing what?"

Tan had played his hand without thinking. Now, it was too late to retreat. "I heard you just now. I wasn't following you or anything. I was just out there coming back from the Five Bends, and I heard you talking."

"About nuking Fenorn?" Sajem broke into a laugh.

"It's not funny."

"What made you think we were talking about that?"

"She said it was going to take nukes to win, like in the old war."

Sajem scratched his stubbled chin. "I see. Yes, I see. She was giving an example of how high tech once won a war. Just an example. No one is considering nukes, I promise you."

"Then what the blast were you talking about?"

Sajem hesitated. "Other tech."

"Like?"

"It doesn't matter."

"I think it does," said Tan, "if it'll end the war quickly, like she said, and without bombing them. Without killing a lot of people? *Is* it better than burning the Bridge?"

Sajem shook his head. "No. Violating tech limitation..."

"But if the *Teacher* says it's all right?"

"Teachers can be wrong." He fixed sharp eyes on Tan, all his dithering vanished. "The problem is figuring out the boundaries. High technology always sounds good. It can perform wonders: cure diseases, travel between planets, smash your enemies. But too much of it destroys *home*: that's the history of humanity. High tech devastated our Mother world. The same was true of Daughter, the first world our ancestors attempted to terraform. Yes, that was thousands of years ago, and I know you'll say our presence here is evidence terraforming works. Of course, high tech can be used successfully—if you call living on this strip of a few hundred miles of habitable land, surrounded by a dead sea, underneath a cancerous sun successful."

At Tan's stare, he waved a dismissive hand. "Of course, high tech can work. Of course, at times, we have to use it. But none of that alters the basic pattern: tech dependence and tech acceleration degrade the living land. You see it now with the Citadel. They should have migrated north long ago, gradually, when the drought began. Instead, they relied on their tech for food and water. Now they're starving and invading, using firearms, so killing becomes easier and wars more devastating."

The hypocrisy struck Tan as glaring. "Then what made it all right for you to bomb the West Men?"

Sajem hesitated. "It wasn't all right. It was a grave mistake. The only good to come out of it was the Convention Treaty. And that's what Enátha is throwing aside."

"I don't know what you're talking about," said Tan, all this history beyond him.

"The Convention Treaty specifies what tech is allowable in daily life and what must be confined to tech centers. We're still in the early stages of spreading this teaching across the Kiri planets. The Convention itself is a fledgling union, and I'll be blasted if I see it discarded right here on Uramésha, the very planet where it began." He stopped abruptly as if surprised by his own vehemence.

The sounds of woodmen's axes poured into the silence, Oak killing grandmother spruce to build blockades against the Citadel.

"*You* sound like a Teacher," said Tan.

"I am a Teacher."

Tan absorbed that for a moment. "You're not. Only women are Teachers." He wasn't sure how he knew that, but he had no doubt.

"There are a few male Teachers too. We're considered useful especially on Uramésha, where men rule, because the leaders are more inclined to listen to other men." He cracked a smile. "Or so they tell me. I can't say it matches my experience."

Tan studied him. "I am sorry for what I said to your father."

Sajem shrugged. "It was clear you believed it, and what you said made sense, given that you believed it."

It was hard to imagine living that way, without resentment or injury. It was like Oneness, that peace of everybody with all. The scripture said, *Loss started in surprise, for now his enemy lay in his hands, he loved him.*

He looked down, embarrassed. "I saw him. Your father. I know it wasn't him, but I *saw him* kill my parents. Grandmother Linóvi thinks I got confused by stories my grandmother told me about the Burner."

"That sounds likely."

"But I *remember* him. I can see it now. I can see the scar on his ear. If I didn't see it, why can I see it?"

After a moment, Sajem said, "I trained to be a Teacher on the world of Green Sky. For a while my sister studied there too. In her final year of advanced lay study, it happened that she was pregnant. Now, she managed to time this rather poorly, so that her graduation celebration coincided with when she was due to give birth. But she made it to that celebration. As huge as a boulder, she stood there with all the rest. I sat with the crowd above the amphitheater and clapped my hands as the Teaching Keeper laid the garland of fir fronds on her head." He gave Tan a wry look. "But it didn't happen."

"I don't understand."

"A few years later, I made some remark about how proud I'd been of her that night. She looked at me like I'd gone insane. 'I wasn't there,' she said. 'My heart rate was high, and the midwife said I needed to stay in bed.' Well, I presume she knows, but I can see it to this day, as clearly as I see you now."

"So is your point that a lot of people are insane? Because I actually agree with that."

Sajem smiled. "The point is the human brain is astounding and imprecise. We interpret our world by focusing on what seems important and letting go of what doesn't. Then, to make sense of those important moments, we create stories to connect them. A few people remember almost everything with high accuracy, most don't. All your confabulation means is that you're like everybody else—well, almost everyone."

Tan felt tired suddenly. He wanted nothing more than to lie down in the dappled shade.

"In the Massacre, thirty-six years ago, my father may well have killed your relatives. I don't know, I don't think he can know. I know he didn't kill your parents, but I don't think there's a person living who could say *exactly* what you saw, any more than I can say what I saw that graduation day."

"But then how can we know anything if no one knows what's true?"

"Do you know it would be wrong to nuke the Citadel?"

"Yes."

"How do you know?"

"Because the kids don't deserve to die. The women don't deserve it."

"There you are, you see. We can know a great deal about a great many things, even with the edges blurred."

It wasn't much comfort. Good luck aiming a gun through a blur, short-sighted like Sho. Yet Sho pulled his weight in C-16...

"My mother wanted to offer the women of Fenorn asylum." Sajem's voice pulled him out of his thoughts. "Thirty years ago, after Jeyza came back with Enátha. But the Kept Worlds' Councilwomen said they would not interfere with Fenorn as long as Fenorn didn't interfere with the rest of Uramésha." He sighed. "Well, now I suppose all bets are off."

"Some of them are Kiri," said Tan. "I think Aunt Ferthi would want to see Blue Gums again. Aunt Togi." Shonco's sister. "Her mother's from Free of Ford."

Sajem seemed to consider this.

"You're sure the Bridge is the best option?" said Tan.

"I'd stake my world on it."

"Then convince your father to take me back, and I'll help you destroy it."

Sajem gave him a sober look. "It isn't my father you need to convince. You need to convince Dawn Rock Apáshan."

Apáshan. Tan felt his whole form going soft like a cheese in the sun. He rubbed a hand across his face, reminded he was still awaiting judgment, justice for Apáshan's *sélnutor*. His wrongdoings kept weighing up like links on a massive chain.

Chapter Thirty-One

"**I** hear you have something to say to the warden."

That was how Hunter Apáshan began, not with his own grievance but the grievance of Oak.

Tan stood in the center of the circle, Borderlanders ranged in front of him and the unseen weight of the Oak men behind. Apáshan stood a little in front of the rest, a finely stitched purple coat over his purple sash and his hair cut short in mourning. At his feet lay a large iron pot.

They won't hurt you like Fenorn, Linóvi had said. *We aren't like them.*

At the very, very worst, she'd said, if they judged him to death, they would put him down quickly. But since he was a child, they should be more lenient, demand some service in atonement. He could do that. He understood service, and he'd ask to serve them at the Bridge.

"I want to apologize to the warden," he said.

"Then why are you facing me?"

Tan took the cue, as Linóvi had told him, and turned around, where the Oak men stood. From the corner of his eye, he could see Sajem and Jeyza, the marshal, the Teacher, and in front of him now, the Burner, a stone-faced king presiding over his property. He sat on one of the tables, his feet on the bench, somehow eerily like the Landowner, standing on the stairs in the wake of the nuclear hoax, looking down on them. *They're all the same*, he thought, *these men in power*.

"Lord Nermártan," he said, as Sajem had instructed, "I made a false accusation. I accused you of murdering my parents. I was wrong. I was a child then, and with a child's eyes, I mistook someone else for you. I beg forgiveness." He bowed his head.

"It is given," said the Burner. "Such outbursts from a child are beneath my indignation."

"Yet he should pay, my lord," the marshal said, not so much with remonstrance as a ritual cadence.

"We must all pay," said the Burner. "I have dismissed him from my service and returned him to his people. That is his payment to me. He is theirs now, and he must answer to them."

So the Burner wouldn't take him back. That meant, if he was going to have any use, Tan had to join Apáshan.

"Thank you for your clemency, Lord Nermártan," he recited. He bowed again and turned back to the hunter. He could feel Linóvi, a white shape to his left, the headwoman beside her.

Standing stolid, arms crossed, Apáshan seemed somehow to gaze down from a height, though, in truth, he was just a little taller than Tan. "And what have you to say to your own people, Knotty Vines Red Leaf Tánashen?"

Beside him, Hérseji took a step forward. "Does it matter, Hunter? He is a mute—or Fenorn made him one. How can we judge if anything he says is true?"

His eyes never left Tan. "As best we can, Blue Gums Winding Root Hérseji. Red Leaf, you have confessed to the murder of my *sélnutor*, Vinter's Delight Dawn Rock Ren. Will you tell me that, too, was a child's mistake?"

"No, Hunter Apáshan," he said. Linóvi had said to speak the truth, and he would, up to a point. "I didn't see that it was Dawn Rock Ren. I had nothing against him. If I had seen it was him, I wouldn't have shot him. I would have called out to him." That last part was a lie. If he'd called, Ren would not have heard him, or not have heeded him, and the boy would have died. No, Tan would have shot him either way, but there was no use telling Apáshan that.

But though his thoughts were blocked, Apáshan's eyes cut through him. "Yet you admit you killed one of your allies, a Borderlander, without regret?"

"I regret I couldn't think of anything better to do. I regret I wasn't smarter or quicker. I saw him about to shoot a child, one of the children I lived with in Fenorn. And I don't hold that against him. It was war, and the boy was an enemy. The boy was armed, he was dangerous. But he was also just a child, and I couldn't let him die. He was just confused. He was trying to run."

"That is all you offer?"

"That's the truth, Hunter Apáshan." Mostly.

"It is a brave man who admits his treachery so openly."

Tan frowned, unable to separate the compliment from the condemnation.

"There is a misstep in your judgment, Hunter." The voice, calm but piercing, belonged to Linóvi.

Apáshan glanced at her. "What misstep, Way Pointer?"

"My *sélnutor*, Red Leaf Tánashen, is a child, not yet a man."

"He is a man by age."

"He has never completed the ritual hunt. In fact, he has lived for such a long time with Fenorn, he knows many of our ways only as a child would."

"Which is to say he is a man from another people, like these Oak men here, yet I would not call them boys. A foreign murderer remains guilty of murder."

"Yet he is not foreign. He is a child of ours whose childhood has been uprooted."

Apáshan shook his head. "I honor the wisdom of your words, Way Pointer, but I cannot see the justice in them. He is a hunter, a killer; he was a tactician in the battle at Blue Gums. This is all man's work. That cannot be denied."

Linóvi inclined her head. "It is also undeniable that both our hearts are unclear. You are grieving for your *sélnutor*. I am frightened of losing mine. I ask the headwoman, then, how do you judge this question?"

The headwoman, too, wore a bright ritual coat, a salamander winding in a green embrace. Her straw hat was woven with brown salamander swirls.

"It's difficult," she said. "You both speak wisely." She fell silent and the circle waited. As the moments passed, Tan's heart ticked faster, the silence, this suspension, more difficult than any speech. The Oak men began to whisper. Apáshan's gaze remained rooted on the headwoman, as if a wall stood between him and Tan.

At last she said, "I judge that he is both a man and child and should stand judgment as a man, and yet with some measure of mercy on his age and mind."

"Then let him feel his burden as a man." Apáshan hefted the iron pot by its two handles and set it before Tan. Linóvi has said it was just a ritual, but the He loomed sudden and dark in Tan's mind. Punishment rituals were rituals of pain. Then again, perhaps pain was what Tan wanted.

He picked up the pot, left arm smarting and left hand weak. He found the best grip for holding it, leaning it right and against his belly to distribute the weight, as Linóvi had said he could.

"May the loss be ours," said Apáshan, "the weight of it be for us to live with. Begin." He nodded to his right.

One by one, Borderlanders came up to him, each bearing a stone, which they laid in the pot. Not everyone stepped forward, only those in grief, but that was still a lot of people. Even though this was not his home village, it seemed Dawn Rock Ren had been well loved.

The headwoman came forward, and her wife. Anji's son came forward, and Anji too. That hurt Tan: to think that he'd wounded Anji, that even as she'd chastised her son for his harsh words, she'd quietly borne her own grudge.

As the stones weighed the pot, Tan felt his muscles quiver, the left side tearing. He tightened on his grip; the veins in his hands swelled blue.

Linóvi did not come forward, and he wondered if that meant she had not known Ren well or simply that she wished to spare him.

In his turn, Apáshan laid his rock in the pot, no larger or smaller than anyone else's. Hérseji laid hers, and those whose names he didn't know but whom he'd robbed of a friend or kin; some of them were children.

The weight of the pot was near the limit of his strength. He leaned back to rest it against his chest, and no one told him not to.

The line of mourners had reached the Oak men, and to his surprise, Sajem came forward and put in a rock, never meeting Tan's gaze. Tan's pulse jumped with a sting of shame. He hadn't known he'd hurt Sajem by killing Ren.

The Burner, too, came and added a stone, none of the other Oak men.

Now, everyone stood back and watched. Tan's arms burned, his fingers numb. The pot shuddered in his grasp. Though the day was mild, he'd begun to sweat, and the He was close, and it filled him with a strange desire to laugh.

You have no idea what lightweights you are. He thought it at them furiously, knowing the thoughts were locked safe in his head. *You have no idea what a butterfly walk this punishment of yours is.* And yet, it was somehow the same, Citadel and Borderlands, crime and retribution, error and the consequence of error. Punishment to maintain cohesion, Tan understood that very well. He'd meted it out, had it meted on him.

He gritted his teeth as the pot began to slip.

There was a kind of Oneness in it, a kind of universal blur named Júzian, Ordan, Ren... Ash. He wanted to let go and let it wash him away with them, down the stream with the memento of Ordan, out in the dusty breeze through the pines.

But he had to hold on. Because his worthiness defined his chance to rescue Ash and help his boys. His worthiness defined his power.

The pot slipped in his sweaty palms. He caught it and kept it, though his arms were bending lower. He tried to shift his footing; it didn't help. A child whispered and was hushed. Murder, he thought, must be very rare—must have been rare till these war times. Tan had never seen anything like this in Knotty Vines. It must be the war that—

The pot clattered down. As it escaped his left hand, the sudden shift in its weight dragged it out of his right. The stones tumbled, some striking his toes and shins like raindrops solidified into pain. He picked the pot up and set it down in front of him, orderly, as Linóvi had instructed.

"As the eldest present *sélnutor* to the dead," said Apáshan, "I am ready to declare my judgment. Red Leaf Tánashen speaks truly when he says that this is war. In war, hunters hunt other human beings; that's the way of it. At the same time, he had promised to serve us at Blue Gums. This has been confirmed by Yowlers Mica Melting Fashen, Blue Gums Winding Root Hérseji, and several Oak people. So, he is killer and trust-breaker both, and the sharp justice of war seems to call for his life." He paused and Tan held his breath. "But when my mind goes to his youth and his own broken *sélnua*, I cannot demand his life. In peace time, murder merits exile, and that is the judgment I ask: three years' exile from the Borderlands. That way, Way Pointer, your *sélnutor* will return to you in time."

Three years! thought Tan. It might as well be death, a lifetime. He could feel Ash flying away from him like a dandelion seed on the wind.

"Headwoman," said Linóvi, "you said pity should be taken on the child part of him. Three years as an outcast is no way to heal a child battered by brutal strangers."

Once again the headwoman was silent a long time, her head nodding slowly as if in conversation—and for all Tan knew, it was, a communion of minds from which he was excluded. "The judgment seems reasonable to me," she said. "Three years is a short exile for murder, even without trust-breaking."

"But where will he go," said Linóvi, "how will he live, this boy who scarcely remembers the rhythms of *mirya* in this land?"

"I will take him into my household." Tan started and glanced behind him. Jeyza looked coolly past him to Linóvi. "He can stay three years with me, then return to you if he wishes."

"Then you must send him away to Oak, Oak Jeyza" said Apáshan, "for I cannot have a trust-breaker in our alliance here in wartime, even if he is counted among the Oak men and not ours."

"Please reconsider, Hunter," said Tan. He knew he was not supposed to speak but the words gushed out. "I will do whatever you say. Just let me rescue my brother."

"You have said that before, so I'm told," said Apáshan. "And within days, your faithful service cost my *sélnutor* his life." He took a step toward Tan. "I understand you better than you know, Red Leaf. I understand you love your brother and those lads you were raised with. I believe what you intend is good. But in war, all that's worth nothing if your *deeds* cannot be trusted. That is all that needs to be said. Be glad of your life and your home with Oak Jeyza. Leave Fenorn to us who have earned each other's trust."

Chapter Thirty-Two

He awoke to the commander's voice. Shit, had he overslept? Why would the commander be here in the barracks?

Then he looked up at the bushes and remembered where he was: a hole in the ground on the outskirts of Salamander. He must have been dreaming.

So far, things had gone to plan. He'd ridden west toward Oak with one of Jeyza's men. Then, per Jeyza's instructions, the man set him free and rode on while Tan doubled back on foot to his hiding place.

"I still owe you your brother," Sajem had said. "If you can help us get him out, you'll be first to know. If not, we'll bring him to you."

But Tan feared that Sajem was out of his depth, offering what wasn't in his power to give.

That was four days ago. Since then, alliance troops had been departing, presumably for the Bridge. From the sounds he'd heard, he guessed thirty or forty had left Salamander, about half of the men who'd been stationed there. If Jeyza didn't come and get him soon, he'd trail them on his own, he had to.

The voice came again—not a dream after all, a Citadel man, right here in Salamander.

Jeyza had given Tan his gun back. He drew it now and listened. He couldn't catch the words, but he knew the cadence of a commander's orders, a measured voice, but too loud for enemy territory, overconfident fool, hadn't reckoned on spies, hadn't reckoned on Tan. He raised his head to get a better sense of direction. The south? It was coming from the *south*?

Not east from Yowlers, but south—from Blue Gums. They'd retaken Blue Gums? After only ten, eleven days? So Oak had burned it for nothing, killed the priest for nothing.

He had to warn the Salamanders—but of what? How many were there, how far out?

It was early morning, dew still wet on the ground. He wriggled his pack onto his shoulders and surveyed the view through the bushes—nothing. From his hundred and twenty unblocked degrees, he could see only forest.

He chose a stand of bushes, then put his helmet on and bolted for it, then the next bush.

"—should be a half mile to the north." The commander's words rang close.

Tan dove to the ground. Lying still, he could hear their footsteps. He crawled forward to get a view over a rise. At first, he saw only trees—but then, he caught some movement and there they were, at least ten, twelve men, marching straight for Salamander.

He slunk back down the rise. As soon as he was out of sight, he ran for the village, banking around the hillside to pop up close to the town center.

He dashed past the stares of Salamanders, past "It's him. Isn't he exiled?" It would do no good to just shout a warning and alert the Citadel troops that they'd been seen. A goat dog barked at him as he sped by.

He bolted into Linóvi's yurt where Anji was just stirring the embers to life.

Jethan leapt to his feet. "What the blast are you—?"

"They're coming," said Tan. "Citadel—Fenorn warriors."

Anji and her son both started talking at once, but Linóvi silenced them with a gesture.

"What warriors? How many?"

"I counted twelve, but I'm sure they have more. They wouldn't march on Salamander with twelve."

"Impossible," snapped Jethan. "If they were coming, we'd know it. The Yowlers Road is guarded."

"They're not coming from Yowlers. They're coming from the south, from Blue Gums."

❧

Not five minutes later, Oak was mobilizing, the Burner giving quiet orders to his men. But where was Sajem, where was Jeyza? As Tan herded three stray children back to their family, he scanned for them but he saw no sign.

A gunshot rang out. The littlest kid squawked and clung to his leg. It seemed like every dog in the village was barking. Tan knelt and held the kid's shoulders.

"Run for your yurt," he said, "don't stop." Oak men and hunters were dashing past them. "Find someone from your *sélnua* and stick to them like pine sap. You," he told the oldest, the Júzian, "don't let go of your sisters' hands." He gave her a light shove and the three dashed for home.

"Tan!"

He sprinted to Linóvi's side, hefting the pack she handed him by habit. Another shot echoed through the hills, a child cried out for her father.

"Let's go," said Linóvi. "We'll make for Creeky together. From there, you can keep heading west—"

"I can't."

"You've been exiled."

"Grandmother—" A surge of hooves interrupted him. He spun and aimed his gun. But it was Sajem on a hill-jack with two little kids before him.

He called the hill-jack to an abrupt halt and dismounted, as she snorted, eyes wide. "Way Pointer, ride with them," he said. "They'll get you out the west road to Creeky."

Linóvi stared at him, at Tan, at Anji nearby.

"Go on, Way Pointer," said Anji. "I'll see you there." Shouldering her pack, she scurried off.

"But Tánashen..."

"I'll watch him," said Sajem.

She looked at the kids on the hill-jack and nodded. She pressed two fingers to Tan's forehead and said, "Luck bless you." Then she let Sajem boost her foot onto the hill-jack, and she was gone out to the west road, leaving Tan with one less worry.

Sajem said, "We need to—"

"Down!" Tan pushed him hard and fired.

The Citadel man fell back, winged in the arm or merely startled, Tan didn't stop to see. He grabbed Sajem's arm and hauled him to the edge of the village circle, down the hill, fast as a pika, into the shelter of the brush.

Sajem slammed under a bush beside him, smelling of dust and hill-jack.

"I have to get to my father," he said. "I'm ordered to stand with him. We have to get you out west, to the Oaks—"

"Where's Jeyza?"

Sajem hesitated.

"Why isn't she here fighting...?" Tan pressed. "Where's Dawn Rock Apáshan?" He'd seen no sign of the hunter either.

"They've gone."

"Where?"

No answer.

"Sajem. Lord Sajem—"

"The Bridge. They'd been preparing for days and slipped away at the first warning of the Fenorn—wait." He yanked Tan back down.

"If they needed you, Jeyza would've gotten you. She'd have gone to your hiding place."

"Except I wasn't there. I was the one giving that warning." Tan pulled his arm free. "Which way did they go? East, near the road? Southeast?"

Sajem's face was grim.

"Fine. I'll find them myself." He moved to go.

"Wait." This time, Sajem's voice was softer. He scrounged in a pocket and pulled out a rumpled paper, a letter or something, and a writing stick. He tore off a blank corner and scratched a few words. "They went south of the road, bearing east. Give this to Jeyza."

Tan stared at the marks, Kiri swirls.

"What's it say?"

"It says to accept you, but I can't promise they will."

Tan took the paper and stuck it away. He started to rise, but something made him stop. He owed him, owed everyone...

"I didn't—" A gunshot drowned his words. Above them, a hill-jack squealed. "I didn't know you were friends with the Dawn Rocks. I'm sorry."

Sajem gave him a blank look. "I'm not—not in particular. They're valued allies, of course, but..." Then understanding came into his face. "I put that rock in the bowl to show them honor, not out of personal grief." His gray eyes were wide as a doorway. For a moment, Tan could see nothing else but those eyes.

"I'm sorry all the same," he said, yet the burden sat a little lighter.

Chapter Thirty-Three

He found a spot in a dry creek bed, sheltered by yellowing chestnuts. In settling there, he only dislodged one stone, a brief clunk and then quiet. It surprised him, in fact, how well the Citadel had prepared him for creeping through the woods. Though the physical space was entirely different, the business of passing unseen was the same; instinct knew when to duck and be still.

He listened, beating back the anxiety that invariably washed over him when only silence answered. He knew they weren't far.

He was right. A man spoke, conversational, just up the hill, a rustle in the grass, the crunch and shuffle of a camp being laid. Day was waning fast, his creek bed turning gray and cooler as the summer heat receded.

When he was sure they wouldn't move again, he took a small drink, waterskin half empty. They'd have to go down to a stream tomorrow, and when they did, he'd contrive to refill it. He slid his pack off his shoulders and scrounged for his supper. Jeyza's provisions were almost gone. He had five chestnuts hoarded in a pocket, along with four roasted grasshoppers and some dried beets in the pack. He'd eaten the last of the flatbread yesterday. He ate a chestnut, chewing slowly and looked around for other options.

The big, brown caterpillars were mostly gone by now—either pupating or just not here this far south. The chestnuts above him were in full white flower; it would be months till they bore fruit, and then they'd need heavy leeching. That he remembered from childhood, leeching acorns and chestnuts. Neither was a food you could just pluck and eat. Plum trees weren't common here, but he'd passed a few, fruit still unripe but edible. There was a grass with a bulbous root, but he wasn't going to chance it.

Gingerly, he turned up some stones in the stream bed and was rewarded with a couple of plump worms. They tasted terrible, but they gave him protein. He chased them down with a beet slice.

Then he remembered and said, "Thank you, worm people and beet people, for giving your life for me."

He had only a vague idea where he was: somewhere east of Yowlers and probably south of it, but still too far north to hear the River, scrubby woodlands, sort of like north of Blue Gums.

He assumed they were making for the Bridge—well, no, he couldn't assume that. For all he knew, they might be following the Teacher's plan, her mysterious tech. But they *were* going southeast, and that meant toward the Bridge, a small group, just six men and Jeyza. A small group made sense for sneaking up to the Bridge. And though he'd rarely ventured close enough to see them, he thought he'd caught a glimpse of large sacks, not just travel packs. The oil sacks, that's what he figured.

ta

Running streams were dangerous. They drowned the ears and masked activity near their banks. This was a two-edged blade for Tan, giving him some license to walk with less caution while also requiring intense concentration not to lose his own quarry. Sometimes, he had to come in sight of them to track them, close enough to catch a glimpse of a leg through the trees or a hat in the sun. Once, he let them drop out of sight for a minute, while he darted down to the bank to fill his waterskin and douse his hot body with water. Then, he was back in the brush, stalking the hillside above them.

He couldn't see them, though. Where had they gone? Already around that bend in the hill or—?

A shout cut across the burbling water. He couldn't make out the words, but the accent was Citadel. A Kiri shouted in answer. Then a question, maybe "What are you doing here?" in Citadel.

Tan moved toward the voices, as swift as he could without breaking his cover in the chestnuts.

He was not quite in sight of them when the shooting started, three quick shots in succession. He froze, crouching low. More shouts, a cry of pain abruptly gutted: the Kiris putting down one of their enemies, probably. Hopefully. *Let them be the victors.*

Then he smelled it—Blue Gums, the tang of mint. A cold sweat fell on him in the heat of the day. The sacks had spilled. If the sacks had spilled, the Bridge plan was dead.

But if the Bridge plan was dead, there'd be another plan, right? He still needed to be here. Whatever happened, he might still be the card they needed to play.

He crept toward them. He could see them now, Kiris, thank the gods. They must have just stumbled on a couple of scouts, but with the sound of gunshots, more might be on their way. Apáshan's people knew that too and slipped off quick and quiet.

He followed them all day, back up into the higher hills, crawling through scrub and sprinting over hot, bare rock. Once away from the overwhelming smell by the stream, he could track them, in part, by the trail of mint, which let him fall back a little and take less care to hide. In the dry-grass dazzle of afternoon, his head throbbed with hunger and thirst. He indulged in one of his grasshoppers and took small swallows of water, spaced to keep himself going.

In the evening, they stopped at a stand of old oaks. With little brush to shelter in, Tan stayed downhill behind some younger trunks, but as night fell, he let himself inch closer to hear them. They'd lit no fire, a wise move in the summer dryness with a cargo of oil and in enemy land. It also meant there was no crackling to cover up their voices.

"—could be enough." That was Jeyza.

"It's not that I doubt your skill." Apáshan. "But lighting the wet underside of a bridge with scarcely enough to paint the piles..."

Scarcely enough? That meant they still had some oil.

"Agreed," said someone else. "Even if every arrow hits home, whether the Bridge burns depends on the piles. We won't have enough oil for all six."

"Well, what's the alternative then?" said Jeyza. "Give up? Go back to Blue Gums? Because they won't help us."

"They won't help *you*," said Apáshan, then added, "No, I'll not give up. We've come too far." He paused. "We have to make every arrow count. Each hit will have to spark a weak point. Blast it, if we only had one of those Free of Ford engineers."

They passed on to discussing the construction of the Bridge.

But arrows? thought Tan. How would they burn a bridge with arrows?

Flaming arrows, like Jeyza had used to rescue him in Knotty Vines, wrapped in oil-soaked cloth maybe. They'd shoot up at the bottom of the Bridge. It wouldn't be enough.

Then he made a decision—not a safe one, but life did not trade in safety.

He spoke up from his place behind a tree trunk. "I can help you, Hunter."

Silence. Then, a single harsh whisper.

Then Apáshan's voice, calm. "Can you really, Red Leaf?"

Tan went still, skewered. The hunter knew his voice, wasn't even surprised. But Tan was in this deep now, he had to press on.

"I can pass for Citadel. I can walk through their guards straight onto the Bridge and dump the oil from above. Poke a hole in the sack, and I can trickle it all over."

"Come up here, Tánashen," said Jeyza. "No use lurking there now."

She was right, and still his feet dragged as he came into their circle. They were black statues against the pre-Ribbon stars.

"Sit down," said Apáshan.

Tan groped for a flat spot and sat. "I have a letter from Oak Sajem."

One man chuckled. "These Oak men and their letters. Fine good that does them in the dark."

There was a rustle of cloth and a scratch and a spark. Jeyza held up a match, her face a flickering shadow. Matches were Citadel products; Tan wondered who'd traded it to her. "Let me see," she said.

"Oak Jeyza," warned Apáshan.

"It's only a moment of light." She examined the paper and blew out the match. "Hm. It says this one gave the alarm when Fenorn attacked Twelve Salamanders."

"You believe him?" said someone.

"Sajem? Yes."

"Are you going to kill me, Hunter?" said Tan.

Apáshan did not answer at once. The night filled the space up, a cricket singing down the hill, oblivious to the wheeling of the planet that he lived on.

"If I had wanted to kill you, Red Leaf," he said, "you would have been dead before now." He sighed. "You gave the alarm, eh? Well, Oak Jeyza said you could be useful."

"Surely, you don't trust him, Dawn Rock Apáshan?" said someone.

"Trust is a matter of circumstance. I trust Oak Jeyza on this journey. On another, I might not. The question is what do the circumstances demand?"

"How much oil do you have left?" asked Tan.

He hesitated. "Two sacks."

Two-thirds of what they started with. Could be worse. "Let me take one."

"And you'll dance in right under their noses?" said Jeyza. "A traitor, wanted by the priests?"

"If he doesn't break trust, he'll get caught," said one man.

"They only perform Oneness in the mornings," said Tan. "If they're not actively looking for me—and why should I be in Free of Ford?—they won't find me if I head in once Oneness is over." At least he hoped not.

"But if someone recognizes you?" said the man.

A thoughtful noise came from Apáshan. "It may not be such a hard adjustment, Red Leaf's plan. We've already arranged for Spy Keskan's people to be in place near the Bridge. We may just need to alter a few of their positions. If we send word to Tracker Fashen at first light, he can send word to the spy."

"How did you arrange all that?" said Tan, so flummoxed he was almost angry. C-16 had no say in where they might be stationed.

"Fashen's good," said Jeyza. He could hear her fishing for something in her pack. "Keskan too." She leaned over and put something in his hand. A crust of bread; he devoured it.

"But let's say Red Leaf gets through," said someone. "Why pour oil from above? Fire burns upward last time I checked. Better to use all the oil below."

Tan had thought about this a lot. "That's where you're wrong."

The man laughed. "It burns down now, does it?"

Chuckles answered.

"The Bridge is old. I've been on it, I've seen. A lot of the wood is dry and cracked. If oil's poured from above, it'll seep into the cracks. It'll go up like tinder."

"That agrees with my contacts in Free of Ford," said Apáshan. "The Bridge is sixty years old and poorly maintained. These Fenorn folk have no love for wood."

"Let me try," said Tan.

"To redeem yourself?"

"It's never been about me. It's my brother—all those boys, they..." He found himself stuck for the right words. *They deserve to be free,* he was going to say. But what did freedom mean for the One, for Dezdenec, for Muned? What did he hope for them? Enough food, some peace, away from Citadel lies, where Oneness could be true—a Garden. "They deserve a better life, and the Citadel can't give it."

Chapter Thirty-Four

The morning mist clung to the river bank. A mile up River, back the way he'd come, a battle impended at Friend of Fennoc—Fennec, Tan corrected himself. Friend of Fennec, the fox town. But it wasn't a real battle. It was a diversion, designed to hollow out the reserves near the Bridge.

His oil sack corked and packed in his rucksack, he picked his way through the mud just out of sight of the River Road. He didn't want to test his credibility with the Citadel until he had to. If someone did spot him along the way, he would claim he was skirting the road to avoid Kiri soldiers, which was, in fact, the only sensible thing for a lone cadet to do. The marks of the drought on the riverbank stood in warning, striations like desert cliffs marking how far the water level had fallen.

The Bridge was only about nine miles away now, so in order to arrive near twilight, he'd need to find a place to wait out part of the day.

He walked through a thin wood, dominated by trees with white, wispy trunks and leaves that clattered in the slightest breeze. From the south came the River's sandstorm rush. Good luck for him; the noise made it less likely that his passing would be noticed. Or perhaps the spirits were inclined to help him.

"I'm sorry I don't know your names, tree spirits," he whispered. "But thank you. Thank you, River."

High above the River, a hawk rode the sky. He was watching her through the branches when he heard the thunder of hooves. He ducked, just in time to glimpse hill-jacks galloping, their riders in Citadel uniforms. *Or maybe they're Oak uniforms*, he thought ruefully, *that just look like the Citadel because I'm crazy.*

Half an hour later, two units of footmen marched by him. He hid behind an inadequate tree for a good ten minutes, till he was confident they'd passed, headed for Friend of Fennec, no doubt, where a fake battle would cost real lives.

⁊

There were no villages between Friend of Fennec and Free of Ford, so Tan had assumed he'd pass no habitations, only soldiers or travelers on the road. It was, therefore, with some consternation that he stumbled on a wooden house. He veered clear of it just to find himself in plain sight of another. They were rectangles, reminiscent of the Grid's Old Town, but ramshackle, built without the benefit of the Grid's industrial machinery.

He could hear men talking, along with axes and hammers. He didn't dare try to sneak past them. A Citadel cadet would not avoid Citadel footmen.

Keeping his helmet low over his forehead, he made his way up to the road. The uniform was his own with the red ray that marked him a captain pulled off. Four remaining brown rays marked four years of service.

"Hold," called a sentry almost at once. "What's your ID, cadet?"

"C-4, Cadet Fourth Year Ren." If he was going to impersonate C-4, it seemed fitting somehow to base his name on the man he killed to save them.

Gun at the ready, the man perused him. "C-4? You got routed at Silver."

"Yes, sir. This medicine in my pack comes from Silver, sir. I was ordered to deliver it to Ark's Town." The Citadel names for Blue Gums and Free of Ford rang old and alien in his ears.

"Let's see that pack."

Tan opened it and stood back as the man rifled through it.

"Smells out to the Gods' Realm." He looked up. "Lost your gear?"

"Had to leave some to fit the medicine, sir. Left more back with our injured guy."

"Injured guy?"

No way had a cadet been assigned to walk the roads alone. "Three of us got put on this delivery detail. But we got jumped by Oak outside Fennoc's Town. One of us got nailed and one got hurt and had to turn back with a busted arm."

"Bad day for the gods, I guess," said the man with a touch of softness. "Oak's making a bid for Fennoc's, they say. But we'll beat 'em, you'll see." He rezipped the pack.

He's afraid of Oak, Tan realized with a touch of surprise. But of course, he was. They'd all been trained to see Oak as the invaders, the wielders of nukes, who'd tried to blow up the Citadel to keep control of the Garden. A half-season ago, Tan had believed that too.

"What's the medicine for?" the man asked.

"I don't know, sir. I only heard people say the gum tree oil's good for a lot of medical stuff."

The man searched his face. Should he look more broken up about his dead companions? Behind the sentry other footmen had paused in their work to stare at him.

"All right." The sentry waved him through.

Tan had trained for years at looking purposeful. He walked steady and not too fast, ignoring the eyes that followed, and hoping he seemed insignificant enough that no one radioed about him.

It bothered him how easily he'd gotten through. But of course it was easy: no one expected a deserter to return. Deserters, by definition, were either running or dead. He couldn't be the first to survive the priests, though. Someone else must have stolen a hill-jack and ridden out of range or been left for dead in a battle like Tan. Yet Jeyza had said he was unique.

Maybe it was the surge that changed things. Now, the Borderlands teemed with Citadel people, not just settlers handpicked to reward loyalty. There would be more Keskans, more successful deserters. A ruse like this one would not pass scrutiny for long.

~

The trees thinned into a sharp-smelling marsh. With no more cover, he stumped along, just a cadet, tired and dull, with the summer sun gathering its heat inside his helmet. Little wooden bridges spanned the River's tributaries, each one breathing a few seconds of cool before he passed it and heat closed in again.

Twice footman units rushed by him, hill-jacks pulling the troops in wagons. They didn't stop to interrogate Tan, but both times men yelled versions of "Where the hell do you think you're going?"

Both times, Tan yelled back, "Medicine needed at Ark's Town, sir!"

They cursed about needing it at Fennoc's. But by then they were a rumble fading off down the road.

In the afternoon, the marsh behind him and ground firm, he rested in the shade of a stand of boulders. They were carved with faded lines now encrusted with white lichen, but he made out the shape of birds in flight. Some people long ago had laid these boulders as mementos. Maybe now they housed guardian spirits. He bowed to them and offered a small piece of dried fruit, though his stomach said it was a waste. Then, he ate and drank from his canteen.

He waited.

He should be about three miles from the Bridge, and he needed to lose about four hours or else he'd arrive ahead of schedule. He drank more. He might as well tank up here; he'd have ample time to piss before going on.

As he waited, Keskan encroached on his thoughts, like a blur on the road slowly coming into focus. To hear Jeyza tell it, most of this plan hinged on Keskan. He was playing a double agent, feeding Shonco bits of information curated by Fashen. He'd got C-16 reassigned to Free of Ford by convincing Shonco his informant would be there. He orchestrated the information leak that diverted the Citadel troops to Fennec.

He's good, Jeyza had said—or was it Fashen? The memory played tricks. He was good, no doubt, much better than Tan. Better leader, smarter person—all of that, all that. In an earlier life, his defeat would have enraged him. Right now, it gnawed at the back of his mind, and that was where he kept it.

After a time, he heard men talking some way off above the River's rush. His heart began to pound, and he couldn't tell why. They weren't nearby, they weren't a threat. After some minutes, it came to him. Hiding here was too much like that day on the rocks above the Grid with Ash and Júzian.

At that realization, he felt a fierce need to run, just get back on the road, get going.

But he waited.

He heard a gunshot, distant shouts, then quiet. After a time, some soldiers marched past him.

He waited.

Then something strange happened out at the River. Its silver ribbon was interrupted by a froth and something rising up, humped and black. Tan couldn't see it clearly, but it curved like the back of a river rat sluicing out from the reeds. But it was huge and slow, like some monster fish. There could be no such fish. All the life in the River couldn't feed it.

Some machine then? His mind went to the Teacher's assertion that what had been forbidden was now allowed. He shrank down where he sat and tried to make himself invisible. The thing churned past him west, up current, and dipped out of view again.

What was it? No one had spoken of such a thing. How could anyone hide a machine so huge?

Then it came to him. It had not been hidden. It had been in plain view in front of the Grid: the tanker. Except it wasn't for carrying water. Quite the opposite. Water carried it. It was an underwater ship.

A ship. That was how they'd retaken Blue Gums. No long march along the River roads; they'd just moved units in by ship.

But if the Citadel could move troops in an armored ship, it didn't need the Bridge at all, and their whole strategy was useless.

Chapter Thirty-Five

The lowering sun on his helmet boiled his head like an egg. The road climbed away from the riverbed, up into a rocky, grassy land, not so different from the Grid. In the distance, he could see Free of Ford, an old, densely built village of stone fortifications. It rose like a chess board stacked with pieces, scarcely like a place people lived at all.

The Citadel's already won, he thought. What if that ship was unstoppable?

But it wasn't Tan's place to undercut months of planning. Losing the Bridge would hurt the Citadel. Minimally, it meant one less means of transport. As for Tan, he just had to fulfill his own part and get Ash, who should be stationed at the River if all went to plan—then leave the future to the future.

He passed a goatherd and fishing boats pulling in for the night and reached the outskirts of the village just as the sun set in a red blaze.

Soldiers bustled about the town. He spotted Codo hauling boxes into a warehouse. That jarred him, but he made himself walk on. Had it really been Codo? There were a number of blond boys in the Citadel. But he knew those ears that stuck out and that stick-thin figure.

Fear was pounding in him now—and strangely, it was not fear of capture. Rather it was fear of Keskan. He found himself hoping the sentry ahead was anyone in the world but Keskan.

It wasn't Keskan. It was Dradam, thin and pinched in a uniform too big.

He's in league with Keskan, thought Tan. *He must be*. But just in case, he pulled his helmet low. It wouldn't fool Dradam, but if it might, well, why not try it?

"What's your ID?" asked Dradam.

Tan went through his story.

Dradam nodded. "Okay, Cadet. Good luck with the medicine delivery."

Tan peered at him a moment as he started forward. Their eyes met, and Dradam, his face like stone, gave him a second nod.

❧

The sky settled into a dull blue-gray. Tan padded on his way, ignored by the people of Free of Ford. Uniformed soldiers talked loudly in the streets, but ordinary folk walked among them, too, many of them Kiri in appearance and dress. A fishmonger was shutting up her shop. A fisher who had been mending a boat packed up his tools for the evening.

Then came a sudden blast of white. Tan started, laid bare in the floodlights.

He walked on, breathing fast, and saw soon enough that the lights weren't aimed at him; they lined the entire street. Once his eyes adjusted, he could see they were much dimmer than the Citadel's lights, small lamps on posts at even intervals. He wondered what powered them. Did they have solar here? He caught no sulfur smell of geothermal.

The buildings thinned until, south of the road, there were none at all, just boats moored at the River. Guards passed in and out of the shadows like spirits, each visible for a few moments only. He could see the Bridge up ahead now, a sketch of black lines across the water. As darkness fell, its silhouette transformed into two rows of battery lights like giant, low-hovering stars.

The streets emptied. A battery whirred. He must have heard that all the time at the Citadel but hadn't noticed. Now, in contrast to the stillness of Salamander, the hum was everywhere. Far off the shriek of a curlew signaled the start of its night hunt for insects. (It was Shonco who'd taught him the name *curlew*.) Now and then, words punctured the quiet, final directives for the day, a laugh. He walked past a cluster of wooden buildings, windowless, storehouses maybe.

As he neared their end, a figure stepped out in front of him.

"Hold. What's your ID?"

Tan took his helmet off and stepped up to meet him. "C-4, Fourth Year Ren." He gazed coolly up into Keskan's face.

Keskan gave him a tight-lipped smile. "What brings you here, Ren?"

"Medicine." *Were they really going to do this?*

"You don't say? You need it or you got it?"

"Got."

"You always talk to sentries like that?"

Tan was done with this. He stared him down.

"All right. Off you go, Cadet Ren." Keskan stepped out of Tan's way with a smirk.

Just then, a cadet came up from a side street. "Captain, we got a report of some unauthorized boats—" He broke off and stared at Tan.

For a moment, Tan could only think *Dezdenec's face is beautiful.*

With a sudden jerk, as on awaking from a dream, Dezdenec's hand made for his gun. Keskan seized him from behind. It happened fast. A squawk, a scrape, a glint of steel, and blood burst from the boy's throat with a sucking gurgle.

Tan stepped back. It was all he could do—stand and watch Dezdenec bleeding out on the dirt. Keskan dragged him, still writhing, into the shadows. When he came out, his eyes were flint, his hands and uniform stained red.

Tan gaped at him.

Keskan held up one glistening finger. "Not a single word from you. I just saved your worthless life." He glanced back at the body. "I'll have to say someone jumped him, and when they start looking, they'll come up with you. I'll give you half a fucking hour, then I have to report this."

Why report—? Because of the blood.

Keskan could claim his uniform got soaked while trying to stop him bleeding out, but only if he found him within moments of the stabbing. Even half an hour was a crazy long delay.

As if edging past a wildcat, Tan crept around Keskan, holding his eyes for as long as he could. Looking away was like turning his back on a gun. His legs were jelly, the concrete clinging onto his feet like a marsh. The lamps threw ghost light across the streets, turning the buildings into scratches of black and white. The space around him expanded like water, and vibrations bounced, as if he'd grown bats' ears to hear shapes in the dark. His body trembled, disconnected from his control.

He tried to keep his mind level. He owed that to Dezdenec. It didn't make sense, but it was true. Dezdenec would have wanted him to fail: he was—had been—a true believer in the One. And yet if the Bridge did not come down, Dezdenec's death would be for nothing.

The road to the Bridge was wide and straight, forming an L with the north road toward Knotty Vines. Every forty feet or so, a lamp cast a circle of light. Passing footmen looked him over but didn't stop.

A faint wail rose across the land and ground its way into his heart—a train, moaning like the voice of the dead. Silence, moan, silence, a distant shriek of rusted wheels on metal. The sound drew him and repelled him at once. In some corner of his mind, he fell into the gods' realm. *Behind the veil, we all are One.* He took several breaths and set his eyes on the road, set his ears on the crunch of his feet on the gravel.

In a lonely shadow between streetlights, he halted and took the oil skin from his pack. He loosened its cork. He could spill the oil that way if need be, but better to let it drip through a leak. He felt his pocket, making sure he had his bore needle handy to quickly make a hole. In his other pocket, he had a flint to light the oil, but ideally that shouldn't be his job. Apáshan's hunters should be waiting to light the fire from below.

The sack heavy in his hand, he made for the Bridge.

Two people stood on watch at the north bank, one tall, one short, a man and a boy. Tan didn't know the man, but he knew the outline of the boy by heart.

Fucking gods, Keskan had made good. He told Fashen he'd get Ash out to the River, and fuck if he hadn't done just that.

Tan felt dizzy, tipping. His steps brought him forward as if against his will.

He steered toward Ash, but the man said, "Hold. Your ID, boy."

"C-4, Fourth Year Ren." He tried to face the man respectfully, but he could scarcely take his eyes off his brother's face.

He went through the rigamarole about the medicine by rote, thinking, *When did his face get older? It's been just over a month since that last night in the tent.* Thinking, *Somehow he knows. He knows I killed Dezdenec.* Though Tan had not killed Dezdenec, he remembered with a shock.

"My captain confirmed this shipment would be coming." Ash's voice sprang out the night like a memory.

"Did he?" said the footman. "It's cleared by Commander Shonco, then?"

"I don't know, sir," said Tan. "I'm acting on Commander Beyo's orders." He was taking a guess that Beyo still commanded C-4.

"My captain said it came from his briefing, sir," said Ash.

Was it Tan's imagination, or did his eyes jab deeper every time he said, "my captain"?

"All right then," said the footman. "I'll escort you up the Bridge."

Fuck. An escort was the last thing he needed. Pulling his eyes away from Ash, Tan followed him.

They climbed the ramp up to the Bridge, its floodlights like dandelion puffs shifting as they neared. The flat clap of their boots on the planks took on a deeper reverberation as they stepped over the water. A few steps more and a clunk came from below, as if something had struck one of the piles. Animal maybe. His comrades maybe, at their boats.

"Stop there," the guard ordered. They both went still, listening to the River's rush. "Did you hear that?"

"Yes, sir." No point lying when it was obvious.

"We've sighted a lot of boats today, more than we ought to. Those invaders retreating from Fennoc's maybe."

Oak men retreating would head upstream toward Oak. But Tan was not about to contradict the footman.

The footman took a hand light from his belt and shone it at the embankment: rocks, dirt, weeds, a glint of lapping water. Tan tensed, ready to drop the skins and pull his gun—no, he couldn't shoot. That would alert everyone. If the man spotted his companions, Tan would draw his knife, like Keskan. Though he was far from certain he could take a large man on his guard, if he let him give the alarm, they were finished. They waited, ears straining.

Finally, Tan said, "Can I go on ahead, sir? I'll be late."

The footman glowered at him. "Come on."

Their feet thunked on the wooden slats. The ground before them seemed to shimmer, ghostly in the white lamps. Think, think. He had almost accomplished his mission. He just needed to start dribbling out the oil. But he couldn't do a damn thing with this footman by his side.

Think.

"Sir, did you hear that?"

The footman stopped, scared. "What?"

"That sloshing below. Listen, sir."

The water swished.

In a low voice, Tan said, "I didn't want to scare the kid back there, but walking over here, I heard scrabbling down the bank. And, you know, there's been unrest up the river in Naimu's Town."

"Had the sub arrived by the time you left Fennoc's?"

Tan didn't know what he meant. "No, sir," he ventured, and the footman accepted it with a nod.

Tan made a show of looking out at the river. To his relief, the man followed his gaze and walked to the rail to look over. Tan took the boring needle from his pocket and punctured his skin. He held it low to the ground to mask the dribble of oil. He swung the skin gently and shifted here and there as if nervous.

"I've got to keep going, sir. I'm late."

He hoped against hope that the footman would tell him to go on by himself while he went back to shore up Ash's position. He didn't, and Tan wasn't senior enough to suggest it. They walked on.

"Smells, doesn't it?" the guard remarked.

"Yes, sir," said Tan. "I guess it's a really strong medicine."

Think.

At some point, he'd simply have to spill the oil. Wait till someone gave the alarm, then spill it fast and jump if he wasn't shot first. Maybe he could make a show of the bag's leaking—run around like an idiot, spilling the oil?

Then, he saw an orange flicker from the corner of his eye, down below the Bridge ahead of him. A curious relief rushed through him. The glow guttered. Was it real? Was it wishful thinking? It came back, a little brighter.

"Sir," he gasped, "I think... that's fire!"

"What?"

"There!" Tan scuttled toward the light, squeezing out oil as he went.

The footman was right beside him.

"Fuck, we're under attack!" yelled the footman.

Shouts erupted. In the chaos, Tan crouched and pulled out his striker, struck it. Nothing. He tried again. Sudden pain flashed in his face. He recoiled and rolled, face buried in his arms, arms smothered under him. Smoke burned his eyes and the overwhelming mint fumes choked him.

"Fire!" Feet pounded.

His leg fell over an edge into empty air. He scrambled back onto the Bridge. No, he was supposed to jump and let his comrades pull him from the water. No, he needed to get back to Ash.

He found his feet and ran for the north bank. A scatter of gunshots sounded. He couldn't tell if any were aimed at him. The Bridge throbbed underneath to the rhythm of his feet. Blurs of orange spiked the night, to his right off at the eastern pile, on the boards beneath him where his shadow danced.

He reached the north embankment and burst through a couple footmen in his way. They shouted something; he didn't heed them.

"Ash!"

He wasn't at his station.

"Ash!"

Maybe he'd already gone down to the boats.

Levering himself against a post, he whipped around and rushed down the slope, skidding on mud and rock in the dark. The flames licked high and hot, and shadowed specters flickered, running, rowing, disconnected from the shouts unifying the night.

"Ash!"

He tried to make some sense of the movement around him, to find the small figure.

"Where are you?"

"Tan!"

He couldn't localize the voice.

"Ash?"

"Here."

He looked around madly and spotted a hand waving in the rocky shallows.

Tan sped to meet him, cracking his knee on a rock. He slipped into the muddy water, up to his calves, the cold filling his boots.

"Ash." He crouched beside him and grasped his hand, needing the solidity of touch in the dark. "We got to go. Those low boats, they're our men, but we've got to get out there before they get shot." He yanked on Ash's arm, met with resistance. "Listen, it'll be okay. There's a place for you, people from our *sélnua*: they're still alive."

"Our what?"

Tan stared. "Never mind. I'll tell you later. We got to go."

"I can't." The fire shadows made a mask of Ash's face.

"Don't be stupid. It's all set, come on."

"I need to stay here and help Keskan."

The words hit him like a slap in the face. For a moment, the sounds of battle receded.

"Ash..."

Ash reached out and touched his cheek. It hurt; he'd forgotten that he'd been burned. "He needs backup, Tan. We can do it. We can win, but he needs me here, and we need you there. I got to go." He rose.

Tan grabbed him. "Ash, I came for you. Look, I'm sorry—I'm sorry about... everything."

Ash crouched again and put a hand on his shoulder. "I got to go and report in before Shonco gets suspicious."

Tan held onto him.

"Let go of me." He tugged against Tan's grip.

A gun went off too close, voices too close... closing.

Tan clung on, grappling him down into the rocks. "Ash, I'm not fucking around."

"Tánashen!" A woman's voice came over the din. Jeyza, Fashen?

He didn't pay attention. He hauled Ash toward the River, slick in the mud. Ash flailed, just like that day when Tan had pulled him away from Júzian. At a wild lurch from Ash, Tan slid and fell. Ash snaked out of his arms. He was slipping away, already a specter in the shadows. Tan dashed after him and tackled him.

Through the fog of their struggle, a word leapt out.

"Dezdenec!"

Tan lost his grip. Ash kicked his ribs, but Tan grabbed an ankle and held him like a vice.

"...he is!" Keskan's voice, uphill somewhere. "He killed Dezdenec..." Something garbled. "...get him, Gomu!"

He looked wildly into the flame-licked shadows. Figures ran everywhere. The heat poured down and he could hardly tell the gunshots from the popping of the fire.

Ash had shaken off his hand and was scrabbling away, stark in the firelight.

"Ash!"

Someone yanked him up. He whirled and punched them. Jeyza stumbled back.

He spun back to face Ash but couldn't see him, only red people running in the blaze, only the blaze giving life to the shadows.

Mint burned in his lungs.

"The Bridge is about to come down, you fool." Jeyza was in front of him. "We've got to get the boat."

He made a dodge to get past her, but someone grabbed him. He struggled now, as Ash had struggled, and for an instant, he was free. Then, something smacked his head, and as he reeled, the hands seized him again.

"Take him now!" Jeyza was several feet away, crouched and aiming her bow in the direction Ash had fled.

"No!" Tan tried to shout, but he was being dragged away, feet losing purchase. The River soaked him to the thighs. The world had broken into pieces—scalding and water, flame and shadow.

The Bridge roared above him, red and gold, like Death and the Way. Pieces of beams tumbled over them, hissing in the waves. Sparks flew. His eyes stung. A scrap of flaming wood fell on his arm; he threw it off. Then, the roar was receding and the fiery rain behind them.

Chapter Thirty-Six

In the summer half-season of Wind Watch, the crush of the heat lasted deep into the evening. Sweat pouring beneath his broad-brimmed hat, Tan slipped and slid up the deer trail, over bone dry dirt and slick husks of bleached grass.

In the month since the burning of the Bridge, the fighting in the Borderlands had only intensified. Where the Citadel once marched troops over the Bridge, now it transported them in its underwater ship, deploying its units anywhere it wished along the River. Stationed with a small group of hunters south of Knotty Vines, Tan was getting well versed in guerrilla defense.

When they'd regrouped after the burning of the Bridge, Ash had not been with Jeyza.

"You Oak men promised you'd get him," Tan snarled.

"From what I saw he didn't want to be got," she said.

"He's a child. He doesn't know what's best for him."

And that might be true, but Jeyza's words were true too. *He didn't want to be got.* Ash wouldn't leave until the Citadel surrendered, so Tan would fight till they surrendered.

When he reached the shriveled chestnut leaves that formed a curtain across the path, a voice said, "None too subtle, Bridge Burner. You're like a boar in the brush."

"Mica Melting Fashen?" He stopped, winded from the climb.

"Get under cover."

Tan joined him in the shade of the chestnuts. "When did you get in?"

Caked with dust and smelling of sweat, Fashen handed him a waterskin. "Morning. And I don't have much time. I've got to get to Batty Hyrax; that's a long blasted hike."

Keskan's village. "Why Batty Hyrax?"

"To get help from the rings."

"The rings?"

"Do you live under a rock? The Hyraxers, they wear rings, yeah? Word is, they've thrown off Fenorn, so if we're lucky, they can spare reinforcements down south."

"So why are you here then?"

"For you, what do you think? The alliance leaders want you, so if you have stuff to finish up here, better get to it fast."

"No, nothing to finish." There'd been a Fenorn camp, only three men, which meant they were scouts on the lookout for Kiri camps. But they were gone now; Tan had shot them.

🐾

The leaders were encamped a day southeast at a cave in the scrub woods. Their sentry had apparently been watching for Fashen's approach because Apáshan strode out to greet them as soon as they were in sight of the camp.

"Red Leaf Tánashen." He folded his hands. "It does my eyes good to see you. Come eat and drink."

Surprised by what seemed his genuine good feeling, Tan greeted him in return and moved to follow, but then stopped short.

He hadn't expected to see Sajem. He should have, Sajem was one of the leaders, but he hadn't. So it threw him to see him there by the mouth of the cave, grubby and older than the last time they'd met, his Oak tunic traded for the deer skins hunters wore, his arms bare to the summer heat. He looked out of place, in the same way Tan was. He gave Tan a weak smile.

Tan cocked his head in unspoken question, he didn't even know what question.

But though there could never be mind-reading between them, Sajem seemed to read his mind. He shook his head minutely and made a gesture that said *later*.

Tan gave him a nod and walked by.

Inside, it smelled of summer and pheasant roasting on a spit. The fire in its pit defied the passing of the day, prolonging the vanished sun's heat. Ample water wet the grass around the pit. It must have been a lot of work to haul it up from the arroyo, but that was the price of a safe summer fire.

At a gesture from Apáshan, Tan skirted the fire and entered the interior. Illuminated with a mix of twilight and flame, woodsmoke swirled lazily. Though four or five hunters ranged outside, the cave itself was empty except for the leaders of the alliance: Apáshan, the Burner, Jeyza, Tan with Fashen, and now Sajem, slipping in behind them.

"Well met, Knotty Vines Tánashen," said the Burner. "Come eat, and then we have much to discuss."

❧

Restored by pheasant and water, Tan felt strangely equal to whatever the alliance wanted. It would be wrong to call him eager or expectant. He was waiting. He felt ready now for what came next: one step and then another. That was all anyone could do.

"Sajem, my son, do you still have objections?"

To what? Tan wondered.

Sajem shook his head, not meeting his father's eyes. "No. Hunter Apáshan is right. The Borderlands can't feed more warriors from Oak."

"Then let's proceed. Lady Jeyza."

She nodded. "We could fight Fenorn for years with our hunters and warriors, and maybe eventually beat them back, but only at the cost of great loss of life and destruction of land—"

"Yes, I said I am done with objections," snapped Sajem.

Jeyza glanced at him coolly and produced a pouch from which she took a cube with some dials and switches, small enough to fit in the palm of her hand. "Or we can stop them now."

"Is that it?" asked Tan, "the device?"

"Our only way to stop that underwater ship."

"How?" asked Tan. "That ship's a giant hulk of steel. You said—Lord Sajem said—your device wasn't a nuke."

"Don't be stupid," said Jeyza, turning the cube in her hands. "What's the great weakness of higher tech? The great dependence?"

"Electricity," said Sajem wearily.

Jeyza held up the cube. "We'll shut off its power."

"With that thing?" said Tan.

"It's an auxiliary antigravity calibrator."

Apáshan laughed.

"If you wanted us to understand tech talk," said Fashen, "tell your Teacher to teach tech use, not its limits."

"In spaceships that use antigravity fields, it's designed as manual backup for adjusting the field if computer control fails."

"Still not helping."

"Then let me try again," said Jeyza. "This particular device has been set to exert a force pushing away from its center. That means, wherever it's activated, lines of force will radiate out from it. Imagine someone pulling your arms and legs apart. It's like that. If it's set in the middle of an engine, for example, it will push the components out of alignment and the engine will malfunction. We could use it to disrupt their electrical lines. We could use it to disable their monster ship."

Tan could not follow all of her words, but his Citadel mind had the essence. If it could disable the ship, then the burning of the Bridge would not have been for nothing. They'd bring the Citadel to a standstill.

"And here's the beauty of it," she said. "If this device fell into Fenorn's hands, the nature of tech limitation makes us impervious to serious harm. The device could kill a human or a hill-jack. It might knock down a building or start a landslide. But we have no electrical lines to disrupt; we have no monster ships, no trains. We could devastate their power, but the worst they could do to us is local damage."

"But if they used it on us over and over?" said Apáshan.

"There, Hunter, you've touched the two-edged sword. Separated from its power source, it can only be used once. Someone has to switch it on, and then that person has to run before the field fully powers up and twists apart their organs. After that, the device will generate its field until it runs out of power, which should be about a quarter hour. Then, it will be drained; it will be useless."

"Could Fenorn recharge it?" asked Sajem.

"It can't be charged by conventional electric current. It's... well, I don't understand what it is, but it needs to be charged in a tech center or onboard a spaceship."

"Have you tested it?" he said.

"The tech center keeper tested it before she released it, Enátha."

"A remarkable tool in theory," said Apáshan. "But only if we can break into a Fenorn stronghold. If a human can outrun it, its range can't be far, yes?"

"About twenty feet."

"So how do we break into the ship?" said Tan.

The Burner cracked a smile.

"From what I've heard, we can't," said Fashen. "It's all over the River and crawling with warriors."

"The Grid is the basis of their electrical supply in the north," said Jeyza. "That ship needs to charge its batteries to run. So does the train. If we gut the Grid's power, we'll eliminate all their mass transport, including their ability to run supplies to the Citadel."

"And the people in the Citadel will starve," said Sajem.

"They've brought that on themselves," said Apáshan.

No, they haven't, thought Tan. His mind, for some reason, flicked to Aunt Tson.

"We'll ensure they won't if their high priest surrenders," said the Burner.

High priest? He must mean the Landowner.

"Even as we speak, Sajem, your mother is in the Oaks, at the tech center, standing by at the radio. She's authorized to offer terms on behalf of the Kept Worlds, including emergency supplies and materials to repair their gardens, their... hydro— hydroponics."

Tan considered that. "Most of their men are in the north now," he said. "The well at the Citadel is probably fixed by now too. That may give the rest some time for supplies to get through."

"Then we target the Grid," said the Burner, his eyes on his son, but Sajem held his peace.

"We can't force our way into the Grid with bows and arrows," said Tan.

Fashen chuckled. "Since when have the Borderlands ever done anything by brute force?"

"We need a ruse," said Apáshan, "one they'll believe. Red Leaf Tánashen, you're our lore-holder on the Grid. Anything you can tell us of their ways may be useful."

Tan didn't know what to say. What ruse would get them into the Grid? They were all hated or held in contempt. No chance could Tan fake his way in again. They'd have to come as captives...

"They know me at the Grid," said Jeyza. "I visited the Citadel decades ago. I could claim to be an envoy, to attempt negotiations—"

"No," said Sajem. "That kind of deception would beggar our attempts at truce. There has to be a weak spot in their defenses."

But for Tan, a realization was unfurling like a flower. "I know the geothermal plant."

"The what now?" asked Fashen. Tan had used Citadel words.

"The place that makes their electricity. I've done work there. I know it. I mean, I don't know a lot about how it works, but I know what it looks like and where the main machinery is."

"Can you draw us a map?" said Jeyza.

Tan had rarely held a pen or brush in his life. "I could maybe draw something, but that doesn't matter. I'll go in person."

"No," snapped Sajem. "You're too well known."

"He's right," said Fashen. "After the Bridge, they're out for you." He measured him up. "Did you actually hit Waxwing?"

"Waxwing?"

"Waxwing Keskan, dimbat."

"Hit him? No." *Not recently*.

"Well, he must be quite an actor." He broke into a smile. "I was on the lookout, you know, as the Bridge was going up, and you could hear his voice all across the valley, shouting at his head warrior how you'd clubbed him and killed one of their men. He puts on a good show of hating you."

Tan felt himself go still and dangerous, unable to pinpoint where his anger at Keskan bled into Fashen or himself. Why should he even be angry at all? Tan knew Keskan had given him the blame for Dezdenec. He'd been right to. If he was going to survive that conflagration without trumpeting that he'd let Tan reach the Bridge, he'd better damn well have a good story. Keep Tan the enemy—it was a good bluff; Shonco knew there was no love between them.

"I agree with Sajem," said Jeyza. "Their priests must surely have their minds bent to find you. Even if we find a weak spot in their defenses, you're the last person we'd want to try to sneak in."

"But I won't be sneaking in," said Tan. "I'll let them capture me."

Sajem made a noise that was almost a scoff, as if Tan had said something to offend him.

But the Burner said, "Go on."

"If Keskan can arrange to be on guard, then all he has to do is get his hands on me, him or somebody loyal to him. He can give me a good shaking and palm the device. After that, it shouldn't be too hard for him to fake an errand in the plant and put the device where it can break things."

"And you?" said Sajem.

Tan shrugged. "They'll probably kill me." They'd probably gut him and eat him, but he wouldn't think about that now. Maybe one of his boys would shoot him.

Jeyza gave a slight smile Tan could not interpret.

"We can't accede to that," said Sajem. "I will not throw away your life."

"What's your big concern with my life?"

Sajem held up a hand as Oak men did to say *wait*. "But using Keskan's team makes sense. Yowlers Fashen, can we fake a reason to get Keskan assigned to the Grid? Maybe one of your trackers could slip him the device."

"We may be able to swing getting him to the Grid." He eyed the ground thoughtfully. "Yes, maybe one more time before it's obvious we're playing their commander. But we couldn't palm him the device, not near the Grid. There's no cover for a meeting. And if we passed it off in Free of Ford, he'd have to hide it for days. Or what if we gave it to him and then he wasn't reassigned after all or was attacked before he got there?"

"People die all the time." Tan was glaring at Sajem. "They die of gunshots and arrows. You've killed them, I've killed them. What makes my life so valuable?"

Sajem gave him a hard look. "What makes your brother's life valuable?"

Inside Tan, a flame ignited. "That's *my* concern. He's my *sélnutor*. I'm not yours. That has nothing to do with this."

"Oak Sajem," said Apáshan. "This choice is his. A hunter who offers himself freely is free to choose his path."

"Then, we're agreed," said the Burner. "We assault the Grid."

Chapter Thirty-Seven

Dawn broke with a quiet pink and trace of dew that would soon vanish. Dressed in a Citadel uniform, a little too big, Tan was ready to depart, and yet not ready. For a moment, as the camp began to stir, he felt nothing but a desire to stay there in this scrubby corner of the Garden, as if he was an old, water-stressed pine, peaceably extending its gnarled limbs across the centuries.

As he sat on some rocks, he heard a step behind him.

Sajem sat beside him. "Beautiful dawn."

Tan made an affirmative noise. All at once, he felt on the brink of tears and fighting a swell of terror.

"I'm sorry," said Sajem. Perhaps he'd sensed Tan's fear, not through mind-reading but something more basic, because his own voice suddenly cracked. "I failed you. I made a promise I haven't honored."

Tan clamped himself down to make sure he would not yell, because, yes, it was all one giant failure, Sajem's and his and everyone's, and it did no damn good to harp on it.

Instead, he said, "They brought me Ash at the Bridge. It isn't your fault he refused to come with me."

Sajem wiped at the tears on his face. By gods, the man cried easily. "I'm sorry all the same. This... You shouldn't have to do this."

"Why do you care so much what happens to me?"

Sajem did not answer at once. "Because you amaze me. You're everything I'm not."

Tan felt suddenly afraid to move, as if his mere human motion would break some porcelain expectation.

They sat in silence for a little.

Then Sajem said, "You're really not afraid of dying?"

"I'm plenty afraid of dying. But then again, dying's something we all have to do." His mind strayed to Júzian. "There are worse things than dying for a good reason."

"I want to promise you we'll get you out."

Tan cracked a hard smile.

"But I know I can't. I know you're right. You'll probably die, and I can't even promise that we'll rescue Ashtyn for you." The sunlight threw a smear of gold across the hills. Soon Tan would have to be leaving. "I can't—I don't want to face that reality. You'll be swept back into *mirya*, and the loss will be mine."

It seemed to Tan he should feel something, but the words bounced off him. Or maybe they hit him like rain on the rocks, bouncing and penetrating both, transforming the dust into a living smell of rain.

It was odd to be valued that way. Shonco sometimes approved of him, but always across a distance. Linóvi loved him because she had to: he was her *sélnutor*. It was the same for Ash. Some of his boys looked up to him—or used to—because he'd taken decent care of them. But the only one who'd really seemed to value *him* for who he was had been Dezdenec.

"I'm not coming back," he said. "But if I come back..." What was he trying to say? "If I come back, I'll come back to you. Somehow."

Sajem glanced at him with some show of surprise. "I didn't mean—you don't owe me..."

Tan rose. "It's not about owing. It's just I'm everything you're not, so I guess you sort of need me."

Sajem gave a small laugh.

"Now, pull yourself together," said Tan. "If I can, you can."

Chapter Thirty-Eight

The River in the Ribbon light had a crystalline flicker as Jeyza plied the oars of the skiff, pulling forcefully against the current. They were east of the Grid, deep in Citadel territory but also away from the heaviest fighting. Up in those gray night hills to the north was Batty Hyrax, Keskan's home. But they were headed toward the southern shore. They'd cross the River as straight as they could, then head by foot, west to the Grid. In the distance, it shone as a halo of white, like a second Ribbon rising out of the earth. He pressed his fingers to the hard surface of the anti-grav device, stitched into a hidden lining in his pocket.

The rush of the current drowned the night, leaving nothing but the flashing waves. Tan had come to fear the spirit of the River. It was his passage into murdering Dawn Rock Ren, the flaming ruins of his bid to rescue Ash. He came back to it like a proving ground his spirit could not cross.

His thoughts were interrupted by a howl of straining metal.

"What is that?" whispered Jeyza.

A little bit north of the Grid, white pinpricks mixed with yellow; then a spark of red and blue coasted like stars in the water.

"They're launching the ship, aren't they?" she said.

The lights glided out and down, vanishing one by one. They watched it for a handful of minutes in silence.

"Let's hope it's headed west," she said.

"No reason to head east," said Tan.

Ahead, the riverbank lay dark and peaceful. There were no towns to fight over here, just Low in Mouth, Lavan's home, a good dozen miles away, and it was faithful to the Citadel. They slipped toward the reeds that were rising now like a fuzz of silver in the mist.

"Shh," said Jeyza, though Tan hadn't said anything. She suspended her oars, the River speaking gently over them.

Then he heard it, a man's voice in Citadel tones. It was Tan's plan to get captured, but it had to be by Keskan, and his rebels wouldn't be this far east.

"I'm going to pull us in as softly as I can," breathed Jeyza, nudging the boat toward the shore, down the sluggish marsh current. "Get down."

He strapped on his helmet and did his best to disappear against the bottom of the boat.

The River rocked against the oars. On the bank, the quiet held. The reeds were brushing past them now, the bright mist like a river Ribbon. He hoped they'd be lost in it.

He was wrong.

A shot rang out and Jeyza hissed, the oar torn from her right hand.

"Out," she commanded as a second shot rang.

Tan seized his pack and went over the side, the chill water stinging and tugging, but his feet were solid in the mud. He reached for his gun and realized he'd just let it get soaked in the water. He drew his knife instead.

Third shot.

He sank low in the reeds, just high enough to breathe. He couldn't see Jeyza. She'd ditched the boat the same time as him but in the slosh and waves, he'd lost track of her.

Beneath the River's rustling, a silence coiled. He waited, seeing nothing but sky and reeds. They waited too, the others.

Then, up in the shallows, something slithered.

Another shot fractured the night, close enough to stun his ears. He couldn't hear what came next, but the water pitched, sluicing silt into his nose. He choked and snorted.

The next sound that came to him was a strangled cry, far and flat to his tender ears—a man's cry, not Jeyza's, then an arrow's thwack.

He waited.

"Tánashen." Jeyza's voice, up on the bank.

He waited. If their enemies were near, she'd just made herself their target.

Nothing happened.

"Tánashen, are you there?"

"Here." He made his way toward her, shivering as he hauled himself out of the water onto the marshy grass.

"Is that you—? Thank luck." Jeyza hurried to him. "I put them down. Two of them. I don't think there are others, but we'd better move. You have it?"

Tan fingered the device in his pocket. "It got wet."

She sighed. "Can't be helped. Let's go."

They headed into the hills, up where the pines glinted silver, and finally settled in a declivity shadowed by a dwarf pine. Tan had some waterlogged bread and dried yams in his pack. He kept two yam slices in reserve and shared the rest with Jeyza, who'd lost her pack when abandoning the boat.

"Did you get hurt?" he asked her.

"Just grazed."

"Let me see." He couldn't see much in the dimness but did his best to get a bandage wrapped around her upper arm.

Shoulder to shoulder, they shivered as the dawn grayed the sky.

"This is as good a place as any to wait out the day," said Jeyza.

Tan felt torn between his legs' desire for rest and his heart's determination to plunge ahead, but the plan was the plan, and it said show up tomorrow. So in the sweet warmth of the morning, rest won out.

He reached into his pocket to assure himself the little cube was still there.

"Do you think the device will work even though it got wet," he asked?

After a moment, she said, "It's very high tech. My guess is it's waterproof. But I should have asked Enátha. Stupid."

Another thought occurred. "If it's anti-gravity, how do its parts stay in place? Wouldn't it blow itself apart?"

"Ah, that I do know. Its effects are reduced in its immediate vicinity, for just a hands-breadth or so. Don't ask me how, I'm not a tech keeper."

She stabbed a lizard that had come out to sun on a rock. They thanked it and split it. She attempted to skin her half, but Tan crunched his half whole.

"That's good," she said. "Assume you'll live. A true warrior always plans to live."

"It's not about living. I'm just hungry."

As the sun penetrated deeper into their hideout, Jeyza took her *shulin* off her head and unwrapped it, draping the wide scarf as a shade across the two of them.

"You need to find a way forward," she said. "You can't live on death."

"Isn't that what we all do, Lady Jeyza?" He gestured at the lizard skin at her feet.

"I'm not talking about *mirya*, clever pants. I mean the mind must bend on living. I'm alive, and I've seen my fill of death. My mother, my brother's widow, my nephews, cousins: the instant the bomb fell on the West Men's city, all of them died, but a piece of them remains as long as I'm living."

She came from the West Men, like her father. In the back of his mind, he'd know that, but he hadn't stopped to think about it. But now, to hear her count off the dead, it snapped her into focus. She'd lost her *sélnua*—or the West equivalent, just like Tan, her home city razed cleaner than Knotty Vines. Yet here she was, undefeated.

"You're Rendyen's daughter," he said, understanding a little better now.

"We were away when the bombing happened, he and I, fighting north of the city."

"Oak massacred your family, yet you live with them."

"Well, I'd be fool to hold a grudge for thirty years just because some stupid—" She broke off. "You think they bombed us on purpose, don't you?"

Tan stared at her, uncomprehending.

She nodded. "I forget how many Borderlanders think that. The Oaks lets them, of course. It's less embarrassing than the truth."

"What truth? Your peoples were at war."

"We were at war with *Noryen*, boy. Think for a minute. The Oaks is just a province of the Western kingdom; we were allies against Noryen. It was them we intended to bomb—well, not me; I didn't know anything about it. It was Nermártan's uncle who was warden in those days. The stupid idiot didn't understand targeting."

"The West Men weren't the target?"

"No, my lad, the Oaks' own king was not their target. They nuked us by mistake. Damn fool was so embarrassed he pretended he had planned it—and massacred the Borderlands to prove he was a real warlord."

Something in Tan went hard and cold.

"The Massacre was a cover for a mistake?"

"It would be easy to say, 'That's *men* for you,' but the reality is it's merely power plus desperation."

"Sajem lied to me."

"Really?" A hint of surprise.

He'd said it was a mistake but... "Maybe his *words* didn't lie, but he never even hinted..."

Jeyza settled back a little deeper in the shade, wincing as she shifted her injured arm. "Well, if he lied, I'm sure he did it badly. He's indefatigably honest and constitutionally incapable of shutting up. But I expect he thought the truth would be too much."

It was too much. Images flooded his mind—Ordan, Ash's accusing eyes, the Burner shooting Dad in the face. He could still damn well see it, but in his mind, Keskan said, *Of course the Citadel killed your parents.*

"This world's built on mistakes and lies," he said. "It... rides them, like a boat."

Jeyza gave a little laugh. "I'll tell you what, that bombing scared the living piss out of the Grid. They'd been our friends, you see, the West Men's friends, I mean. My father helped found the Grid. It was their easternmost base." She fell silent. "Looking back, I expect that the bombing was the start of the Citadel's militarizing. They must have figured they'd be next."

"Funny," said Tan. "That's what they always said. Those blasted, blasted liars, and you're telling me that's the truth."

"I don't think I've ever met a lie that didn't have a core of truth. And maybe I've never met a truth that wasn't slightly lying."

❧

Blue Aldu-la rose in advance of the Ribbon, a spark heralding the silver night.

Jeyza rose. "All right. Remember to unbutton your pocket before they can detain you. And when you get out, you and Ashtyn both, remember, we'll have men waiting in the southeast." She pressed his hand in the dark. "I think you may live."

"But if I don't, you'll help Ashtyn—if you can?"

She hesitated. "I'll help defeat the Citadel, and that's what he wants, isn't it?"

He watched her make her way up River, bow on her back and quiver half empty, until she was lost in the shadows. Then he began to pick his way up higher in the hills, as if retracing that last day of Júzian's life.

Did your spirit tell me to come? To finish what you started and get Ash free?

But only the chill of night answered.

As his steps crunched across the rocks, he reviewed the plan. The story Fashen had established with Keskan was simple and, like many lies, not so far from the truth. Keskan would tell Shonco that his contact (Fashen) had informed him of a Kiri plot to break into the Grid through a weak point in the fencing. Keskan would request to be on guard at that place. He'd give the Kiris a signal that it was safe to advance, and then the Citadel would close in—that's what he'd tell Shonco.

That was one place the plan might break. Shonco or his superiors might demand that Keskan describe the place and assign others to go on guard instead. There was no guarantee C-16 was even at the Grid. They'd been stationed out at Friend of Fennec when Fashen and Keskan had last met.

But no use worrying about that now.

Tan's stomach complained, but he didn't know the terrain well enough to gather food, and he guessed it wouldn't amount to more than a few herbs in any case.

Maybe Keskan would shoot him. If that happened, then it was out of his hands, and good luck to Keskan pulling off all the rest.

Would Keskan shoot him? Could he be that kind?

Or would it have nothing to do with kindness? Maybe if Tan tackled him hard enough, maybe he'd just shoot by instinct...

In the waning night, the first songbirds woke and ignited a nauseous fear in Tan. It had come, the final day. But as the horizon grayed, he breathed the mist and began to walk bolder through the pine stubble. His legs no longer shook. The body was strange that way, breakable and strong, a piece of *mirya*.

≥⋆

Even though he intended to be caught, he grew cautious as he neared the Grid. He had never approached the Grid from the east, and though he knew it well by map, rock by rock, it took concentration to pick his way. He had to keep low; it wouldn't do to be caught by the wrong soldier. The morning had gotten away from him, and the land was now almost fully lit, too bright for hiding and already beginning to soak up heat.

He saw the plumes of steam before anything else, as if the crags spewed their own cloud cover. The terns had been dogging his steps for some time, shrieking and winging like spirits awaiting revenge. Voices popped in and out of his ears, subject to air currents or the placement of a hill slope.

The morning surrendered to the terns and beneath their wings the earth lay still. Like peace, he thought, like the desert evening. Maybe peace was nothing more than a pausing in the violence.

He could smell the sulfur now. He could hear the rumble of the power plant and the buzz of the electric grid. That was one of the signs Fashen had given. If all went to plan, he'd find Keskan by an electric tower. Tan pointed his steps toward the sound. He could see it now, like the statue of the He self-unified in sanity, symmetrical lines locking into elegant triangles. Cresting a hill, he saw the fence, three layers of wire. How could Keskan even bluff the idea that they'd break in? How could they break in? No, there would be no Kiri attack, not unless the Grid collapsed in such chaos that they could just bludgeon down the main gate.

But Tan didn't need to break in. He saw the place, a stand of discarded square-hewn stone hard up against the outer fence.

He saw no people. That told him they were watching for him. Any ordinary day at the Grid, its perimeter would be far more obviously guarded.

He crouched down and unbuttoned his pocket to make the device easy game when he fell.

Then he crept toward the fence. He'd been armed with a small set of shears for cutting through the fence if he got that far, but he had lost it when they capsized. What if he got to the fence? What should he do, pretend to fumble for his lost gear, dig for an opening?

The barbed wire loomed before him and the tower whirred like a hornets' nest.

"Stop there."

Tan froze. The words were Kiri but heavily accented, not Keskan's voice and too low to be anyone from C-16.

"Do not move."

"You!" The yell broke so furiously Tan jumped. "You fucking traitor shit, you're mine!"

Tan spun just in time for Keskan's fist to smash his eye socket. Sparks danced in his eyes. He hit the ground, rocks gouging his arm and hip. By instinct, he rolled and got an elbow jab in, but a second later Keskan had him slammed on his stomach. As his vision swam back, he felt a hand groping at him. He strained to get up. A piece of him remembered this assault was the plan, but his body could not understand it. He got a knee under him and elbowed Keskan again. A footman was shouting. Then, the weight left his pocket and knee struck his back, sending a numb shock down his legs.

"He's mine, the fucking deserter!"

"Get ahold of yourself, Cadet!" The knee was gone from his back. "This isn't your personal vendetta."

"I want him dead, sir, nice and slow."

Tan rolled over to see Keskan, arms pinned by the footman, eyes blazing with a Dezdenec light. Tan couldn't look away. They were black, he knew that. How could they shine like silver? How could two such different men glow with the same hatred?

❧

They tied his hands, stripped off his helmet, and marched him alongside the fence. People appeared around them, as if born from the rocks, a few footmen but mostly cadets. Someone who looked like the ghost of Muned strode up and spit in his face.

"You traitor! You murdering shit!" He had lost so much weight, his skin clung to his stolid bones.

Gomu appeared before him, a fresh bruise making his scars stand out stark. His nose looked wrong and snubbed, like a hyrax. "I will eat your marrow, fucker."

"Steady, boys. He'll pay all right." Keskan's voice came low.

He saw Lavan from the corner of his eye, gaunt and ghoulish. But no Ash.

No Dradam, no Tarnto, no Fendo, no Codo, no Sho.

No Ash?

His heart began to hammer.

"Is Ashtyn dead?" he asked no one in particular.

"Shut the fuck up!" spat Gomu.

There were other boys. Replacements? He tried to count them.

He walked a long way, and his feet kept slipping, as if his boots had lost their tread. The heat piled up in his head and flowed down his throat. Ash was dead—that was the obvious explanation. He was dead and all this shit meant nothing. Even burning the Bridge, what had that accomplished but starving his boys to the bone?

The Grid was weirdly quiet when they marched him through the gate. A handful of soldiers stopped to stare, but the scattered remnant went about their business.

A man he didn't know said, "You're too late, kid. The assault is already underway."

Tan didn't know what assault he meant, but he could imagine the underwater ship pouring troops out, maybe even as far west as Oak.

The gibbet stood before him, plain metal with none of the spirit of the He. That bothered him somehow, that he'd end his life strung to a piece of steel with no spirit. Its lines filled his vision.

Then he was past it. He glanced back in surprise, but Keskan or someone shoved him and kept him walking forward.

Where was Shonco?

When they reached the geothermal plant, it seemed to Tan they were mocking him, taking him right to the heart of the mission, old and lost and late.

"You wait here." Tan couldn't make out who the footman was speaking to, but all the boys fell back, and two footmen marched him through the doors and down the stairs into the bowels of the complex.

The growl of the generator closed around him. In the cold, white lights, the prison bars cast tilted shadows. A door clanged open and crashed behind him. The footmen left. He stood in the cell, six feet of concrete to a side, staring at the figure in the neighboring cell.

Ash lay crumpled on his side, unmoving.

Chapter Thirty-Nine

"Ash?" Tan called. "Ash?"

No response.

He got down on the floor, his body shaking, and reached an arm through the bars, as far as could. Logic said it wouldn't be far enough, but he had to try. He could get his fingers within a foot of Ash's face, but he couldn't reach him. He drew back.

"Ash!"

The face didn't even stir. Was he dead? If he was dead, why lock him up here? Tan watched for the rise and fall of his breaths. Yes, he was breathing. Tan fixed on his face, the hollows under his eyes, the thin stretch of his cheeks. His body told Tan, *You are a failure. You have failed to keep your own baby brother from starving.*

Maybe he *was* starving. Maybe that was why he was out cold. No, it didn't work like that.

Tan himself was not hungry. He had been, but he wasn't now. He'd been beat up, but he scarcely felt it. He was running in some other zone, parallel to his body.

He settled cross-legged and rested a hand on a bar. "Ash, I'm so sorry for all of this shit, I..." He shook his head, the words, like Ash, unreachable.

It was cold down here, with an earthen deadness he'd never really heard before. Deep below, the generator pounded like the heartbeat of an unrestful spirit or the Realm of the Gods when they were lost in despair.

Words came to him from the gods, so it seemed, and he sang,

Landowner's phantom entered into the heart of Loss.
And Loss embraced the phantom as brother, as self,s
Wondering and human in his tears,
And they were unsundered.

Ash stirred and groaned.

"Ash?" Tan started forward and gripped the bars.

Ash's face screwed up, and he blinked blearily. "Tan?" He took in Tan's face, then rolled over, looking around the cell. "Where...?"

"We're in the geothermal plant—or right next to it technically, I guess."

Ash stared. "They got you."

"They were supposed to, Ash. Didn't Keskan tell you?"

Ash shook his head, not a straight denial, Tan thought, a sense of pieces missing. Then, he rubbed his temples, obviously in pain.

"Are you all right? How'd they get you?"

"I was getting ready to go out with the unit. Then, I got so woozy."

"They drugged you. Why? Why you? If they knew this was a setup, why didn't they just drag you off? Why didn't they drag off Keskan?" He was asking himself, not Ash.

Ash merely looked at him bleakly. After a moment, he said, "I guess Commander Shonco knows I let you by at the Bridge."

"You think Keskan told him?"

"Keskan wouldn't."

Like hell, thought Tan. He'd tell him anything if it furthered his plans.

"Maybe Shonco guessed," said Ash. "The story was you knocked me out. I even whacked my head with a stone." He pointed to his brow where a little scar stood out red.

"You're a brave kid, Ash. That was smart." But not smart enough, it seemed, and if Ash had been thrown in prison for helping him. "What about Dradam? He let me by too. Is he...?"

"He died in the fighting after the Bridge."

"He's dead?"

A tight nod.

"Dradam's dead..."

It shouldn't surprise him, yet somehow it did. Why were they doing this if not for people like Dradam? He'd worked so hard, that skinny kid, just so he could go home and live again. He was supposed to go back to Dip and trade in crayfish with Lavan in Low in Mouth.

"How did Lavan take it?"

Ash scoffed. "Well, he didn't turn us in—unless he did. He said he wouldn't—unless he had to. Keskan gave him this look, like, *are you going to be a liability?* And Lavan said, 'If something happens to me, I got friends who know who to look for.' Damn, even Keskan looked impressed."

"Then things got too hot, and he ratted you out, fuck him."

"Fuck *him*? But it was okay when you did it to Juz?"

The words smashed him to the ground. He couldn't find which way was up. "I never said it was okay, but Júzian was captain. He ran out on C-16."

"He didn't."

"Ash, for gods' sake, you were there."

"He wasn't running out. He wasn't. He was going to pick up men in Blue Gums and bring them back to free the others. That's what he told Keskan."

Tan stared at him.

Júzian was going to pick up Kiri troops in Blue Gums and bring them back to storm the Grid? The absurdity made Tan want to laugh; it made him want to cry. It was the sort of thing a kid would plan, a kid with nowhere else to turn.

Then he was crying, the tears sliding out without permission.

Tan swiped at them. "That's a shit plan. We all would have died."

"Maybe. But we would've tried. I'm not sorry that I tried, Tan. The only reason you got this far—the only reason you reached the Grid at all is all the times I kept people busy while Keskan met with that spy, Fashen. It almost worked, maybe, maybe it will work, and I'm not sorry—" He broke off and took a ragged breath.

The room's cold lay around them like the whole universe. So many other places they might be, yet to be here in this room was all that existed.

"Me neither," said Tan. "What I'm sorry about—I'm sorry about Júzian. I'm sorry."

Ash reached his hand through bars, and Tan grasped it.

"I told him I'd protect you. I'm sorry." He pressed Ash's hand to his forehead and held it in both of his own.

"S'okay," said Ash.

It was so not okay that it made Tan laugh, a quiet rumble more felt than heard. But Ash's hand against his forehead soothed him. In some way, things like that were the only things that mattered.

They sat there like that a little while.

In the generator thump of this netherworld came peace.

"Tan." Gently, Ash pulled his hand away. "We got to be ready."

Palms empty, balance tilting, sundered, Tan tried to organize his thoughts. Ready for what? For anything, the next thing.

"Ash, does Commander Shonco believe Keskan?"

"He'd be a fool to."

Tan's head snapped around at the familiar voice. Shonco stood in the corridor that led down to the center of the plant. He looked the same. But, no, he didn't. His eyes gleamed out of hungry circles and a bandage wrapped his right hand and wrist.

He pulled out a set of keys and unlocked Tan's cell, only Tan's, not Ash's. The clank of the door as he yanked it open echoed down the hall.

Tan stepped out. "Let me stand for him." He nodded at Ash. "Let me take the deserter's punishment. He was just following his captain's orders. Keskan..." *Think fast.* "Keskan told him I was a spy working for the Citadel—"

"Tánashen, enough. I am not going to execute you."

Tan stared at him. "Sir, I don't think you have the authority to pardon a deserter."

Commander Shonco eyed him a moment, then laughed. "And *that* is why. *That* is why we need you. Tánashen, you make a poor traitor. Come with me." He started down the hallway.

"Ashtyn..."

"He's safe enough here. For now."

Tan held Ash's eyes a moment before he followed and wished to the gods he had the Kiris' telepathy so he could say something real, like *I love you. I'll save you.*

Commander Shonco led him to a rec room, one of those small subterranean spaces with a table and four chairs. He gestured for Tan to take one and sat opposite.

The commander folded his hands. "I have to say I was a little surprised that Keskan was willing to collaborate with you. I suppose I shouldn't have been. He worked with you as his captain for over a year. He's... opportunistic."

"How long have you known?"

He shrugged. "Well, there's 'know' and there's 'suspect.' I knew when you came back to us at Reason's Town that you hadn't deserted. But I couldn't take you back—or that's how I judged it. I may have judged wrong, gods know we do. With Keskan declaring you an enemy spy, when you'd already run once with Júzian..."

"But isn't that why you have to kill me now, sir?"

A knock sounded on the door.

"Come."

A footman stuck his head in. "We've finished searching him, sir, and put him in the cell by the boy."

"Good. That's all."

The door clicked shut behind him.

"Keskan, sir?" said Tan.

Shonco studied him a moment. "To tell the truth, I wasn't sure he was working for the Kiris till the Bridge. I had suspicions, of course, back as far as the Kiri ambush outside Reason's, but that young man—" He shook his head. "He's such a plausible climber I'm still not sure how much the climbing is part of his game. Did the Kiris make him a better offer? Lord of a village or something?"

"They offered him freedom, sir, freedom from the Citadel." Tan took a certain satisfaction in looking Shonco right in the eye.

"It's a pity," said Shonco. "He could have been a real asset to us. Never mind." He fished in a pocket and pulled out the device, turning its small apple shape in his hands. "This is?"

Tan looked at it. He looked at Shonco. He groped after a clever lie, a misdirection that would rescue the whole plan and Ash with it.

"Sir, with respect, why should I tell you? I'm with them. You know that."

Shonco replaced the device in his pocket. "What if I make *you* a better offer?"

Like lord of a village? He didn't say it. He had too much regard for Shonco.

"Do you really want to live under Oak?"

"Not particularly, sir." It occurred to Tan he didn't know what the Borderlands would be like without the Citadel—with Oak, taxes, men grabbing goats and women...

"I'm glad to hear it," said Shonco. "Because in the end, we will defeat them. They can burn the Bridge. They can send a surge of troops..."

Yet at the Citadel, you said our troops were surging to meet their surge, a surge that hadn't happened yet.

"I suppose they might even overpower our shield with their nukes someday."

No, thought Tan. *You knew they didn't nuke us.*

"But if they nuke the Garden, they lose the land they're fighting for, and we are far too deep in the Garden for anything else to uproot us."

That's probably a lie, thought Tan. *And yet it's probably the truth. They've been in the Garden, some places, for generations. Shonco's own mother's from the Garden. They can't really stop being part of us now. Knotty Vines is theirs now, it's not coming back.*

Shonco leaned forward. "I want you back on the winning side, with Ashtyn."

"Sir, you can't trust me." He found himself speaking as if to a child. "And even if you did, your superiors wouldn't."

Shonco nodded. "I am, in fact, running some risk in displeasing my superiors. I find you worth the risk."

Tan almost laughed. "What for?"

"You're a decent fighter, Tánashen. You're perceptive and intelligent, but no more than a number of other cadets. Dezdenec exceeded you in intelligence. Gomu exceeds you in fighting skill. Ashtyn may exceed you in perception, and Keskan exceeds you in all three. But in one area you surpass any cadet I've ever led—and I hardly know how to put it in words. Honesty? Integrity? A dogged commitment to serving your men?"

Tan's face settled into stone. "You think too highly of me, sir."

"That quality cannot be replicated," said Shonco. "It cannot be taught. Add to that your Kiri background, your ability to negotiate between our peoples. And add to that Keskan's treason. He branded you a traitor. Now that he's exposed as one, his word is meaningless. I can make a case you were maligned. I can make a case you were delivering this to us." He held up the device. "Of course, not everyone would believe it. I couldn't reintegrate you into C-16, but that's not where I mean to send you. I've made my argument to certain priests. You can be sent as a settler to the Garden. Now. With the submarine, we're on the cusp of ending this war. By sheer numbers, we hold all the villages from Twelve *Lányti* east. We cannot be rooted out. You can be an interpreter between our peoples. I've been laying that argument for some time, hoping you'd come back to us. You can prove me right."

Was he right—about the numbers? Even with the ship defeated, were there too many to drive out?

Some of what Shonco said sounded reasonable, and yet the Citadel had no word for 'salamander.' It had no Citadel name for Twelve Salamanders, not yet. It didn't own this world. It would never own it.

Memories of Knotty Vines played through Tan's mind—*Reason's Town*, its hillsides carved into featureless rows, slope bleeding into slope, wider and yet somehow smaller than the place where he was born. No knotted vines, no vines at all, no red leaves, no home for a boy of Red Leaf. No, there was no salvation there. There was no kind of safety.

"What are you going to do with Ashtyn?"

Shonco sat back. "The question is what are you going to do. Ashtyn is a traitor."

"So am I."

"Not by choice. I don't say it with malice, Tánashen. He's a good boy, but he disunites us. The safe thing would be to execute him."

Tan felt his jaw set. "Then you'll have to execute me too."

"But there is a justification for letting him live, and I think you can probably guess it."

Because he was young? Misguided? No. It wasn't that kind of calculation. "To make me obey?"

"For myself, I know that once you give your word, you'll keep it."

Then you don't know me very well, thought Tan.

"But there are those who regard me as partial to you. And they're not mistaken, Tánashen. I like you, but having Ashtyn in reserve would assuage their concerns."

"So he'll just stay in a cell?"

"For a time, he'll have to. But as you earn trust, you'll earn privilege as well. In due course, we can have him transferred to your settlement in the Garden, under custody, of course. Once the war is over and the land is unified, there's no reason he couldn't be released. The more you can assist with that unification, the sooner he'll be free."

Did he really believe the land would ever be One? Maybe he did. Maybe. But he didn't know Apáshan; he didn't know Linóvi. Yet Shonco had known his own mother and father; in a way, his existence made the two peoples one.

"And if I refuse, he'll be executed."

Shonco met his eyes. "As traitors are, yes."

Tan's mind could not hold the idea of Ash's torture. His own he could hold. He could dissect it, his agony, his burnt remains in Gomu's mouth. But at the thought of Ash, his mind revolted. In momentary bursts, he could see Ash tied and screaming, then the vision snapped shut. An impossible thing. Júzian he could sacrifice, Ash he didn't dare to.

But in the end, it was Ash's choice, not his.

Ash wouldn't sacrifice the Borderlands to save himself. And he was right. They could not sacrifice the Borderlands to the Garden.

"Sir," he said, "back in the Massacre, did Oak kill your mother's *sélnua?*"

Shonco frowned at him, wary. "They did."

"I'm really sorry, sir," he said with sincerity. "I am really very sorry."

They were flimsy, these aluminum tables. He'd upended one of them at Keskan, easy.

"They've killed your people too," said Shonco.

"Yes, sir. They have."

Tan surged to his feet, thrusting the table at Shonco, a bit to his left to leave his right flank exposed. Shonco scrabbled out of his chair, hand going for his gun, just in time for Tan to grab his bandaged wrist and twist it. Shonco grunted and bent under the pain, and Tan kicked him down and stamped his wrist. The commander yelped and tried to roll. Unbalanced, Tan went down, his knee striking Shonco's hip, but his hand grasped Shonco's gun. He drew it and fired twice point black at his chest.

Chapter Forty

Tan didn't look. He couldn't. He kept his eyes on the edge of Shonco's jacket as he felt inside his pocket and pulled out the device.

He heard feet pounding down the hallway.

"Sir, is everything all right?" That footman was outside the door. Tan aimed the gun at it.

If he positioned himself right, maybe he could shoot him too as the door swung open. He darted to the side of the door.

But more gunshots would bring more footmen...

The door smashed open. Tan fired, hitting him dead on. The man shot, too, and missed but the report of the shots echoed down the hall. Others would be here in seconds.

Where was the nearest intercom? He'd seen one by the cells, to call for backup probably. He ran, scanning the walls. There it was, intercom and alarm. He flipped up the heavy lever of the alarm. At once, the siren blared.

He hit the red comm button.

In a deep and even voice, he shouted, "Attention, all personnel. This is Commander Shonco. A bomb from Oak is about to blow. Evacuate the installation! Repeat: evacuate. This is not a drill."

He hoped enough people had seen the device that the story rang true. He hoped the blaring alarm outweighed the fact his voice was not like Shonco's.

"Let us the fuck out!" In a cell two down from the intercom, Keskan clung on to the bars.

The keys, dammit.

Tan dashed for the rec room.

"Tánashen!" Keskan hollered.

Rounding the corner, he nearly ran into a footman. They skidded to avoid each other.

"Evacuate!" Tan yelled, though he was running the wrong way.

"Deserter!" The man went for his gun.

Tan fired. The man fell. Tan shot him again in the head, realizing only when he looked down that his own thigh was bleeding thickly. Can't just stand in the hall. He ran to the rec room. His thigh didn't hurt, but his gait was lopsided. Behind the door with two corpses, he took off his belt and tightened it around his thigh to slow the bleeding. Then, half sprawling, he got to the ground and felt around Shonco's pockets till he found the keys.

He met no one on the way back, though the echo of distant shouting reached him.

He unlocked Keskan, unlocked Ash.

"All right, —go," yelled Keskan, words half lost to the alarm. He pounded down the hall, stopping only to grab the gun from the fallen footman.

"Keskan, wait!" called Tan. "Let me get Ashtyn a gun."

To his surprise, Keskan slowed to an agitated hover while Tan dove once more into the rec room and snatched the guard's gun.

"Are you okay?" said Ash as Tan gave him the gun.

Tan grunted and ran after Keskan.

At the entrance to the manufacturing deck, they skidded to a halt, barreling into a wall by the door as several footmen dashed up the ramp to the exit without glancing in their direction. When they'd gone, Keskan poked his head into the hall. He gestured them forward and they dashed down the corridor.

Stairs or elevator? A little tech lim voice said stairs—less parts to break. But if they met soldiers, the elevator was better. They might have to shoot getting in, getting out, but on the ride, they were safe.

Keskan apparently thought the same. He hit the elevator button and they trained their guns.

It was empty. Of course. Evacuations used the stairs.

The ride up was like being plucked out of reality, with only the blaring alarm soaking through. They hid at the sides of the door, guns ready. Tan felt blood squish in his boot. When the door opened, Keskan sprang out, making a sweep of the room. They saw no one, a dead concrete floor, dead metal, and the living alarm.

"You know where to plant it?" Keskan yelled.

Tan nodded and made for the central piping. His leg dragged as he went up the ladder. He holstered his gun to pull himself with his hands, the device bulging in his pocket. At the upper level, the metal ramp sprang under his steps. The piping on either side radiated heat so that his cheeks flamed like he was in the full sun.

All right, there: a narrow ledge held up a mishmash of pipes. He could set the device there and hope it did its work.

Once he flipped the switch, he'd have a minute maybe to get out of range before it twisted up his organs.

He flipped it and set it down, heat blazing on his fingers. But the moment he took his thumb off the switch, it snapped back to *off*. He frowned and flipped it again. The same. Again.

"Come on!" yelled Keskan. "What the fuck are you doing?"

"Switch broke!" Tan shouted. "I'll have to hold it down. You go!"

"No!" Ash cried out.

Keskan shouted something but Tan couldn't make it out.

He flipped the switch with his thumb and held it. He set his hand on the ledge, the heating pouring into it. Almost at once, he felt ill, his stomach turned, his sight losing focus. He concentrated on keeping his hand in place. Metal growled around him.

He fell to his knees and threw up, the device still clutched in one hand. His heart pounded and the contents of stomach dripped through the grate beneath him. Pin pricks of fire touched his skin. He threw up bile.

After that, he wasn't sure what happened. He was flying but something ripped his arm and struck him on the head. Something scalded the flesh on the back of his arm. He jerked back, pipes all around him, and scrabbled, clawing for escape. A moment later, he crawled out onto the open floor, lights pulsing before his eyes.

"Where's the —ice?" yelled a voice.

"I see it!" Ash. Feet dashed past him.

Ash? He forced his eyes to focus. He could just make out a bit of Ash crawling under the pipes and out again with a cube in his fist.

"Stop," he said, probably no one heard him.

He must have passed out and dropped the device as he fell.

Ash was darting up the ladder. Tan got up on his knees and made a bid to follow. He fell. He crawled forward.

"Ashtyn, it'll happen to you too," cried Keskan at the foot of the ladder.

"No, it won't!" yelled Ash. "Get Tánashen out of here."

Tan reached the ladder and hauled himself upright, shouldering Keskan out of the way. He could see Ash above through the metal grating: he'd slipped his belt off and was using it to tie his hand against the switch. With a jerk, he pulled it tight.

Again came the low growl of metal.

"Go!"

"Ash!" Tan put a foot on the ladder.

But Keskan yanked him back and slugged him. They grappled briefly, but his guts were spinning. He heard metal groaning, a hiss of steam, a cry of pain.

"Ash!"

The room was hot and sticky, white and sticky, his feet kicked on the floor. Then, he was off the floor like a sack, thumping against

Keskan's shoulders. The white of a corridor zapped black and the alarm got buried in the groan of dying steel.

Outside, the air rang with gunshots and shouting. He choked on a soup of sulfurous smoke, a flicker of fire in a sea of pale rock.

☙

He awoke with a splitting headache on the dirt behind a curve of metal: a water drum, several drums. He lay among them, obscured from sight, as the sounds of battle barked around him. No sign of Keskan. He must have dropped him here, the limits of his loyalty to Ash's request—

Ash. Tan needed to go and get him.

He made a lunge and struck one of the drums with his shoulder. Its dull reverberation seemed to suck out all his strength.

Ash was dead.

If he'd been lucky, the antigrav stuff knocked him out before the bursting pipes scalded him and choked him.

Even so, Tan had to find him. He had to see his body. Maybe Ash had fallen like Tan, maybe he was breathing under some rubble. No. The pipes had burst. Nobody could survive that. He'd be broiled, he'd be Ordan. He'd be melted and gone, spirit *mirya*-changed into a piece of that place.

Tan's stomach seemed to float up from under his ribs. He couldn't bring himself to move. The reality of Ash's death settled on him like a coat soaked in the River. He lay there for a long time, numb.

He would just keep lying there and wait for the end.

Except Ash had made Keskan rescue him. Ash wanted him alive. But what did that matter if Ash was dead? But it did matter. The dead always mattered. He could feel Júzian just out of sight, looking down behind his shoulder. He had to get out because Ash had said so. What would it mean if he did less than Keskan to honor Ash's final wish?

He looked around. He seemed well hidden, but if there was fire, they'd come for the water drums. Had to get out. His head swimming, he dragged himself forward to peer around a drum, saw dust and gravel, the edge of a building. He collapsed back down. He couldn't feel his leg. It was hot to the touch but didn't feel his touch at all. But he would need it if he was going to run. He loosened the tourniquet of his belt. The blood flowed, scraping like sandpaper through his leg. He'd have to wait till he could move it. No, he couldn't wait. He began to crawl away.

❧

He awoke again to a throbbing head and someone shaking him. "Captain."

Off somewhere, everywhere, a ruckus of battle rose and fell in his ears like a dream. His vision swam onto a pair of oversized eyes under brown hair.

"Fendo?"

"I've got to get you out of here."

Get me out? I killed your uncle.

Fendo hauled him upright. "Keep low, okay."

They stumbled through the smoke.

It lay like a fog over everything now, ghosting the buildings and the noises of war, more distant now, intermittent. Tan tried not to fill his lungs, but the air got into his throat. He coughed. Fendo seemed to know where they were going, and Tan let himself be led, focusing on making his legs operate. His pant leg was drenched in blood, his throat an aching passage straight to his dry head.

"Fendo. Water?"

"Hang on a sec."

They lumbered on until, abruptly, Fendo deposited him on the ground. Then a canteen was in his hands. He gulped, remembering only when it was mostly drained that he'd better leave some for Fendo. Where'd he gone?

He heard a snap and then another. Peering through the smoke, he saw Fendo's figure against the wire fence. Wire cutters. Tan watched him, mesmerized.

"Okay, this way." He pushed Tan at a crawl through one layer of barbed wire, two, three.

"Why are you here?" asked Tan.

Fendo just tugged him the last few feet till the Grid lay behind them. Before them, the rocky plain soon began to climb into craggy hills.

They made for the cover of the boulders, each step a shock of pain in Tan's head. Then, they were between two boulders, crouching.

"Why *you*?" said Tan. "You're the nephew of an officer."

Fendo looked sallow, wasted. He didn't meet Tan's eyes. "My mama used to say, 'When you get home, come back and get me,' home to Ark's Town—Free of Ford, she meant. But I was going to die before getting home. I almost died; the Citadel didn't care. Only you did."

Funny thing was, Tan couldn't remember caring. That is, he had cared, but it surprised him that Fendo had noticed.

"So you're with the Borderlanders now?"

Fendo hesitated. "Things in the Citadel weren't working out, were they?"

Tan found nothing to say.

"Your rendezvous's up southeast, right?" said Fendo.

"How do you—?"

"Keskan said. I'm going to try to find your Kiri guys and send them to come get you."

Tan looked at his birdlike face, the same pointed chin as Shonco, same hollow cheeks as Ash.

"Ashtyn's dead," he said.

Fendo looked down. "Yeah, Keskan said. I'm sorry."

Fendo left and Tan lay on shards of rock, his body throbbing to the beat of his heart. What time of day was it? Was it still the same day? The light was an unchanging sulfur fog. He began to shudder with cold. His limbs shook so violently that his teeth clacked. As he tossed and turned on the ground, he saw Fendo's canteen beside him. He laid a trembling hand on it but couldn't get a firm enough grip to twist the cap off. He tried again, rested, tried again. It finally gave and he swallowed what remained of the water. It went raw down his throat.

He floated in and out of dreaming: the canteen kept coming back into his hands and the cap slipping under his fingers. His joints ached, and flies tickled his face. The light began to dim, though he wasn't sure if it was the falling day or the darkening of his eyes that did it.

Júzian put his hand on his shoulder.

Then, his mother came and carried him away.

Chapter Forty-One

His right arm burned. He lay there for a while, perceiving the burning, unable or unwilling to move. At some point, who knew when or why, he opened his eyes to a curving, cave-like chamber. It reminded him of the mess hall when the lights were down low. But while the hall had been lit in a uniform brown, this space danced with oil lamps. He could see one of them clearly and a flicker from another near to his feet. He didn't have the energy to turn his head to look at it.

He was not alone. Laid on other bedrolls, he saw other figures, asleep or dead, IVs dripping into them. An IV dripped into him too, just above the bandage on his scalded arm, and that was when he knew the Citadel had reclaimed him. Maybe he was deep in the Citadel itself, where there was no escape for their chosen.

The thought scarcely touched him. He was too tired to care. Ash was dead, Shonco dead. He knew it but it floated away. If this was dying, he was ready to let go.

Then Oneness came, as if fit to the moment, the loudspeaker's crackle and the mournful, joyful horn, vibrating through his chest and his aching skull. It said the ocean will sweep you free. Then, through the static, the words arrived like traces of the Gods' Realm.

How can it be we walk through fires yet remain?
That the sundered is restored to its primeval Oneness?

Pain swept into insignificance. The room washed away into unsundered reality.

And Loss embraced him as brother, as self.

They were with him, his brothers selves. He knew their names—Sho, Tarnto, Codo, Keskan, Muned, Fendo, Lavan—knew the feel of the priest—it was Codo's father—and the patients lying half awake beside him, and of others he knew and did not know by name. Their names marked their selves, and their selves points of light on the Golden Way.

❧

When it was over, he thought back on it, on the wholeness and the hole where Ash no longer existed. Strange how that absence didn't matter in the One. Yet now it mattered, now it was a gash in the earth of his life, the gash of Júzian, the gash of Ash, and Tan balanced on the slice of land that stood between those gashes. The fact he was still breathing laid a duty on him.

He reached over to the IV in his arm and pulled it out. He saw that he wore a loose medical gown. A bed pan slipped uncomfortably beneath him.

"Where are you going?" said a footman in a nearby cot.

"Are we at the Grid, sir?" said Tan.

"Where else would we be?"

With some burn and tear of muscle, Tan turned to face him. "I thought we were at the Citadel," he said truthfully, "but the Landowner wasn't there."

The man leaned back into his pillow, blinking in pain. "He is still there. He'll bring us home."

Tan hauled himself up and got bare feet on the ground. "We're in the ship, aren't we?" It was the only place that could look like this.

"Damn Kiris took it over."

"I need to go help."

"The *Kiris*?"

"My unit."

One breath, another, then he pushed off the bed. One step and another. He found a uniform folded on a shelf, and half-collapsing back on his bed, he twisted into it like an earthworm. He found his boots beneath his bed.

"You're an idiot, kid," said the footman as Tan fell in a heap on the floor and went to work on getting his boots on.

After a few tries, he got himself pulled back up, and then was out into a corridor lit by smoking oil lamps in alcoves not built to hold them.

A few more steps and his legs went out. He struggled up, one knee underneath, and then another.

A shadow blocked the corridor. Tan froze.

"Tánashen."

He melted in relief. It was Sajem beside him, his arms like fire around Tan's burns as he lifted him, carried him back to the bed.

"No, take me out," said Tan. "I need to see it."

*

Sajem supported him up a winding stair into a waning day. They sat on the rim of the open hatch. It was almost like riding a vast fish. The rise and dip of the ship against the sluggish River made a sleepy sound like cascading sand. A tern shrilled and fled away, back up the River.

A Borderland guard on the bank was watching him. When Tan looked his way, he put his palms together in greeting. "Are you Red Leaf?" he called.

"Yes," said Tan, his weak voice lost on the River. "Yes, I am," he repeated louder.

The man bowed. "The spirits of your *sélnua* will remember your sacrifice."

"The Oaks will as well," said Sajem.

Farther off, the bones of the Grid lay before him. The air hung thick despite the River breeze. The fencing had been hewn down, and marks of fire and refuse lay everywhere. The buildings, however, were much as they had been, their stone and metal hardy. And tents still stood and people moved ant-like, some Kiri, some Citadel, even women and children.

"How long was I out?" Tan asked.

"This is the third day."

No steam came from the great vents of the power plant, though from the outside, the geothermal plant appeared almost untouched: a bit of roof a little caved. But the stillness of those vents marked the death of the beast. The generator no longer rumbled; its threat had gone out, and the whisper of the River had come out of hiding.

"Did we win?" said Tan. "We won, didn't we?"

Sajem didn't reply at once. "We'll see. Right now, the villages are in chaos. The fighting is fierce; there are so many Fenorn warriors north of the River."

"Jeyza. She saved my life." The memory was a patchwork of sulfur fumes and pain, and her face, dirt blackened and a hill-jack, and that was all. "Is she all right?"

"She is, she's here, helping me oversee the Grid. And the Grid—well, you can see. Without the Bridge, they can't ship enough food from the north bank. Without power, they can't run the train to ship any to the Citadel, which means the Landowner is stuck."

"He'll die," said Tan dully.

"My mother, the Convener, she's working on a truce." He paused. "Keskan said your brother died. I'm sorry."

Tan felt tears prick at his eyes. "He died for this."

He was looking out over the rubble, but he couldn't have said what *this* actually was: just destruction and death—or the stillness, the quiet rushing when the hum and churn stopped, when the work stopped and the world resumed its walking.

At the Grid, at least, the walls that had kept the world in pieces had crumbled. Sand met sand, and water water. The dead and living lost their difference, the currents of *mirya* swept all things.

> *And Loss embraced the phantom as brother, as self,*
> *Wondering and human in his tears, and they were*
> *unsundered.*

Ash had done that. He'd said he wouldn't leave until his work was done, and he'd proved it.

Tan began to shake with sobs. He was filled with a wonder that stretched out wide, to the earth, the air, the sun, the Ribbon, to Sajem's hand on his shoulder, but it orbited Ash. Because Ash had understood—this was the work of becoming unsundered.

Chapter Forty-Two

Jeyza nodded curtly to the guard at the gate and motioned for Tan to follow her. "Mind you, Tánashen, food and land are scarce. Not everyone's going to end up dancing in dandelions, but you tell me who's good for what, and I'll do what I can to find a place for them."

Tan understood the realities well enough. He didn't expect a happy outcome for everyone.

Funeral pyres flowered across the Grid, black tendrils of smoke curling skyward. The smell of roasting flesh pressed on him; he fought the impulse to gag. This was the Oak way, he reminded himself, just cremation, just like composting, not the punishment it felt like.

He followed her through debris and soldiers; they spoke Kiri now, not Citadel, but the staccato of orders never changed. He strained to see familiar faces among the mishmash of Kiri and Citadel clothing. He named off a few he knew for Jeyza—a couple of boys from C-12, an officer from F-13.

"They're loyal Fenorn people," he said. "They'd do best at the Grid, I guess. Or back in the Citadel."

She wrote notes in a book as he talked, as if catching people's futures in those little letters.

He named some more but saw no one from C-16.

The sun broke on the gravel in shards, like a shattered pane of glass. When he glanced up the hill at the Old Town, he made out a single pointed shoulder of the He peeking over a roof, another fragment. In a pile of junk, a hammer clanked.

"We can stop for some food," said Jeyza, "and then we'll find..."

But he'd stopped listening, his eyes on the young cadet in the junk pile. The boy took off his helmet to wipe his face and his blond hair glinted in the sun.

"Sho?"

Tan hurried toward him, denying his knees the right to buckle.

Sho turned at his name and stared, mouth open, a cut across his nose. Tan barreled into him and clung on tight, his arms sinking into the uniform's stiff fabric, Sho's tentative fingers on his back in return.

"You okay?" said Tan.

Sho nodded, his face thinner, older. "Ashtyn—"

"I know. And I know Dezdenec's dead, and Dradam, but you got to tell me about the others." He sat him down on a steel beam. "Fendo, is he okay?"

"Fendo? I think—I thought maybe I saw him. There's so many people, Captain, and they're not in units anymore. They're called meets. Gomu, I..." He broke off and stared at his feet.

After waiting a little, Tan said, "Spit it out, Sho. Don't let it poison the inside."

"Captain, I did like you said."

Tan frowned. "Like I said?"

"I overheard Keskan: he was telling Fendo about that bomb thing."

"What bomb thing?"

Sho gave him an incredulous look. "That thing you used to take out the power plant."

Tan nodded. "Oh. Okay." A dread was settling in his heart.

"So I told Commander Shonco, like you said."

Tan froze, not trusting himself to move. It came back at him like an unrestful ghost: he had told Sho to report on Keskan. Sho had followed his orders. It was Sho who had informed on them.

"Did I do the right thing, Captain?"

"Yeah." Tan put a hand on his shoulder. "Yeah. You did good."

"But the power plant got blown up, and Ashtyn—"

"It wasn't your fault. You did good."

Sho said nothing. The morning clacked as they sat in silence. What had happened to Jeyza? When Tan looked up, she was still there, waiting.

"Captain..." Sho stopped.

"Yeah?"

"Did you desert us?" His eyes on Tan were as blue as the sky that tied the whole world together.

Tan pulled him close again. "Never."

For a moment, it seemed they were only people living, two as One.

Then came the crunch of a foot in the debris pile above them.

Tan started.

"Ma!" The voice was a man's. "Ma, it's Tánashen!"

Nearby, a boy jeered, "Aw, he wants Mama!"

"Go fuck yourself," said Codo mildly. Tall as a rake and brown with dirt, he plopped down on the beam beside them. "Where the hell did you come from, where the hell you been? Lavan said you joined some alliance. That right?"

"Tánashen!"

Tan turned. "Aunt Tson?"

She clambered down the rubble and hugged him hard. He scarcely recognized her, thin and plain in a beige work dress, not like a priest's favored woman.

"When did you get here?" Tan asked her.

"Early summer. Codo's pa came down as priest and brought me with him. It's beautiful—I mean, the river, just lovely, but Togi never told me the Garden would be so dark and grubby."

"Aunt Togi, is she...?"

"No, not here yet. Don't know if they'll ever send her now. Don't know what's going to happen." Tears brimmed in her eyes as she strove with partial success to get her arms around all three of them.

ε&

Codo led Tan down a path through the rubble. "Lavan's been in and out of Ark's Town. Probably has his own farm already, little cocksucker. Haven't seen Fendo at all. But we might as well start with the cages, right?" He paused. "You know, I was actually captain of C-16 for a day or such after they locked Keskan up. Wouldn't go back to that, not no how."

"You won't have to." Tan hesitated. "Aunt Jeyza told me Keskan is out with the Kiri soldiers. Have you seen—?"

"Dunno." said Codo shortly. "'Aunt Djeyza'? You mean the old barbarian stalking us? That aunt?"

"You better be nice to her," said Tan. "You want a nice farming life? She's got the power to decide it."

"That old weed?"

"Careful. She speaks Citadel," said Tan.

They were out in the hinterland, the south part of the Grid, where Ash had tried to escape through the fence after Júzian. It had once been used for troop maneuvers; now bits of rubble had been converted to house prisoners, four or five to a cell.

"Where do you think you're going, Fenorn scum?" Sword in hand, an Oak guard blocked the way. Then he glanced at the figure behind them and immediately fell back. "My lady."

Jeyza eyed him coolly.

The prisons were damn insecure, thought Tan. Steel bars and slabs of walls thrust snaggletoothed into the ground. Like Knotty Vines, but, no, this wasn't the work of the Citadel. It was done to the Citadel—by Oak, by the Alliance. Citadel rubble to imprison the Citadel: so maybe it was Citadel work, he didn't know.

Codo led them to one of the cages, where five figures in stained uniforms sat on dusty blankets.

"Hey, Muned, Tarnto," called Codo.

Two seconds later, the makeshift bars shuddered as Tarnto barreled into them.

"Fucking traitor!" he screamed at Tan, who took step back by instinct. "Gomu's blood is on you, you fucker! I will beat your skull to bloody pulp. I will drink you dry—"

"Tarnto, it's—" began Codo.

"Shut your mouth, fucking collaborator shit—"

"That's enough," said Jeyza in Citadel.

Tarnto, of course, kept shouting, till, at a nod from her, a guard stepped up and jabbed a club into his chest. He fell back, gasping for breath.

Jeyza crossed to the figure standing quietly by, his cold, brown eyes fixed on Tan. "You. Muned."

His eyes flashed to her.

"You believe in the Landowner?"

He just stared at her, implacable.

She turned to Tan. "This one we may be able to save."

"You have to." Tan held her eyes. "He's steady like—like steel, or like earth. He's..."

She squeezed his shoulder as if to say she understood him.

Tarnto was still on the ground, swearing at him, wispy and straining to get air in his lungs.

Tan nodded at him. "Him, he's just a kid."

"I think you know better."

"Let him go back to the Citadel."

A smile flitted past her face.

"He'll be a gun there, pointed at your face."

Tan glanced at Muned. "Maybe two, maybe more. That doesn't matter. Anyway, I'm not going back."

Chapter Forty-Three

Tan was spreading compost on the bean bed. No one seemed to know why so many pods were stunted. The soil seemed okay; bees were flying through the greenhouse. He was puzzling on that when the gardener went out and he realized he was alone. Where had everyone gone?

He turned. Where was Ash? He should be right here. Had he run—?

Then he remembered.

He sat on the edge of the yam bed. The C-4 boys had taken the harvest to the kitchens, just as Tan had ordered them. Ash, of course, had not been there. The morning sun of late summer filled the room with fever heat, and he was working because work was the bedrock of sanity, because feeding people was good work.

He was still sitting, a bit calmer, when the Gods' Realm touched the human. It came like an old friend in the bass horn's rumble, resonating in his chest. But they had shared Oneness yesterday; it wasn't due again for four days.

Nevertheless, like everybody who was One, he dropped what he was doing and went outside. The campus swarmed, some frightened Kiris shouting orders at the burgeoning crowd, but the Citadel people, by and large, stood hushed, attentive to the slow notes flowing out of some loudspeaker.

The notes faded, and the voice that boomed next was not a priest's but a woman's, speaking Kiri.

"This is Leki of the Oaks, the Convener of the Kiri Worlds, speaking to you by radio from the tech center of the Oaks. I have been given leave to suspend tech limitation so you can know that the Alliance and Fenorn have agreed to peace." She immediately repeated the words in Citadel, heavily accented but fluent and correct.

The music swelled again, and the voice that followed cracked Tan's heart. He almost fell onto his knees in relief.

"My people," said the Landowner, faint with radio hiss, but still himself, invincible, "it is the nature of the gods to burst and contract. Like stars, they splinter and then fall again toward wholeness. Today marks the end of a splintering age. The sundering begins to be undone and the Age of the Garden suffuses us like the dawn. That age marks the end of bloodshed. Today, the baskets begin to fill, and I summon you home to a time of plenty."

Then, he spoke the scripture:

> *How can it be we walk through fires yet remain?*
> *That the sundered is restored to its primeval Oneness?*

The strings rose low and soothing, the static behind them calm like autumn leaves underfoot.

"Listen to the wisdom of your leaders," he said, "and they will lead you home in peace."

Tan found himself waiting for Oneness. He could see it in the others too, the straining of their backs, the fingers brushing tears. But the music faded and the loudspeaker went silent, leaving them still sundered.

He started when the loudspeaker crackled once more.

A Kiri man said, "This is Nermártan, warden of the Oaks. As we turn to sending men and supplies back to Fenorn, remember, my people, that the war is done. This is a time of work and healing."

A time for work, for healing. Tan should go back and attend to the beans. Instead, he put his straw hat on. It felt strange and Borderlandish to put aside his assigned duty. But his feet were calling him somewhere else, and the beans wouldn't suffer from a composting delayed.

&

He hadn't been to the geothermal plant since that day, three weeks before. Its quiet mass sat at the periphery of his daily rounds, a dead thing trapped in the husk of its old life.

It was off-limits but when he said he needed to remember his brother, the Borderlander on guard, who knew him slightly, waved him through.

He descended the scuffed ramp, his footsteps clacking. The light from the open door waned quickly. He'd have to go back for a candle. Or maybe...

He cracked the door of a supply closet and rummaged in the dark. There was a flashlight on the shelf behind the door, like standard. He clicked on its pale light, ducked under the rope that blocked off the stairs, and went down the shuddering stairway to the prisoner block. The door to the room where he'd shot Shonco stuck on its hinges but gave to a shove. The body was gone—both bodies, the footman he'd killed too, though the blood still shadowed the floor.

He wanted to say he was sorry, but the words would be cheap. Instead, he sat on the floor, his flashlight on the red-black blood, and thought about what Shonco told him—how his dad had been afraid when Oak bombed the West Men. Had he been lying? He had been a liar, yet Tan believed that part was true.

At the plant itself, piles of concrete glued up holes where the pipes had fractured. It gave the impression of a vast machine rising out of a range of rocky hills in stark light of the rising Ribbon—it gave the impression of the Grid itself. He climbed toward the center of the rubble, the light beam shaking to the movements of his hands.

Ash had been near here when the pipes had burst. His body would have been here when they trucked in the concrete. They had no choice but to bury him. It would have been too hot to retrieve him. Pour the cement and get out.

In places the concrete was warm under his hands. He searched and searched through the chunks of rock and lingering sulfur. There was no sign of Ash. He was boiled and buried.

Then, beneath the broken ramp, in a jumble of rough concrete and metal, he caught a corner of something dark, not pale rock, no metal shine. He put his hand out and touched the charred leather of a boot.

He gripped it tight, his brother's boot.

You were right, Ash. There's a job we can't leave undone, a job that's bigger than a brother, or a sélnua, or a whole people, even a people who's One. It's for this planet, Uramésha, for all the living land and all the beings who live in it.

&

"Take those sweet potatoes out to the tracks," said Tan, "and help load them on the push car if they tell you to. Then you can get in the supper line."

"Yes, Captain," said Sho, though Tan was no longer his captain. To the Oak men, he was *handler of a meet*, much the same.

"Say hi to your ma for me."

After Sho had gone, he took a moment to taste the stir of autumn. Though thicker and wetter than in Knotty Vines, the message he read in the breeze was the same: renewal after the long, dead waiting of summer. It must be the half-season of Acorn Fall in Knotty Vines—if there were acorns to fall.

"Tánashen."

He turned at the welcome voice. With his beard grown to cover his chin, he looked more Kiri—Borderlandish.

"Lord Sajem. How's Free of Ford?"

"Still very dark." Sajem came to stand beside him. "Those new stone hovels were built for electric lights. Are you done here?"

"I have to send my meet to supper."

"I'll send them. You have somewhere else to be; your way pointer's arriving."

ᴥ

He knew three of the four people in the boat, and it gave him a sense of his worlds colliding: Linóvi tall and dressed in white, flanked by the incongruous pair of Fendo and Lavan. The fourth was a Kiri youth Tan did not recognize.

Linóvi's face lit up when she saw him. She held out a hand, and he helped her out of the boat. Lavan handed her a gnarled walking staff, and she leaned on it heavily. She'd been old before but was older now. "Tan. Mica Melting Fashen said you were alive, but to see it's a whole different reality."

His throat closed up. "Ash is dead, Grandmother."

"He told me that too." She pressed her fingers to his forehead in blessing. "May the loss be ours. But you yourself are living hope. I had almost given you up for dead."

"He saved me."

A tear gleamed in her eye and she hugged him. Fendo fidgeted with the knapsack in his hands. Lavan watched coolly with the other boy behind him.

"Why did you come here?" Tan asked her.

"For you, lad, what do you think? And for Ash, to do the rites." She hesitated. "I was sent word you were alone here, remembering your brother alone."

"I'm glad you survived Salamander," he said.

"The Alliance has taken it back. When we're done here, I can take you home—to Salamander, I mean. Life was good to me there before the Citadel came. It can be good again for our *sélnua*."

"Grandmother," he said gently, "I'm exiled. Don't you remember?"

She gave him a puzzled look. "No one's told you?"

"Told me...?"

"They must have been waiting for me." She took his hand. "As Dawn Rock Ren's closest kin, Hunter Apáshan asked your exile be rescinded. The Salamanders agreed, of course. They say you've proved a trust-keeper."

Tan felt like the world was tipping over. He had to catch himself to keep from falling. A snide smile passed over Lavan's face that Tan could not interpret.

Needing to say something, he said, "Grandmother, they've put up a tent for you. Fendo will get you settled."

Fendo gave him a questioning look but said merely, "Do you come with me, *bezo*?"

Though he spoke in halting Kiri, the word he called her was Citadel. Tan suspected she didn't understand it and was glad. He couldn't imagine she'd want to be called "owner," like a priest.

"Fendo," Tan called after them. "When they get a caravan going to the Citadel, they're going to pick up your mother. Oak Sajem told me."

"To come to the Grid?"

"Probably Free of Ford, if you want."

Fendo nodded. "She'd like that."

When they'd gone, Lavan took a step toward him. "'*Bezo*.'" He shook his head. "So you're off to Twelve Salamanders?"

The youth with him was standing a little way off. Tan could see the fish tattoo on his bare arm now, a Low in Mouther, one of Lavan's folk.

"Whose side are you on?" Tan asked Lavan.

All trace of a smile slipped from Lavan's face. "Whose are you?"

"I'm just trying to clean up the damage—"

"—you caused."

Tan closed the space between them. "The Citadel caused it—and Oak. You refused to help us, then you show up with *my sélnuta*. I just want to know what you want."

"I *want* to go back to Low in Mouth and start cleaning up the rubble from your fucking revolt."

"Rubble? Low in Mouth wasn't even in the fighting."

"We've traded with the Citadel for generations; now we can't get nails, we can't get bricks. We got refugees and no way to build houses but cut down the woodlands we never had much of to start with. So you go fuck off to Twelve Salamanders, have a happy old life, but don't get righteous with me."

Tan hesitated. "We'll fix it. We're fixing it."

Lavan scoffed.

"You know Dradam's dead?"

"And?"

"Don't you care?"

Lavan's face froze. He stared at Tan, still as the steel He while the seconds dripped. "Fuck you." He hefted his pack and nodded for the Low in Mouther to follow him.

જ

The next day, with Sajem's permission, they crossed into the restricted zone of the geothermal plant, Linóvi and Tan, with Fendo and Lavan, an odd little cobbled Kiri group passing for Ash's *sélnua*. At first, Tan had bridled at Lavan's presence, but Linóvi had observed that he was one of Ash's people, and she was right. They'd lived in C-16 together for more than two years.

As they walked to the plant, Tan attempted a peace offering. "You're welcome here."

"I don't need you to welcome me," said Lavan.

With two walls knocked in, the plant had become an L housing a jumble of pipes and cement. Tan could not decide if it resembled more some strange, semi-unsundered He and She or a mound of guts turned into stone.

"He's in there," he told Linóvi softly. "I worry he's trapped."

"He's not the one who's trapped." She gave them all a sad smile. "Come. Let's begin to free ourselves."

Since they had no trees, she had proposed chiseling the shape of a grape leaf in the cement above Ash's remains. She went to work on it now with a *tap-tap-tap*.

Tan did not know how to chisel, but he cleaned up the debris as the others stood by, as more distant kin would.

It was Tan's idea to use blood. Each of them opened a vein to blend the life of their *sélnua* with the wet cement, Tan and Linóvi, then Lavan and Fendo. Lavan made a cut right below his fish tattoo, as if to say, *Don't forget I'm Low in Mouth*, or that was how Tan saw it.

"The gift is ours," intoned Linóvi.

With only the four of them and all of them hungry, they did not give much blood, only enough to stain the mixture pink.

She and Tan took turns troweling the mix into the chiseled forms of three grape leaves. Without her having to say it, Tan knew the leaves represented his brothers and him, and it relieved him that he could leave a piece of himself here, since a piece of him had already gone with them.

As they were smoothing the final edges, new steps crunched across the gravel.

Tan glanced up and started. There stood Apáshan—with Keskan beside him, hands folded in the Borderlands way, waiting for Linóvi to finish her work.

"You should add your blood," said Fendo to Keskan. "You were C-16 too."

Keskan glanced at Tan, whose inclination was to tell him to fuck himself. Instead, he gave a curt nod.

Swiftly, Keskan drew a knife and sliced his palm. Tan saw a ring on his left index finger, like the Hyraxers wore. His blood reddened his brothers' *sélnua*.

Linóvi sang,

> *No loss to mirya.*
> *No. No loss.*
> *No loss to mirya.*
> *Knotty Vines Red Leaf Ashtyn,*
> *May his loss be ours.*

They bowed, and Tan helped her to her feet.

"There," she said, "Pink Leaf *sélnua*."

Apáshan smiled.

"It's a good memento to him," said Keskan. "It's a pity one of his *sélnuti* is a murderer."

For a moment, the silence rung, and then Tan burst out laughing. The past, he reflected, never, ever let you go.

"Mind your tongue, Waxwing," said Apáshan. "Ren's death has been paid for."

Keskan's eyes bored into Tan. "Has it? I must have been misinformed."

Tan waited.

A slight, slow smile spread over Keskan's face, but he said nothing more, as if silence were victory.

"Let's go and leave these spirits in peace," said Linóvi.

"He isn't talking about Dawn Rock Ren," said Tan. "Or my leader Shonco, or Dezdenec." Why had he said Dezdenec? He hadn't killed Dezdenec. "He's talking about my brother, my older brother."

Fendo broke in, the Kiri words labored and quick. "Tánashen don't kill him. Júzian choose run away. Not his fault."

"Yes. It is," said Tan. "I turned on him to save myself. If I'd shot him myself, it would have been kinder."

Fendo looked away, while Lavan eyed him coolly. Apáshan was visibly stunned—Linóvi not. Her unsurprise was the heaviest condemnation.

"So you see," said Tan, "I can't go to Salamander with you, Grandmother. I'm sorry, but he's right. I killed him."

After a moment, Apáshan raised a hand, a gesture that might have been a blessing or farewell, and wordlessly, he walked away. Tan watched him till his dwindling figure disappeared behind a quonset.

Lavan bowed to Linóvi and started back toward the dwellings, with Fendo behind him.

Tan looked at Keskan. The smile had fallen from his face. Then, he too, walked away, as if a thread had broken.

&

A minute later—or maybe ten—Linóvi put a hand on his shoulder. He flinched.

"Help me sit," she said.

He helped her down to the rocky ground, the pink leaves rising above them.

"Now," she said, "where will you go?"

"To Oak." He hadn't thought about it clearly, but in the back of his head the choice was already made.

She squeezed his hand. "Yes, you need to, don't you?"

Tan frowned. "Can you read my mind?"

"You're mute as ever, and yet I can see that you're drawn there."

Tan felt vaguely insulted. "I'm a Borderlander."

"Always. What will you do there?"

"Pay for Júzian, for Juz."

"Pay?" She considered the word. "I'd rather ask how will you heal what's broken?"

He wanted to say *this can't be healed,* because he didn't believe it could be. But saying so was a coward's way out.

He thought about it a while. "I guess it's, well, the Landowner, at the end of the day. He... He's not what you think. I don't know what he is. But I know he believes, I can feel—I've felt, he's not about to give up on the Garden, the Borderlands."

Linóvi nodded. "I think about it too. There are so many Fenorn people in our lands, so many more than before, far too many for even Oak to round up and send south again. Even when they run out of bullets, even then..."

She fell into thought.

Tan groped for words but couldn't find them. They were buried somewhere beneath the pink leaves, buried in the power plant, in the bull's skull of the Citadel.

"Juz..."

She waited for him to go on but he couldn't.

Finally she said, "In time."

They sat a while in silence.

At length, Tan said, "Oak is pretty far away, but they have power. They have warriors."

She nodded. "And the Convention Treaty calls on them to defend us—which they have."

"And they'll have to again. And they'll—what's the word?—tax us for it. I think they're kind of like the Citadel, Fenorn, in some ways. They're bigger than us. And I think I could learn from them, and teach them maybe about how to... to *be* with our people. Maybe teach them about Fenorn. I don't know. I don't know how to say it. But I think, somehow, it's what Ash would want. If he were here, he'd say, 'I belong in the Borderlands, and you belong in Oak. They need you there.' I think he'd say that. I—I don't know what Juz would say." He looked away, embarrassed.

Linóvi took Tan's hands in hers and lifted them to her forehead, the red sand dying their flesh.

"I'm still yours," he said, "your *sélnua*. I just can't, I just don't belong in... I don't belong."

"You're a brother of many. You can be," she said. "Your spirit will remember where the Red Leaves lie."

Acknowledgements

THIS BOOK IS THE WORK of many minds. Thanks to the late Susan DeFreitas for her conceptual advice. Without her input, this would be an entirely different story. Thanks to Hailey for early draft feedback and Erik Grove for the beta reading, even though it creeped him out! Thanks to my editors, Erin Wilcox and Bailey Potter, for helping me reshape and refine the story and everyone at Indigo Editing. Thanks to David C. Perez for the meticulous proofread (and J.B. for recommending him).

For the visuals, thanks to Xavier Aguirre for the fantastic cover art and to my long-suffering partner, Glenn Peters, for the cover design and his unflagging support. The background cover-texture photo is courtesy of Dave Hoefler on Unsplash.

Thanks to Z.A. for the moral support and encouragement and T.K. Greenleaf for the encouragement and expert marketing help. To everyone, thanks for your input, patience, and faith. And, of course, to William Blake.

Don't miss out!

Visit the website below and you can sign up to receive emails whenever Arwen Spicer publishes a new book. There's no charge and no obligation.

https://books2read.com/r/B-A-NPLEC-OYUAI

BOOKS 2 READ

Connecting independent readers to independent writers.

About the Author

Arwen Spicer is a writer, educator, and mother from Sonoma Mountain, California. She writes ecological and psychological science fiction and fantasy, often exploring guilt and reparation. Her short fiction has appeared in the Ursula K. Le Guin-inspired anthology, *Dispatches from Anarres*, Dragon Soul Press's *Timeless II*, and the Fabled Collective's *Women of the Woods*. She currently lives in Portland, Oregon with her partner and kids.

Read more at www.arwenspicer.com.